the vacation mix-up

THE MIX-UP SERIES
BOOK ONE

K.M. GOLLAND

For my daughter

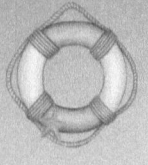

You only live once. Apparently. Unless you're a cat... or Bill Murray in *Groundhog Day*, because without divine intervention or a feline righting reflex, one lifetime is all we have.

Until recently, I thought "only living once" was exactly what I was doing—following my dreams of becoming a publisher in New York—by working my ass off from morning 'til night six days a week.

I live in my mother's apartment, own a somewhat desirous closet, and my bank balance is... healthy. Not Jeff Bezos healthy. More like sweetened oatmeal healthy, but healthy nonetheless. It gets me by, considering I have no children, husband, or hobbies.

And speaking of health, I'm the picture of it. I don't smoke, drink, or party on weekdays... nor weekends. I commute to work by train and foot, eat at least one substantial meal a day, and I exercise my brain with a balanced mix of words and caffeine. My life rides a sturdy track to success, but apparently, that's not what "only living once" is all about. According to my mom, it's just a fraction—a small slice of the life pie—and her dying wish was for me to have the whole thing with cream, sprinkles, and even a cherry on top.

So that's what I'm trying to do—live a fuller, less career-driven, and sturdier life for her.

"Big boat!" my Uber driver exclaims as he pulls into the drop-off point on the dock at Cape Liberty.

I glance out the window and correct him. "It's a ship."

"Same thing."

Technically, he's right, but I don't have time to discuss his inept choice of adjective and noun. If I get into a grammatical debate with him, I'll be late for my allocated boarding time, and that's not an option. I'm never late for anything. Not my train, not my job, not even my period.

"I'll help you with your luggage," he says, opening his door and exiting the car.

Staring at the ship, I marvel at what will be my floating home for the next few weeks. "I'm really doing this, Mom," I whisper, hugging my bag to my chest, unable to suppress a small, anxious smile.

Embarking on a European adventure is far outside my well-constructed comfort zone. I've never left the country, let alone sailed to another continent, so while I'm excited, I'm also nervous. I'll be alone—but then, that isn't unusual, given my career-driven existence.

"Seven countries in sixteen days," Mom said excitedly when her frail hand placed the ticket into my palm.

I remember fumbling with it as if it would burn my skin, as if taking it would seal my acceptance of her unfair and undeserving fate. I also knew I couldn't abandon my job for that long just to take a vacation. My boss, Georgia Peters—head of publishing at Duxley—would never allow it. I'm her right *and* left hand, her twenty-four-seven go-to, her eager and opportunistic slave.

Uncharacteristically, as it turns out, Georgia has a compassionate bone in her body and was surprisingly supportive of my trip—provided I worked on a couple of manuscripts in my downtime.

Stepping out of the Uber, I double-check that I've left

nothing on the back seat before collecting my luggage from the driver.

"Bon voyage," he says, saluting like a sailor.

I smile politely but have zero time to waste. My appointed check-in is only minutes away, and I need to ring the agency temp who'll be filling my role while I'm abroad. Every T must be crossed, every I dotted. Quite literally. No stone—and I mean absolutely *no* stone—can be left unturned, because being *the* personal assistant of one of the country's most sought-after publishers isn't an easy feat, and it's certainly not for the faint of heart. Georgia Peters is meticulous and indomitable, and yet I somehow manage to endure her Miranda Priestly tendencies.

If *that* devil wore Prada, then Georgia wears Hermès.

Nudging my large suitcase with my knee, I awkwardly sling my bag over my shoulder and dial the office on my cell, counting how many times it rings before the temp answers.

"Georgia Peters's office, you're speaking with Freya. How can I assist you?"

I draw in a frustrated breath. "Freya, it's Riley. You need to answer quicker than that."

"I picked up as soon as I could." She sighs as if my request is impossible. It's not; I do it day in and day out.

"We've been over this," I say sympathetically. "Two rings. No more. Trust me, it's for your own good."

"Yes, Riley, I understand."

"Did you collect her coffee?"

"Yes. Double espresso, turmeric, ginger, and honey."

I wait for her to continue, and when she doesn't, I come to a complete halt. "Please tell me you also asked for steamed milk."

"Shit!"

"Freya!" I shriek, exasperated.

"I'm so sorry, Riley. I forgot that part."

"I wrote it down in the Memorize-This-If-You-Want-to-Live bible I left you."

"I know!" she whines. "But I was in a panic this morning, and the milk bit slipped my mind."

Knowing my absence from Georgia's life will spell trouble for everyone at the office, I glance at my watch, wincing at the time. "Has she arrived yet?"

"No."

"Then go."

"Huh?"

"*Go!* Go and get her the coffee she requires. It's life or death, Freya. Her Golden Latte is the catalyst for the day to come."

I shut my eyes—because headache—debating whether boarding the white monstrosity before me is a wise move or not. But then I remember my mother's pleading, heavy gaze as she handed me the ticket, and I know I have to set sail. For her.

"Go. I'll call ahead. It should be ready by the time you get there."

Ending the call, I immediately dial the coffee shop to order Georgia's liquid lifeline, informing Casey, the barista, who it's for.

No more needs to be said.

My stomach twists with unease, but I pocket my cell and continue walking as a family of four, all wearing **I Love to Cruise** printed T-shirts, marches past me.

As I shuffle out of their way, a train of suitcases in their wake, the older son knocking his sister's hat off her head and laughing as she falls behind to pick it up.

"Loser!" she calls after him.

"No fighting!" their mother barks before visibly forcing herself to take a deep breath. "Smell that fresh sea air. Isn't it wonderful?"

I take a whiff, wishing I hadn't. All I can smell is apprehension and fish.

The mother bends down, picks up her daughter's hat, and then cups the little girl's cheek, their loving exchange thickening my throat as I swallow. Momma often cupped my cheek too, her fingers warm and nurturing. No matter the day I had or what lay

4

ahead, that subtle gesture always brought me peace, even if only momentarily.

Blinking back tears, I nudge my suitcase once again, following the family to where cruise staff wait to take our luggage. They check for ID tags and cabin numbers, which were printed and attached at home, and then heave my case onto a large metal cart.

I hug my tote bag to my chest again, relieved I kept my most valuable items with me.

"What's your check-in time, ma'am?" one of them asks me.

I glance at my watch as the alarm I set starts to vibrate my wrist. "Uh... now."

"Please proceed to the elevator and then head to the counter."

"Thank you." I sigh, relieved he doesn't berate me for being late. It's nice, considering I'm accustomed to being criticized for the smallest of things.

Noticing the doors to the elevator closing, I call out, "Hold the door!" while scurrying forward, almost tripping in my heels as a muscular arm scrawled in ink slides across the steel, preventing it from shutting.

"Thank you," I huff out, slightly breathless as I wiggle into the cramped elevator car, my ass brushing the man's thigh as I squish in tighter to allow the doors to close. "Sorry." I glance over my shoulder at him, once again hugging my bag to my chest as I smile apologetically. "I probably should've gotten the next one."

He nods but doesn't quite smile back, so I look forward, no stranger to cramped elevators, except they normally comprise like-minded, professionally attired people, ready to start or leave work. Not large-brimmed hats, carry-on suitcases, or flustered mothers cradling babies.

Please, God, I don't want a cabin next to a crying baby. I'll never get any work done.

Staring at the polished steel doors, my reflection a blur of color, I silently pray my cabin neighbors are over the age of sixty. The elderly are quiet, mostly. At least my mother was. Mostly.

My cell rings from within my pocket, so I slide it out, my stomach lurching at the office's number on my screen.

Damn it!

I thumb the Accept button and press my phone to my ear. "Yes, Freya?"

"I have her coffee, but she's already in her office."

"Shit!" I blurt, once again glancing over my shoulder, this time mouthing, "Sorry," to the other occupants.

"What do I do, Riley?" Freya asks, voice drenched with fear.

"You need to take it to her... now!"

"Okay, but what do I say?"

"Nothing. It's too late for that." I close my eyes. "Open my bottom drawer. You'll see a container with cookies. Take two out."

"Oh." She pauses. "Did you make these?"

"Yes. I baked them this morning and dropped them off on my way to the dock. They're organic and contain chamomile tea, berries, and dark chocolate. Great for stress relief. Georgia thinks I buy them at the health food store on the corner. The recipe is in the bible."

"You want *me* to make these?"

I massage my temple. "Yes."

"But I can't bake."

"Well, you have two days to learn."

"Two days?"

"Uh-huh, they stay fresh until then."

"But I—"

"Was there anything else? I'm about to board my ship."

She stutters, "Um... no."

"Excellent! You'll be fine. Just read the bible. It's all in there."

"Uh... Riley?"

"Yes?"

"When are you getting bac—"

I end the call, slip my cell back into my pocket, and accidentally elbow the tattooed man in the rib. "I'm so sorr—"

"It's fine," he coughs out, shuffling to my side and once again sliding his arm across the doors as they open, gesturing I exit before him.

Wincing, I mouth, "Thanks," and as I pass him, he leans down and murmurs, "Your cookies sound delicious."

I blink all the blinks. "Excuse me?"

"Your stress-relief cookies." He smirks, his neatly cut moustache and trimmed beard lifting, the skin around his lovely eyes crinkling. "I could use a few myself."

"Oh." I nearly choke on my laughter. "Trust me, they're *not* delicious."

"They're not?"

I shake my head vehemently. "No, but my boss loves them."

We join the check-in line and are immediately directed to counters beside one another.

"Do you have your boarding pass?" our attendants ask simultaneously.

We both hand over printed tickets.

"Welcome, Riley," they once again say in unison.

My face scrunches with amusement—he's a fellow Riley. I laugh. "How homonymous."

He cocks his head as if he has no idea what I just said, and by the rugged, blue-collar look of him, he probably doesn't.

"May I have your passport please?" my attendant asks as she clicks her computer mouse.

"Yes. Of course." I rifle through my bag, snag the important little book, and hand it over.

She glances at the other attendant's screen, then back to hers. "Oh. You only need one of us to check you both in."

Seems peculiar, but perhaps this is a new system put in place to streamline the embarkation process. I've always wondered how cruise lines manage to get thousands of passengers on board in such a short window of time, so processing multiple people concurrently is feasible... I guess.

She hands my paperwork to the other attendant and then calls for her next passenger, so I awkwardly scoot closer to the other Riley.

"I love that you both have the same name," my new attendant says as if she's delighted. "It's cute, but I'm guessing it's sometimes confusing."

Other Riley pulls a what-is-she-smoking face, and I shrug. A lot of people have the same name, so how it's confusing is beyond me.

"Funnily enough," she continues, snort-laughing, "I went to school with two Jane Does." She swishes her hand at us. "Don't worry, they're both alive."

This time, I pull a what-is-she-smoking face, and the other Riley chuckles.

The woman merrily processes our check-in, then hands us both cabin cards attached to lanyards. "The suitcases you checked in downstairs will be delivered to your room before the ship sets sail. Once you're through security and on board, you're free to explore the ship and grab a bite to eat on Lido Deck. It is, however, a requirement that you watch the safety briefing video in your room and report to your muster station before we leave port, so please do not forget to do so."

I nod.

"Any questions?"

Other Riley and I shake our heads.

"Excellent! Enjoy your cruise."

We thank her, take our lanyards, and then make our way to the security line, where I'm held up because of what—or who—is in my bag.

"I have a letter from the crematorium," I explain when the officer carefully lifts Momma's urn.

He reads the document together with her death certificate, then carefully inspects the small pot. My stomach lurches, fearful he might drop it and scatter her remains across the terminal floor and not in the ocean as she requested, which would be disastrous and, quite frankly, horrifying.

"I'm sorry for your loss," he says, placing her back inside my bag before handing me my paperwork.

I nod, my expression somber. "Loss" is hardly an adequate adjective for the death of a loved one. Someone who is lost could potentially be found. I haven't "lost" my mother. She was taken. She's gone. And although it's lovely for him to offer his condolences, he shouldn't be sorry for my "loss." He should be sorry for life's only certainty—death—and that her death was premature.

"Ma'am?"

I blink. "Yes?"

"We're all done here. You may board the ship now."

"Oh. Thank you."

Once again hugging my bag to my chest, I shuffle forward, cross the gangway onto the ship, and enter the lobby.

Brass rails glitter under slightly dimmed lights, a myriad of crew in white uniforms together with passengers scuttling about. I step out of their way and tilt my head way back. "Wow!" I whisper, exhaling as I slowly turn in a circle, absorbing the extravagance of the grand atrium and the glass elevators moving between various decks.

"Can I direct you to your cabin?" a steward asks.

My cheeks stretch, excitement over my expedition finally hitting me for the first time. "Yes, please. I'm bound to take a wrong turn. This ship is colossal!"

"Don't worry," he assures me. "You'll find your way around quicker than you think."

"I hope so." I show him the card on my lanyard, seeing also for the first time that it has my photo and all sorts of other information on it.

"You're on Deck Ten, midship." He points to his left. "Head toward the stern to the elevators opposite Guest Services. When you step out, turn right into the corridor. Your cabin is port side."

"Which side is port side?"

He chuckles. "It's the left side of the ship when facing forward. Starboard is the right side."

"Port is left, starboard is right," I mutter to myself.

He kindly pats my shoulder. "Enjoy your cruise."

Heading in the direction he instructed, I make it all the way to my cabin, slide my cruise card into the lock, and push the door open, straining under its solid weight as I enter the room.

This is nice—quaint, but not too quaint.

Desperate to see the view from the balcony, I gently place my bag on the perfectly made, queen-sized bed and then step outside, taking in the Lower Manhattan skyline across the bay. The air no longer smells of fish and apprehension. Well, maybe a little fishy still, but it's more fish and liberation now, which is ironic considering the stony presence of Lady Liberty in the distance.

"Oh, Momma," I say, blinking back tears as I grip the balcony railing. "I wish you were here with me."

Time is a delicacy we take for granted, and I'd give anything to wind it back and share this trip with her. To go on an adventure and see the world with her by my side, laughing, conversing... living. In a morbid way, she will be with me, but it's not the same. She won't see a glacier or eat at a patisserie in Paris. She won't hear the chime of Big Ben or potentially see the Northern Lights.

She won't experience the slices of life pie she insisted I devour.

Wiping my damp cheeks, I will myself to stop crying. Mom wouldn't want me to be sad. Her hopes and aspirations were for this trip to be a happy one—for me to step outside of my work bubble and see the world. And at the very least, I owe it to her to try and achieve that.

"Okay, Riley." I fan my face. "No more tears. You're here. You're ready. You're going to have an amazing time."

Nodding, more to myself than to Lady Liberty, I hear the sound of a toilet flushing, followed by a door opening and then closing behind me. A chill stiffens my spine, so I spin on my heel, swipe the curtain aside, and step into the cabin... coming face to face with the tattooed stranger from check-in.

"What are you doing in my cabin?" I yell. "Get out!"

chapter two

OTHER RILEY

The woman from check-in screams at me, and I almost crap my pants.

"*Your* cabin?" I scratch the back of my head, confused. "This isn't your cabin. It's mine."

"No, you're wrong." She glares at me, snatches up her lanyard from the bed, and shoves her sailing card into my face. "Room 10143. See? Now, get out!"

I study the details, almost going cross-eyed because she's practically rammed the card up my nose.

Riley Wilson. 10143.

I'll be damned.

Raising my hand, palm out, because she looks about ready to either barrel me over or take a dive off the balcony just to get away, I lift my lanyard from my chest and show her my own card. "Mine says the same. Room 10143, see?"

"What?" Her brows pull together, her posture losing its I'm-gonna-kick-your-ass rigidness just slightly before she huffs, tugs my card closer, and nearly severs my neck from my body as she inspects the details.

I breathe in her perfume for the second time today, a mixture of flowers and coconut. She smells amazing—unlike the stench of Upper Bay.

"Wait a minute," she says, letting out a relieved sigh, her hand clutching her chest as her eyes meet mine. "They've printed my card twice and given one to you. They both say Riley Wilson."

Our heads are mere inches apart, and although the lanyard is practically cutting into my nape, I can't help the grin that breaks across my face. She's cute, and a little clueless.

"I don't think that's what they did," I explain.

"Yes, it is. Look." She flips the card and shows me what I already know. "Yours says Riley Wilson too."

"That's because I *am* Riley Wilson."

"What?"

"Yeah." I step back and run my hand through my hair. "This explains the weird Jane Doe comment in the terminal."

"Oh." She cups her cheeks, her stormy eyes wide. "Your last name is Wilson too?"

"Yep."

"That's crazy."

It's not; I bet there are more Riley Wilsons in the world other than us.

She bites her lip. "What does this mean, then?"

"It means we need to head to Guest Services and sort this out."

"Yes!" She stabs both of her pointer fingers at me and then delicately collects her bag off the bed. "Let's do that."

"After you." I gesture toward the door, allowing her to go ahead because I'm a gentleman, then both of us stride along the narrow corridor—my eyes glued to her incredible ass.

"I'm sorry for screaming at you," she says, glancing over her shoulder. "You scared me, is all."

I snap my eyes to a respectable height. "No apology necessary. I'm surprised I didn't scream too."

She laughs and stops at the elevators, and my insides cringe. I *hate* these oxygen-lacking death boxes with every fiber of my being.

"So, where are you from?" she asks after pushing the button.

"Buxtonville."

"Nice! I've been through there once. It's lovely."

"It is," I agree. "How 'bout you?"

"Manhattan."

Fighting my urge to scoff, I don't offer the same compliment, because where she lives isn't lovely. Manhattan is a concrete jungle, and I prefer my jungles to have trees.

"You don't like the city?" she probes when I don't answer.

"Not particularly." I eye the stairs, tempted to take them, but I'll look like a weirdo if I abandon her now. So I lean against the wall and wait, praying the elevators are out of service. "I like peace and quiet," I explain. "More oxygen, less people."

The elevator dings and opens, and my gut churns.

"Can't say I blame you. Manhattan is many things, but environmentally friendly isn't one of them." She enters the death box and then pokes her head back out when I don't follow. "You coming?"

"Yep," I mutter, pushing off the wall.

Riley squints at the buttons on the panel. "What deck is Guest Services on? I don't know which deck we actually boarded the ship on."

Not wanting to be in here longer than I have to, I lean across her and press the button for Deck 4, and she gasps when my arm brushes her bag.

"Whoa, you got a bomb in there?" I joke, even though bombs —especially in elevators on a ship—are no joking matter.

"No! Of course not." She steps back. "Just something very precious and... delicate."

I eye her suspiciously.

By the looks of her non-vacation-type clothing—white blouse and tailored gray pants—I suspect her "precious and delicate" thing is an expensive pair of shoes, like the ones on her feet, or perhaps something from that Tiffany store. Krystal, my ex, often came home from weekends in Manhattan with one of those bank-breaking blue bags.

"Fair enough," I say, letting it go. "So long as it's not a bomb."

"It's not." She laughs the kind of laugh that isn't convincing, then asks, "So why are you on a cruise?"

My face scrunches with confusion. "Huh?"

"You just said you like peace and quiet and fewer people, yet you're about to embark on a journey with a lot of people."

Yeah. Three and a half thousand, or thereabouts.

"I need to get away," I explain.

She nods, as if she needs to get away as well, and I'm curious as to why, but the elevator doors open, and my speedy exit takes priority.

"After you," I say, holding my arm across the door.

"Thank you." She goes to exit but stops, unintentionally holding me prisoner as she studies my ink. "I like your tattoo. The font is beautiful. Is it a name?"

My chest tightens, and I retract my arm. "Yes," I snap.

Riley startles at my harsh tone, her cheeks flushing pink before she frowns and scurries ahead.

Goddamn it.

I clench my fists, because I didn't mean to be a jerk. This trip across the Atlantic is supposed to help ease my anger and resentment, and I'm certainly not off to a good start.

Knowing I should apologize—or make up a ridiculous excuse —I choose to bite my tongue instead, keeping a safe distance until we reach Guest Services, where a guy in a suit kindly greets us.

"Welcome aboard. How can I assist you today?"

I open my mouth to answer, but Riley beats me to it, which is fine. She seems like the type who can adequately explain our dilemma.

"You've made an epic mistake," she blurts, finger pointing, eyes menacing. "Epic!"

The guy inches back, clearly alarmed, and I press my lips

together to prevent myself from laughing. Maybe I should've handled this.

"I'm sorry," she inserts, splaying her hands apologetically. "What I mean is, both of us—" She gestures to me, and I offer a polite wave before resting my arms on the counter. "—have accidentally been booked into the same cabin."

"Oh dear." The guy pouts as if we're two lost puppies looking for our owner. "That can't be right. Let me look up your details." He holds out his hand. "Can I have your sailing cards please?"

We lift our lanyards from around our necks and hand them over to him. He scans them into his computer, his eyes narrowing at the screen. "They both say Riley Wilson."

"Correct," I say, tapping the counter. "That's our name."

His complexion turns blotchy. "So... you're not traveling together?"

"No," we both snap.

"We don't know each other," Riley adds.

"I see." He rubs his chin, and I know that's not a good sign. I often do the same when I've royally fucked up a piece of furniture I've been working on. "It appears you've both been allocated the same cabin," he explains.

"No shit," I huff out.

"I'm terribly sorry for this. We'll get it sorted. Just bear with me while I speak to my supervisor." He pushes a bowl of candies toward us. "Help yourselves. I won't be long."

Obliging—because who doesn't like candy—I offer one to Riley as well. She scowls, so I shrug and pop one into my mouth just as the guy returns with a woman in a crisp-white naval uniform.

"Thank you for your patience, Mr. and Ms. Wilson."

"We're not married," I rumble, my patience wearing thin. All I want to do is go to a bar and relax. That's what I booked this damn cruise for.

"I wasn't implying you were," the supervisor says. "But please forgive me—I meant no offense."

Riley glares at me. "What he's trying to say is that, up until minutes ago in the cabin, we'd never met."

"I see." The supervisor clicks her mouse a few times, eyes locked on the screen. She exhales and shakes her head. "Hmm... I don't know how this happened. I mean, you both have the same name, so obviously that's *how* it happened, but—" She chews her ruby-red lip. "—it shouldn't have. How strange."

She keeps digging for an answer that, frankly, doesn't matter to me. I don't care how it happened. I just want it fixed.

"Listen, I'm happy to move cabins," I offer. "Riley can have the one you've given us, and I'll just move to another. Easy."

The supervisor's eyes meet mine, and she relaxes a little. "Thank you for your understanding, sir. I can't express how sorry I am for this. What I can do is offer you a full refund for your inconvenience."

"Sweet," I say, pleased I volunteered first.

"I will have to downgrade you though, sir."

My satisfaction dissipates. "How much downgrading are we talking about?"

"The stateroom you booked is a premium mini-suite with balcony. Unfortunately, we don't have any of that cabin class available. The ship is at capacity."

"Okaaay," I drawl, not quite processing what she's saying.

"What we do have are interior cabins, aft, on Deck Three."

A chill runs the length of my spine. "I'm not moving to an interior cabin in the bowels of this boat. No goddamned way. I'm claustrophobic."

The woman winces. "Right. That certainly won't work then."

We all look at Riley, and she takes a step back. "S-So am I. And... And I get seasick and need to be midship." She crosses her arms over her chest. "I'm not moving cabins."

"I understand." The supervisor sighs and taps her chin. "Would you be willing to share the cabin, then? I can offer you both a partial refun—"

"Absolutely not!" Riley barks.

I'm a little offended, but she's right. No fucking way. I spent a good portion of my savings on this trip. It's my bachelor getaway—my freedom vacation—and I'm not about to share my room with a stranger.

"Nope," I agree, shaking my head. "Not sharing."

"Unfortunately," the woman says, "the only other option is to cancel one of you and book a new cruise for a later date." She checks her watch. "But we'll need to do it ASAP. We set sail in less than two hours, and we'll have to track down your luggage."

Riley whirls on me. "It'll have to be you."

I laugh. "Sorry, sweetheart. No can do."

"Neither can I. It was hard enough getting this time off work. I'll never get the opportunity again."

"That makes two of us."

"But...." She hangs her head and bends over, hands gripping the counter as if it's the only thing keeping her upright.

Fearing she's about to hyperventilate, I ask, "If we share, how much of a refund do we get?"

"Fifty percent," the woman answers.

Riley snaps her head up. "I'm not sharing!"

"Could you give us a second?" I clasp Riley's elbow and gently pull her aside. "That's nearly eight grand. Each."

"I don't care. This trip is... special. It's personal. No offense, but I don't want to spend sixteen days sharing a cabin with you."

"I don't want to either. But what choice do we have? You won't cancel, and I won't cancel. So... what? Are they going to flip a damn coin?" I run a hand through my hair. "Do you like those odds? Because I sure as hell don't."

Tears spill from her eyes, and she clutches her bag to her chest as if it's the only thing anchoring her.

I swallow hard, almost on the brink of caving, when she wipes her cheeks and says, "Okay. If we don't have a choice, we'll share."

Relief sweeps through me, which is weird, because I'm *not* relieved. Far from it. "Are you sure?"

"Not really," she deadpans. "But if we have to, we're getting *more* than a fifty-fucking-percent refund."

Caught off guard by her sudden I-want-to-spill-blood mood shift, I move out of her way as she storms back to the counter.

"We'll share," she says, "but we want free Wi-Fi as well. And the all-you-can-drink package. And separate beds—moved to opposite sides of the cabin. And... And as many shore excursions as we want"—I lift my brows at that. *Good idea*— "And... a damn apology letter. It's the least you can do."

"Rest assured, Ms. Wilson, we can certainly arrange that."

"Good."

"Thank you so much for your understanding. And once again, I really am sorry for this."

"And don't forget that refund. I want my money back before the end of this cruise, or I'll..." She squares her shoulders. "I'll make this ridiculous error public on social media."

"Of course." The supervisor smiles awkwardly. "Let me fix this up for you. I'll send a steward to your room immediately to reconfigure your beds, set all excursions as $0 in your daily schedule on the ship's app, and I'll add a drinks and Wi-Fi package to your accounts. Everything will be updated on your sailing card, so you won't have to worry about a thing."

I internally applaud Riley's negotiation skills. Free drinks? Awesome. "I'm impressed," I whisper.

"I'm not," she hisses.

The supervisor hands our lanyards back. "All sorted. And if there's anything else we can help you with, please don't hesitate to ask."

"We won't," Riley grumbles before striding away.

I thank the woman and fall into step beside my marching cohabitee. "Hey, I know it's not ideal, but it might not be that bad. We now have free drinks, which would've cost over a thousand dollars each if we actually purchased the package, free unlimited shore adventures, plus more money in our banks. And I'm a good roommate. I promise."

"Do you snore?" she asks.

Shit.

"No," I lie.

"Thank goodness."

She wipes her damp eyes once more, and my chest tightens at her distress. This trip is obviously more than just a vacation for her. It is for me, too, but she seems to be carrying more than just her precious bag. Either that, or she's extremely emotional—like my niece. *God help me.*

"We're going to have to lay down some rules and boundaries," she says.

I wrap my arm around her shoulders and hug her to me. "No sweat."

"Starting with"—she shrugs out of my grip—"respecting each other's personal space."

Raising my hands, I nod. "Fair enough."

"Toilet seat down. Pick up after yourself. And don't touch my things. Especially *that*." Riley points to her bag, which is sitting on the desk on her side of the room. After the steward rearranged the beds and left the cabin, Riley had all but drawn a line down the center of it.

"Why? What's in it?" I reach out to pick up her treasured bag, but she snatches it away.

"I said don't touch."

"Okay, okay." For quite possibly the hundredth time since meeting her, I once again raise my hands in surrender. "I won't touch your shit."

"Good. And no sleepovers."

"Come again?" I collect the TV remote and move it to my bedside table.

"No bringing some random girl back to *my* room."

I laugh; she's funny. "It's not *your* room. It's *ours*."

"Fine. No bringing some random girl back to *our* room." She unzips her suitcase and carefully lifts out an evening dress, the shiny purple material skimming the floor.

I stare at it, my imagination forming a picture of it draped over her body, her long dark hair cascading over her bare shoulder. "I'm a grown-ass man, sweetheart," I say, clearing my croaky throat. "If I want to hook up with a woman on my vacation, I will."

"Good for you. But you can do it in *her* room. Not this one."

My natural instinct is to argue and tell her where to go—back to Manhattan—but the last thing I want to do right now is... argue. That's all I've done for the past two years, and quite frankly, I'm exhausted.

"I'm going to the bar."

She lays the dress on the bed, spins to face me, and shoves her hands onto her hips. "But we need to set some boundaries and—"

"What I need is a drink. Boundaries can wait."

"But—"

"Later, sweetheart."

"Stop calling me that."

"Fine. Later, *cookie*." I wink and head to the door, waving without looking back.

"Riley!"

"How bad can it be?" I mumble under my breath as I close the door behind me. *Ha! Bad. This can end up being very bad.*

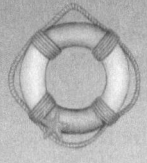

chapter three

C ookie? *Did he just call me... cookie?*
 Balling my fists by my sides, I growl as the door slams
shut, tears bursting from my eyes, my shoulders wracking as I sob
uncontrollably, almost as much as I did the day Mom died.

This vacation is for her as much as it is for me. It was what she
wanted most before slipping away, and now it's ruined before I've
even left the shore.

"I'm sorry, Momma," I whimper, "but this is.... It's a
disaster!"

Slumping onto my bed, I cover my face with my hands and,
through my sobs, release every ounce of sadness and regret I've
been holding in, until a cool breeze blows in from the balcony and
gently caresses my knuckles, a caress like my mother's—reassuring, comforting. I blink and peer through my spread fingers,
feeling her presence. Deep down, I know it's stupid. She's not
here, even though I want her to be. *Need* her to be.

If she were here, she'd rub my back and tell me everything will
be okay, that disasters happen, and that people live and die
because that's the way the world works. She once said to me that
when a plant perishes, sow a fresh seed, and when we make a

wrong turn, we should explore our new surroundings and experience what we wouldn't have if we had gone our planned route.

Mom believed life was a gift but that we don't always get what we ask for, and when we don't, smile appreciatively and make do, or... regift. That notion always warmed my heart, because she had a shelf in our linen closet that was stacked with presents she'd been gifted by friends, presents she didn't warm to or simply had no use for. Presents she'd pass on to someone else: the doorman, the lady down the hall, the homeless guy in the park across the street.

My mother was a giver. An optimist. A realist, but also a dreamer. She saw light and love and grasped it with both hands, and she always did it without complaint. When she was delivered her terminal diagnosis, she didn't kick or scream. She simply treasured what she'd already lived through and embraced what she could still give.

Me? I'd kicked and screamed. Repeatedly. I'd embraced hostility at life, God, abnormal malignant cells, and at my father. He was a ghost I'd never seen nor known—a summer fling Mom had willingly left on the beach in her early thirties. A nobody, as far as I was concerned, because at no time in my thirty-two years had he been a somebody. Momma was all I had, and she loved me irrevocably and unconditionally, as I had her.

Wiping the tears from my face, I push up from the mattress, cradling my waist as I walk around the bed to where my bag is sitting safely on my bedside table.

"Hey, Momma," I say, gently taking out the urn, warmth once again settling over me. "Wanna see my cabin? It's rather lovely, and surprisingly spacious." I sniff back my sorrow, trying to sound upbeat and enthusiastic. "It has a desk, a closet, a sofa, and a TV." Holding her out like a trophy, because she is one, I show her my surroundings. "The bathroom is modest, but there's a bath, so I can't complain. Not that I'm complaining, Mom, not at all. I'm ever so grateful. I'm sure this cruise will be incredible. But

—" I swallow, my throat thick. "—I have to share it with a stranger. A *male* stranger."

She doesn't answer, of course, but if she could, she'd no doubt say, *"Is he handsome? Single? Does he have manners?"*

I laugh. "I'm not sure about the last two, Mom, but he's certainly handsome."

The other Riley's short brown hair and how he runs his fingers through it flickers into my mind. I like his hair: clean, neatly cut, a little product. A lot can be said by how a man keeps his hair. That he cares about hygiene and presentation. And that's important. It's not only courteous but also shows self-appreciation.

Thank God he's not an odorous slob.

His kind, albeit mischievous eyes also flicker into my mind, and much like hair, a great deal can be determined by a person's eyes. They seldom hide our inner truth. A lie detector of sorts. And so far, his eyes haven't set off any alarms.

I try to recall if they're gray or blue. Possibly blue. But every time I've been close enough to tell, I've looked away, embarrassed I'd be caught staring in the first place.

"Later, cookie."

Ugh!

"On second thought, Mom, no, he doesn't have manners. And he walked out on me."

The thought of being roomed with an inconsiderate, pigheaded jerk churns my stomach. I won't cope; I'm already fragile and at my breaking point. Just being here, away from work and everything I've ever known is a giant leap of faith for me.

Why did I agree to share? It's a terrible idea.

"Mom," I groan. "What have you gotten me into?"

Again, as if she's in the room with me, I hear her loving rebuke. *"Riley Alessandra Wilson, stop this nonsense. Any given moment is what you make of it, so seize and embrace. Stop sulking and unpack your suitcase. And don't forget to eat something."*

I puff my cheeks and exhale. "Fine. Jesus, Mom!"

Scrunching my nose at her, I kiss the urn, place it back inside my bag, and remove my cosmetics bag from my suitcase before making my way to the bathroom. There isn't a lot of room, but I set about my perfume, makeup, and hair accessories, confident Riley won't mind if I occupy most of the space. He's a man, after all, and even though he has well-kept hair, he's certainly not Ralph Lauren billboard material, so I doubt he'll own many toiletries.

But what if he does? What if he's a hair stylist, or works at Ulta?

I recall the standard man-texture of his skin.

No. He's definitely not cosmetically confident.

Satisfied I'm one-hundred percent within my rights to commandeer the bathroom, I plop my toothbrush into the glass on the vanity, smiling satisfactorily until I catch a glimpse of my reflection in the mirror. Besides my red-rimmed eyes and tear-streaked cheeks, I look ready to take part in an editorial meeting, not a transatlantic cruise.

"I need to change," I mutter, releasing the pins securing my hair to my head, the tendrils falling past my shoulders.

Had Georgia seen me in anything but my corporate attire when I stopped by the office earlier, she'd have been most displeased, disgusted even, and I couldn't take that risk. Impressing her is a fine art I attempt to excel at despite the stress it causes me. But she is a means to an end, and I'm hoping that end is near.

Sighing as I massage the tension in my scalp, I kick my heels off, neatly place them in the bottom of the closet, and then unpack the rest of my things, hanging my clothes before settling Mr. Snuffles against the pillows on my bed. He's been my "pet" since I was seven years old. Not the living, breathing puppy I always wanted, thanks to Mom's allergies, but a comforting, synthetically stuffed confidant all the same.

I pat his head, undress, and then tug on a pair of denim shorts, my fingers freezing on the zipper, my head snapping toward the door, now acutely aware Riley could barge in at any moment. "Shit!"

Wrestling my T-shirt over my head, I make a mental note to add *knock before entering* to the list of rules I'm yet to finish going through with him.

Sharing a cabin will no doubt be difficult and a nuisance, at least at first. But if we stick to the rules and respect each other's space and privacy, we should be able to make this work. We must. We're both adults. And so far, he doesn't seem like the axe-murdering type. A playboy, maybe, which is unfortunate. But if he keeps his promiscuity out of this room, I don't care—he can play all he wants. Plus, we have no choice but to share. There's no way in Hades's hell I'm canceling this trip or risking having it canceled for me. Nor am I bunking in an interior cabin at the back of the ship for two and half weeks. So, yeah, no choice but to stay put.

I'll lock him out if I have to.

Turning in a circle, I rest my hands on my hips and survey the room. "Okay. I've unpacked. I've settled Mr. Snuffles. I've changed into something more comfortable. What next?"

"It is a requirement to watch the safety briefing video and visit your muster station before we leave port."

"Ah... yes, safety first!"

I search the desk for the remote control, lifting the room service menu and opening a few drawers. Frustrated, I pivot, ready to dial Guest Services and tell them they've messed up again, when my eyes land on the black device atop Riley's bedside table.

"Oh no you don't," I grouch, stomping to his side of the room and snatching it up. "This belongs with the TV, where it's going to stay." If he thinks he's going to lay claim to items we should share, he has another think coming.

Taking a seat on the sofa, I press the Play button and watch the video, memorizing important directives and the location of our muster station. Then I take out my cell, open the ship's app, and scroll to the deck plan, mapping my route.

Ready to head out, dread climbs my spine like a perfidious spider when I catch sight of my bag containing Mom's urn. I can't just leave her out in the open, unprotected, on my bed... and yet I don't have the heart to lock her inside the pint-sized, tenebrious safe in the closet.

"Damn it!"

I decide to take her with me; it's the safest option. So I gently sling my bag over my shoulder and follow the map until I'm standing outside the Lagoon Bar and scanning my sailing card at the muster station.

"Hello, ma'am. Did you watch the safety video?" a steward asks.

"I most certainly did," I answer, proud of myself. "A continuous alarm will sound in the event of an emergency. If that happens, I'm to go to my room, get my life vest, and then proceed here, to Muster Station 5."

He smiles. "Correct."

I continue, "Smoking is strictly prohibited outside of designated areas. But that's okay because I don't smoke," I admit, winking. "Oh, and if I see a person go overboard, I must shout 'Man overboard' three times and then find the nearest telephone and dial reception." I scratch my head. "Have I missed anything?"

"No, ma'am. I'm confident you'll be the safest passenger aboard."

"I hope so. This is my first cruise, and I want to be prepared."

He chuckles. "You're off to a great start."

After thanking him, I'm about to leave and explore when I spot Riley at the bar, hunched over a glass of amber-colored liquid. He looks miserable, and I can't say I blame him. I was miserable too, given our situation. Still am to an extent. But what good does it do to mope over the things we cannot change? If Mom taught me one thing, she taught me that. And while I'm still trying to master that particular lesson, I've learned to choose my moping battles more wisely—our vacation mix-up being one I can wave a white flag at.

Unable to walk away and just leave him there, I make my way to the bar instead. We'll be spending a lot of time together, so why not break the ice, put our dilemma behind us, and get to know one another over a drink?

Splendid idea.

"Hey," I say, as I awkwardly climb onto the barstool next to his.

He mutters, "Hey," then rotates his head in my direction, and I swear a low growl reverberates in his throat when he realizes it's me.

Recoiling just slightly, I fear I've made a mistake in joining him and that a white flag isn't sufficient protection. Perhaps I pissed him off in the cabin when I told him he couldn't have sleepovers. But then... it was a reasonable request. The cabin sleeps two, not three. And if anyone should be pissed, it's me. He called me "cookie," for Pete's sake. Who does that?

Choosing to ignore his rudeness, because I have just as much right to be here as he does, I pick up the cocktail menu and inspect what's on offer. "What are you drinking?"

"Bourbon."

Yuck!

I pull a sourpuss face. "I think I'll have a... Manhattan."

Take that, you Big Apple hater!

Riley's brow hitches, but he doesn't say anything, so I order my drink and then spin my stool away from the bar, admiring the tropical, novelty decor. "Have you done much exploring yet?" I ask him.

"No."

"Well, you'll have plenty of time for that, I guess."

He nods, and I get the impression he doesn't want company, his answers clipped, his attention still fixed on his glass.

"First cruise?" I ask, continuing to make unwanted small talk.

"Yep."

"Me too."

He doesn't offer anything in return, so I persist. We need to get to know one another—it's vital, since I won't be able to fall asleep with him in the same room as me if I still view him as a complete stranger. "What destination are you looking forward to the most?"

"All of them."

"None in particular? Personally, I can't wait to see Paris. And Greenland. Oh, and Nova Scotia. There's a Titanic museum there. I love all things Titanic," I confide, and when Riley chuckles, I relax a little and spin back to face the bar. "What's so funny?"

"You're about to go on a transatlantic cruise, and you love all things related to an ocean liner that sank in the Atlantic?" he points out.

"Well, when you put it like that...." I accept my drink from the bartender and take a sip, almost choking as it burns my esophagus.

Oh my Lord! What is this? Moonshine?

I'm not normally a "drinker." The odd glass of wine and celebratory Cosmo, yes. Pure ethanol, no.

Subtly pushing my glass aside, I eat the cherry garnish instead, then continue, "Modern-day ships are perfectly safe. Watertight bulkheads. Advanced radar technology. Sufficient lifeboats...."

"They can still sink."

Nonsense. "Not cruise ships."

"2012. *Costa Concordia*," he deadpans, swirling his drink and downing the rest before gesturing to the bartender for another.

That's somewhat uncomfortably recent.

Frowning, I protectively clutch my bag to my chest.

"You gonna take that thing everywhere you go?" he asks, side-eyeing me.

I squeeze it tighter. "What's it to you?"

"Nothing. I'm just wondering if you've smuggled your pet chihuahua or rabbit onto the ship."

I let out a small laugh. "Nope. Guess again."

"Cocaine?"

I shake my head.

"Dead boyfriend?"

My insides freeze.

Riley's eyes light up comically, and he points his empty glass at me. "That's it, isn't it?" he jokes. "Asshole ex is in there. You offed him, and now you're getting rid of his remains."

"That's—" I swallow thickly. "That's not funny."

"Sure it is!"

"No, it's not."

"You don't have much of a sense of humor, do you?"

Sliding off the seat to stand, I want to tell him *he's* the asshole, but all I can manage is "I'll see you around."

AFTER I LEAVE RILEY TO WALLOW IN HIS MISERY—OR to pick on some other poor passenger—I explore the ship, book some shore excursions, and sign up to do a behind-the-scenes tour. It's a first come, first served basis, and despite Riley being an inconsiderate jerk in the bar, I sign him up for the tour as well. He could've refused outright to share the cabin, potentially forcing me off the ship, but he didn't, and I can't ignore that.

The app has both of our accounts listed for the same cabin, which I suppose would be super convenient for a family or friends who want to book things to do together. I mean it's convenient for me to book him on the tour too, so I can't complain. Plus, he seems the type who'd enjoy the tour and would be disappointed he missed out because he chose to get drunk instead of seizing the opportunity. If I'm wrong, he can cancel and offer his spot to someone else. No harm done. Especially since I scored us unlimited excursions at no extra cost.

A mild breeze whisps across my face as two glass doors part, allowing me to step outside onto the fourteenth deck. Island-themed music blasts from speakers surrounding the pool, kids excitedly chase one another, and parents relax on sun lounges, brightly colored cocktails in hand. I weave in and out of the chaos and take a seat under the shade of a cabana, when I'm instantly approached by a waitress.

"Can I get you a drink, ma'am?" she asks.

I shake my head. "No, thank you."

She nods and moves on to the next passenger until someone accepts her offer, so I set my bag down and take out my laptop, when another waiter approaches.

"Can I get you a drink, ma'am?"

Holy alcoholism! Do they want everyone drunk on this cruise?

Feeling obligated to say yes, I order a Cosmopolitan, hoping it will deter any more waiters from bothering me when they see it on my table. We're due to set sail at any moment, and since the Wi-Fi connection is strong while we're still in port, I need to check my emails. Georgia hasn't texted or called, which is unusual, given her penchant to dismiss personal time and space, so when I open my laptop and find a message from her flagged **Urgent**, I'm not at all surprised.

Of course, it's urgent. Everything to do with her is urgent.

Slumping back in my seat, I click on it to find two attached manuscripts with a request for me to give them a "**quick read-through**" while I'm gone.

"You've got to be kidding me!" I spit out, glaring at the screen.

It all makes sense now. The Wicked Witch of the East has already given me two submissions to read through, hence why she was atypically accommodating of my leave. But it turns out she plans to work me just as hard, whether I'm in the office or not.

Stabbing my finger on the touchpad, I open the first attachment, taking note of the word count.

One hundred and thirty-eight thousand words?

"Peanut butter!" I curse under my breath, already fearing that pacing will be an issue.

"I'm sorry, ma'am?"

Blinking, I snap my attention to the waiter standing beside me, serving tray in hand, my Cosmo balanced on top of it. "Pardon?"

"You said peanut butter. Did you want that cocktail instead?"

"No, no." I swish my hand at him. "I'm just cussing," I explain.

Momma hated the F-word, so she taught me to swap "motherfucker" for "peanut butter."

"Wait a minute! There's a peanut butter cocktail?" I ask.

"Yes."

My tummy twirls with excitement as I stare at him in awe at the possibility.

"Would you like one, ma'am?" he prompts.

Tempted to say yes, because I *love* peanut butter, I bite my fingernail and decline, opting not to get inebriated on day one. I'm fond of my liver, and I'd much prefer it not to dissolve. "No, thank you. Maybe next time."

He places my drink down, kind of bows, backs away, then turns to collect a few empty glasses on a nearby table.

Picking up my glass, I sip my pretty pink drink while reading the genre of the first manuscript: a modern-day, Greek mythological romance. My curiosity piques. I adore Greek mythology.

Confused, because Georgia would normally automatically reject a romance submission of one hundred and thirty-eight thousand words, I scroll further to the agent's name, a frustrated sigh whooshing past my lips.

No wonder she sent this to me. It was submitted by her sister— the Wicked Witch of the West.

Knowing I'll have my work cut out for me when I shouldn't, I stab the touchpad again when a male voice suddenly bursts from the speakers above my head, scaring the absolute bejesus out of me.

"Welcome, cruiselings! My name is Paul, and I'm your cruise director. We'll be setting sail in just a few minutes, so I hope you're ready for a fantastic vacation. While the captain navigates us out of the harbor, the party is about to get started on Lido Deck. So head on up, grab yourself one of our delicious cocktails, and put your dancing shoes on. I'll see you all soon."

The engines rumble to life, so I finish reading Georgia's email and type a reply, obediently telling her I'd be glad to read over the manuscripts, even though "glad" couldn't be further from the truth. And by the time I snap my laptop shut, the ship is slowly drifting away from the dock.

Collecting my bag and what's left of my drink, I make my way to the railing, the water swirling and bubbling below. A mix of excitement and melancholy twists within my chest, my heart skipping over its usually sullen beat.

Leaving my motherland to explore other parts of the world is both daunting and exhilarating, mostly because I'm culturally and ethnically challenged—a side effect of strict goals focused solely on fiction and publishing for as long as I can remember. School, college, internship, NYC—it's all I know. I can identify a sentence written in passive voice and make it active without a blink, but ask me to voice a sentence in any language other than English, and I'd fail miserably.

Actually, that's a lie. After receiving my cruise ticket from Mom, I googled how to say "Where is the bathroom, please?" in French, so, perhaps I wouldn't fail and ultimately soil myself.

At least... I hope I won't.

Taking the stairs to deck sixteen, I shade my eyes from the sun, marveling at the Verrazano-Narrows Bridge as we cruise toward it, the grand structure majestically spanning New York Harbor, growing more prominent and imposing the closer we get to it.

Exhilaration peppers my skin.

The ship's horn blasts.

I almost pee my pants.

Giggling, the realization of why my mother desperately

wanted me to go on this cruise hits me—just like her often swift but lovingly playful slap to the back of my head.

A lump of regret forms in my throat, and I swallow. She knew my life was all work with no play. No adventure nor culture. I just pray she didn't think I was unhappy, because I'm not.

Lonely? Sure. But happy? Mostly.

At least, I *was*... before she died.

chapter four

OTHER RILEY

After Riley left me in the bar, I felt like an asshat.

It wasn't her fault the cruise line fucked up. It wasn't her fault my life had gone to shit and that my wife of fifteen years ditched me for her hot-shot lawyer colleague. And it wasn't her fault I was getting a divorce. Hell, it wasn't my fault either, and yet for some reason, I felt responsible, because I struggled to direct my anger at the correct target, which isn't my new roommate.

"You suck, Wilson," I mutter, as I swirl the glass of bourbon in my hand before draining the last drop.

For the past two years, I've become bitter and lost, constantly mourning a life I adored and worked hard to achieve, a life my wife Krystal ruined.

We'd been together since high school. Two peas in a young, naïve, lovesick pod. We'd built a home together, shared our life's aspirations, and we'd been inseparable since the moment we met. She owned my heart for as long as I could remember... until she ripped it from my chest and tore it to shreds.

According to her, we'd "grown apart" and "lost our spark." Apparently, our small-town, "simplistic" life wasn't enough for her anymore. She wanted hustle and bustle instead. A corporate adventure.

More like an adventure between her legs on her office desk several times a week with Finn.

Cracking my neck from side to side, I roll my shoulders, willing my anger and tension to ease, a trick my sister Roni has been helping me master. She says it releases trapped emotional trauma, or some shit like that. Do I believe her? Not really. But I do it anyway, because she's the champion of Zen. She has a room full of gems and crystals, and she often burns plants from the garden and fumigates my home. It's outright annoying and stinks, but I don't stop her, because nothing else I've done so far has worked.

Since my split with Krystal, my vision has been nothing but red, black, and then red again, but thanks to Roni and her pushy Zen-like ways, I've slowly come to realize my divorce is a clean slate—I just don't know what I'm supposed to do with it. My life was paved before me, my future set, my heart whole... until it wasn't. And now my sister and mother are helping me piece it back together, most of those pieces once again intact, with the exception of one, which will always belong to my daughter, Imogen.

A child runs past the bar, her laughter echoing throughout the room. I smile, but my face is tight. Strained. My sweet baby angel never saw the light of day, never squeezed my thumb or burped on my shoulder. She never laughed as I chased her, and she never would.

At twenty-six weeks' gestation, Krystal and I were forced to say goodbye to her four years ago, and perhaps that's when we said goodbye to our marriage as well. Regardless, that life as I knew it is over, and I have the divorce papers in my suitcase to prove it.

I just have to seal them with a signature.

Roni suggested I get away and live it up on a whirlwind cruise to reset and sow my wild oats, because my oats had always been domesticated. In all honesty, I have no idea how to sow wild oats. It's not a lifestyle I've ever entertained nor ever *wanted* to entertain. According to my sister though, I owe it to myself to at least try.

So that's what I'm here doing—trying to enjoy the single life. Trying to put the past in the past where it belongs. And trying to leave my resentment and anger back in the States, which I haven't quite managed to do yet.

Slamming my empty glass on the bar top, I hang my head. Riley didn't deserve me being a jerk to her. She'd been great about the cabin mix-up, when most wouldn't have. Sure, she tried to dump a bucketload of rules and boundaries on me, but I can't blame her for doing so. We're gonna need them—*some* of them—and I'll agree within reason. Whatever she needs, because she could've refused to share the cabin, and she didn't in the end. Credit where credit is due, I guess.

She's also undeniably hot as fuck.

Damn!

I draw in a deep breath, my throat rumbling on the exhale as I recall her legs and ass in those tiny denim shorts. Perfect skin. Sleek. Slender. I'd been ready to sow my wild oats all over her on top of the Lagoon Bar, but she doesn't seem like the wild-oats-sowing type either. There's something fragile and sad about her—her eyes red from crying—and it pains me to think I'm the cause because my presence is ruining her "special" trip.

No doubt I am, but in a way, she's also ruining mine.

Maybe I'm wrong and she's just a spoiled, stuck-up snob. A well-to-do Manhattan princess. My gut tells me that's not the case, and instead, like me, she's been through something, recently —the telltale signs are hard to miss.

"Would you like another?" the bartender asks as I trace the rim of my empty glass with my fingertip.

I look up and shake my head. "No thanks, man. I've had enough for now."

He nods, so I leave him a tip, then make my way out of the bar, knowing I need to unpack, have a shower, and then scope out the ship and, apparently, "the local talent."

When Roni helped me plan the cruise, she pointed out several singles' events on the itinerary: a singles' nightclub, speed dating, and some fancy High Tea on the Seas. Just the thought of doing that shit feels desperate, but then what would I know? Until two years ago, I'd never been a single adult.

"Going up?" a woman asks as I'm about to bypass the elevator for the stairs.

If I were any good at being a single, wild oat-sower, I'd respond with, *"I prefer going down."* But I'm not any good, not yet anyway, so I blurt, "Yep," and reluctantly follow her into the death box.

"What deck?" she asks.

"Ten, thanks."

She presses the button for me, and we smile at each other, her long eyelashes fluttering. They remind me of spider legs, and it kinda gives me the creeps.

"Enjoying the cruise so far?" she prompts, casually leaning back on the railing while propping her foot against the wall.

I chuckle; what a stupid question. "We haven't cruised yet."

"The ship, silly." She giggles. "Are you enjoying the ship?"

Her spidey eyes skate over my chest and arms before landing on my face again, and even though I've been a married man for almost half of my life, I'm not naïve enough to mistake her unmistakable flirting.

"The ship is great," I say. "But I haven't seen much of it yet. Just a bar."

"Good place to start."

I nod. "It is."

Focusing on the illuminating numbers on the panel above the door as we ascend the decks, I will them to move faster. Elevators are the devil's cubbyhole, and if I ever end up stuck in one when it breaks down, I'll more than likely pass out.

Heat surges the length of my spine, simmering at my nape.

Why didn't I use the stairs?

I shuffle from one foot to the other.

Roni, that's why.

She's spent the past year encouraging me to take small leaps of faith, because life is short, and if you don't leap every now and again, you won't go anywhere. Thanks to her, I've leapt into five fucking elevators today. Five! And I'm far from feeling liberated.

"You here with family?" the woman asks.

I shake my head. "No. I'm flying solo."

Her eyebrows rise, and I wish I hadn't been so forthcoming. But then isn't that what I'm here to do? Be forth-cumming?

"How 'bout you?" I ask.

"I'm travelling with my bestie."

I nod again as if to say, *"Of course."*

She drops her propped foot to the ground and twists a lock of her hair around her finger. "I'm about to get my swimsuit on and check out the adult oasis. You should join me. It's looks amazing."

"I—" The elevator dings, and the doors spring open, so I waste no time in getting the hell out. "Yeah. Maybe I will."

"Looking forward to it."

Fluttering her spidey lashes again, she waves her fingers, so I wave mine, immediately dropping my hand once the doors close.

What are you doing, Wilson?

Although tall and with a delightful chest, she's not my type. Too young, too eager. But then maybe young and eager is what I need—what Roni thinks I need.

Surely not!

Considering the woman's offer as I slide my card into the door lock, I decide I'm not in the mood for a swim, instead preparing for a potential Riley "rules and guidelines" attack.

"Riley, you here?" I ask, tentatively stepping inside the cabin. "Hello?"

When she doesn't answer, I exhale my relief, remove my lanyard, and toss it onto my bed, my hands coming to rest on my head as I scan the room. A suitcase is propped against the wall, pajamas neatly folded on her bed, a stuffed dog placed in front of her pillows. I'm tempted to pick it up and give it a squeeze, but she explicitly told me not to touch her stuff, especially her bag.

I search the room like a sniffer dog looking for drugs, eager to find it. Not knowing what's inside is fucking irritating. None of my business, of course, but I want to know what she's hiding. Maybe it's because we're sharing a room, and if she's an international drug smuggler, I could be implicated. Accessory before the fact, or some shit like that. Not that she seems the narcotics-dealing type, but then Krystal didn't seem the cheating-whore type either.

Fuck it! I'm done with lies and secrets. Not at home, not with Krystal, and certainly not on my vacation.

Practically ransacking the room, I search under her bed and in the drawers of her bedside table but come up empty-handed, most likely because she still has the damn bag glued to her side. So I give up—for now—and enter the bathroom to take a piss, stopping dead in my tracks.

"What the hell?" I breathe deeply, turning in a circle, bottles of perfume, lotions, and potions scattered across the sink and shelves like a Macy's store. "Gee, thanks for leaving some space for my stuff."

I lift the toilet seat with a snap and piss, annoyed with all the girly shit surrounding me. Women waste so much money on junk. Krystal once bought a lipstick that cost more than my hammer drill. A damn lipstick! A drill makes me money and is put to good use; her lipstick probably ended up around Finn's cock.

Performing a hygienic shake, I prepare to close the lid like I always do when I leave it up instead. Screw her! This is my bachelor getaway, and if I have to lift the seat, Riley can damn well put it down. Fair's fair.

I grin, pleased with my act of rebellion, then have a shower, using Riley's shampoo. It smells like mint and flowers, and I'm okay with that. Plus, we're meant to be *sharing*.

Stepping out of the dwarf-sized shower-bath, I grab a towel

and attempt to tie it around my waist, but it barely secures at my hip. Baffled, I wonder if I've accidentally picked up the bathmat instead, so I grab another towel and unravel it to find it's the same size.

Why is everything so damn small? Yeah, I'm a big guy, but Jesus... this is ridiculous!

Not knowing how to neatly roll it up again, I do my best to fold and twist it like a fucking artistic donut before tossing it onto the sink. I collect my clothes and head into the room, dropping them onto the bed and discarding the poor excuse for a towel on the floor, aware Riley could barge in at any moment. To be honest, I don't care. I'm not ashamed of my body, and I'm not about to stress over whether or not I should get undressed in my own damn cabin. If she doesn't want to see me naked, she can cover her eyes.

"Welcome, cruiselings!" a male voice blasts throughout the room. "My name is Paul, and I'm your cruise director."

I jump out of my skin, cup my junk, and turn in a circle, searching for Paul, when the speaker above my head crackles.

"We'll be setting sail in just a few minutes, so I hope you're ready for a fantastic vacation. While the captain navigates us out of the harbor, the party is about to get started on Lido Deck. So head on up, grab yourself one of our delicious cocktails, and put your dancing shoes on. I'll see you all soon."

Sounds like a plan, so I unzip my suitcase, rifle through it for a shirt and pair of pants, and get dressed. Roni took me shopping for "cruise clothes" a few weeks ago, because apparently plaid shirts, varnish-stained denim, and work boots aren't appropriate for a vacation. I put up a fight to begin with, but as always, my sister was right—I would have looked like an idiot if I packed what I usually wore.

Gathering my new suit and shirts, I make my way to the closet and open the door. "For fuck's sake!"

Dresses, blouses, and more girly shit occupy almost every hanger apart from three on the end, one of them broken.

"Not gonna happen, sweetheart!" I shove her clothes across the rail, bunching them together, before hanging my suit and one shirt. If she thinks she's going to hog our entire cabin, she's sorely mistaken.

Krystal used to pull this shit as well—assume I wear the same thing day in and day out and therefore require no hanging space. Granted, back at home, I do wear the same thing day in and day out, but that's not the point.

I'm supposed to be getting away from this shit. Bachelor lifestyle, remember?

Glaring at Riley's clothing, I pull one of her shirts off the hanger and replace it with my own, and then I close the door and lay hers on her bed, happily rubbing my hands together before opening the top drawer in the closet to find it full as well.

"Fuck me!" Steam practically billows out of my nostrils until I wrench open the next drawer, which is empty.

Drawing in a deep breath, I hold it, count to three, then slowly exhale.

Calm the hell down, Wilson. She hasn't completely disregarded you. She's not Krystal.

I close my eyes and crack my neck, then head out onto the balcony and stare over the bay toward Lower Manhattan, where my ex is currently working. A disgusting smog floats on the horizon, nothing but concrete, glass, noise, and traffic below it. New York City is a smokescreen, full of rats and contamination, and I sure as shit can't wait to get out of here. To escape and explore other places.

When Roni suggested the cruise for "sowing my wild oats," I instead grasped the opportunity to further my knowledge for work. That said, I reluctantly embraced her objective as well, because she often knows me better than I know myself.

Maybe I do need to put myself out there again. Maybe not. Regardless, I'm looking forward to a change of scenery.

The ship's engines rumble, the water below bubbling like a murky jacuzzi. Seaweed floats to the surface among a slick of oil and some empty plastic bottles and potato chip bags. I scoff, grinning at the garbage—not because it's polluting the water, but because it's reminiscent of this cesspool of a city.

"Good riddance," I mutter under my breath to a place I resent and a woman I once loved.

Good riddance to bad garbage and bad people.

By the time I've reached Lido Deck, every man, woman, kid, and crew member has also made their way outside, the sailaway atmosphere now in full swing.

A band plays nautical-themed music while kids run around the pool, ice creams in hand, crewmembers mopping up in their wake. I dodge passenger after passenger, avoiding their novelty drinks with useless paper umbrellas.

Hopefully, when we're out to sea, everyone will disperse, scattering to the many hubs of the ship. The kids will go to kids' club, the gamblers to the casino, the shoppers to the shops, and the sun lovers by the pools. Once that happens, and I pray it does, I'm sure it won't feel so crowded and suffocating, because I need to let go and breathe—something I haven't properly done for many years.

Spotting the Verrazano-Narrows bridge looming ahead, I take the stairs to deck sixteen and walk closer to the bow, when I catch sight of Riley, shielding her eyes from the sun, ready to look up as we pass beneath it. Her denim shorts hug her ass, showcasing her sexy legs, her T-shirt snug against her breasts. She has a body that could make a grown man cry, and if I were a crier, no doubt I'd be sobbing where I stand. But... I don't cry—not anymore. My tears dried up four years ago, and they haven't fallen since.

I wander closer, wanting to speak to her, because she's the only person I kinda know, but also because I was a dick to her in the bar and don't want things to be more awkward than they already are. Apart from her barking orders at me and hogging ninety percent of our cabin, she isn't all that bad to be around. So I step up beside her, the noise of the traffic on the bridge roaring overhead, then echoing as we sail underneath it.

I read on a forum that the *Oasis of the Seas* is too tall to pass under the bridge, even at low tide, and the only way it can is because it has a retractable funnel. Our ship isn't as tall, but I do know there's not much more than ten feet from the tip of the radar mast to the road deck of the bridge. It's impressive, or maybe stupid. There's not much room for error.

I open my mouth to speak, then close it again, because it's useless—she won't hear me anyway. So I watch her instead as she sucks in a nervous breath before smiling her relief as the shadow of the bridge disappears and the sun once again hits her face. She's cute, her eyes lighting up like a kid on Christmas morning, her cheeks forming into little apples.

"Holy shit!" she whispers, clasping her chest. "That was close."

I lean down, my mouth hovering near her ear. "Lucky it's low tide."

Riley shrieks and stumbles, so I reach out and grab hold of her to prevent her from falling on her pretty ass, pink sugary shit spilling from the glass she's holding.

"Jesus!" she says, her wide eyes searching mine as if I'm either Superman or a sexual predator. "You scared me."

Unable to tell which one she suspects I may be, I help her steady herself and quickly let her go. "Sorry."

She puffs out a breath. "I nearly fell off the ship."

I chuckle. "You can't."

"What do you mean I can't?"

"It's impossible to *fall* off the ship."

"No, it's not. People go overboard all the time."

"Unless you climb the rails, someone throws you over, or you step onto a chair or some stupid shit like that, you can't just accidentally fall overboard."

She blinks as if what I'm saying is a bunch of baloney.

It's not.

"I'm serious," I say. "You can't."

Placing her now-empty glass on a nearby table, she reaches into her bag, and I get ready for her to pull out whatever it is she's hiding in there—a taser, perhaps. But she pulls out a tissue instead.

My anticipation deflates.

"Should I be worried you know so much about falling off the ship?" she asks, side-eyeing me suspiciously while wiping her hands and legs.

"Should I be worried you might test out my theory?"

"So it is a theory then?"

"Theoretically, yes."

Riley laughs, then tosses her tissue in a nearby trash can. "Feeling better, are we?"

I run my hand through my hair, readying my apology. "About before, I—"

"It's fine. I get it. Neither of us planned for our vacation to be the way it's shaping up to be. I was mad; you were mad. It is what it is."

Shocked, I press my lips together, a grin spreading across my face. I'd expected her to force me to my knees, to grovel and beg for her forgiveness. And hell, I might've done it for the sake of peace.

"Okay then," I choke out. "Truce?"

She holds out her hand. "Truce."

We shake.

"You look nice," she says, eyeing me from top to toe. "Where are you off to?"

"*We're* going to dinner," I say as if she doesn't have a choice.

"We're? As in you and me?" She shakes her head. "Nuh-uh. No thanks. I'll pass."

"Sorry to burst your bubble, cookie, but we have a reservation in the main dining room."

Her head tilts with confusion, and I get the impression she

knows nothing about the sailaway dinner, which strikes me as odd. She seems the type who would carry an hourly planner with scheduled bathroom breaks.

"A reservation?" she asks, one eyebrow raised. "What are you talking about?"

"The sailaway dinner."

She slides her cell from her back pocket and checks the cruise app, as if to call my bluff. "Huh. You're right. I must've missed that."

"Yes, I know."

Rolling her eyes at my audacity, she continues to scroll her screen. "What time is the reservation?"

"In an hour."

"Oh. Okay. Perhaps I will go then. But I need to shower and get ready first."

"I just had one, so knock yourself out."

In keeping with our ceasefire theme, I could be honest and admit to using her shampoo. But she might try severing my head from my neck again, so I save that little mishap for another time.

"Thanks. I better head downstairs then." She goes to turn but stops instead. "I take it there's a dress code tonight?"

"Sure is. Smart casual."

"Well—" She subtly rakes her eyes over my body. "—you've certainly nailed that."

Blushing like a teenage boy on his first date, I slide my hands into my pant pockets and rock back on my heels.

She smiles. "See you there."

I smile back. "You will."

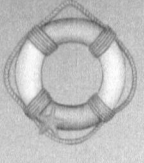

chapter five

Holy shit! Maybe he could be Ralph Lauren billboard material.

The grumpy Gargamel certainly does clean up impeccably well: a crisp white shirt with navy buttons and stitching, collar up, cuffs rolled to his biceps, charcoal pants hugging his thighs and ass. I'm tempted to glance back for a second look but hurry to the cabin instead.

Freshly showered in reasonable time, I smooth my dress down my thighs while waiting in line outside the main dining room, then I stretch onto my tiptoes, trying to spot him. When he said he'd see me here, I assumed he'd wait for me and we would eat dinner together, get to know one another better, and then go over some more rules and boundaries. But maybe I got the wrong idea. Maybe he meant we'd see each other in passing, or maybe he only informed me of the sailaway dinner on the off chance I didn't know about it, which, strangely enough, I did not.

When it comes to preparation, I'm methodical. Diligent. I have an annual subscription to Daily Planner, and I'm a seasoned color-coder and annotator, so I'm mystified at how I missed this "unmissable" event. Then again, my plan for the next eighteen days is to simply eat when I'm hungry and to order room service here and there. Mealtimes are never a priority, because I seldom have time. Eating is always an afterthought really.

Scanning the line again, I give up my search. The guy is certainly polarizing. Hot and cold. Engaging one minute, stand-offish the next. So I guess it's no surprise he's ditched me to eat alone... or with someone else.

He's also grossly untidy.

When I returned to the room to get ready for dinner, his clothes and towel were on the floor, and the toilet seat was up. I slammed it down and then refolded a towel he rolled into a ball and had thrown into the sink as if it were a laundry hamper. And then I found my blouse tossed onto my bed, which sent my blood boiling... until I went to hang it back up, only to find I'd uninten-tionally taken up most of the hanging space.

Oops! My bad.

Most guys don't need the space women do, but perhaps I'd been wrong about that as well.

What am I doing here, alone, waiting in a line for dinner I don't particularly want to eat?

Contemplating leaving and grabbing a quick bite from the buffet on my way back to the room, I inch out of the line when the couple in front of me are escorted into the dining room.

"Next please," the hostess says, waving me toward her.

I perform an impromptu what-do-I-do tap dance before abandoning my escape and shuffling forward.

"Hello, ma'am. Welcome. May I have your room number?" she asks.

"Uh, yes. Of course. It's 10143."

She scans her computer. "Ms. Wilson?"

"That's me."

As I'm about to say, *"Table for one, please,"* she collects a leather-bound menu and cradles it to her chest. "You're the last to arrive. Please follow me."

Last?

I look at my watch; I'm not even late. I'm never late. And if I'm *last* to arrive, who's first, second, third, and....

Wait! Does she mean I'm the last diner for the session? Oh goodness, how embarrassing.

"I'm sorry I'm last," I say, scurrying behind her and past waiters and waitresses rushing about, carrying trays the size of hula hoops stacked with dishes covered in domes.

We stop and move aside, allowing one of them to pass, his head barely visible above the tower of food he's so expertly balancing.

She continues walking, so I follow, the clang and clatter of cutlery and crockery playing a culinary melody. Chandeliers sparkle two floors above, while large gold pillars etched with aquatic mythological figures gleam on either side of the room. It's rather grand, chaotic... and rocky.

Skipping a few steps to avoid landing in a gentleman's lap, I have no choice but to use the back of his chair to balance myself.

"I'm so sorry," I say.

He chuckles. "Someone hasn't found her sea legs yet."

I pull an *eek* face. "I'm not sure I own a pair."

"First time cruising?"

"Yes, I'm afraid so."

"Just give it a day or two. You'll find them in no time."

"I hope you're right." I let go of his chair and summon the sheer will to walk with at least a little bit of poise.

No doubt resembling a penguin, I continue to totter, splaying my hands out at my hips while silently cussing myself out for wearing heels.

Five-inch stilettos on a floating structure.... Are you crazy, Riley?

"Here you go, Ms. Wilson," the hostess announces as she pulls out a chair at a large circular table, numerous strangers seated around it.

I stumble again before bracing myself on another poor gentleman's chair. "I think there's been a mista—"

Other Riley stands and takes the hostess's place.

"Oh! I didn't see you. Th-Thank you," I stutter, offering everyone a meek wave.

"Can we order now?" a little girl asks.

I recognize her from the dock, sans her **I Love to Cruise** tee.

Her mother pats her leg. "Yes, Avery."

"About time. I'm starved," her brother grouches, his face buried in his iPhone.

I lower into my seat, and Riley pushes me in before taking his seat next to mine.

"Do you know these people?" I whisper.

"No," he whispers back.

"So why are we sitting with them?"

"Because, apparently, that's what sailaway dining is all about... meeting other passengers."

"Right." I sit up straighter and pick up my menu. "Hello."

"Everyone, this is Riley," Riley says, and I can't tell if his clipped tone is because he's as hungry as the kids and I've unintentionally made them wait to order, or because we're "meeting other passengers" he doesn't want to meet.

Two men sitting opposite us narrow their eyes curiously, one of them flicking his wrist and swirling his finger at us. "You're both named Riley?"

I glance at my namesake, my lip quirking. "Yes."

The man grins as if we're newborn babies and then unfolds his napkin and lays it over his lap. "Pleased to meet you. My name is Hugo, and this is my husband, Immanuel, but you can call him Manny. We're on our honeymoon."

"Congratulations," I offer. "Pleased to meet you both."

The mother beside me butters a bread roll and slides the plate in front of her daughter. "I'm Kathy. This is my husband, Oscar, and these are our children, Avery and Zachary."

"Zach," the boy snipes, his focus still glued to his screen.

She playfully rolls her eyes. "Teenagers."

I smile as if I understand what teenagers of today are like, but apart from once being a teenager myself, I haven't the slightest clue. I never owned a phone back then, and I was scarcely ill-mannered toward my mother.

"Do you have kids?" she asks.

I shake my head. "No."

"I'm eight," Avery interrupts. "How old are you?"

"Thirty-two."

"Avery!" Kathy pats her leg again. "Don't be rude."

The little girl shoves the bread roll into her mouth and goes back to coloring her picture, practically murdering her crayon as she aggressively mashes it into the paper.

"The name's Ben, but most people call me Horse, 'cause I'm hung like one," a boisterous voice says from the other side of Riley.

I lean forward to get a better look at the self-proclaimed Mr. Ed, but he leans back instead and holds out his chubby calloused hand behind Riley's chair.

Anyone who feels it necessary to discuss the size of their genitals to strangers at a dinner table is certainly not someone I'd normally shake hands with, but I do it anyway, graciously lying when I say, "Nice to meet you."

"Ditto, love." He waggles his eyebrows, then rests his arms on the backs of Riley's and Manny's chairs. "So where we all from?"

"Jersey," Hugo says.

Ben snaps his fingers at him. "Yankees or Phillies?"

I cringe; I *hate* finger snapping with a passion. It's obnoxious. Georgia does it on the daily, and it grates my nerves.

Hugo hesitates as he says, "Phillies?", his eyes wide as if his answer could somehow be incorrect.

Riley tips his glass of beer toward him. "Good man."

"How 'bout you, Ben?" Manny asks, angling his body closer to his husband and away from Ben's intrusive dangling arm. "Where are you from?"

"Michigan."

"Tigers?" Riley asks.

"Fucking damn straight."

Hugo covers his mouth with his hand and dips his head, his eyes bouncing in their sockets.

Unable to bite my tongue, I hiss, "Ben!"

"Yes, love?"

I tilt my head toward the kids, and mouth, "Language."

His brow pinches before he realizes what he said. "Oops. Sorry, squirts."

Zach doesn't bat an eyelid, and neither does Avery. In fact, Kathy and Oscar don't either, both of them intently studying their menus.

Okaaay, then.

"And how about you two?" Hugo asks Riley and me. "Where are you from?"

We both go to speak at the same time, so I close my mouth and offer my hand for Riley to answer first. "You go."

"No, ladies before gentlemen."

Huh. Perhaps he does have manners.

Smiling appreciatively, I place the menu down and lay my napkin across my lap. "I'm from Manhattan."

"And I'm from Philly," Riley offers.

Ben scrunches his face. "Long way to go for hook-ups."

"Oh, we're not together," I explain. "We just met. Actually, it's a funny story."

Riley scoffs. "I wouldn't exactly call it funny."

I let out a mild laugh. "I suppose not."

"Mom, I'm hungry," Avery whines.

"Okay, sweetie." Kathy tuts and waves a waiter down, almost grabbing his shirt as he hurries by. "Can we order? My children are hungry."

"Uh, yes, ma'am. I'll be right with you," he says, graciously flustered.

I offer the waiter my thanks, something Kathy failed to do, before he hurries off again. The service staff buzzing about remind me of bees, each table a flower they must visit, their duty essential for the enjoyment of others. I've always been fond of bees: such harmonious, unappreciated, hard workers.

"What are you going to have, dear?" Kathy asks her daughter.

"Pizza."

"Why don't you try something else?"

"I don't want anything else. I want pizza."

"Of course." She winks. "You can have what you want."

The waiter hastily returns, apologizes, takes our orders, and buzzes off again.

"So, what's the not-so-funny story?" Hugo asks me.

"About how Riley and I met?"

"Yes. Do tell." He snuggles into his husband's side and lifts a glass of red to his lips, which is when I notice a Cosmopolitan in front of me.

Pointing to it, I ask, "Is this mine?"

Riley slides it closer to me. "It's what you were drinking on deck, right?"

"Drinking?" I laugh. "More like spilling." I take a sip. "Thank you."

"Tell us the not-so-funny story already," Hugo urges. "I'm dying here."

Giggling at his eagerness for gossip, I take another quick sip and fill him in. "We were booked into the same cabin by mistake."

Ben bellows. "That *is* funny!"

"Not really," I add. "Because we have to share."

Kathy stops fussing over Avery and frowns. "Are you joking? That's outrageous! Surely they have other cabins."

"One of us would have to accept a severe downgrade, and neither of us wanted to," Riley explains.

She wrinkles her nose. "That's unacceptable."

Oscar shakes his head. "We spend good coin on these cruises, and this is what we get... double-booked cabins and tardy table service."

I understand their vexation; I was mad too. But I wouldn't exactly say the table service is tardy, because it's not. There are at least two hundred people on this level of the dining room alone, most of them pleasantly eating already. Not to mention Guest Services was extremely apologetic about the double booking. If they said, "Bad luck," and offered no remedy nor form of compensation, then yeah, it would be outrageous and unacceptable.

Kathy tuts again. "I hope you got a refund."

"We were looked after," Riley offers before I can answer.

"So, you're sharing, eh?" Ben claps Riley on the back, his eyebrows dancing, his grin sexually insinuative.

I all but snarl, as does Manny.

"We're sharing the cabin, yes." Riley leans back in his chair and squashes Ben's dangling hand, the obnoxious man promptly removing it and subtly stretching his fingers.

I hide my satisfied smirk behind the rim of my Cosmo, Manny and Hugo doing the same behind their glasses of red.

"So," Manny prompts after taking a sip, "all's well that ends well then?"

Riley and I lock eyes, and I shrug. "So far, I guess."

He clinks my glass with his, just as our appetizers are promptly served together with the kids' meals, everyone happily eating while entertainment staff visit tables, performing magic card tricks.

"Where are you from?" I ask Kathy and Oscar as I dip my spoon into my soup.

"The Buckeye state," Oscar says with pride.

Ben points his fork at him. "Home to the country's best-ever athlete."

I know who Ben's referring to, because my mother was married to an NBA assistant coach when I was fifteen. And although I'm a huge fan of LeBron, I disagree with Ben that he's the best-ever athlete to be produced by the State of Ohio. I also don't like Ben. He's arrogant, creepy, rude, and crude.

Knowing I probably shouldn't bait the guy, I can't help myself, and say, "You must be referring to Annie Oakley."

He scoffs. "Annie Oakley? She wasn't an athlete."

"Of course she was."

"She was a performer, love."

"Athletes are performers."

He scoffs again. "I'm talkin' about the GOAT."

I narrow my gaze on him, my spoon midway to my mouth. "She was, *love*."

Manny presses his lips together, amusement shining in his eyes.

"She was no LeBron," Ben snipes.

I sip my soup, ladylike. "Not the GOAT, I'm afraid."

Riley chuckles.

"Let me guess," Ben spits out, his arrogance stronger than the pungent aftershave wafting from him. "You're a Bulls fan."

A sugared smugness quirks my lip. "No."

He furrows his brow. "Knicks?"

I nod.

"Well, if LeBron isn't the greatest basketball player of all time, who is then?" He crosses his arms over his chest while glancing at the other men as if I'm a dim-witted woman with no expertise.

I deadpan, "MJ, of course."

Hugo raises his glass. "Here, here."

Oscar shrugs.

Zach drops his phone on his grilled cheese.

Kathy stifles her indigestion.

And Riley simply says, "Slam dunk."

AFTER AN UNUSUAL BUT MOSTLY PLEASANT DINNER, Ben desperately tries to encourage us all to accompany him to one of the nightclubs. I'd rather shave my head and do The Hokey Pokey naked, so I decline and slip away, making my escape to the theatre.

"Wait up!" Riley calls out from behind me.

I stop until he catches up, then continue walking, my steps impatient and unsteady.

"Where are you off to in such a hurry?"

"The Welcome Show."

"Me too." His eyes crinkle at the corners. "You do realize it doesn't start for another twenty minutes, right?"

Momentarily fixated on the cerulean swirls of his irises—*his eyes are definitely blue, not gray*—I divert my gaze. "I do."

"So why are you rushing?"

"Because I don't want Ben to change his mind about the nightclub and follow me instead. And because I want to get a good seat before they're all taken."

"Fair enough."

The ship tilts with the swell, and I stumble before righting my footing.

"Do you need help walking?" he mocks.

"No," I snap, and he holds his hands up defensively, an arrogant but endearing smirk lifting his lips. Wanting to change the subject, I say, "Dinner was... interesting."

"Your choice of footwear is even more interesting." He glances at my feet as if my heels are hideous.

Offended, I gripe, "There's nothing wrong with my shoes."

"I didn't say there was anything wrong with them. I just said your choice to wear them is interesting, given we're on a ship in the middle of the ocean. You can barely stand, much less walk."

"I can stand and walk just fine, thanks."

He smirks again. "Whatever you say, cookie."

I halt my unsteady steps, still managing to stumble. "Stop calling me that."

"Why? What's wrong with cookie?"

"My name is Riley."

He deadpans, "Yeah, I know."

"So call me Riley."

"It's confusing."

"How is it confusing?"

"Because I'm Riley too."

"So? I'm managing just fine. Why can't you?"

He runs his hand through his hair. "Because I can't. It's weird... and because I like cookies."

My eyebrow hitches.

"Ease up. I don't mean it like that."

"Is that so?"

"You bake cookies. It's fitting."

"It's annoying." I continue walking, focusing on balancing my stride.

"You look like you're performing a WAT."

"A what?"

"Exactly."

Exasperated, I shake my head and rub my temple. "What's a what?"

"A Walk-and-Turn test... for an officer... to prove you're not inebriated."

"Ha-ha. Very funny. I'm just trying to find my damn sea legs."

"Where'd you lose them?"

I clench my fists, almost ready to punch him or, alternatively, *jump* overboard. "Are you always this irritating?"

"Are you always easily riled?" His eyes light up, and he points at me. "That's it! Riles. That's what I'll call you."

I suck on my teeth. *At least it's not cookie.* "Fine. I can live with that."

We continue toward the theatre, soon entering the grand, three-story auditorium with luxurious velvet curtains and seats, brass railings, and sculpted architraves.

"Wow!" I exclaim, carefully descending the steps toward the stage, my hand secured to the railing. "This is extravagant."

"It's what we've paid *good coin* for," Riley says, his tone pompous.

Glancing over my shoulder, I shoot him a knowing smile. "You heard Oscar say that too?"

"I did."

"Like I said, dinner was interesting."

"Yeah. A bunch of spoiled, self-entitled fools."

"Hey, Hugo and Manny are nice."

"Yeah, you're right. They are."

Taking a seat midway to the stage, Riley sits beside me, even though there are plenty of empty seats available. Not that I mind... as long as he doesn't revert back to calling me cookie.

"Do we always have to share a table with them?" I ask.

"I assume so. It's prebooked for the same time every night."

"Surely we can choose who we eat with? Just Manny and Hugo, for instance."

"I think you'll find Team Ohio won't go back there again."

"True. That just leaves... *Horse.*" I facepalm. "What an idiot."

Riley leans back in his seat and rests his ankle on his knee. "So, MJ's the GOAT, huh?"

I chuckle. "He sure is."

"You know your NBA."

"Kind of."

"Do you play?"

"No, not really. Well, I haven't in a very long time. My stepfather was an assistant coach for the Knicks when I was a teenager, so we lived and breathed the game for a while."

He pulls an "impressive" face. "He still coach?"

"No. I don't think so. Last I heard, he retired. He's no longer my stepfather. Hasn't been for many years."

"Right." He raises his hand to his chin and rubs it. "So other than being a cookie-baking, heel-wearing Knicks fan, what else are you into?"

"Firstly, I'm not a cookie baker. I just bake them for my egomaniacal boss. They contain ingredients that placate her, which is best for me." I rest my hands on my lap and awkwardly tap my fingers. "And secondly—"

"So you roofie your employer?"

I snap my head toward him. "I do *not* roofie my employer."

"Sounds like you do."

How rude!

Crossing my arms over my chest, I silently pray the show will commence.

"I roofie my niece," he says as if it's perfectly fine to do so.

"I beg your pardon?"

"My niece. I roofie her with hot milk before bed."

Blinking, I shake my head, confused.

He smiles. "She's six and doesn't know how to shut up. Talks my ears off for hours. She also doesn't appreciate a bedtime before midnight, so... I roofie her."

"With milk and only milk?"

He chuckles. "You should see your face. Yes, of course with only milk. Who do you take me for?"

I relax into my seat. "Well, I don't exactly know you, do I? You could be a pervert."

"So could you."

Taking umbrage, I hiss, "I'm not a pervert."

"Neither am I."

"Good."

"Good."

We sit in silence as the lights dim, and our cruise director, Paul, takes the stage, welcoming us aboard.

"Good evening, cruiselings. We have a very special show for you all tonight. It is one of many and my personal favorite."

The lead-in of "We Will Rock You" by Queen blasts from the speakers, Paul stomping his foot twice and then clapping once to the beat, prompting the audience to do the same.

I oblige; I like Queen.

"So without further ado," Paul shouts, "please put your hands together for our entertainment crew!"

He backs off the stage as four men and four women dance onto it, all of them dressed in leather costumes with studs, their hair teased with no doubt an entire can of hairspray. They sing and dance for the next forty-five minutes, covering songs from

Bon Jovi, Bonnie Tyler, Guns N' Roses, and Def Leppard to name a few.

I happily sing along, because I love '80s rock—Mom was a big fan. When I was younger, every Sunday afternoon, she'd blast her favorite albums while cleaning the apartment, often using the broomstick as a microphone while she was "Livin' on a Prayer." If I wasn't helping her with the housework, I was cramming for an exam to "Is This Love" by Whitesnake.

The show catapults my nostalgia, but I embrace it, knowing Mom would want me to. If she were here, she'd be rocking an air guitar, embarrassingly so. I dip my head, missing her silly antics.

Riley doesn't sing along, instead occasionally tapping his fingers on his thigh, his knee bouncing to the beat. I figure he likes '80s music too. Either that or he's bored.

When the show ends, we follow the crowd out of the theatre like ants leaving a nest.

"That was great!" I chirp, still on a high. "When I get back home, I'm going to make it a priority to see as many Broadway shows as I can. Would you believe I've only seen *one*?"

He slides his hands into his pockets. "And you live in Manhattan?"

"I know. It's pathetic. I'm a recluse. Mom is always on my back about—" I cut myself short, nearly choking on my words— I'd spoken them in present tense.

"Your mom is always on your back about what?" he asks.

"Nothing," I blurt.

Heat climbs my limbs and simmers at my chest, my sea legs now grief legs, my balance much worse than before. I close my eyes and suck in a deep breath, desperate to stay calm or disappear into thin air. If I vanish, I won't have to admit out loud to a stranger that Mom is no longer in my life, that she can longer talk to me and tell me what I should and shouldn't do. That she can no longer hug me at any moment. No longer breathe. I'm not ready for that conversation, for the pity, for the truth.

Trying to breathe—because I can and I should—I feel like the air entering my lungs is almost non-existent, containing no actual oxygen.

"You okay?" Riley asks, his hand gentle as it squeezes my shoulder.

"Uh...." I step back and blink, the foyer tilting. "Um... no. I feel sick. It's too... uh... rocky. I think I'll go back to the room."

Spinning on my heel, I don't wait for him to respond.

I need to be alone.

I need to cry.

And I need my anti-nausea meds.

chapter six

OTHER RILEY

R iles stumbles off toward the elevators, and I feel the need to go with her, to find out what's wrong and if she's okay. We're not exactly friends—we've only just met—but my mother taught me from a young age to be kind, understanding, and to help someone in need. And Riles sure looks like she needs some form of help, at the very least with walking.

My gut tells me to leave her be though. Not to mention if she is going to puke, I'm happy to stay well away. I can't stand puke, especially someone else's. Half-digested food and stomach acid should never see the light of day. When Poppy was a baby and regurgitated on my shoulder for the first time, I all but regurgitated too, much to Roni's amusement. Thankfully, it was pretty easy to get used to baby spit-up. Puke though, another thing entirely.

Stifling a body shudder, I make my way outside for a night walk on deck, the ocean breeze fresh but pleasant. Waves lap at the side of the ship, nothing but darkness as far as the eye can see. I welcome the eerie peace and slide my hands into my pant pockets as I head toward the stern, weaving around lovey-dovey couples strolling in the opposite direction. It wasn't long ago that I made up one half of a similar pair, fingers interlaced, not a care in the world as Krystal and I laughed over mundane things.

Comfortable.

In love.

Happy.

Drawing in a deep breath, I let it out again, expelling the memories into the passing wind, when I spot Ben up ahead, cigarette in hand as he leans against the railing in one of the few designated smoking sections on the ship. My feet fumble for a change of direction, but he raises his chin and makes eye contact, and it's too late for me to sprint away or dive overboard.

Fuck.

"Riley!" he hollers.

I give him a curt nod. "Ben."

"You smoke?" He offers me his packet.

"Nah, man. That shit'll kill you."

"Probably." He pockets the cigarettes and waggles his eyebrows like he did at dinner.

"What?" I ask, glancing over my shoulder, expecting to see a runway model.

He chuckles, greedy-like. "You're a lucky son of a bitch."

"Why?"

"Being shacked up with that hottie."

"Riley?"

"Damn straight! Have you seen her...?" He puffs out a fat cloud of smoke and fondles his chest. "What I wouldn't give to be buried in those."

I agree; I'm a man, after all, and her breasts are superb, especially in the tight dress she was wearing tonight. It took balls of steel not to stare at them, which I didn't, because I do have balls of steel.

Clearly, Ben doesn't.

"So—" He draws in a lungful of toxins, voice strained. "—you gonna do her?"

"Come again?"

"Riley... are you going to make a move?"

I laugh at his foolishness. "No. I've only just met her."

"So?"

"So... that's not me."

"Well, it's me. All day, every day."

It doesn't take a rocket scientist to know he's not kidding, but for some reason I can't explain, the thought of him making a move on Riley irks the shit out of me. So, I lie.

"On second thought, man, hands off. I'm simply biding my time."

He grins at me as if he knew that's what I was doing all along. "Well, don't bide for too long, or I'm cutting in."

I'm confident his "cutting in" skills are pathetic. Not to mention she'd no doubt knee him in the balls or sever his head from his neck if he tried. And even though that's something I wouldn't mind witnessing, if I can save her the annoyance of having to do so, then lying and telling him to back off so I can have a crack at her is the gentlemanly thing to do.

"Like I said..." He claps me on the back just like he had at dinner. "Lucky son of a bitch."

Burying the urge to punch him in the face, because I don't feel like being thrown in the brig on day one, I step around him. "I'll see you around."

"Nah, man." He throws his arm around my shoulders and tugs me to his side. "You're coming to the nightclub with me."

Jesus fucking Christ!

I pry myself loose. "Some other time."

"Don't be a pussy. There's plenty on offer in there while you're... biding."

I'm not in the mood for what's on offer, nor am I in the mood to indulge in it with this dipshit. "Not interested."

"Look—" He sticks his cigarette into the butt stand beside him. "I haven't lucked out so far, and I can sure use your help. The ladies love a pretty boy like you until they realize they need a man like me." The idiot winks at me. "Come on. Help a guy out."

He definitely needs all the help he can get, and then some.

My bro code rears its ugly head, and I stupidly relent. "Okay. One drink."

"Sweet!"

We enter the nightclub, strobe lights and heavy-bass dance music attacking my eyes and ears. It's been several years since I stepped foot into a hellhole such as this—the last time with Krystal. It wasn't my jam then, and it's not my jam now.

"What are you drinking?" Ben shouts over the music.

"Beer."

"Fuck that. I'm hitting the hard stuff."

He orders me a Bud and himself a whiskey on the rocks, then rests his back against the bar, wasting no time scoping the place out, nodding his head to the music and grinning like the Joker at every woman who passes by. They all ignore him or scowl. It's humiliating, and before long, I feel marginally sorry for him—he doesn't stand a chance.

"Check out the ass on that one," he says, his elbow colliding with my ribs, my beer sloshing onto my shirt.

I no longer feel sorry for the dick.

Brushing myself off, I take note of the woman he's leering at, recognizing her from when I rode the elevator earlier in the day, her spidey eyes locking with mine. They light up as she waves and coaxes her friend to follow her in our direction.

"I saw her first!" he shouts over the music before taking a gulp of his drink.

I want to tell him he didn't, that I did. But I honestly couldn't give a shit. He can try his luck; little good it'll do him.

Trying my damn hardest to be welcoming, I manage to lift one side of my face when spidey woman sidles up to me and shouts, "Hi there!"

I shout back, "Hey!"

Ben frowns for the slightest of seconds but then turns to her friend, his face once again opportunistic. "Hey, princess."

The friend all but goes cross-eyed. "Heyyy."

"Can I get you a drink?" he shouts.

She holds up her cocktail. "Already got one."

"Want another?"

"No, thanks." She dips her head and sips from her straw, looking everywhere else but at him.

"I didn't see you by the pool," Spidey tells me.

"I didn't have time for a swim," I reply with a shrug.

She pouts.

"I'm Riley, by the way," I say, offering her my hand, because I'm polite like that.

"Brittany."

We shake, and she sips her drink again, her colorful cocktail disappearing as she seductively sucks it down her throat.

"Want another?" Ben asks her.

She looks at him, then at me. "Sure."

"What are you drinking?" he shouts as the music gets loud again.

"Something fruity," she yells back.

All the hollering is giving me a headache.

"And how 'bout you, beautiful?" he asks her friend.

"Already got one, remember?"

Brittany glares at the other woman, and the friend glares back before sighing and calling out, "Whatever she's having."

Ben beams. "Comin' right up."

I internally celebrate his small victory, when Brittany asks me something I can't hear over the music.

I raise my hand to my ear. "What?"

She leans in, pressing her chest to my arm. "I said, where are you from?"

"Oh. Philly."

"Cool! We're from Florida."

I nod.

"You been there?"

"Once."

"Only once?"

"Yeah, I took my niece to Disney World."

"Cute."

Puppies and babies are cute. Grogu is cute. Chaperoning my sister and her daughter to Disney World because I'd never be able to take my own daughter is definitely *not* cute.

About to call it a night and finish my deck walk, I chug my beer and set down the empty plastic cup on the bar when Ben shoves another one into my hand.

"Let's grab a booth," he says. "I can't hear a fucking thing here."

Brittany point to the back of the room. "There's an empty one over there."

If I could hear her friend over the godawful racket, I'd bet my left nut she just groaned... like me.

Why did I agree to this?

Trudging behind them through the crowd of dance monkeys to the far end of the club, I contemplate my odds of successfully slipping away when Brittany latches onto my shirt.

"We nearly lost you," she says.

"Yeah, nearly." I stand back and let them slide into the crescent banquette so I can sit at the end and escape when the time is right.

"So, what's your names?" Ben asks them.

When Brittany's friend doesn't respond, she answers for her. "I'm Brittany, and this is Whitney."

"Brittany and Whitney?" He grins, all teeth. "That's hot." He stretches his arms out and not so subtly drapes one behind Whitney's back. "I'm Horse."

Laughter bubbles in my throat, but I stifle it.

"Uh..." Whitney stiffens, her eyes damn near popping out of her head. "I'm gonna dance. Britt, you comin'?"

She practically shoves Brittany onto my lap as she tries to scoot back out of the booth, and if I were an evil fucker, I'd stop stifling and laugh my head off, and then laugh some more. But

I'm not evil, so I bite the inside of my cheek and stand up instead, enabling Whitney's escape.

"Wanna dance?" Brittany asks me.

"Nah. Got two left feet."

She pouts again, and I wonder if she's got some involuntary issue with her lips. Krystal got some shit injected into hers once, and she looked sulky for weeks.

"Okay, Mr. Two-Left-Feet. I'll be right back."

I nod but plan to be gone before that happens.

"She wants me," Ben says as I take a seat again.

"Who?"

"Whitney."

This time, I do laugh. "What makes you say that?"

"Look at the way she's shaking her ass for me."

Glancing at the girls, both of them sway their bodies in unison as if they're extras on the set of *Dirty Dancing*, it just enforces that I don't want to be here. Especially when Ben sticks his chubby fingers between his chubby lips and wolf whistles.

"See?" he prompts, practically bouncing in his seat. "She wants me."

I chuckle, then lie. "I think you're right."

"You know the other one?"

"Nah, not really. I met her in the elevator today."

"Lucky. Son. Of. A. Bitch."

Ben's definition of luck is grossly different from mine. Luck is winning the lotto, catching a cancer diagnosis before it becomes inoperable, or finding a four-leafed clover. Having to share a cabin on a cruise ship for a few weeks with a stranger is not the result of luck, and neither is meeting Brittany in an elevator the size of a shoe box.

"I'll be between her legs before daylight," he says before chugging his whiskey and wiping his mouth with the back of his hand.

I can't help myself and finally burst into uncontrollable laughter. "You're delusional."

His head drops, showcasing his second chin. "Am not."

"Yeah, you are. There's no chance in hell you'll be fucking Whitney tonight."

"O ye of little faith."

"It's got nothing to do with faith, man."

"Fine. O ye of little Benjamins."

Little Benjamins?

Confused, my eyes bounce from left to right. "What are you talking about?"

Ben rubs his hands together. "I'm loaded. And when Whitney finds out, she'll be all over me. Brittany too. Like I said, the ladies love a pretty boy like you until they realize they need a man *like me*."

Wait! What? The bastard outright played me.

Somewhat impressed but also dubious of his logic, I say, "You think that just because you've got a lot money they'll sleep with you?"

"Damn straight."

I glance at the girls again, and Brittany winks at me while shimmying down and then up Whitney's body before tugging her toward the booth.

"Watch and learn," Ben murmurs as the girls stroll back and retake their seats.

I wait for my so-called lesson in fuckery as Brittany sips her cocktail dry again.

"Did you miss us?" she asks.

"Every second of every minute." Ben nods to her empty glass. "Want another? You can have whatever you like. Your drinks are on me all night long."

She winks at Whitney. "We can have anything we like?"

"Sure can, princess. And after you're done, we can go have some fun in the casino or at the shops." He makes a show of adjusting his Rolex. "You see, I have too much money, and I need your help spending it."

Turning her body toward Ben, Whitney grins seductively and

walks her fingers up his chest. "In that case, I'll start with a... Blow Job."

He pats his lap, and fuck me stupid, she slides on top of him. "You can have all the Blow Jobs you want, gorgeous."

Brittany giggles, then drops her hand to my leg and squeezes. "Would you like a Blow Job too?"

I blink. *What the fuck?*

My dick stirs in my pants, letting me know his thoughts on the matter. And while I assume she's referring to the alcoholic drink and not oral sex, her spidey fingers and lashes suggest otherwise.

Not wanting to let my dick down, I draw in a ragged breath, but I'm just not ready... for that... with her, so I reach down, collect her hand, place it on her thigh, and exhale. "Some other time."

Her jaw drops, her mouth nice and wide, and for a split second, I rethink my answer.

No, Wilson. You don't want this.

"I'm off," I say, pushing up to stand. "Have a great night, guys."

Ben chuckles, pleased with himself. "Pussy."

Snaking my way through the dance floor until I'm clear of the club, I head back out on deck, finally able to breathe again.

Do I want to get naked with a woman after so long? Sure. I miss soft curves, plump lips, and tight grips. I miss the feel of fingertips skating my skin and sweet moans in my ear. I miss the intimacy and not being alone. But Brittany reminds me of what I despise about Krystal, and I'm not doing that again. Replacing toxic with toxic is lethal. It gets you nowhere other than back where you started—full of regret and hating yourself for it. Dead, inside and out.

I'm done with fatal attraction. I want to feel again. Love again. I want to find a connection that runs so deep it doesn't end. And I can't do that if I'm merely chasing pussy for the sake of chasing it.

If this is what sowing my wild oats is all about, I'm not doing it.

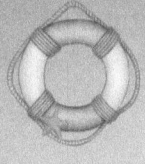

chapter seven

RILES

Heart thumping, I shoot upright in bed and wake to what sounds like a commuter train rumbling by my ear. Confused, because I went to sleep on a ship out to sea and not on the subway, I rub my eyes and fumble for my cell, blinking until I can focus on the godawful time of three thirty-seven.

Are you kidding me?

I tap on the Flashlight button and illuminate the room, aiming the ray of light toward the sound. Riley's log of a body is fast asleep and vibrating with every breath he inhales.

"You lying asshat!" I grumble, flopping back onto the mattress. He snorts like a hog doing a line of cocaine, so I spring back up, astonished. "Jesus!"

The stench of alcohol wrinkles my nose, and I want to scream bloody murder.

Great! Just... great! I'm bunked with a single party guy who suffers from sleep apnea.

Turning onto my side, I use the corner of the pillow to cover my free ear, muffling his locomotive swine grunts.

Jerk!

Never in my life have I felt so helpless and frustrated, so lost

71

and alone. Tears sting my eyes, threatening to erupt and stream down my cheeks, so I puff out a long breath and count to five, forcing my despair down and tucking it away, because I don't want to cry anymore.

After I left Riley at the theatre, I cradled Mom to my chest on the balcony and sobbed for over an hour, and then I struggled to get to sleep, my eyeballs on fire, my head swimming with nerves over my pending first night in the cabin with a stranger. I hadn't known what to expect, which was somewhat terrifying. Actually, that's a lie. It was so terrifying that I swiped a butter knife from the buffet restaurant on my way back to the room and placed it under my pillow... just in case.

My fingers graze the stainless steel. I'm tempted to bonk him on the head with the handle just to knock him out and shut him up, but I open my bedside drawer instead and place it inside. Clearly, I don't appear to need it for self-defense, because he'd rather torture me with sound than physically attack me in my sleep. An encouraging thought, I guess.

Lying there, utterly depleted, exhausted, and running on fumes, I stare at the shadowed ceiling. And speaking of fumes, yuck! Did he down a full keg of beer?

Swiping the air in front of my nose, I kick my feet and fling my comforter off, and then I march to the balcony door and wrench it open for some much-needed fresh air and white noise before climbing back into bed again, the soothing sound of the ocean and gentle movements of the ship once again sending me to sleep.

Sunlight spears through the open door, coaxing my heavy eyelids to open. I rub them with my knuckles and roll onto my back, Riley's snoring now a soft rumble.

Propping myself on my elbows, I glare at him before climbing

72

out of bed, pillow in hand. How dare he sleep peacefully when all he's done for the past several hours is disrupt the peace? How dare he just lie there without a care in the world? Well-rested. Blissful. Comfortable.

Inching along the side of his bed, I raise my pillow behind my head but pause as my eyes settle on his bare leg poking out from underneath his sheets. A nicely sculpted leg. Muscular. Tan. A virile sprinkling of hair.

I stare at it, captivated, as if I've never seen a man's leg before.

He snorts.

I freeze.

He snorts again, eyelids spasming before relaxing again.

Despite how freaking annoyed I am at him, I can't deny his rugged good looks. I also can't help but wonder if he's wearing any underwear, because I can't see any sticking out from under the sheet.

Wait! Is he naked? I step back. *He better not be!*

Slamming the pillow down on his face, I wrench it back again, and shout, "Wake up!"

Riley releases a cacophony of grunts, blinking as he wrestles with his sheets until he's upright and leaning back on his palms.

I whack him again for good measure. "You liar!"

"What the fuck?" He raises his hand, shielding himself from further blows.

"Yes, what the fuck indeed." I stab my finger at him. "You snore like a damn freight train."

The jerk searches the room and then looks at me as if I'm an imbecile. "Freight trains don't snore."

"Whatever! You do!"

Growling, I whack him again, then storm to the closet and collect my clothes for the day.

"What time is it?" he grumbles as if it's too early to be awake.

"Time you moved cabins."

"Wait! What?"

"You heard me."

"Come on, Riles. You don't mean that."

I wrench open the bathroom door, step inside, and allow it to slam behind me, shouting, "I most certainly do!"

"I'm sorry," he calls out. "I don't usually snor—"

"Liar!"

Growling again, I slam the toilet lid down, lay a towel over it, and place my clothes on top before boxing the air like Mike Tyson's uncoordinated twin. I'm not normally the violent type. Frustrated air-boxer? Yes. Physically connect my fists with someone else? No. Yet, for some reason, Riley makes me want to kung-fu his ass. Twice over.

Clenching the edge of the vanity, I grit my teeth and stare at myself in the mirror, my hair awry, my eyes puffier than a pufferfish. *Oh my God! I look like Beetlejuice.*

I groan, turn the faucet on, and grab my toothbrush, scrubbing my teeth like a mad woman before spitting out the froth more forcibly than intended, white foam spraying the mirror.

Tempted to leave it there, because Riley seems to think mess is acceptable, I end up wiping it away, since the clean freak within me won't stand for it, and then I secure my shower cap and step into the shower, hot water massaging my shoulders and neck and slowly easing my volcanic tension.

I press my palms against the wall, hang my head, and exhale, once again counting to five—a stress-relief technique I picked up not long after starting my job with Georgia. It's a daily ritual I perform, but I certainly didn't anticipate having to continue it on vacation. Then again, what would I know? I never go on vacation. Perhaps they are stressful.

No, they're not. Vacations are enjoyable. My vacation will be enjoyable, just as Mom wanted it to be. Riley and his snoring be damned.

Today, we dock in Halifax, Nova Scotia—one of my bucket list ports of call—and I plan to visit St. Mary's Basilica, the Fairview Lawn Cemetery, and the *Titanic* exhibit at the Maritime

Museum of the Atlantic. Ever since I was a young girl and watched *Titanic* at the theatre with Mom, I've been fascinated—borderline obsessed—with the ill-fated maiden voyage. More than fifteen hundred people tragically died on April 15, 1912, and what's worse is their demise could've been avoided.

I'm also a hardcore Leo DiCaprio fan.

Humming "My Heart Will Go On" as I psych myself up for the day ahead, I finish showering, then I spend the time needed to put on my makeup and do my hair when a knock on the bathroom door has me almost poking my eye out with my mascara wand.

"What?" I grouch.

"Hurry up! I need to piss."

"Piss over the balcony." I swipe on another coat of mascara then bite my lip, contemplating whether he'd be the type to do just that, which I think he would, so quickly add, "No! Don't! Use the toilet in the lobby instead."

He groans and murmurs, "Fine," and by the time I'm done, he still hasn't returned, which only elevates my frustration with him. We need to go over more rules and boundaries. "Sleep with your mouth closed" a new one added to my list.

Not having the time nor patience to wait any longer, I say a quick goodbye to Mom before placing her in the safe with Mr. Snuffles as company, then I collect my bag and passport and head to the buffet restaurant for a quick breakfast.

The smell of pancakes, toast, and bacon heavily permeates the air as I dodge person after person rushing about with plates and bowls in hand, some of them lining up at food stations while others try to find empty tables.

"Holy cow!" I murmur. This place is busier than Times Square.

Making a dash for the coffee machine, desperate for my elixir of life, I scoot to a stop and wait in line for a short while before pouring a cup, and then I weave my way to one of the food stations to grab a bagel. My chances of finding an empty table seem slim, but I scan the room nonetheless, when Riley raises his hand and waves me over to where he's seated.

Huh. So this is where he disappeared to.

I consider flipping him the bird but don't, instead acknowledging him with a single head nod as I chart a path in his direction.

"Morning, sunshine." He tips his mug to me, his twinkling blue eyes annoyingly wide and fresh.

I decide I no longer like them.

"It's been morning for me since three-thirty when your hog call woke me up," I say, sliding into the spare seat and releasing my plate onto the table with an intended clatter.

"Hog call?"

"Yes."

"Wow! That's insulting."

"It's meant to be."

"Brutal."

"That's what happens when I've had little to no sleep."

"Sorry." He dips his head and sips from his mug. "Must've been the beer."

"Good guess, Einstein, because I was nearly drunk off the fumes."

"That bad, huh?"

"Yes," I grumble. "That bad."

"Sorry," he murmurs again.

His apology seems genuine, but it doesn't change our dilemma. "You said you didn't snore."

"I don't... usually."

"Well, you did, and it's a problem." I spread cream cheese on my bagel and take a bite, mumbling, "I'm not spending the next few weeks with no sleep."

"It won't happen again."

"I don't believe you."

"It won't."

Scoffing, because you don't just magically stop snoring

because you say you can, I sit back and cross my arms over my chest. "How can you be so sure?"

"I have a plan."

"You do, do you?"

"Yes."

"Speaking of plans, we need to revisit the rules and boundaries."

Riley groans. "It's too early for that."

"I'm serious. Our situation is already unconventional and uncomfortable. The least we can do is set some guidelines to make it a little easier."

He stretches his arms toward the ceiling, then locks his fingers and rests them behind his head. "Fine. What are your rules and boundaries besides the ones you've already stipulated?"

"I—" My treacherous eyes lock onto his biceps, and I almost choke on my bagel.

"You okay?" he asks, brow raised.

"Yes"—*cough*—"I'm fine." I thunk my chest with my fist, then take a sip of my coffee. "You need to knock."

"What?"

"Knock... before entering the cabin."

"But I'll forget."

"Then try not to. I might be getting changed, and I don't want you barging in on me."

"Why not?" He leans forward, picks up his toast, and points it at me. "You've got nothing to be ashamed of."

Heat blooms in my cheeks, and I can't help squirming in my seat. "I'm not *ashamed* of my body, Riley. I respect it, and that means not flaunting it naked in front of strangers."

"I wouldn't exactly say we're strangers anymore."

"That's not the point," I say, gritting my teeth.

"Okay. Ease up." He chuckles. "I'll try to remember to knock."

"Thank you."

"Anything else?"

I take another bite and mumble, "Toilet seat down."

"Why not toilet seat up?"

"Because I can't sit on the rim of the bowl."

"And I can't piss when the seat is down. If *I* have to lift it, why can't *you* put it down?"

I go to drink my coffee again but pause, the side of the mug resting against my lip as I deliberate his rebuttal of how gender biased toilet etiquette can be. But then I remember hygiene trumps all.

"Because it's unhygienic to leave it up," I deadpan. "Poo particles."

He bursts with laughter. "Poo particles?"

"Yes. They become airborne and land on your toothbrush."

Riley shakes his head but doesn't argue. "Fine. I'll put the seat down." Then he adds, "And the lid, if the poo particles concern you so much."

I lift my brow, because that's actually fair. "Good. I will too."

We eat in silence for a moment, and when he doesn't say anything else, I ask, "Do you have any rules or boundaries for me?"

"Yeah, stop hogging all the space. I have stuff too and nowhere to put it."

I wince. "Sorry. I didn't realize how much room in the closet I'd taken up until I found my *very-expensive* blouse thrown on my bed." I smile the kind of smile you smile when you don't want to smile.

"I didn't throw it."

"Looked like you did."

"I assure you, I didn't."

Engaged in an eye-locked showdown, I slowly exhale. Maybe he's telling the truth. "Do you need more closet space than you currently have?"

"I don't know. I haven't finished unpacking."

"Well, when I get back from the city today, I'll free up some room just in case."

He smirks. "Thank you."

I smirk back. "You're welcome."

Riley runs his hand over his beard, studying me.

"What?" I mumble, fearing I've smeared cream cheese on my face.

"You feeling better?"

"Huh?"

"You said you felt sick last night."

"Oh. Yeah. I did." I divert my gaze. "It came and went. I'm fine now."

"Good. Because another one of my rules is no puking in the cabin."

I laugh. "What?"

"No puke. If you need to, do it overboard or somewhere else."

"I'm not puking overboard. That's disgusting. It might land on someone below. And anyway, I have anti-nausea meds. I'm not going to puke."

"Sweet. So are we all sorted then, cabin cop?"

"For now." I down the last of my coffee, stand, and collect my bag. "If there's anything else, I'll let you know."

He stands too, and murmurs, "I'm sure you will."

I gift him a sarcastic smile.

"What are your plans for today, cooki—" He cuts himself short and grins at me.

I don't grin back. "Sightseeing."

"Me too."

Despite how annoying he can be, I consider asking if he wants to sightsee together, but he probably doesn't. Like me, he planned to cruise solo, so I'm guessing he won't want company.

"Where are you headed to first?" he asks as we make our way out of the restaurant.

"St. Mary's Basilica."

"Me too."

I snap my head at him. "Really?"

"Yeah."

"Are you Catholic?"

"No. I just like cathedrals. I appreciate the architecture and design."

I stop at the elevator, but Riley turns toward the stairs, so I follow, curious about his answer to the question I want to ask next. "What do you do for a living?"

"Third generation carpenter. I have my own furniture business. I do restorations and build things from scratch."

"Like what?" I ask, holding onto the handrail as we descend the stairs.

"Chairs, tables, cabinets... one-of-a-kind pieces. You know, furniture that tells a story."

My steps pause at his lovely words. "Wow! That's... impressive."

He smirks. "You sound shocked."

"No." I continue down the steps, finding myself eagerly chasing him. "I'm not shocked. I mean, I figured you'd be a laborer of sorts, given your size and build."

"My size and build?"

I blush. "You're not exactly Danny DeVito."

"But?"

We step off the last flight of stairs and head toward the gangway. "No buts. I'm just impressed with how you described what you do, that you want your art to tell a story."

For the first time since meeting Riley, his entire face lights up. Not with mock humor at my expense, but with genuine joy, and I can't deny it's endearing.

"May I have your sailing cards please?" a crew member in charge of letting passengers off the ship asks.

We remove our lanyards for him to scan, and he does just that.

"Ship leaves at five on the dot." He hands them back. "Don't be late. The captain waits for no one."

I recoil. "Really?"

"Yes. Unless you're on a shore excursion you booked through the ship and your whole group has been held up. We'd either wait, if it won't be long, or we'd set up transportation for your group to meet us at the next port. Happens more than you think."

I hang my lanyard around my neck and follow Riley down the ramp and onto the dock. "The ship leaves you behind if you're late? Holy crap! How awful."

"Why should three-thousand-plus passengers and crew be delayed from sailing just because some idiot lost track of time?"

"Because said idiot might end up being you or me, by accident. We'd be stranded, and that's... that's the stuff of nightmares."

The pit of my stomach drops, and my knees nearly buckle. What if I'm stuck on land, and Mom is locked in the safe and sets sail without me?

Should I go back and get her? Would they even let me take her off the ship?

"Are you okay? You're as white as a ghost." Riley places his hand on my shoulder and gently squeezes, much like he did the night before. "We won't get stranded, Riles. I promise." He removes his hand and rotates his wrist. "Look, I'll set an alarm on my watch."

Drawing in a breath as I look up at the intimidating vessel, I try to pinpoint our cabin's location while deliberating whether I should stay or go. I desperately want to see the *Titanic* exhibit, but I can't bear the thought of the ship setting sail without me.

"It'll be fine," he adds. "Trust me. You can't spend the entire cruise on the ship for fear of being left behind."

"I'm not scared of being left behind. I'm scared of leav—" I shake my head. "Never mind. You're right. It'll be fine. We'll be back in plenty of time. I'll set some alarms too. Keep us on a schedule. I'm good at schedules."

We continue walking toward the city center, and I gather we are, in fact, sightseeing together, which I'm not mad about. Like he said, if the two of us set alarms and stick together, we're more likely to make it back on time.

"Schoolteacher?" he asks, pressing the button on the traffic light as we wait to cross the road.

I point to myself. "Me?"

He nods. "You said you're good at schedules."

"No. I'm not a teacher."

"Delivery driver?"

I laugh. "I don't even have a driver's license. No. Guess again." The last time I probed him to surmise something about me flickers in my mind, and I fear he'll respond with something along the lines of funeral director or hospice nurse. "I'm a publisher," I blurt before he has a chance to answer. "Well, publishing assistant. I hope to run my own small press one day. That's why I liked what you said back on the ship... about your furniture telling stories. I live and breathe stories."

"Publisher?" He purses his lips as if impressed. "Have you helped publish any books I might've read?"

"You read?"

"Again, Riles—" He side-eyes me. "—you sound shocked."

We cross the road and head toward a gothic-revival church spire a short distance ahead.

"If I'm going to be completely honest, then yes, I am shocked," I admit. "But I mean no offense."

"None taken."

"It's just that, sadly, reading is a dying art in an overworked world. No one seems to have time to sit, relax, and read a book from cover to cover anymore. Trust me, if it weren't my profession, I'd never have the time either."

"So you're a workaholic?"

"You could say that."

"Is that why you're on the cruise? To take a break?"

"Not exactly." I divert my gaze to the sidewalk beneath my feet, not wanting to elaborate. "How about you? Why are you cruising?"

"Why *not* cruise? You only live once, right?"

We turn the corner, St. Mary's Basilica towering before us, and once again I stop walking, snagged by his words.

"You only live once, Smiley Riley," Mom said as I sat beside her hospital bed, holding her hand. "So promise me you'll live it to the fullest. See the world. Meet new people. Fall in love...."

"She's a beauty, isn't she?" Riley prompts, shielding his eyes from the sun as he looks up.

I find my feet again and step forward, stopping beside him. "Y-Yeah. I love these old churches. I can't wait to see Westminster Abbey and St. George's Chapel when we dock in Southampton. Then there's Notre Dame and Montmartre."

"You're doing a day trip to London?"

"Of course. Aren't you?"

"Yeah. I just haven't booked anything yet."

My face scrunches in horror—how unorganized. "You haven't booked any tours?"

"No."

"Are you crazy? They're filling up fast. You'll miss out. And I got them for us for free! What are you waiting for?"

He runs his hand over his beard, which he seems to do when in contemplation. It's a cute habit, and it tickles my chest.

"What's so funny?" he asks.

"Nothing. You coming?"

I walk ahead and enter the church, Riley catching up to me, his heavy footsteps echoing throughout the cathedral together with hushed voices as other people wander around. Careful not to bump into anyone or anything, I tip my head back, drawn to the arched ceiling and shimmering stained-glass mural.

"It's so pretty," I whisper. "Don't you think?"

When he doesn't answer, I turn around, finding him bent over a few yards away, caressing a church pew, his hand gliding along the wood, much like I'd do to a Birkin if I had the chance to touch one.

I shuffle closer and murmur, "What are you doing?"

"Admiring the handiwork. These old cathedrals provide some of the best inspiration."

Huh. I suppose they would.

Leaving him to fondle the furniture, I meander for a while, take a few photos before heading back outside to wait for him, the splendid sunshine equipoising the mild breeze.

"Fancy seeing you here, love."

My body spasms at the sound of Ben's voice, and I reluctantly swivel in his direction, faking a smile. "Hello, Ben. Are you here to atone for your sins?"

He stubs out a cigarette with his foot and winks. "After last night, I probably should."

I shudder.

"Ain't that right, pretty boy?" he adds, glancing over my shoulder.

"What's that?" Riley asks as he stops beside me.

"I said, after last night, I should atone for my sins. I was a bad, bad boy. Too many blowjobs."

Bile almost rises to my throat, and I have the overwhelming urge to gag.

"Dope night. Whitney and Brittany were *very* friendly. Ménage à trois, if you know what I mean." He lands a few playful punches on Riley's arms and abdomen.

So that's what Riley was doing last night... getting drunk with Ben and doing God knows what with Tittney and Spitney, or whatever their names are.

Charming!

Personally, I'm not a fan of a one-night stand; I simply don't get the point. I mean, I get the point of having sex. I like sex, very much, just not with some creep I've shared a few drinks with and know nothing about. I've regretfully done it once before, and I promised myself I'd never do it again: the walk of shame the next morning, that violated feeling afterward. No, sir-ee—once was more than enough.

"So where are we off to next?" Ben asks.

We? As in him, Riley, and me? Hell no!

"Okaaay," I drawl, giving them both a double wave as I back away. "I'm gonna leave you two to discuss whatever it is you're discussing. Have fun."

Turning on my heel, I scurry off to explore on my own.

F *or fuck's sake, Ben.*
         He's like a bad smell that won't go away. And sure, Riles gets riled up at me easily, but I'd much rather sightsee with her than spend the day with him.

"What did I say?" the irritating jackass asks as he pulls out a cigarette and lights it while Riles scurries off like a frightened mouse.

"What didn't you say?"

"Too much?"

I scoff. "Yeah, maybe a little."

He brushes it off and draws in a lungful of smoke. "I think my dick is about to fall off."

I scoff again. "Bullshit!"

"Not bullshit, dude. I dropped a few grand in the jewelry store last night, and Whitney and Brittany were very appreciative. Best few grand I've spent."

My jaw plummets.

"Yeah." He grins and cups his junk. "You missed out. Big time."

I didn't. I don't pay for sex, ever, not with cold hard cash nor extravagant gifts. But to each their own.

"So where we going next?" he asks as if we're the best of friends.

I hadn't planned on going anywhere with him, but now that Riles has abandoned me and I've seen all I wanted to see in Halifax, I shrug. "Your guess is as good as mine."

"Let's go to the pub. There's one down the road."

My liver cringes, but I've got nothing better to do. "Lead the way."

He claps me on the back.

"Do that again, and I'll break your arm."

Ben chuckles as if I'm kidding.

I'm not.

"I like you," he says. "You're funny."

We walk a couple of blocks to an Irish-themed pub, dark oak hardwood lining the floors and walls. A man plays a fiddle in the corner by the fireplace, flames smoldering, people laughing as they chatter among themselves.

I beeline for the bar, admiring the beveled edges and intricate carvings.

"Mornin'." The jolly bartender slides two coasters across the bar. "What can I get you?"

"Two pints of Guinness," Ben says as he takes a seat on a stool, the maple creaking under his weight.

My insides cry—the poor girl needs a restoration.

Unable to help myself, I squat down and take a closer look.

"What are you doing?" Ben asks, peering down, brows pinched. "Looking for gum?"

Bane of my fucking existence. The number of times I've come across gum underneath chairs and tables... it should be considered a criminal offense.

I look up, a shit-eating grin on my face. "Why? Do you want some?"

He grimaces. "Do you?"

"Nah." I chuckle and take a seat beside him. "I was just checking the joins."

"Why? You think it's gonna break?"

Quite possibly.

I shake my head. "No. It'll hold."

"How do you know?" He sets one foot back onto the ground, and by the worry etching his face, I get the sneaking suspicion it's happened to him before.

"I'm a carpenter," I explain.

"Dude! I own Mason's."

I nearly fall off my stool. "Mason's? As in the hardware store?"

"Yep."

"All of them?"

"Yep."

No wonder he's throwing money around.

Not knowing what else to say, I simply congratulate him. "Well done."

"Not really. Family-owned business for decades. The old man did the hard work. I just inherited it."

"Still. You're running it now though, right?"

"Me?" He laughs. "Pay white collars to do that shit."

To be honest, I'm not surprised. Ben gives the impression he couldn't run a bath, let alone a chain of hardware stores.

The bartender places two glasses of Guinness on our coasters, and Ben picks one up, clinks the other, and says, "Cheers," before chugging nearly half of it.

"Thanks." I pick mine up too. "Cheers."

"So what do ya build?" he asks before wiping his mouth with the back of his hand.

"Anything made of wood."

"Houses?"

"No. I specialize in building and restoring furniture, but I did build my own home."

"Not much money in housing anymore anyway."

"I didn't build mine for the money."

He scoffs. "Everything these days is done for the money."

"And that's the problem," I mutter.

"Why's it a problem?"

"Because no one appreciates the simpler things in life anymore. It's all about the finer things."

"Damn straight it is. I appreciate fine things, especially fine ass." He chugs the rest of his beer. "And you, my friend, missed out on some exceptionally fine ass last night. But I'm not complaining. More for me."

I rest my arms on the counter. "They're all yours, Ben, if that's what they want. I'm not interested."

He laughs, but it's less boisterous than usual. "Look at me. I don't think I'm what they want. Girls like them want you, not me."

"So why waste your money on them?"

"It's not a waste. I got my dick wet, didn't I?"

I eye him suspiciously over the rim of my glass. "Did you?"

"You don't believe me?"

At first, I didn't, but I do now, given he's Mr. Mason's.

"I believe you," I say.

He sets his glass down and turns to face me. "Why didn't you hang around last night?"

Staring at the O'Brien crest hanging above the bar, I confess, "I'm getting a divorce."

"More reason to have stayed."

"Nah."

"Are you crazy? What better excuse to fuck 'em, then chuck 'em?"

"Jesus, Ben." I close my eyes momentarily, shake my head, then turn to him too, unblinking.

"What? It's the truth. You're free now. Fucking enjoy yourself."

"You can't just say shit like that."

"Why not?"

"Because it's not right."

"Women have never treated me right, so I give what I get."

Again, I mildly feel sorry for the guy. Mildly. "Well, what you get is always what you're gonna get if you feel that way."

"That's rich, comin' from you. I bet all you have to do is flash those pearly whites and washboard abs, and you could have any woman you want."

"Not true."

"Bullshit." He faces forward again and waves down the bartender.

"It's not. Trust me." While I've never had a problem getting a woman's attention if I wanted it, which I haven't, forming a connection isn't about a perfect smile or whether you lift weights. "Not all women care about looks, Ben. At least, not the ones who are in it for real."

"Your ex not in it for real?"

I don't want to talk about Krystal, but I've stupidly opened that can of worms. "She was, but not anymore."

"Fuck her."

I give him a look, one that says, *"Be careful."*

"What she do? Fuck your best friend?"

"Ben," I warn.

"My cousin's wife did that."

"No. She didn't fuck my best friend."

Close enough though.

"Nice women don't exist," he says, tilting his empty glass. "They're all 'get away from me' until I tell 'em I'm loaded. Then they're all 'yes, Horse, yes.'"

I massage my forehead, an idiot-induced headache forming.

"So I take what I want," he continues, "and they get what they want. Win-win."

"Doesn't sound like a win-win to me."

"Don't really have a choice, do I? I've never met a real nice woman who digs me for me. They only ever dig for my gold."

"That's because you're offering your gold to be dug, and because you're scaring the *real* nice ones off with your inappropriate mouth."

"My mouth isn't inappropriate."

I raise a brow at him.

"You're right. It is." He smirks, then orders another two pints.

"Nah." I hold up my hand in protest. "Not for me. Got shit to do."

Other than buy Poppy a stuffed moose toy and get Riles some earplugs, I plan to go for a walk along the waterfront and then head back to the ship. It's only day two of the cruise, and I don't intend to spend it with a hangover.

"Come on, just one more. Don't be a pussy."

Rubbing my beard, I give in to the poor fucker. "One."

He grins. "So, why'd hot stuff run away at the church?"

"Riley?"

"Yeah."

"Probably because you mentioned blowjobs."

He dismisses my valid point. "I doubt it. She's an adult. Plus, I was talking about Blow Jobs, as in the shots. You know that."

"But she didn't. Either way, it was inappropriate, Ben."

"She a prude?"

"No. I don't think so. But that's not the point. There's a time and a place to talk about blowjobs. And with someone you don't know, especially in public in front of a place of worship, is neither that time nor place."

We're served our next round of beer, and both of us drink as a patron gets rowdy over a game of baseball on the TV.

"She's gotta be a prude," Ben says, deflecting the blame. "Such a fucking shame *that* is." He sets his glass back on the coaster. "Great legs!"

I agree but keep it to myself.

Ben grows silent for a moment, then says, "You think if I don't mention blowjobs again, I'll have a chance with her?"

I almost spit-take my beer, hysterics itching to burst out of me. "No, I think that *ship* has *sailed*."

"Ha! I see what you did there." He goes to slap me on the back but thinks better of it, pointing at me instead.

I point back, acknowledging his restraint.

"But what if I—"

"No. Riles is off limits."

He frowns but then grins. "Ahh, that's right. You want a piece of her."

I hang my head. "And that, right there, is my point."

Staring at me dumbfounded, like a puppy who thinks you've stolen its ball, I offer him advice he desperately needs, advice I feel will fall on deaf ears.

"You don't just 'want a piece' if you want something real with a woman. You've got to get to know her first and let her get to know you."

"But you said I say the wrong shit."

"So don't say the wrong shit."

"But that's me. That's who I am. I say what I say. Why should I change?"

The dickhead makes a dickhead point; I can't deny him that.

"I guess you need to find a woman who says the wrong shit too. Otherwise, you're gonna end up with a lot less money in your pocket."

"Money talks."

I give up!

Downing the rest of my beer, I set the glass down when it's completely drained. "I'll see you around, Ben. Thanks for the drinks. Next time, they're on me."

"Yeah. Cool! Next time." He salutes me, and I leave while I can.

WHEN I GET BACK TO THE SHIP A COUPLE OF HOURS later, I go to the shore excursions desk and book the Stonehenge tour. I also ask about the behind-the-scenes ship tour, but the assistant tells me its fully booked without even having to look at the screen. Apparently, those spots were all taken yesterday.

Pissed I didn't do it earlier, I sign up for a few other things, not wanting to make the same mistake and miss out. I even register for Irish dancing lessons. Why? Because my sis wants me to step out of my comfort zone. Not to mention the tour desk clerk magically convinced me to give it a try.

Feeling like I've somehow been swindled, I head back to the room and have a shower. Riles isn't back yet, so I can take my sweet time and regrow my balls before she returns.

As I pop the lid of her shampoo, I recall hearing her hum the *Titanic* theme song while she showered before we disembarked. It was kinda adorable. Stupid, but adorable. She seemed really excited when talking about going to the museum, and I'd be lying if I said I wasn't hoping to see her there when I quickly walked through the place before heading back to the ship. But I wasn't going to wait there like a stalker. No doubt she'd peg me for one anyway—she seems the conclusion-jumping type.

Washing the suds from my hair and face, the alarm on my watch chimes, so I turn the faucet off and get out, wondering if I should head back into the city to try and find her. She looked terrified at the prospect of being left behind, and I promised she wouldn't be.

A man of my word, I dry myself off with the intent to track her down before we set sail when the cabin door opens then slams shut. Relief swims through me, so I tie the stupid little towel around my waist and exit the bathroom, casually strolling out.

"You made it back in time," I say with a smile.

"I—" She shoots up from lying on her bed, eyes wide as they scan my body. "Shit! Sorry, I-I forgot to knock."

Pleased she fucked up before I did—because I'm bound to—I smile proudly. "Yeah, you did."

Riles doesn't move, her mouth open, her face beautifully flushed.

Amused, I ask, "Are you going to watch me get dressed?"

"No! Of course not. Sorry, I-I'm.... I'll leave and give you privacy."

Not wanting her to leave, because I like the effect I'm having on her, I toss her the earplugs I bought at the drugstore. "I got you these."

She tries to catch them but fumbles, her arms flailing like a first-time juggler.

"They're to help you sleep."

"Th-Thanks." She picks them up from the floor, wrinkles her nose, then places them on the bed beside her.

"So, did you go to the *Titanic* exhibit?"

"I did. It was great. Lots of flotsam recovered from the ocean. Very interest—"

"Flotsam?" I scratch the back of my head. "What's that?"

She stares at my arm, then blinks. "Uh... what?"

"Flotsam," I repeat, "I don't know what it is."

"Oh, it's wreckage and items from the ship."

"Cool!"

"Yeah." She blinks again. "Did you know three hundred and twenty-eight bodies were recovered in the waters near Halifax, and of those three hundred and twenty-eight, two hundred and nine were buried in Fairview Lawn Cemetery, including J. Dawson?"

I go to say no, but she keeps rambling.

"I thought it was *the* Jack Dawson from the movie, but according to the exhibit, and much to my disappointment, Jack is indeed fictional, because the headstone belonged to a coal shoveler named Joseph. I mean, what are the odds, right?"

I nod. "Right."

She nods too. "Right."

Smirking, because I'm enjoying flustered Riles, I stay where I am, waiting for her to make the next move.

"Right." She springs up from the bed like a grasshopper and goes to step around me, one way and then the other, before bumping into the wall.

I chuckle. "You okay?"

"I'm fine."

I stand my ground.

Her nostrils flare. "Are you going to move out of my way?"

Eyes locked on hers, a droplet of water leaves my hair and lands on my chest. She watches it fall down my stomach, her throat bobbing as she swallows, her breasts rising and falling.

Heat flushes through me, and I have the sudden urge to kiss her, my dick stirring beneath the towel.

"Move!" she growls.

I laugh. "Okay, okay. Ease up, Riles."

"You ease up!" She stabs her finger at me, her apple cheeks ripening. "And... and... put some damn clothes on!"

Moving aside, I let her storm past me and out of the room, my eyes glued to the closed door as I slump onto the edge of my bed, the towel splitting apart.

"What the hell am I doing?" I ask no one, chuckling as I flop back onto the mattress and cover my face with my hands.

Ever since finding Riles in my cabin, I haven't had the faintest idea what I'm doing. I've just gone with the flow, completely out of my comfort zone, yet somehow still comfortable.

None of it makes sense.

I've only ever been with Krystal. Shared with Krystal. Cohabitated with Krystal. Other than my ex-wife, I've never spent time with another woman like this. Never stood before one, half-naked, desperate to kiss her.

"Jesus!" I sit up again, scrub my face with my palms, and then stare out the window.

I wasn't ready to "move on" with someone like Brittany.

But perhaps I could try with Riles.

Perhaps *she's* what I need.

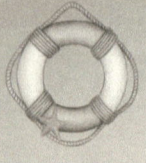

chapter nine

RILES

Peanut butter!

Pressing my back to the cabin door, I fan my face with my hand, cheeks burning, heart thumping.

What in God's name was that?

I consider going back in there to make up an excuse for the hot mess I just was, but I flee to the Vista Lounge instead, ready to play trivia. Hopefully, general knowledge questions will reset my brain, because it certainly requires a reboot. My cerebrum needs to focus on Nobel Peace Prize winners, one-hit wonders, and ancient cities of the world. Not impeccable lines, sun-kissed skin, and a sumptuous happy trail leading down to—

Why didn't I knock? Jesus, Riley!

Taking a seat after ordering myself a health juice, I suck in a mouthful of pureed beets, apple, and pomegranate, then settle back into the plush club chair, my heart rate finally easing, the fire in my cheeks no longer ablaze with embarrassment. Gosh, it's been a while since I've seen a wet, mostly naked man in the flesh, my unusually voracious hands itching to explore every bump and groove, my typically subdued body screaming for a release I didn't realize it needed. And boy did he have some delicious bumps and grooves.

Peanut butter, peanut butter, peanut butter!

I swallow my fruity mouthful and fan my face again, this time with the trivia game sheet, when I notice a couple of flustered women sitting by the windows and doing the same thing, no doubt for entirely different reasons than mine. Then again, who knows? Maybe they too just came face to face with a freshly showered man barely wrapped in a towel.

Swiftly placing the sheet of paper down, I set the pencil on top and gather my bearings.

"Two more minutes," the trivia host singsongs into his microphone.

I welcome his jovial distraction as he enthusiastically dances around the lounge area, welcoming passengers of various ages, some in teams of six or more.

My solitary ass is going to get royally kicked, especially if he asks questions about geography or sports other than basketball. I can hold my own with music, movies, and literature, but ask me what the capital of Norway is, and I'm bound to write **No Clueville**.

"Are you on your own, dear?" an elderly lady sitting at the table beside me asks. "Because if you are, you're more than welcome to join us."

I'm about to take her up on her kind offer, when Riley plops down into the chair opposite me.

"Oh, never mind," she adds. "Good luck!"

"Thanks, you too." I chew the inside of my cheek before giving him a curt nod. "Glad to see you put some clothes on."

"Only because you asked me to." He drapes his arm across the back of the chair and casually surveys the room, as if what happened back at the cabin didn't happen at all. "Looks like we've got some stiff competition."

Grateful he's not making a big deal of the hot mess, and also a little shocked he wants to join in, I ask, "You're gonna play with me?"

"Sure." His eyebrow hitches seductively, and my insides curl.

So much for not making a big deal.

I curse my treacherous insides and narrow my gaze, needing to change the subject. "Do you know the capital of Norway?"

"I do."

"Well... what is it?"

"Oslo."

I have no idea if he's correct or not.

"Did I pass?" He winks confidently, so I assume he's right.

"Yes."

"Do you always run an aptitude test for potential partners?"

I snatch up the game sheet, tap it on the tabletop, and then set it down again. "The stakes are high, so yes."

"What are the stakes?"

"That." I nod toward the gold plastic ship-replica trophy sitting on top of the piano beside the host. "I want it."

"Whyyy?"

"Because it's the prize for winning."

"You do realize you can buy one in the gift shop, right?"

"You can't. Not gold ones." I rub my hands together greedily. "Plus, we get bragging rights."

"For winning trivia?"

"Yes. Don't you want to win?"

"Honestly, I don't care. It's supposed to be about having fun."

"Exactly! We'll have more fun if we win, so pay attention." I collect the pencil, ready to write a team name on the sheet of paper, when I pause.

"So what are we calling ourselves?" he asks.

"I-I don't know. The Unfortunates?"

Riley chuckles. "Nah. Too negative."

"What do you suggest then, smarty-pants?"

"How 'bout R'n'R?"

"Rest and relaxation?" I scrunch my nose—his team name is awful.

Riley bends his elbow, supporting his head with his hand, his fingers partially covering his eyes. "No. Not rest and relaxation. Who in their right mind would call themselves that?"

"No one!"

"Exactly."

"Do you mean Rock 'n' Roll? Because that's not too bad, I guess."

"No." He belly-laughs. "Riley 'n' Riley."

"Ohhh!" I bite my lip, suppressing my idiocy, then jot the name down and scoot forward, ready for the first question.

"Maybe I should've ran an aptitude test on *you*," he mutters.

"Maybe you should zip it so I can hear."

He runs his pinched fingers across his lips, pretending to seal them.

I sneer.

"Okay, trivia buffs, my name is Carlos, and I'm your daily trivia host. Woot!" Carlos pumps the air with his fist. "Don't forget to write your team name on the top of the sheet. And *no* cheating. Cell phones in pockets, and your arms will remain in their sockets." He gives us all a playfully menacing look. "Are you ready?"

We call out, "Yes!" and he drums his hands on top of the piano he's standing next to. "First question: Which singer's real name is Stefani Joanne Angelina Germanotta?"

"Ooh. That's easy." I scribble down **Lady Gaga**, pleased we're off to a good start.

Riley leans forward and assesses my answer, but he doesn't have to, because I know I'm right. So I flip the page over so no other teams can see what I've written and then smugly sip my juice. One question down, nineteen to go.

Carlos hums "Poker Face" while waiting for everyone to finish answering the question, and I roll my eyes, annoyed.

"He's giving it away," I grouch. "That's so unfair."

"Ease up, Riles. It's just a game."

"No, it's a competition."

He scoffs. "Let me guess... you were Homecoming Queen?"

I clench my jaw. "No."

"Class President?"

Damn it!

"As a matter of fact, yes."

"Thought as much."

I continue sipping my juice, ignoring him.

"Next question," Carlos announces. "According to Greek Mythology, who was the first woman on earth?"

I flip the page quicker than a fish flips out of water and I jot down **Pandora**.

Riley leans forward, assessing my answer again. "You sure?"

"A hundred percent."

The corners of his eyes crinkle, and I have to look away. They'll distract me, and I want that damn trophy.

"Question number three. What is the chemical symbol for iron? And I'll give you a clue." Carlos places his hands on his hips. "It's not I-R."

Pencil to paper again, my hand pauses.

Crap! I hated Chemistry.

"Cat got your fingers?" Riley asks.

"No. And it's cat got your tongue," I say, correcting him, "not fingers."

He gently slides the pencil from my hand, his knuckles momentarily brushing mine, before he writes down **Fe**.

Fe? Wouldn't that be Fluorine or something?

"Are you sure?" I ask, tempted to scribble it out.

He stares me down, much like I had him, and mimics my previous response. "A hundred percent."

I snatch the pencil back and point it at him. "You better be."

He chuckles. "I am."

"Because if you're not, you need to tell me."

"Trust me. It's correct. My sister was a middle school science teacher."

"Really?"

He nods.

Curious about his personal life, I ask, "How many siblings do you have?"

"Just the one. Veronica... Roni. She's two years older."

"Are the two of you close?"

"The closest."

My heart warms at the sincerity in his eyes. "That's lovely."

"How about you? Any brothers or sisters?"

I shake my head. "No. I'm an only child."

At least I think I am. Who knows if the sperm donor that is my biological father donated more sperm?

"Are we ready for question number four?" Carlos asks.

Everyone in the lounge, except Riley, shouts, "Yes!" and I wonder why he's taking part if he's not overly into it.

Carlos's eyes widen with exaggeration. "Eager bunch, aren't you? I like it. Okay. What bones are babies born without?"

Glancing to my left out the window, blue ocean as far as the eye can see, I try to recall if I've ever heard of boneless babies, which I haven't.

Again, Riley's knuckles gently graze mine as he takes the pencil out of my hand and scrawls **Kneecaps**.

"How on earth do you know that?" I blurt.

His sparkling crinkly eyes return, but this time, they're not as animated, instead serene. Somewhat desolate. "I just do. And I have a niece, remember?"

"Oh, yeah. The one you drug to go to sleep."

"That's the one."

"What's her name?"

"Poppy."

"That's sweet. I love floral names."

"So does my sister. She has a cat named Marigold and a car she calls Lavender."

I laugh. "Is it purple?"

"The cat? No."

"Not the cat, the car." I roll my eyes when I realize he was messing with me.

"Yes." He chuckles. "The car is purple."

His sister sounds fun, unlike her irritating brother.

"This next question is for all you sweet tooths," Carlos says, singling out a child as he points his microphone in her direction after he asks, "Do you like chocolate?"

She nods emphatically.

"I don't have any, sorry."

The girl pouts, and I feel sorry for her, until Carlos pulls a Hershey's bar out of his pocket and tosses it to her. "Just kidding." He winks, then adds, "The next question is... what is the rarest M&M color in a standard packet?"

Pulling an I'm-not-sure face, I look to Riley, and he does the same.

"Well, there's red ones, orange, yellow, green, blue, and brown," I declare, picturing them in my head.

"Always bet on red," he tells me.

"Isn't the saying 'always bet on black'?"

"Is there a black M&M?"

"No."

"So bet on red."

"But brown is the closest color to black."

"It's not 'always bet on brown,'" he deadpans.

"Okay, question number six," Carlos says, and I panic and jot down **Red**, even though I think it's brown. "Name the song and artist who sang this."

The drumbeat of "Invisible Touch" blasts through the speaker, so I quickly scribble the title followed by **Phil Collins**.

Riley leans forward and shakes his head. "You're wrong."

"I am not. I know this song."

"The song is correct, but the artist isn't."

"Yes, it is."

"No, it's not." He goes to take the pencil, but I snatch it back. "Riles, trust me, you're wrong."

"I am not. Listen. That's Phil Collins singing."

He holds out his hand. "Are you going to give me the pencil?"

I stubbornly press it to my chest. "No."

"Suit yourself."

We answer more questions, Riley taking the lead on the sports-themed ones, while I handle anything to do with literature and chick flicks. We complement each other well, except when we disagree on stupid questions like *"How many hearts does an octopus have?"*

He said eight, and I said one.

We went with four.

"Okay, trivia buffs, last question, and then you'll need to swap your sheets with the team next to you."

Smiling at the elderly lady beside me, so she knows I'm going to swap with her, she smiles back in acknowledgement, her lips pressed together with anticipation.

"What is the capital of Norway?"

Laughter bursts out of my mouth, and I roll backward into my seat, nearly kicking my empty juice glass off the table.

"You want me to answer that one?" Riley asks, a cocky—albeit sexy—grin on his face.

I bite my lip and sit upright again. "No. I've got it."

Scribbling down **Oslo**, I double-check we haven't missed any answers before passing our sheet to the lady and taking hers.

"What did they write down for question number six?" Riley asks.

I scroll down the list. "They left it blank. Why? Which question was that again?"

He smirks. "You'll see."

Shooting him a puzzled look, I dismiss him and check what they wrote for the M&M question. "They chose blue M&Ms. Crap! Do you think it's blue?"

"Nah."

"It could be." I keep scrolling, confident we've at least beat *them*. A lot of their answers are blank, a couple definitely wrong.

"They said Madonna for question number one." I pout, feeling sorry for them.

Riley darts forward, snatches up the cocktail menu, covers his face with it, and slides down his seat.

I glance from side to side, because he looks like a fool. "What are you doing?"

"Hiding."

"Why?"

"Horse."

"Huh?"

"Ben," he murmurs. "Six o'clock."

Snapping my head back, my insides squirm as Ben approaches the lounge, his arms draped over two women's shoulders, the women giggling and happily swinging Tiffany & Co. bags from their fingers.

I follow Riley's lead and slip down in my seat, almost sliding onto the floor as they pass.

"Have they seen me?" Riley asks.

"Not yet."

I sneak a second look, wondering if the women are the same two Riley got drunk with the night before. They look young, given how gravity is still their "breast" friend. But then, what would two youthful, beautiful women see in Ben? His mouth is filthier than a pig troth. And not the good, smutty romance book filthy. No. His filth is outright insulting. He could also learn to button up his shirt properly. And brush his hair.

Riley peeks over the menu. "Are they gone?"

"Not yet."

"Shit!" he whispers.

The trio keep walking, and when they disappear behind a pillar, I sit up and relieve Riley of his surprisingly successful camouflage tactic. "You're good to come out now."

He lowers the menu, repositions himself, and runs his hands through his hair.

I smirk. "Tittney and Spitney, I take it?"

"Whitney and Brittany, yes."

"They seem... perky."

"I wouldn't know. I didn't hang around long enough to find out."

"Wait... what?"

"Not my crowd."

Surprised, I ask, "Then who'd you get drunk with last night?"

"I didn't get drunk."

"But you came back to the cabin in the early hours of the morning reeking of alcohol."

"That's because Ben spilled my drink all over me, and because I went for a long walk around the ship and chatted with some crewmembers before coming to bed."

I blink all the blinks.

He snickers. "You seem shocked, Riles."

"I am."

"Why?"

"You just strike me as a single, party guy."

"Who said I'm single?" he asks, lifting a brow.

For some reason, my stomach twists. "You're not single? I... I just assumed. I'm sorry." I shake my head. "Wait! What does your partner think of us sharing a cabin? You've told her, right?"

"No."

"Riley! You have to!" I chew my thumbnail. "Not that anything is going to happen. I'm not like that."

"I'm not like that either," he says, smirking.

"Good. She has nothing to worry about then." I point the pencil at him. "You should still tell her. It's the right thing to do."

"I agree. It is the right thing to do."

Still smirking at me as if he's Veronica's cat, Marigold, who got the cream, I frown. "Wait! When I set the rule that you couldn't bring back a random woman to the cabin, you said you're a grown-ass man who can hook up if he wants to."

He nods. "I did."

I narrow my eyes at him. "I'm confused."

"Clearly."

"Okay, trivia buffs," Carlos calls out, interrupting a conversation we need to revisit. "The time has come. Let's go through the answers. Question one: Show of hands, who wrote Lady Gaga?"

I spear my hand into the air, but so do many others.

"Excellent!" Carlos performs Gaga's iconic monster dance, and I giggle. He seems fun. Carefree and spontaneous. Someone who loves his job. I envy him. Not that I don't love my job, because I do. I just never have fun while I'm doing it. Never laugh.

Never dance.

"Question two: According to Greek Mythology, who was the first woman on earth?"

"Pandora!" I call out.

He points at me. "Very good!"

Riley slow-claps.

"I told you I was one-hundred percent sure," I say, smiling sweetly at him.

"Question three: The chemical symbol for iron is...?"

Someone shouts, "R-N!" and Carlos shakes his head.

"No. Sorry. Incorrect. The answer is F-E."

I pull a "not bad" face, and Riley simply shrugs.

"Question four: The bones babies are born without are—" Carlos points to his legs. "—kneecaps. Apparently, they start off as cartilage and ossify to bone when they're toddlers."

This time, I slow-cap Riley.

"I told you I was one-hundred percent sure," he mimics my response.

Playfully narrowing my eyes at him, I divert my attention back to Carlos when he asks, "What M&M color is the rarest? Why, it is brown, of course."

I groan. "Told you."

Riley raises his hands, palms facing me. "Easy mistake."

"No, it wasn't. Red was a stupid answer. The obvious answer. The wrong answer."

The speakers crackle, and "Invisible Touch" once again blasts through them, Carlos murdering the lyrics. "What is the name of this song?"

A few of us shout, "'Invisible Touch'!"

"And who sang it?" he asks, eagerly.

I jump in first. "Phil Collins!"

"Wrong!" He points the microphone at me, and it may as well be a "loser" spotlight.

What?

My stomach plummets, heat crashing into me like a tidal wave. "But that is Phil."

Riley slowly shakes his head. "Genesis."

Peanut butter! Of course.

My eyelids fall until they're pressed shut, my face scrunching with humiliation.

"You were saying?" he prompts, his voice infuriatingly arrogant.

Snapping them open again, I divert my gaze from him and cross my arms over my chest. "That was a trick question. Phil Collins is the lead singer."

He chuckles, and it annoys me even more. We should've gotten that question correct, and it's mostly my fault we didn't.

Choosing not to apologize, even though I know I should, I shrug it off as Carlos runs through the rest of the answers. And by the time he's finished, we only got three wrong.

"We did better than I thought," I say, scanning the room to see if anyone else is boasting. "Stupid octopuses. Why do they need three hearts? One is sufficient."

"Is it?" Riley murmurs, his knuckles white as he clenches his fist before relaxing.

Curious, I go to ask him what he means by that, when Carlos says, "We have come to the moment of truth. Hands up if you got fifteen correct or more."

I spear my hand into the air, as do members of four other teams.

"Now keep them up if you got sixteen or more."

Three hands drop, and I inch closer to the edge of my seat.

"Seventeen or more."

Mine and one other team's stay up.

"Eighteen?"

I reluctantly let my hand fall, but the other team member keeps hers victoriously raised. "Damn it!"

"We have our winner!" Carlos points his microphone at the other team. "Come on up and collect your one-of-a-kind trophy. Everybody else, please give them a round of applause."

Sullenly clapping—because I'm not a bad sport—I slump in my seat.

"We'll get 'em next time, Riles," Riley says, his voice mildly patronizing.

"We better," I mutter. "Because I'm not leaving this ship without a gold trophy."

He stands and stretches, the hem of his T-shirt lifting just enough to remind me of his sexy happy trail. "What are your plans for dinner?"

"I'm not sure." I look away and stand too. "I don't particularly want to eat with Ben again though."

"Why not?" he prompts, mockingly. "He's charming once you get to know him."

"Says you, who practically had a coronary when he walked past before."

"I did not."

I laugh. "Yeah, you did."

"In all honesty, he's not that bad. Just says stupid shit because he's insecure."

"Insecure?" I scoff. "Did you see him with Tittney and Spitney? There was nothing insecure about him."

"Smoke and mirrors, Riles."

"More like smoke and liquor."

Chuckling, Riley drops his arms and slides his hands into his pockets. "I'm probably just going to grab a burger at The Grill and eat out on the top deck to watch the sunset. Want to join me?"

Visualizing the sun melting into the horizon, something I don't often get to see, my body fizzles with excitement. "That actually sounds really nice."

chapter ten

RILEY

R iles detours us into one of the atrium's glass elevators, and even though I can see out of it, the confined space still jitters my pansy-ass knees.

"I love these things," she says, peering down as she presses herself to the glass like a demented starfish.

I stay near the door. "Y-Yeah, they're cool."

She lets go of the railing and faces me. "You don't sound convinced."

"That's because I'm not."

As she assesses me through the slits of her eyes that are full of suspicion, the turning cogs in her head must click into place as she blurts, "You were serious when we went to Guest Services... about being claustrophobic?"

"I was. Clearly, you weren't."

"Of course not. I just didn't want to be moved to a cabin on deck three." She dismisses her fib as if it's irrelevant. "Is your claustrophobia bad?"

"It can be."

"Why do you keep getting into elevators then?"

"Because my sister told me to."

Riles steps forward and clasps my forearms, her grip firm but kind.

"What are you doing?" I squeak like I'm going through puberty as she coaxes me forward, my balls bouncing up deep into the pit of my stomach.

"Come closer to the glass."

Until now, I've managed to keep my cool while traveling in the death boxes, rooting myself near the door, focusing on the numbers lighting up, and acting as if I were any other passenger. My dignity has remained intact, my phobia private.

"Nah," I choke out, trying but failing to remain impassive. "I'm good near the door."

"You won't feel so enclosed if you look out into the atrium." She gently tugs my arms, her smoky-gray eyes encouraging and without judgment.

I go to back away, but I'm fucking cornered.

"Trust me," she says. "I promise."

Unable to escape, I let her lead me to the glass while stupidly sucking in a breath and inhaling her please-lick-me perfume. My head swims, my knees unlock, and I nearly fucking collapse.

"Is this helping?" she asks.

Hell no!

"S-Sure," I stutter, willing the damn elevator to stop so I can get the hell out.

"See?" She gestures to the atrium, her chest rising as she inhales. "There's no walls closing in on you. Breathe, Riley. Embrace the vast space."

I do as I'm told, breathing in and out, my balls the size of acorns.

"Phobias are awful. Trust me, I know. I'm equinophobic."

Diverting my gaze from her breasts, which are providing a better distraction than the vast space I'm supposed to be embracing, I choke out, "What's that?"

"Fear of—" She pauses and smiles the kind of cheeky smile Poppy is exceptionally good at. "—horses."

Laughter leaves my throat in a whoosh, and for the slightest moment, I forget where I am.

"Kidding. I love horses. Just not the ones named Ben." She winks at me when the doors open, then pats my back as if I'm a kindergartner who refrained from pissing his pants. "You did good."

"Thanks," I mutter, attempting to stride confidently out of the glass prison.

"Hey! Don't downplay it. I'm being sincere. You did good. Phobias are silent stranglers. An invisible noose."

I scoff. "I rode an elevator up six floors, Riles. That's hardly good."

"Nonsense. You're facing your fear, which is more than I can say for myself."

Curious about what she's afraid of, apart from the ship setting sail and leaving her behind, I ask, "How so?"

"I might not be equinophobic, but I am chronomentrophic."

Chrono-whatever-she-just-said isn't something I've heard of before, so I scratch my head.

"Fear of clocks," she explains.

Clocks? What's so scary about clocks?

We enter The Grill, and Riles scans the menu on the board as if she didn't just admit a timepiece terrifies her.

"Clocks?" I probe, trying not to laugh, because she didn't laugh at me.

"Yeah. But not all clocks. Just the ones that tick loudly. It's as if they're a bomb ready to detonate. It scares the bejesus out of me."

My favorite childhood book springs to mind. "Perhaps I should call you Captain Hook, then?"

Her head slowly turns in my direction, exorcist style, her eyes narrowing menacingly. "Please don't."

I raise my hands. "I'm joking. I wouldn't."

"Good. Because if you do, next time we're in an elevator together, I'll hit the Stop button."

Every nerve ending in my body sparks with dread, mostly because of the don't-fucking-mess-with-me look on her face. But the thought of being in an elevator with Riles again, provided it's moving and made of glass, doesn't petrify me as much as it should. In fact, I can think of a few things to do as a distraction.

"Riley!"

Blinking, I meet her eyes. "What?"

"I said, what are you having?" She gestures to the waiting server behind the counter.

"Uh..." I rub my beard. "Double beef, double cheese, L-T-M, fried onions, and barbeque sauce. Fries on the side. And a Bud."

"Ooh, me too." She spins back to face the guy. "Sorry, can I have that instead? But no Bud. I'll stick with my Pepsi."

"Certainly. Coming right up."

We wait a few minutes before our burgers are ready, and then we head outside to the deck, finding a free table in the corner by a window.

"This is a great spot," she says, setting down her plate and soda. "No wind. No kids."

I take a seat opposite her. "You don't like kids?"

"No, I do. I just prefer to eat my dinner away from their splashing. I think I drank chlorine with my Cosmo yesterday." She takes a sip of her drink. "How 'bout you? Do you like kids... when you're not drugging them?"

A passing passenger almost trips and performs a double-take at me.

Riles smirks.

I smirk back. "Yeah, I do."

She awkwardly lifts her burger—which is almost as big as her head—and assesses it, ready for a bite. "Do you and your partner have any?"

My throat goes dry, so I pick up my beer and take a long swig, mentally calming myself to say, "No. I'm single."

Her enthusiastic munching stops, and she mumbles, "But you said—"

113

"I didn't say I was or wasn't."

"Wait!" She swallows, sauce dripping onto her chin. "So you don't have a partner?"

"Not exactly."

"What does that even mean?"

"I'm getting a divorce."

"Oh." She dips her head and takes another bite. "I'm sorry."

I dunk a fry in ketchup and pop it into my mouth. "I'm not."

Riles doesn't insist I elaborate, even though I can tell she's itching to by how her eyes—swimming with the reflection of the water in the pool—bounce back and forth. But she doesn't request further information, and I appreciate it.

Everyone I know knows the truth. The pastor. The coffee shop owner. The local handyman. Every damn person in Buxtonville. They know about Krystal and Finn, about Imogen and how neither of us recovered from losing her. They know everything. All I want is a conversation with someone who isn't aware of the deepest, saddest parts of me.

And I finally have that.

She takes another sip of her soda, and the sauce on her chin glares at me like a beacon. I have the overwhelming urge to wipe it off for her, so I go to reach out when she collects her napkin, presses it to her mouth, and hums, "Yum. You chose good."

I chuckle. "I can see that."

"Don't judge me. I'm starving."

"How can you be starving? There's an endless supply of food on this ship."

"I know! But all I've eaten today is that bagel I had at breakfast. Oh, and a juice."

"That's it?"

"Yeah." She swishes her hand at me. "I was too busy seeing all the things I wanted to see in Halifax."

"And you forgot to eat?"

She shrugs. "I'm used to it. Happens all the time. As long as I get my coffee first thing in the morning, I'm fine."

For as long as I can remember, Mom made it her priority to make sure Roni and I had a hearty breakfast and ended our day with an even heartier dinner.

"A full belly leads to a full day and a good night's rest, kids. Eat well, live well," she often said while placing home-cooked meals on the table. So hearing Riles "forgets" to eat as if it's perfectly acceptable churns my well-nourished stomach.

"You shouldn't skip meals," I remark.

Her brow bunches. "It's not like I do it on purpose. Most days, I grab something on the run. Other days, I'm too preoccupied. Like today."

"Food is important."

She steeples her fingers, one solitary eyebrow hiked. "Are you saying I'm too thin? Because thin-shaming is as bad as fat-shaming."

"I'm not body-shaming you, Riles. Your body is perfect."

Her cheeks flush pink, her jaw dropping just slightly before she snaps it shut and awkwardly rubs her neck.

Enjoying my ability to make her blush, I control the satisfaction that wants to burst onto my face and continue speaking so she understands what I *am* trying to say. "Food is fuel, and we need fuel to function."

"Ahh..." She pops a fry into her mouth. "You're one of those fitness-freak types, aren't you?"

This time, my eyebrow hikes. "Are you fitness-shaming me?"

She giggles. "No. Clearly, it's working for you."

Stretching back, I think I fucking blush too, so I look out at the ocean, the sky dotted with orange clouds, the water beneath it a rippled mirror. Canada, as big and beautiful as she is, sits as a blip on the horizon. And for the next day, there will be nothing but sea and sky.

"So you're a fitness junkie?" she probes.

I shake my head. "No. I just look after myself."

"Well, believe it or not, I look after myself too."

I'm not sure I believe her, especially if nutrition is an

afterthought for her, so when I don't agree or argue back, she takes another monstrous bite of her burger and grins sarcastically at me, lettuce and beef poking out from between her teeth.

I laugh.

"Did you grow up in Philly?" she mumbles.

"Yeah. Born and bred."

"Does Veronica and Poppy live there too?"

"They do. They live with Mom, two streets away."

"And your dad?"

"He passed away years ago."

Riles chokes, so I stand, ready to pat her back.

"I'm good," she coughs out, raising her hand.

I retake my seat and slide her soda closer to her.

"Thank you." She takes a long sip, her eyes bouncing from mine to her cup and back again. "I'm sorry about your dad. I shouldn't have pried."

"It's fine. He was a heavy smoker, and that's what killed him in the end."

"How old were you?"

"Twenty."

She swallows, her palm resting over her heart, her bottom lip pouting. "I'm so sorry, Riley. That's awful. You were so... young. Barely an adult."

I nod.

"I never knew my dad. He was a jerk. I'm glad you got the time you did with yours though, even if it wasn't the lifetime you both deserved."

Memories of Dad and me in the shed, planing and oiling hardwood together, hit me as if they're happening in real time: the sound of sandpaper scraping wood, the smell of cedar... and tobacco.

I swig my beer. "He taught me everything I know."

"About carpentry?"

"Yeah. I was his apprentice. When he died, I took over the family business."

"Wow! That's a lot of responsibility."

"It was. But Roni now helps out in the store."

"That must be nice... the two of you carrying on his legacy. I bet every time you complete a piece of furniture, a part of him has completed it with you."

Eyes locked on hers, I pause, my burger midway to my mouth. In just that one sentence, Riles has understood a part of me that Krystal never did. Why I work so much. Why I love it. Why I chose to run the business when the business struggled to make ends meet.

Blinking, I take a bite and mumble, "Yeah."

Her eyes soften for a moment, but then she brushes her hands together before pulling out her phone and tapping the ship's app. "I wonder what's happening in the theatre tonight."

Again, I appreciate her ability not to probe beyond a point I'm not ready to talk about, which only enforces what I already suspect... that she too shares some form of grief. Heartbreak speaks to heartbreak or, in most cases, doesn't speak when speaking isn't required.

She frowns. "It's an opera performance."

"You don't like opera?"

"No."

"Me neither."

"Maybe I should go and check it out anyway," she says, chewing her fingernail. "I'm supposed to be trying new things on this cruise."

"Why's that?"

Riles freezes, much like she did last night. And even though I want to know what she's not admitting, again... heartbreak speaks to heartbreak, so I pay her the same respect she did me by not prying.

"I'm sure you'll try a lot of new things on the cruise, whether you watch the opera or not," I offer, changing the subject for her.

Her shoulders relax, and she nods, more to herself than to me. "True."

"Have you checked out the casino yet?"

"No." She sets her phone down. "I'm not a gambler."

"Probably a good thing. No doubt you'd bump into Ben."

"I'd rather bump into a cactus."

I chuckle. "Did you know he owns Mason's?"

"The hardware chain?"

"Yes."

Riles's eyes nearly bug out of her head. "No, I didn't. But Tittney and Spitney's interest in him makes more sense to me now."

"Are you money-shaming him?" I ask, deliberately baiting her as I pop another fry into my mouth.

"No! Well... okay, maybe I am."

Shooting her a judgmental look, I continue goading, because it's kinda fun. She's overly defensive, and it intrigues me as to why she feels she has to justify herself so much.

"What's that look for?" she asks.

I wipe my mouth and hands with my napkin, then toss it onto my plate. "I'm not giving you a look."

"You are."

"I'm not."

"Lies! You're insinuating I'm judgmental when I shouldn't be."

"Are you?"

"No! Ben is just... rude, and not who girls like Tittney and Spitney normally pursue. There had to be more to it, and there is."

"That's judgmental."

"How's it judgmental?"

"Because you don't know Ben, nor *Brittany* and *Whitney*."

"Neither do you."

"Correct."

She frowns at me, pushes her drink aside, and leans back, crossing her arms over her chest, something she does when I'm grating her nerves.

Forcing down my pending grin, I try not to stare at her cleavage, which is now elevated in full sight.

"I'm not a nasty person, Riley, if that's what you're imply—"

"I'm not. I—"

"In fact, I think it's wrong to use people for their money. But it's also wrong to use people *because* you have money."

"Correct."

"And isn't that what that particular ménage à trois—Ben's words, not mine—are doing?"

"Correct."

"So what's your problem?"

"I never said I had one."

She outright growls at me, like a cub, and I can't help but laugh.

"You're so infuriating. Has anyone ever told you that?"

I lie. "No."

"I find that hard to believe." She sips the last of her drink and gestures toward the horizon. "The sun is setting, so I suggest you stop goading me or you'll miss it."

Smirking, I nod my thanks, push my chair back, and then exit our small alcove. We step up to the railing out on deck, the sun sinking behind the water, a glorious amber glow warming the sky. I breathe in the unusual peace settling around and within me, finally realizing why Roni wanted me to temporarily hang up my tools and get away—for moments like this, not for sowing my wild oats.

"I haven't seen a sunset like this in years," Riles says as she rests her arms on the railing beside me.

"Me neither."

The wind whips into an invisible lasso, lashing my face and T-shirt. Riles clasps her top, holding it firmly to stop it from flying up and over her head. Her brown hair frantically thrashes about her as loose strands escape her ponytail. Chaotic but beautiful.

"And to be frank," she gripes, "it pisses me off."

I go to ask her why, but she answers before I have the chance.

"I've missed out on so much because of my boss. Sunrises. Sunsets. Going out with my friends. Shows with my mom. Dates."

Her reference to dating, or lack thereof, piques my curiosity. "Your boss interferes with your love life? Sounds like an HR issue to me."

She scoffs. "What love life?"

Something inside me weirdly blooms to life, but I suppress it when Riles lets out an embarrassed laugh, her cheeks once again flushed.

"Not that I want a love life," she blurts. "Not now, anyway. Too complicated. But that's not the point, you know? Georgia steals a lot of my time. Time I need to stop willingly giving her. If I've learned anything recently, it's that you can't get time back. Once it's gone, it's gone."

Leaning forward, I rest my arms on the railing as well and watch the swell come and go, much like time. "You can say that again."

She draws in a deep breath, then lets it out. "And that is why I'm vowing to see every sunset every day of this cruise."

I turn my head toward her and smirk.

"I'm serious. I'm not going to miss a single one. They're too precious to miss." She smirks back at me. "I'm a woman of my word. When I make a promise, I keep it. You watch me."

Even though I don't know Riles all that well, she appears to have a point to prove, if not to others then definitely to herself, so I don't bait her this time, because I hope she succeeds. Determination is a powerful tool. When used for good things, it shouldn't be messed with.

Silence settles over us until the sky is gray, nothing but the sound of lapping water and distant music from the poolside bar.

"I think I'll get an ice cream," she blurts. "Do you want one?"

Weird question, but okay. "Sure."

"I love ice cream."

"Who doesn't?"

"Georgia."

Turning my back to the water, I rest my ass against the railing. "Your boss sounds like a piece of work."

"She is."

"So why do you continue to work for her?"

"Because she's a means to an end. And because, despite her tyranny, she's the best at what she does. I've learned a lot working for her."

"Surely there are other publishers less witch-like that are great at what they do?"

"There are."

"So why not pursue careers with them?"

She sighs. "Because Georgia thickens my skin, and that's important for a young woman who wants to make her mark. I respect her for that. She successfully worked her way up the corporate ladder in a once male-dominated field, and sadly, she wouldn't have achieved what she has if she weren't the evil queen."

I nod, also respecting her response.

"Do you like vanilla?"

"Huh?"

I'm about to say, *"Yes, I like all sex, even the boring kind"* when she says, "Vanilla ice cream."

Shaking my head, because of course she meant ice cream, I stutter, "I-I guess. Yes."

"I had some yesterday, and it was amazing."

I try not to laugh. "That good, huh?"

"Yeees," she practically moans. "It was as if my mouth made love to a delicious cloud." She clasps my arm and tugs me with her. "Come on. You have to try it."

I follow her eager steps until we're standing outside the ice cream bar, where I order vanilla, even though I want butter pecan.

"Well?" Her eyebrows rise in anticipation as I spoon some into my mouth.

Holy shit!

I spoon some more, no words needed.

"Told you," she singsongs. "It's the stuff of miracles, or sorcery. It must be."

"I think you're right. This is the nicest vanilla ice cream I've ever had. Better than Mrs. Parberry's."

"Who's Mrs. Parberry?"

"She owns an ice cream parlor where I live. And thanks to Poppy, I've had my fair share of the stuff."

We continue strolling along the deck, adjacent to the railing, my cup almost empty, her cone dripping onto her fingers. She sucks them into her mouth, and I fight to keep my thoughts clean.

"So what's your favorite piece of furniture you've built so far?" she asks.

"My sister's rocking chair."

"A rocking chair? How lovely."

"I built it for her when she was pregnant."

"Aww. That's sweet."

I shrug, feeling proud but strangely bashful. "I also built Poppy's crib."

"You're a handy sibling to have for a mother-to-be."

"I help with furniture; she helps with chemistry-based trivia."

Riles nudges my shoulder with hers. "Speaking of trivia, I owe you an apology."

I smirk. She does, but I was happy it let it slide.

"I should've listened to you when you said it wasn't Phil Collins. I can't believe I got that wrong."

"I can't believe you got that wrong as well."

"Hey!"

"I'm kidding. It was an easy mistake."

"More like a stupid mistake."

"Ease up, Riles." I stop by a trash can and toss my empty cup inside. "It's just a silly trivia question."

"Perhaps." She pops the last of her cone into her mouth. "But you owe me an apology too."

"Me?" I run my hand over my beard just in case it collected some ice cream. "What for?"

"You were wrong about the red M&M, and I was right."

I stare at her, dumbfounded. *Is she serious?*

When she doesn't laugh and say she's joking, I'm left with no other option than to say, "Sorry?"

"Apology accepted." Riles smiles as if all is right in the world, but then scrubs her hands up and down her bare arms as she shivers.

I go to offer her my shirt, when she yawns.

"I think I might have an early night."

Guilt twists my gut, and I pray to God I don't snore again tonight like a hog freight train, or whatever it was she called me. "Yeah, no sweat. I won't be too far behind you. I'll give you some privacy to get settled first."

"Thanks, Riley. I appreciate it." Stepping backward, she lifts her hand in a subtle wave. "Goodnight."

I wave back, but unlike when I did it to Brittany outside the elevator, this time feels perfectly normal. "Night."

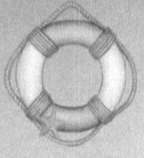

chapter eleven

RILES

My cell vibrates on the bedside table next to me, pulling me from a sleep I'm desperate to cling to, my eyelids sore and heavy, my limbs barely ambulatory.

I smack my fingers at the screen to shut it up, then roll onto my stomach and bury my face in my pillow, muffling my murderous scream as I pummel the mattress beside my ears.

Groaning, "Kill me now!" I lift my head and take a deep breath, then pluck the useless foam earplug out of my ear and toss it into the center of the room. Where the other one is, I have no idea—probably stuck to my armpit for all I know.

At some time in the early hours of the morning, between opening the balcony door, strangling the air in front of me as if it was Riley's vibrating throat, and then climbing back into bed and eventually falling asleep again, it must've dislodged itself from my ear.

Earplugs will fix the problem, my ass!

The inconsiderate jerk snorts in an inconsiderate breath he doesn't deserve to take, which tips me over the edge. So I shove up to my hands and knees, glare at him, and snatch up my pillow, ready to deplete him of oxygen.

Storming across the room to his bed, I wrench the pillow over my head, but unlike the morning before, I don't hesitate before slamming it onto his face... multiple times. "Wake the fuck up!"

He jolts and wrestles, defending himself in the same way he did the last time I pillow-attacked him. "What the— Jesus! Rile—"

Growling, I toss the pillow at his blinking, stunned face.

He catches it and then drops it onto the bed beside him before scrubbing his palms over his eyes. "Shit! Did I snore again?"

"Yes!"

"Sorry. I'll—"

"Shut up. Just—" I massage my temples, trying to keep calm. "Shut. Up."

He does as he's told, his mouth opening, then closing, not one word being said.

I sigh, march to the closet, collect a pair of sweatpants and a hoodie, and throw them over my pajamas.

"Where are you going?"

"Coffee," I grouch. "Because if I don't drink some in the next sixty seconds, I *will* kill you."

Again, he doesn't argue, which is a smart choice, because I'm a woman of my word. Okay, perhaps I'm not a murderer, but I'm definitely capable of inflicting permanent damage to his genitals.

By the time I return from the café, fully caffeinated and a little less homicidal, Riley is nowhere to be found, so I change into my bathing suit and prepare to take my laptop poolside to get some work done, when he comes through the door, a gift-shop bag in hand.

"Before you say anything," he says. "These are for you. I don't know if you have any, but these ones are noise-cancelling."

I narrow my eyes at him and take the bag from his outstretched hand. "What are they?"

"AirPods."

"What?"

"Do you have any?"

"Not noise-cancelling ones."

I lift out the box, suspecting the pair he bought are expensive, so I hand them back. "I can't accept these."

"You can and you will." He steps around me, refusing to take them. "Sleep is just as important as food, and I'm the cause of you not getting any. Please, Riles, just try them out. If they don't work, I'll take the shitty cabin in the bowels of hell. Not that I want to, because I'll probably die a horrible death. But I will if it means you'll get some sleep."

My jaw drops.

Wow! That's... That's chivalrous and remorseful.

Chewing the inside of my cheek, I slump onto the sofa, unwrap the box, and pull out the earbuds, feeling guilty for being a light sleeper.

"And if you download this white noise app thing that the lady at the counter suggested, you shouldn't hear me at all." Riley pulls his cell from his pocket and shows me his screen as he takes a seat beside me. "Apparently, it has over a hundred different sounds that promote peaceful sleep. Fans. Rain." The corners of his mouth lift just slightly, and I don't know if I want to laugh or punch him in the arm when he adds, "A ticking clock."

"Very funny." I reach for my cell to download the app. "Okay, I guess I'll give it a try."

"Sweet," he says, slapping his thighs before standing. "Honestly, I never used to snore. Not before Krys—"

Riley cuts himself short, and my sympathetic heart twinges a little. "You didn't snore before your marriage broke down?"

He clenches his jaw. "No. Not as far as I'm aware."

Scrunching my face, unsure if that's actually the case, I can't help but ask, "Maybe you did, and that's one of the reasons—"

"You think I'm getting a divorce because I snore?" He laughs humorously, but it turns bitter. "Trust me—it's not. If I snored, Krystal would've told me. It would've been high in her arsenal against me."

"Sorry. I didn't mean...." I shake my head regretfully. It was a stupid thing to say. "Thank you for buying these, but... they look expensive. I can't let you pay for them. How much do I owe you?"

"Don't worry about it. It's my fault you need them in the first place." He slides his hands into his pockets, his eyes roaming over my white bathing suit cover-up. "You going for a swim?"

"Maybe." I stand too. "But I have to work first."

"You're working on your vacation?"

"I have to."

"You have to, or you're choosing to in order to please your bitch of a boss?"

I draw in a deep breath, hold it for a moment, then let it out. "I have to."

Riley presses his lips together, his eyebrows rising as he rocks back on his heels, but he doesn't question me further, which I appreciate. Defending my choice to appease Georgia is draining, and I simply don't have the energy to do it right now.

"I'll see you later," I say, hitching my bag over my shoulder before heading out the door and making my way to the adult oasis, choosing a cozy cabana by the pool.

The late morning sun sparkles above, heating my alabaster skin, so I lather on some sunscreen, open my laptop, and dive into work, making notes and suggestions for improvements where the manuscript is lagging. Other than some mild repetition here and there, her prose is eloquent, the character vernacular on point. She also knows her Greek Mythology, which is refreshing.

Completely enthralled in the love triangle between Dyetee, Persei, and Aydon, I startle when Riley asks, "Good book?"

"Huh?" I snap my head in the direction of his voice, my mouth agape at his casually reclined position on the lounge chair beside me, chest bare, abs impeccably rippled, taut legs crossed at the ankles, both arms raised behind his head, biceps flexed.

Oh, holy freaking peanut butter!

My hand slips across the keyboard, and I almost delete a portion of the manuscript. "Shit!"

Quickly amending my mistake by clicking the Undo button, I

save my notes and edits before closing the screen. "Y-Yes, it is good! Her writing voice is strong, and the story is engaging."

"What's it about?"

"It's a modern retelling of Aphrodite, Persephone, and Adonis. Set in Greece in the twenty-first century."

"A modern retelling?"

"Uh-huh. Much like Baz Luhrmann's *Romeo and Juliet*." I divert my eyes from his delicious body and focus on the pool. "You going for a swim?"

"In a minute. You?"

"Not yet. I need to finish the chapter I was working on."

He lets out a "Hmm."

I ignore his disapproval. "I'll let you test out the water first."

"What's to test? It's water."

"It might be cold."

"Are you aquaphobic too?"

"No." I smirk at his witty playfulness. "I just don't like cold water."

"Fear not, Riles. It's heated."

As I contemplate a quick dip before resuming my work, Ben plonks himself on the lounge chair next to Riley. "What's happenin', kids?"

I internally groan.

He bites his knuckle, his prurient eyes shamelessly raking the length of my legs. "Lucky son of a bitch."

I blink. "I beg your pardon?"

"Never mind, love." He winks at Riley and nods toward the pool. "You guys going for a swim?"

"No—"

"Yeah, we are," Riley says, cutting me off while basking in my scowl. "How 'bout you, Ben?"

"Is the Pope a religious fuck? Of course I am."

Oh my God! What is wrong with this guy?

Riley closes his eyes and slowly shakes his head. "You did it again, Ben."

"Did what?"

"What we talked about in Halifax."

"I did?" Ben winces. "Fuck! I suck at this." He balls his fists, then relaxes. "Let me try again. Yes, friends. I'm going for a swim."

Peeking one eye open, Riley grins.

"Better?" Ben asks.

Riley chuckles. "Much."

Okay, that was weird.

"You play volleyball?" Riley asks him.

"Do I look like I play volleyball?"

"That's not what I asked."

"No, I don't, but I'll give it a go."

"Good man."

Ben looks out over the pool and scratches his scruffy head. "Where's the net?"

"There isn't one."

"Then how we playin'?"

"Use your imagination." Riley swings his legs off the lounger and turns toward me. "You coming?"

"Not yet."

"Suit yourself."

"Have fun," I singsong sarcastically.

"Oh, I will." He winks devilishly, and my insides curl.

Damn, he's handsome.

Suspecting he's up to something, I lower my sunglasses to the tip of my nose as he strides to the edge of the pool before effortlessly diving in like an Olympic swimmer.

"Show off," Ben mutters before scooting over to Riley's vacant lounge chair, closer to me. He collects my bottle of sunscreen, pops the lid, and tilts it in my direction. "You need me to do your back?"

I want to tell him I don't have a back, but that would be... well... ridiculous. "Uhh," I stutter. "No thanks."

"You sure? Skin cancer kill—"

"Ben, you coming or what?" Riley calls out.

"Yeah, yeah." He places the bottle down again and rests his meaty arms on his head, trepidation ghosting his face. "Why'd I agree to this? I haven't played a sport since seventh grade. Pretty boy is gonna kick my ass."

I study him for a moment, and for the first time since meeting the inappropriate douche, I suspect Riley may be on to something regarding Ben lacking confidence and being insecure. It flicks my heartstrings. Delicately. As soft as butterfly wings. And despite not liking the guy, I can't help but feel begrudgingly sympathetic.

Insecurity chains us to a place devoid of strength, and we don't fight those chains because we've been groomed to accept them. We're taught to measure our appearance against what society deems perfection, and that only ever leads to failure and disappointment. A demoralizing sense of self-worth. A losing battle we shouldn't be fighting in the first place. It dooms confidence before confidence has a chance at prevailing, and quite frankly, it's unjustifiably unfair.

"You look strong," I offer, encouraging him. "Aim for his pretty head."

Ben rears back. "You think I look strong?"

"Sure." I nod toward Riley. "Hit him where it hurts."

Standing, he links his fingers together before stretching toward the sky, his trunks slipping down past the top of his ass. And even though society wrongfully deems his appearance less than perfection, his ass crack isn't something I appreciate in such close proximity to my face.

I lean back, push my sunglasses up the bridge of my nose, close one eye, and angle my face away, blocking the unwelcome view. "Go get him, tiger."

Ben roars like a big cat and charges toward the pool, belly-flopping the water like a breaching whale.

Laughter bursts from my chest.

"Jesus!" Riley complains, wiping droplets from his face as Ben resurfaces. "You could've killed me."

Ben flexes both biceps. "We playing imaginary fucking volley-ball or not?"

"The ball is behind you," Riley deadpans. "Serve it."

Wading through the pool, Ben collects the ball and gives it a useless squeeze, then he tosses it into the air and smacks it with his open palm, roaring like a tiger again when it rockets barely an inch over Riley's head.

Oops!

I bite my lip as it skims the surface of the water, bounces out of the pool, and rolls to a stop by my lounger. I'm tempted to toss it back but get up instead and take it to the edge of the pool, where I wait for Riley. His strong arms sweep the water back with each step toward me, reminiscent of a *Baywatch* lifeguard.

"Dickhead nearly killed me. Twice!" Riley spits out.

Giggling, I squat and hand him the ball. "Go easy on him. He's insecure, remember?"

He cocks his head just slightly. "Did you tell him to do that?"

"Do what?" I prompt, feigning ignorance.

"Aim for my head?"

I shrug.

His eyes widen with a wicked glint, and before I can leap back a safe distance, he grasps my wrist and tugs me into the water, his arms cradling my body and preventing me from completely submerging.

"Riley!" I shriek, wiping my eyes before slapping his chest. "You jerk!"

"What goes around, comes around, sweetheart."

"My cover-up! It's soaked." I slap him again, wrestle free of his grip, and plant my feet on the bottom of the pool, trying to remain somewhat pissed at him, but I honestly can't. I haven't had this much spontaneous fun since... well... for as long as I can remember. "That was a cheap shot."

"You telling Ben to aim for my head was a cheap shot."

"Why?"

"Because he nearly decapitated me."

Laughing, because he's absolutely correct, I scruff his wet hair. "Afraid of a little competition, are you?"

"Is that a challenge?"

"Maybe."

His eyes crinkle as he calls out to where Ben is ogling a sunbather at the other end of the pool. "Hey, Michigan. Riles is on your team."

Ben turns to face us. "Don't worry, love. I'll protect you."

"Protect me?" I mutter under my breath. "More like try to molest me."

Riley chuckles. "If it comes to that, *I'll* protect you."

"I don't need protecting. I can protect myself." I playfully shove him, then wade to the edge of the pool and take the steps out of the water.

"Where are you going?" he asks.

"I can't play in this, can I?" I explain, bunching the seam of my cover-up after peeling it from my stomach. "And I refuse to be at a disadvantage."

Continuing to the cabana, I awkwardly grapple with the drenched material plastered to my arms and back, twisting as I pull it over my head before wringing it out and neatly setting it on the end of the lounge chair. I then turn back to the pool, finding Riley's eyes glued to my body like a magnet, his Adam's apple bobbing as he swallows.

Heat sweeps my skin, and I'm tempted to wrap myself in a towel or ask him if he's ever seen a woman in a swimsuit before, when the ball slams into the side of his face.

"Two points to me," Ben boasts.

I burst with laughter and quickly slip back into the water, high-fiving my partner. "Great shot!"

"He doesn't know what he's gotten himself into. Pretty boy is gonna pay."

Nostrils flaring, Riley cracks his neck, then snatches up the floating ball with force, ready to pummel his serve—I'm guessing directly at Ben—when he takes a breath and gently taps it toward me instead. I spring out of the water, attempting to set the ball up, but completely misjudge my leap and hit nothing but air.

"What was that?" Ben prompts, frowning at me.

"I slipped."

"No shit!"

"Hey! I'm just warming up."

Truth is, I've never played volleyball in a pool before. Once or twice on a court during my sophomore year, but that's as far as my volleyball prowess extends. Still, I have drive and determination. And I'll be damned if Ben is going to dub me our weakest link.

Game on!

Swimming toward the ball, I frustratedly snag it then stand before tossing it up and gently serving it to Riley. He slices through the water and spikes the ball, powerful and poised like Poseidon, and once again, my head is in the Greek mythological clouds.

A crack of thunder sounds from behind, and I wonder for a second if Zeus has joined us.

"My gut," Ben groans. "Fuck! I think you just broke my gut."

"Shit! Sorry, man." Riley raises his palms but winks at me. "My bad!"

I spin toward Ben, a ball-shaped impression instantly reddening his fleshy stomach, laughter once again bursting from my chest.

"Hey! Whose side are you on, love?"

"Sorry." I cover my mouth with my hand and gain my composure. "Yours. I'm on yours."

"Then put some elbow into it. None of this soft, girly serving shit."

I'm ready to tell him to shove his words up his ass, because "girly" and "soft" are adjectives that shouldn't be used when describing something weak. But I choose to bite my tongue, instead brushing off his insult in preparation for him to eat his sexist comment.

"Let me try again," I say, gesturing for him to give me the ball.

Ben obliges, so I toss it up, this time aggressively slapping my palm to it and forcing Riley to lunge to his right, the ball hitting the water just shy of his hand.

"Thatta girl."

"Thank you, Ben," I say proudly.

Tucking the ball under his arm, Riley smirks. "So this is how it's going to be, huh?"

I lift my chin, confident. "It is."

"All right then." Riley spins the ball on the tip of his finger, all cocky-like.

I roll my eyes, unimpressed—my stepfather taught me that trick too.

"My princesses," Ben coos, arms wide, as Brittany and Whitney walk by the pool, one of them waving at Riley, the other taking a selfie before blowing Ben a kiss.

Ben pretends to catch it, then slides his hand down the front of his trunks.

I all but throw up in my mouth, gagging and coughing.

"You all right, love?" he asks, turning toward me.

I cough again. "Yep, just swallowed some water."

"Here, let me help." He goes to rub my back.

"Heads up!" Riley shouts as the ball careens past Ben's ear.

Taking the opportunity, I step back out of Ben's 'harm's' way as he angrily scoops up the ball and slams it back at Riley. "I wasn't ready," he grouches.

"Not my problem."

"Two against one?" the tall brunette prompts, placing her manicured hands on her slender hips. "That seems unfair."

"It's not." Riley serves the ball again, Ben and I almost colliding as we lunge and miss, both of us plunging beneath the water.

Planting my feet, I push up and stand, blinking water from my eyes, when Ben chastises me.

"Love! You gotta call for it."

I chastise him back. "You call for it!"

"I did!"

"Did not."

He turns his back on the women, his macho bravado waning as he mutters, "I'm sorry. I just.... We need a game plan. I don't want to look like a fool."

I glance over his shoulder at the blonde who blew him a kiss, my heart softening for him as she settles on a lounge chair and takes another selfie, completely engrossed in herself and not Ben. He's wasting his time with her. If he wants to impress a woman, he's better off trying to impress someone who's after more than just his money. Someone interested in his heart, because funnily enough, he seems to have one buried under a load of insulting bullshit.

"I agree," I say, patting his shoulder. "We need to work as a team. You stick to that side of the pool, and I'll stick to this side. You be LeBron, and I'll be MJ. Two GOATs, okay?"

Before I can duck and dive, he pulls me in for a hug. "Two fucking GOATs! Let's do this."

Thinking I'm going to have to pry myself loose before his hands roam where they shouldn't, he surprises me when he releases his grip and swims toward the ball.

"Mind if I join in and even it up a little?" the brunette asks as she slides into the water, her bikini almost flossing her vagina. "I'm Brittany, by the way. And you are?"

"Riley," I offer.

Her eyes flick from Riley to me and back again.

"Yes," he deadpans. "Same name."

She adjusts her bikini top. "Do you know each other?"

I go to say, *We do now,* when Riley waves me toward him. "Riles, you partner with me. Brittany, you partner with Ben."

"No!" Ben snaps, hugging my shoulder to his armpit. "We're GOATs. You don't mess with GOATs."

Riley scrubs his palm over his face, and Brittany playfully splashes him. "Hey! You can't get rid of me that easily."

My eyebrows hike, as do Riley's.

I laugh.

He doesn't.

"Can I serve?" Brittany asks, clapping for the ball, her breasts also applauding.

Ben grins, his eyes bouncing to the beat of her chest.

"Throw her the ball," I grouch.

"I will. Just give me a sec—"

"Ben!"

"Okay, okay." He tosses her the ball. "Spoilsport."

"Just focus. The blonde is finally watching you."

He freezes. "She is?"

"Yes."

To be honest, I can't tell if she is or if she's simply admiring her own legs.

"Okay," Brittany says, twiddling her fingers, "here we go. I may be a little rusty though. I haven't played since high school."

By the looks of her, I ascertain that wasn't too long ago.

She tosses up the ball and serves, and before I can position myself to hit it back, all I have time to do is shield my face with my arms before it slams into me.

"Shit!" Riley hisses. "You okay, Riles?"

I keep my arms where they are, embarrassed but also fuming. "Yep."

"Sorry, Riley!" Brittany squeaks. "I forgot how good my serve is."

Dropping my arms and offering her the sweetest of salty smiles, I turn my back on her and Riley and emit a low, feral growl.

Ben smirks.

"What?" I snap.

"If only we had some Jell-O." He waggles his eyebrows, and at my blank expression, he explains, "For Jell-O wrestling."

"Just serve the damn ball."

"Sure thing, MJ." He tosses it into the air and serves to Brittany. She sets it up for Riley, and he spikes it at Ben, who lunges but misses.

"Yes!" Brittany squeals, launching herself onto Riley's back, her legs wrapping around his waist. "Great shot!" She plants a kiss on the side of his head, then lets go. "We've got this."

He chuckles awkwardly and momentarily makes eye contact with me as if he's done something wrong.

He hasn't. He can piggyback whoever he likes.

"Want to serve, love?"

I shake my head.

"Suit yourself." Ben lobs the ball and serves it to Riley, who returns it but with less vigor, the ball casually sailing toward me. I jump back and set it up for Ben, who slams it toward Riley, but Brittany leaps in front and pops it toward me.

Surging forward, I dive for the ball, but I'm not quick enough to stop it from hitting the water.

Damn it!

"Yes!" she squeals again before draping her arm over Riley's shoulder. "We make a great team."

Pissed, I throw the ball at them, deliberately aiming just shy of where they're standing, sending a spray of water into their faces. "Your serve."

Brittany frowns, wipes her eyes, snatches up the ball, and serves it back. I spike it with force, but she returns it.

I hit it again.

She returns.

Repeat.

Repeat.

"Stop hogging it," Ben says as he crosses into my space and hits it back.

"I'm not."

"Classic Jordan."

Riley pops the ball up, so I spike it, hard, watching as if in slow motion as it slams into Brittany's shoulder and ricochets into the side of her head.

Oopsies.

"My eye!" she cries, covering her face with her hand.

Subduing a revengeful giggle, I call out, "Sorry, Brittany! I forgot how good my spike is."

chapter twelve

RILEY

"Ow! It stings," Brittany whines.

I wade closer and pry her hand away from her face. "Let me see."

"Is it bad?" she asks, her spidey lashes damp, the skin around her eye angry and red.

Wincing, I dip my head and gently wipe the pad of my thumb over her eyelid, when her eyelashes break free and stick to my hand.

I stare at it. *Da fuck?* "Uh... your eyelashes just came off."

She blinks her good eye and collects the creepy thing from my fingertip. "They're fake."

"Fake?"

"Yes, they're false lashes. They're glued on." She glares over my shoulder at Riles. "Or they're supposed to be."

I try to make sense of gluing something to your eyelid, when Riles swims to a stop by my side.

"Are you okay?" she asks. "I'm so sorry. I didn't mean to—"

"I'm coming, princess!" Ben hollers like an idiot, sending a tidal wave crashing into us as he dives forward and scoops Brittany into his arms. "I've got you."

She groans and slaps his chest. "Put me down!"

"You okay, Brit?" Whitney calls from her lounge chair as she flips a page of her magazine.

"No. I can't see."

"You should probably see the nurse," Riles says, her thumbnail clamped between her teeth.

"You think?" Brittany flaps her hands like a spasming bird. "Can you take me, Riley?"

"Sure," Riles says. "It's the least I can d—"

"Not you," she growls, glaring one-eyed at Riles before pointing at me, "him. *You've* done enough."

"Me?" Riles rears back. "It was an accident."

"I doubt that. You aimed for my head."

"I did not!"

"You did!"

I put myself between them before all hell breaks loose. "I'll take you to the med center, Brittany."

"Thank you! Can we please go now? It's stinging so bad."

I sigh. "Sure."

"You'll have to guide me," she says, looping her arm beneath mine. "I can't see."

I'm no anatomist, but when you have two eyes and one of them is closed, you can still see perfectly fine. But I don't argue my accurate point, instead guiding her out of the pool and wrapping my towel around her shoulders.

"Where are you going?" Whitney calls out.

"Riley's taking me to see the nurse."

"Want me to come?"

"No. You stay."

"'Kay." Whitney blows her a kiss. "Love you."

Sniffling, Brittany rests her head on my shoulder. "Thank you."

I fake a sliver of sympathy. "No sweat."

Poppy broke her finger in a doorjamb when she was four, and she didn't milk the situation as much as Brittany currently is, so to say her woe-is-me acting is grossly over the top would be an understatement. But I'm not a jerk, so I reluctantly play along.

"We'll be back soon," I say to Riles, Ben, and an unfazed Whitney, as Brittany whines again.

God, help me!

AFTER TAKING BRITTANY TO THE MED CENTER—a claustrophobic dungeon I do not want to visit ever again—and then escorting her to her room at her request, I make my way back to the pool, but neither Riles, Ben, nor Whitney are there. So I head to the cabin, hoping Riles will be working, or at the very least catching up on the sleep I keep depriving her of.

Those damn expensive AirPods better work, because even though I said I'd move cabins if they don't, I'm no longer confident I can uphold my end of the bargain, especially after spending so much time below sea level in the medical center. I sure as shit wouldn't cope, the air down there thin and suffocating, the walls and ceiling a constant crushing threat.

Knocking on the bathroom door before entering—just in case Riles's in there—after she doesn't answer, I step inside, take a piss, and have a quick shower, tangling myself in her bathing suit, which is hanging to dry on a cord above my head.

What the fuck?

The glue-like material sticks to the side of my face, so I wrestle with it, almost slipping and falling on my ass before eventually smacking the suit to the floor and kicking it aside. *Jesus!* Why she can't hang it out on the balcony is beyond me. It'll dry faster out there and be out of my damn way.

But since Roni constantly badgers me over being a messy slob, I collect the bathing suit and my shorts and drape them over the chair outside, pleased with my efforts. And then I close the balcony door behind me and head to the closet for my clothes. The safe inside is open, and wondering what Riles stores in there, apart from her passport and maybe some jewelry, I bend over to get a better look, but it's empty.

Weird!

"Why would she take her passport out?" I mutter to myself. "It's a sea day."

Maybe she has more than one and isn't who she says she is?

I shake my head. "Nah, that's absurd." Riles isn't a criminal; I'm sure of it.

Then again, she was a little wacky during trivia.

Dismissing my paranoia, I decide I should store my passport in the safe as well, because it's the smart thing to do, so I retrieve it from my bedside drawer, place it inside, and close the door, the mechanism locking and beeping a few times. I press some buttons, but it doesn't open.

Shit! I don't know the passcode.

Making a mental note to ask her what it is when I see her, I head out of the cabin, wandering around aimlessly for hours, Riles nowhere to be seen. A little bored, I grab a pizza, drink a few beers at the Lagoon Bar, listen to some live music, and eventually return to the room where she's fast asleep—AirPods firmly secured in her ears.

Fist-pumping the air, I mouth a silent, "Fuck yeah!"

Sweet dreams, Riles.

THE NEXT MORNING, I WAKE WITHOUT HAVING A pillow repeatedly slammed against my head, which is marvelous.

I yawn, sit upright, and stretch, surprised to find Riles still sleeping. Relief and excitement sizzle through my well-rested body, so I sweep my covers aside and scoot my ass to the edge of my bed, stealthily creeping toward her like the Pink Panther.

Her chocolate hair is splayed in a mess, her mouth slightly open, her wrist resting against her forehead. I graze my hand over my beard, tempted to sit on the edge of her bed and stare at her.

She's undeniably beautiful and has a killer body, especially in a bathing suit. Damn, I almost drowned when she removed her white shirt thing by the pool. My stupid throat wouldn't work, my limbs, lungs, and brain suddenly useless. I honestly felt like a teenage boy again.

Smiling, because I liked my teenage self and how I felt back then—young, dumb, and full of... hormones—I know what I'm feeling now isn't as simple as that. I'm no longer a boy; I'm a man. A man who has been through his fair share of emotional turmoil. A man who delves below the surface in search of what he's looking for. A man who isn't simply pussy-whipped by a stunning body in a bathing suit.

I'm more than that. I *want* more than that.

For so long, I haven't been able to see the fun in things, my thoughts murky, cynical, and destructive. Never light, never comical. When I'm with Riles though, she has an uncanny way of reminding me that life isn't all doom, gloom, and infidelity. She makes me laugh when I usually wouldn't, play when I'd resort to fighting.

She makes me want to flirt... with her.

Murmuring something that sounds like "Momma," Riles unconsciously seeks out her stuffed dog, hugging it to her chest. It's adorable and reminds me of Poppy when I carry her to her room after her milk roofieing. The same sweetness and innocence —a calm purity that comes with peaceful slumber.

I exhale my relief and thank God the AirPods appear to have worked, although I can't be entirely sure until she wakes and turns into the Hulk or not.

I should get her a coffee, just in case!

Ever the fan of a back-up plan, I quietly leave the cabin, make my way to the café, order us coffees, and return as quickly as possible to use hers as a peace offering.

Gently clicking the door shut, I pause at the daylight streaming through the open curtains, her bed sheets ruffled... and empty.

Shit! Here goes nothing.

"Is that you, Riley?" she calls out from the bathroom.

Preparing for an attack, I hold up both paper cups as a deterrence, but her non-demonic, pleasant tone relaxes my posture, and I let out the breath I sucked in for dear life. "Yeah. I have coffee."

The bathroom door flies open, nearly smacking me in the nose.

"You do?" she gasps, peeking her beanie-covered head out. "Oh my God! You're a lifesaver."

Clear goop dots her face, so I hand over her cup, then step back. "What's that?"

"What?"

"On your face."

She ducks back inside the bathroom to check her reflection, then pokes her head out again, laughing. "Moisturizer."

"Looks like a jellyfish ejaculated on you."

"Riley!" She laughs. "That's disgusting!"

Quickly rubbing in the semen-like substance, she takes a long sip of her drink before moaning her delight.

"How'd you sleep?" I ask, my chest tight with anticipation for her answer.

"Like a baby! That app is amazing. Thank you."

"Good to hear."

Wanting to tap dance with my utter relief and joy, even though I can't tap dance to save my life, I keep my cool instead and pick up the daily newsletter Riles has already collected from outside our door. We visit Qaqortoq, Greenland today, a tiny seaside village set within a system of fjords. I've never been to Greenland—never set foot in Europe—so I'm looking forward to the Viking-inspired carvings and Nordic architecture.

"Is it cold outside?" she calls out. "The captain announced the temperature has dropped."

"I don't know. I'll check." Opening the balcony door, a blast of fresh air all but freezes my balls, so I immediately close it again. "Yes."

"Isn't it supposed to be summer in Greenland?"

"Their summer isn't like our summer, Riles."

"You're right. I suppose it wouldn't be."

Knowing I'll need a jacket, I make my way to the closet, when she says, "Have you seen my bathing suit? I hung it in here to dry yesterday."

"I moved it out onto the balcony with mine to dry faster."

"You did *what?*"

Her witch-like screech slices through me, and I'm suddenly hesitant to repeat myself. "I... uh... moved it."

"Did you bring it back inside?"

"N—"

Riles bursts out of the bathroom and shoves past me before wrenching the balcony door open and stepping outside. "Where'd you put it?"

"On the chair."

"It's not on the chair, Riley."

"What?" I follow her, confused.

"It's gone!"

"Gone? What about my shorts?"

"They're gone too. Oh my God! I can't believe you left them out here. What did you think would happen?"

"I...." I run my hand through my hair, eyes scanning the balcony. "Shit! I didn't think they'd disappear."

"They didn't *disappear!*" She leans over the railing to see past the partition into next door, one foot lifting from the ground.

"What the hell are you doing?" I lunge forward and yank her into my arms, my heart thudding manically in my chest. "You'll fall."

"I thought you said I couldn't *fall*."

"If you lean over the damn railing, you might. Jesus, Riles. Be careful."

"Be careful?" She shoves my chest, then slams her hands onto her hips. "You be careful. Because of you, my swimsuit blew away."

"My shorts blew away too!"

"That's because you left them out on the balcony of a ship sailing at twenty knots."

Stunned by her knowledge of how fast we've been traveling, I burst into laughter.

"It's not funny!"

"Come on, it kind of is."

She growls and storms back inside.

"I'm sorry," I say, following her. "I wasn't thinking when I put them out there."

"No shit!"

"I'll buy you a new one."

"Oh, I know you will. And you'll do it before we get to Iceland. I've booked a shore excursion at the Blue Lagoon, and despite the popularity of nudity in Nordic regions, I'm not bathing without a swimsuit."

This time, I can't help but double over.

"Damn it, Riley!" She giggles. "It's not funny!"

"It is."

The flaming-red of her cheeks settles to a blush-pink, and she slumps onto her bed. "I can't believe you did that."

"What can I say? I'm an idiot."

"You're not an idiot. Well—" She holds her thumb and fore-finger roughly an inch apart. "—maybe a little."

"I'll take you shopping before we get to Iceland. I promise."

She sighs. "Don't worry about it. I probably needed a new bathing suit anyway."

"No, I insist."

Huffing, she gets to her feet and retrieves her coffee. "What are your plans in Qaqortok today?"

"Not much. I'm just going to wander around the village. How about you?"

She bites her lip, a wave of joy spreading across her face. "I'm

146

taking a helicopter charter over a glacier. I'm so excited. I've never seen a glacier. I've never even been *near* a helicopter."

I blink. "You're flying over a glacier?"

"Yeah. Didn't you see the shore excursion on your booking profile?"

I shamefully shake my head. Stupid, uninterested me hadn't given the booking profile the time of day, and now my level of regret is as high as the Arctic Circle.

"Have you booked any shore excursions yet?"

"Only the Stonehenge tour."

"Riley! You *must* book the Blue Lagoon. You absolutely cannot visit Iceland without going there."

"Okaaay," I drawl. "Maybe I will."

"No. Do it now, or you'll miss out. Here, give me your phone." She holds her hand out, so I slide my cell out of my back pocket, unlock it, and pass it to her. Tapping the cruise app, she scrolls then taps, scrolls then taps, then hands it back to me. "There. You're lucky they have a couple of spots left. I read that you usually have to book several months in advance."

"What's so good about this Blue Lagoon?"

"It's a geothermal pool with healing properties."

"I have nothing to heal."

"Nonsense. We *all* have something to heal. Our bodies, minds —" She pauses, her eyes landing somewhere beyond my shoulder. "—hearts and souls."

Skeptical that a pool of water can cure the broken parts of me, I thank her anyway. "Thanks."

"You're welcome." Riles gathers her bag. "My charter isn't until ten, so if you want, we can wander around the village together, unless—"

"Sounds good."

"Great!" She grins. "Are you ready to go?"

"I am. I just need my passport. Which reminds me... what's the code to the safe?"

Her grin falters. "You don't need it. I got your passport out for you last night. It's in the drawer of your bedside table."

"Thanks." I retrieve it and slide it into my jacket pocket. "But I'm still going to need the code."

"Why?" she snaps.

Confused and a little taken aback, I frown. "Because I'm not keeping my passport in the bedside table."

"Just give it to me, and I'll put it in the safe."

"No. Just give me the code."

"No."

"Riles, this is my room too."

"I know, but…"

I tap my foot, waiting for her to elaborate.

"I have something precious in there."

"Okay. Care to explain what that is exactly?"

"No. It's none of your business."

Facepalming, I groan and then drag my hand through my hair. "Just tell me. I'm not going to steal it. Fuck, who do you take me for?"

"I know you're not going to steal it."

"Then tell me the damn code!"

"No!"

Taking a deep breath, I'm ready to lose my shit but rein it in, because I did lose her swimsuit. "Fine!"

"Good."

I grit my teeth. "Good."

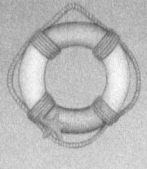

chapter thirteen

RILES

The thing about dodging metaphorical bullets is that those bullets tend to continue flying around, locked on their target, until they eventually hit.

I knew Riley was entitled to the passcode for the safe. Of course he was. But had I given it to him, he would've found Mom, in her urn, and I wasn't ready to explain why she was in there and why I had her with me.

It was a bullet I was happy to dodge, for now.

I also couldn't risk him having access to the safe and accidentally leaving it open. Because of him, my bathing suit was somewhere in the Labrador Sea, so trusting he would keep my most precious possession secure wasn't something I felt confident trying. Trust cracks your armor, and I've been forging mine for as long as I can remember.

After eating breakfast in the buffet restaurant while waiting for our tender tickets to be called, we scanned our sailing passes on our way out of the ship, then took the short trip by ferry to Qaqortoq, a quaint, picturesque village on the southern tip of Greenland.

"Oh wow!" I say, enthralled with the steep rolling hills dotted with brightly colored houses. "They look like little Legos. How pretty!"

Riley leaps off our boat onto the pier and offers me his hand. "Watch your step."

I stop marveling at the fairy-tale scenery, place my hand in his, and focus on my footing. Before the cruise ship dropped anchor, we passed a couple of tiny icebergs, so I don't fancy taking an unintentional dip in the icy water.

"Thank you," I say, gripping his fingers tightly.

"No sweat."

His hand is warm and soft but with rough edges only a hard-working hand possesses, and I like the feel of it in mine, foreign but protective. So much so that I'm tempted to link my fingers with his and skip along the pier, our arms swinging.

What has gotten in me?

I release his hand and awkwardly reposition my beanie, needing to busy my stupid fingers. Perhaps I'm just elated I'm in Greenland, that I've seen icebergs, and that I'll be flying over a glacier by day's end. I've never seen anything like Qaqortoq, and being here, so far away from the confinement of my office, feels euphoric and surreal. Hand-in-hand-skipping surreal.

"I can't believe I'm here," I say, excitement bubbling through my veins as we walk the short distance to the shore.

"Me neither."

I draw in a deep breath, the sea air clean and fresh. "It's so different from NYC."

Riley scoffs. "You can say that again."

Brushing off his disdain for my home city, I'm too overjoyed to pick a fight. "Do you know they eat seal and whale in Greenland? For real! It's like their steak and chicken."

"No, I didn't." He slides his hands into his pockets, probably to prevent me from latching onto them again. "But it makes sense, I guess."

"Would you eat it?"

"Probably."

I cringe. "I don't think I could."

"Why not?"

"Because seals and whales are cute."

He chuckles. "And cows and chickens aren't?"

"Not really. Plus, seals are lovers. They're loyal; they bond for life. I'd hate to think I'm eating someone's spouse of fifty years."

Riley stops walking, nose bunched. "Sorry to burst your bubble, but I don't think that's true."

"It is!"

He shakes his head.

"I swear it is. They're romantic and devoted and—"

"Okay, okay." He raises his hands. "We won't eat the loved-up seals."

"Good."

We keep walking, and I try to recall where I gained such seal information—possibly the movie *Happy Feet*. But then maybe I'm getting them confused with penguins. Still, seals are cute and cuddly, and I don't want to eat them.

"So where'd you disappear to last night?" Riley asks. "When I got back from the medical center, I couldn't find you."

Guilt tightens my chest. "Was Brittany okay?"

He rolls his eyes. "She was fine."

The pit of my stomach twists, because I don't want him to think I'm violent. Sure, I'm competitive by nature, and I like to stand my ground and fight for what I believe, but deliberately causing someone injury, whether I like them or not, well... that isn't me. I'm a lover, not a fighter.

Okay, maybe not a *lover*.

Twisting my fingers together, I murmur, "I didn't mean to hurt her."

He side-eyes me. "I know."

"You do?"

"Of course."

"Oh." I stop twisting.

"So what did you do last night?"

Avoided you like the plague and spent time with my mother, because I felt awful.

"Not much," I say flippantly. "I ate some sushi, checked out the art gallery, and then I sat at a karaoke bar until my ears could no longer stand it."

"Did you join in?"

"With the karaoke? Nooo. I can't sing to save my life."

"Isn't that the point of karaoke?"

"I suppose, but I much prefer to watch other people make fools of themselves."

Riley gives me his judgy-judgmental look.

I narrow my eyes. "Don't even try to bait me on this."

His eyes crinkle mischievously. "I didn't say anything."

"You didn't have to. Your face speaks for you."

He chuckles, and warmth blankets my defense. He has a great chuckle, and it's hard not to be infected by it.

Unable to hide my smile, I focus on the rainbow of houses again. "This place is so vibrant and charming, like the illustrations in a children's book."

"If Poppy were here, no doubt she'd say it reminds her of sprinkles on a cake."

"Yes!" I laugh. "It does kind of look like a cupcake."

Riley laughs too, but his smile doesn't quite reach his eyes.

"You miss her, don't you?" I ask.

"I do. She makes me want to pull my hair out every damn day, but she's also the sweetest little thing. Roni's done a great job raising her on her own."

"Where's Poppy's father?"

"Killed in action."

I swallow the lump in my throat. "I'm so sorry."

His nod is solemn, but then he points to where the ship's photographers are goading passengers to take a picture in front of a novelty Qaqortok sign. "Want a photo?"

I shrug. "Sure."

We position ourselves on either side of the sign, and just as the photographer takes the shot, Riley swats at his face.

"What was that?" I ask.

"Bug."

"Oh."

The photographer snaps more shots and then hangs his camera around his neck and gestures that we reduce the space between us. "Closer, yes?"

We inch nearer.

"Closer."

Wondering whether I should say, *"We're not a couple,"* I don't get the chance when Riley drapes his arm over my shoulders and hugs me to his side. Shocked, I beam at him as the photographer takes the shot.

"Perfetto!" He gives us a chef's kiss gesture, then ushers the next lot of passengers to take our place.

"So, what do you want to see first?" Riley asks.

"I don't know! I was just planning to wander around until my helicopter flight."

A bug flies past my face, almost settling on the tip of my nose, so I swat at it.

"Looks like there's a market over there." Riley points ahead of us, then swats at his face too. "Want to check it out?"

"Sure."

Following him to a line of umbrella-covered tables with local foods and handmade trinkets, we both continue to repel bugs with our swishing hands when a friendly local says something that sounds like "Hi."

I respond with "Hello," hoping she understands my greeting.

"Did. You. Make. These?" Riley asks as if talking to a toddler.

She grins from ear to ear and nods.

He picks up a pink-beaded bracelet. "You're. Very. Clever."

I bite my lip, suppressing my pending giggle.

"How. Much. For. Three?" he asks, holding up three fingers as he reaches into his pocket.

She points to a sign that reads **DKK 70**.

"How much is that?" Riley murmurs to me.

This time, I do giggle. "I have no idea."

Shrugging, he hands over two purple Danish banknotes. The woman goes to give him some coins in change, but he refuses. Once again, warmth waves through my body. He's wholesome... or stupid, because he could've just paid a hundred dollars for all I know.

"Pick one," he says, turning to face me, his palm open to showcase the bracelets.

I blink and touch my chest. "Me?"

"Yes. But not the pink one. That's for Poppy."

Hesitating, because I'm sure Poppy would love all three, I keep my hand pressed to my body. "Are you sure?"

"Just pick a damn bracelet, Riles."

I bite my thumbnail and choose the blue one, and he gently stretches the bracelet and loops it onto my wrist.

"Thank you," I say, adjusting it and running my fingers over the beads. "That's very sweet of you."

"No sweat."

Another damn wave of warmth ripples through my body, and if I don't look away from his crinkling eyes, there's a good chance I'll combust. So I rotate my arm, admiring my gift. Georgia certainly wouldn't approve if I wore it to work, and that act of potential rebellion strangely thrills me.

"Where to now?" I ask, still happily eyeing my new pretty accessory.

"I read online there's some stone carvings, so maybe we could find tho—" Riley chokes, spits, and then gags.

I jump back. "What's wrong?"

"Bug," he croaks, clearing his throat.

"Did you eat it?"

"Yep." *Cough.* "I think so."

"Nooo!" I cover my mouth with my hand.

He spits again, then swipes at his face like a madman. "What the fuck? They're attacking me."

Cradling my waist, I double over as he turns in circles, ducking and weaving.

"Leave me alone." Swat. Swipe. Spit. "Jesus!"

Laughing uncontrollably, I snort in a breath, choke, and immediately snort it out again.

He stares at me.

I stare back.

"You too?"

I gag, not once but twice, then quickly turn my back on him and blow out all the snot before covering my nose and mouth with my hand and turning back around, horrified. "It went up my nose."

He bursts into laughter. "At least we can say we tried a Greenlandic delicacy."

"I'd rather eat seal," I mumble.

Continuing to swat the pesky fly-like bugs, we hurry along gravel roads and paths, past colorful building after colorful building, eventually finding a grocery store, where we buy some repellent. Then we hike up a hill to the highest viewpoint we can find and take in the harbor, our grand ship idle and somewhat incongruous amongst the arctic landscape.

"It's as if we're on top of the world here," I say, awestruck by the view.

His rests his hands on his head. "We pretty much are. Greenland has the northernmost land point in the world."

"It does?"

"Yeah."

I take a seat on a rock and confess my lack of culture. "I'm not very good at geography. This is the first time I've left the States."

"Me too. Well, North America."

"Really?"

He twists his head to look back at me, the corners of his mouth quirking. "Shocked again, are we?"

"You just seem... worldly."

"I'm not." He kicks a small stone, and it tumbles down the hill. "I've been to the Bahamas, but that's it."

"The Bahamas sound lovely. When did you go there?"

He dips his head. "On my honeymoon."

"Oh." Guilt clenches my chest. "Sorry."

"It was a long time ago."

Not wanting to dredge up memories he may not want to revisit, I can't help but pry. "How long were you married?"

"Fifteen years."

"Fifteen years! How old are you?" I blurt, then raise my hand, realizing how rude I'm being. "Sorry. That was inappropriate. You don't have to answer."

He chuckles. "It's fine. I'm thirty-six."

"So you got married when you were—" I do the math in my head. "twenty-one?"

"Nineteen. We've been separated for two years."

"Wow! You were just a baby."

"I was," he says, taking a seat on the rock beside me. "And so was Krystal. In hindsight, we were naïve and stupid."

"I wouldn't say that. Fifteen years is a long time to be married. Some don't even make it to five."

"I suppose."

"Do you regret getting married so young?"

"I do now."

Silence settles over us, so I pick at some moss and bury my curiosity.

"How 'bout you?" he asks. "Ever been married or engaged?"

I scoff. "No. All work and no play, remember?"

He scoffs too.

My eyes settle on his, an unspoken sense of mutual sorrow and regret spiraling around us with the breeze. His gaze drops to my lips, and mine to his, my heart thudding as I wonder what he would feel and taste like.

As if magnetized to him, my body inches forward, when the

wind seems to intentionally intervene, whipping my hair across my face and snapping me out of the moment.

"W-What time is it?" I ask, lifting my wrist to check my watch. "I... I better head to the helipad."

He blinks, stands, and offers me his hand. "I'll walk you there."

CHECKING THE BUCKLES ARE SECURED ON MY SEATBELT as the helicopter engine roars to life, I grip my seat, equally terrified and ecstatic as we elevate off the ground.

The wind from the rotor blades gusts around Riley, and he holds his beanie on his head while waving with his other hand. I lean closer to the window and wave back, my smile so ridiculously immense that I'm sure he can see my molars. But as thrilled as I am about adventuring to a glacier, I'm also disappointed he's not sharing the experience with me. It's a once-in-a-lifetime opportunity, and he's missing out.

After discovering he's as untraveled as I am, and that he seems anguished by it, my heart had splintered for him. Regret is a constantly wedged blade, tearing into the present. An emotional Excalibur of sorts, embedded until someone comes along and wrenches it free. And like me, he too needs a King Arthur of sorts to draw it out.

I make a mental note to make sure he books more shore excursions.

"Helicopter Six, climbing to altitude," the pilot says through my headphones, the nose of the aircraft dipping just slightly as we soar forward over the village, toward the mountains.

I squeal like my nine-year-old self on Christmas morning when I unwrapped my copy of *Harry Potter: The Prisoner of Azkaban*. And as I did that snowy December day twenty-three years ago, I can't suppress my childlike glee.

Thank you, Mom. Thank you for championing me to see what I haven't until now. Thank you for directing my eyes beyond a desk and the pages of a book.

Bouncing in my seat, I turn to the couple huddled together beside me, both of them peering out the window, the woman excitedly pointing to the landscape, her partner gently kissing the side of her head. My smile falters. I have no one to kiss or to kiss me. No one to make memories with or huddle against in the event of the helicopter crashing.

Jesus, Riley, why would you think that?

Shaking away the dreaded and foolish thoughts, I gaze out my window again as we approach the ice shelf, nothing but rocky peaks and a sheet of white on the horizon.

"In just a few minutes, we'll be flying over the ice cap," the pilot explains. "Over eighty percent of Greenland is constantly covered in ice, with the southern tip only accessible via air or sea. There are no roads beyond the villages, so the only way to travel is by boat or aircraft."

I eagerly stare at the scenery below, the snow and ice so white and bright it's almost blinding. "Holy cow!" I murmur, squinting with the glare.

"No, there are no cows. As you can see, they have no vegetation to graze."

"Oh. I didn't mean—" I go to explain to the pilot that he heard me wrong but decide to just shut up and listen. "Never mind."

Lost for words, as no words could justifiably describe the ethereal landscape, at best, I would liken it to heaven. Pure and fresh. Overwhelming. Spiritual.

My chest tightens, and I know my mother is here with me, soaring above the earth, sharing this magical moment. I can feel it to my core, her presence tangible yet angelic, a force so strong I can barely breathe.

I inhale a shuddering breath, my fingers trembling as I wipe happy tears from my eyes with my sleeve and just... be.

Be one with the moment.

One with nature.

One with my momma.

ROUGHLY AN HOUR LATER, WE SET DOWN IN Qaqortok, a palpable sadness and sense of loss spearing my chest, and yet I'm equally beholden by the experience, to feel so close to my mother again and to have her with me in spirit.

I'm also shocked to see Riley waiting for me at the edge of the helipad.

"How was it?" he shouts over the noise of the engine as it powers down.

"Incredible!" I shout back. "I have no words."

"A publishing assistant without words?"

"I know! Crazy, huh? Words don't do what I just experienced justice, so I'm not even going to try."

"Did you take pictures?"

"Is the Pope a religious fuck?"

Riley bursts into laughter. "No, not you too? You team up with Ben just once, and now you're talking like him."

I giggle. "I can assure you I will never, *ever*, say that again."

We walk along the road toward the dock, past streaming creeks edged with rocks and wildflowers, the beauty and simplicity too special to take for granted. Curious, I step off the path and squat to feel the temperature of the water.

"Whoa, that's cold." Standing back up, I dry my fingers against my pants. "It's so clear, like glass."

Riley waggles his eyebrows. "Fancy a dip?"

"Are you insane?"

"Maybe." He removes his sneakers and socks and rolls his sweatpants to just above his knees.

"You're not seriously going into the water, are you?"

"That's exactly what I'm going to do."

Covering my eyes with my hands, I peek through my spread fingers as he steps off the bank and onto a submerged rock.

"How is it?" I squeak.

His jaw tightens. "It's... not that bad."

Amusement quirks my lip. "You're lying."

"Fuck! Yes. Yes, I am." He quickly makes his way out and then jogs in a circle, stopping to jump on the spot.

"I told you it was cold. The pilot said this water melted from the glacier."

"And you didn't think to share that information before I stepped in?"

I shrug. "Not particularly."

"Jesus! I can't feel my toes."

Snickering while he redresses himself, I bend down and pick a wildflower, removing the petals one by one. "So what did you do while I was gone?"

"I made friends with many dogs."

I laugh. "What?"

"There are a lot of dogs in Qaqortok. They're everywhere."

"That's strange. Why dogs?" Horrified, my fingers hold still on a petal. "I hope they don't eat them."

"They don't. According to one of the locals in a café, they use them to pull small sleds in the winter so they can get from house to house."

"Huh," I say, both relieved and impressed. "That makes a lot of sense."

"It does."

"What else did you do, other than befriend canines?"

"I tried raw whale."

"What?" I nearly topple onto my ass.

"It tastes like tuna fish."

I poke my tongue out, pretending to gag. "I can't believe you ate it raw. Yuck!"

"You're supposed to."

I shudder.

"I thought you liked sushi?"

Impressed he remembered that, I say, "I do! But raw whale? Nope. Just... nope. Please tell me you didn't eat seal too."

He rubs his belly, and my jaw drops.

"Riley," I gasp.

"I'm kidding." He chuckles. "I didn't eat seal. They're too cute, remember?"

My heart stupidly thumps in my chest again, something it feels the need to do around him, and I have to tell it to settle the hell down.

"You ready to head back to the ship?" he asks, shaking his arms to heat his body temperature.

"I guess so. You?"

"Yeah, I'm done. I saw everything I wanted to see. Plus, there's some Truth or Dare show in the theatre." He side-eyes me and smirks. "And there's prizes."

My ears prick. "Prizes?"

Riley grins as if he knows what I'm going to say next.

"A gold ship trophy?" I ask.

"Maybe."

Jumping to my feet, I march past him. "Let's go!"

<hr>

WE FILE INTO THE THEATRE, COCKTAILS IN HAND, WHEN I spot Ben several rows ahead, waving at us to sit with him.

I wave back, albeit less enthusiastically. "Looks like Ben has saved us some seats."

Riley gives him a curt nod, and Brittany turns in her seat next to Ben and smiles, the bruise on her eye barely camouflaged by the eyeshadow attempting to disguise it.

My stomach knots.

"We don't have to sit there if you don't want to," Riley says when I don't take the next step.

"No. It's fine. I need to apologize to Brittany."

"You already apologized."

"I know, but I don't think she took me seriously."

"It wasn't your fault, Riles. It was an accident."

"Accident or not, she has a black eye, and that's awful."

He places his hand on the small of my back and gently encourages me forward, and I appreciate the support. And while Brittany and her friend appear to be using Ben for his wealth—which I certainly don't agree with—my childish retaliation physically hurt her, and that doesn't jive well with who I am at my core.

"Hi," I say as we stop at the end of their row. "How's your eye, Brittany?"

"How does it look?" she snaps, lip snarling.

"Sore," I admit. "I really am sorry."

She doesn't say anything more, so I stand there awkwardly, waiting for the three of them to scoot along one seat to allow Riley and I to sit at the end of the row, but none of them budge.

Okaaay. I guess I'll climb over them.

Shuffling in front of Brittany, I almost trip when Ben pats his lap. "Come and sit on my knee, love."

Riley clasps my arm and tugs me back. "Nice try, Michigan. Move up a seat. It's easier."

They scoot along, so I take the seat between Riley and Brittany.

"Where have you kids been?" Ben asks.

"We spent the day on shore." I sip my drink and snicker. "Riley ate whale and bugs. And I flew in a helicopter."

Ben gives Riley an animated yet disgusted look, which, of course, I find amusing.

"What did you do?" I ask him.

"Chartered a boat through some mountains. Boring as bat shit."

"Doesn't sound boring."

"It was, love."

"Why'd you eat a bug?" Brittany asks Riley.

"It wasn't intentional."

I snicker again, and he playfully prods me in the ribs.

"Hey!" I nudge him back. "I nearly spilled my drink."

He prods me again.

"Stop it! I'm ticklish."

Brittany shuffles back into her seat, and I wonder if Riley realizes she likes him. It's obvious, given the way she looks and acts around him, so maybe he does. Then again, men are normally clueless where women are concerned, so perhaps he doesn't. Plus, he's in the process of getting a divorce, so he may not be interested.

He did say he'd hook up with a woman if he wanted to though. I side-eye them. *Surely, she's too young for him.*

Uncrossing my legs, I fidget uncomfortably before crossing them again, when our cruise director jogs onto the stage.

"Welcome, cruiselings." He claps his hands, then waves to the crowd. "Did you all have a wonderful day in Qaqortok?"

A resounding "Yes!" echoes throughout the auditorium, followed by an obnoxious "Boo!" bellowed from Ben's throat.

I dip my head, embarrassed.

"It sounds like most of you did, which is fantastic. What a spectacular place, huh?" He nods passionately. "Now, before we get to this afternoon's fun and games, don't forget that tomorrow is a sea day as we journey to Reykjavik, Iceland. But sea days are glee days, right?"

We all answer "Yes!" and this time, Ben whistles like a manic kettle.

"We have plenty for you to see and do tomorrow. Bingo with Eddie will be held here in the theatre at nine, and for those booked to do the Behind-the-Scenes Ship Tour, there will be five sessions. You'll find your session allocation either in your cabin box outside your door or on your app."

Keeping my eyes trained on Paul, I lean in to Riley and whisper, "That reminds me... I booked you on that tour with me. I hope that's okay. You don't have to do it if you don't want—"

"Are you shitting me?"

I snap my eyes to him, fearing I've overstepped my mark. "No. I just thought—"

"Riles, you're an angel!"

"I am?"

"Yes," he says, leaning closer, our cheeks almost pressed. "I tried to book that tour, but it was full. I was pissed I missed it."

Thrilled he's appreciative, my face flushes. And if I were an angel, no doubt I'd flutter my wings with pride. "Well, you didn't miss it," I say, winking at him. "And, you're welcome."

Brittany shushes us, so I apologize and refocus on Paul.

"Tomorrow is our first formal night, so please don your finest attire and cruise in style. Captain Katarina has also informed me there's a chance we will see the Northern Lights, sometime around midnight. Given it is late summer here, we're very fortunate for the opportunity. So, set your alarms. Glue your eyelids open. Drink lots of coffee. Whatever you do, be awake and on deck. You will not want to miss this extraordinary phenomenon."

I squeal like a banshee, then cover my mouth with my hand and murmur to Riley, "I'm so excited! I really want to see the Northern Lights." I squeal again, this time more subdued. "Oh my God! I hope we do."

Brittany glares at me as if I'm an idiot, and I'm baffled, because who wouldn't want to see the Aurora Borealis.

"*What?*" I mouth to her.

She rolls her eyes in response, so I sip the last of my drink and ignore her. She's starting to grate my nerves anyway.

"Okay, cruiselings," Paul continues, "who wants to play Truth or Dare?"

A bazillion hands shoot into the air, mine included. Riley's remains on his lap, so I lift it too and wave it about, his tense muscles fighting my enthusiasm.

"Wave, damn it," I hiss, flapping harder. "I want that trophy."

He grunts and reluctantly waves.

"Excellent!" Paul says, pacing the stage. "Now, how this works is we will randomly choose a cabin number, and if you're in the theatre and want to participate, please make your way to the stage. Don't be shy, cruiselings. We have some brilliant prizes up for grabs, including a relaxation package for two in our Lotus Spa, which is valued at fifteen hundred dollars."

"Oooh." I drop our hands. "That sounds nice."

Riley's face crumples.

"What? It does! I love spas."

"Have you all met Carlos, the best trivia host on the high seas?" Paul asks.

Carlos skips onto the stage and performs an animated twirl before waving.

I nudge Riley. "Look, it's Carlos!"

Paul applauds his colleague. "He will be my assistant, and that fancy iPad he's holding will select our lucky cabins. Are you all ready?"

I holler, "Yes!" and Brittany turns in her seat and looks at me as if I have feces on my face.

"What?" I mouth again.

Shaking her head, she shields her face with her hand, so again, I ignore her—she's a sourpuss.

"Let's see who our first participants will be, shall we?" Paul drums his feet on the stage as Carlos taps his iPad.

I sit straighter with anticipation, craning my neck to get a better view.

"Cabin number... 10143," Paul announces, trumpets blaring from the speakers.

Squealing, I shove my empty glass into Brittany's hand, jump to my feet, and turn to Riley. "That's us!"

"Shit," he grumbles, wincing as he sinks into his seat.

"Oh no you don't," I hiss, grabbing his arm and yanking it. "Get. Up."

chapter fourteen

RILEY

R iles drags my ass down the aisle, nearly detaching my arm from its socket, her grip firm, preventing my escape.

Screw you, Carlos! Screw you and your stupid iPad!

I hadn't planned on playing the damn game, instead comfortably spectating while others made dicks of themselves. And now here I am, the dick in question, and there's nothing I can do about it.

Jogging up the steps to the stage, Riles tugs me along with her, and I nearly trip into Carlos before he checks our lanyards and then directs us where to stand.

"I want to win," Riles murmurs behind her hand. "Take no prisoners."

Normally, I'd find such a threat lighthearted, but after our trivia experience, I have no doubt she's dead-serious.

"The next cabin number is... 7097," Paul announces.

Riles squints and shades the stage lights from her face with her hand as she seeks out our opponents. I can't see shit, so I just bow my head, praying this will all be over soon.

"They look old," she whispers. "We've got this."

Her competitiveness is hilarious, and I can't help but chuckle... so long as she doesn't give one of them a black eye. If she does, I'm going to have to haul her over my shoulder and get her the hell out of here before blood is spilled.

The thought of Riles, hauled over my shoulder, her ass in my face, isn't all that bad, and I'm suddenly not so opposed to intervening when she proverbially takes her gloves off. And I can bet my left nut that she will.

I glance over at her bouncing on the spot as if she's ready to take on Tyson Fury.

Yep. We're fucked.

Sucking in a deep breath, I close my eyes and compose myself. I hate being the center of attention—Roni was always the overachiever, not me.

"What are you doing?" Riles murmurs.

"Taking a moment."

"For what?"

"For what we're about to do."

"Good." She clasps my hand. "Channel the win."

Channel the win? I'm channeling the ability not to shit my pants; that's what I'm channeling.

She squeezes my fingers, then lets go. "You and I are going to the spa, gold trophy in hand."

A fuzzy kind of warmth spreads over me, and I snap my eyes open and stare at her, amused. Mousey and shy when she wants to be, she's also a firecracker ready to spark, take flight, and explode. It's a curious combination—exciting but also terrifying.

I'm also still stunned she thought to book me on the Behind-the-Scenes tour. She must've done it on embarkation day, after I was horrible to her in the bar. And even though being in the spotlight in front of a roomful of strangers about to play a stupid, childish game isn't high on my bucket list, I decide I'll give it my all... for her. She deserves that, at the very least.

"Okay. Lucky last," Paul teases. "Carlos, will you do the honors?"

Carlos taps his screen, drums his feet, and shouts, "Cabin number 12022."

This time, I squint and shade my eyes with Riles as two young, fit-looking guys jump up from their seats. They fist-bump, chest-bump, then jog toward the stage.

"What are *they* going to do with a spa voucher?" Riles grumbles. "I bet they don't have any chest hair, so they can't even get a wax."

I choke on my laughter, link my hands behind my back, and straighten my shoulders. "If you think I'm going to get a wax if we win, think again."

"I don't," she deadpans, eyes steadfast on the guys. "What I think is you should leave your chest hair exactly where it is."

My head slowly rotates in her direction, the corners of my mouth lifting. "You do?"

"Yes. Now focus, Riley," she hisses. "We can't let them beat us."

"They won't."

"I know. Over my dead body, they will."

Hopefully, it won't come to a life-or-death situation. Then again, I seem to be partnered with Muhammad Riley.

God, help me!

"Welcome, Truth-or-Dare cruiselings." Paul holds his arm out, presenting us to the audience. "Please give our participants a round of applause."

The crowd claps and whistles, Ben's drawn-out war cry the loudest of all. "Riiileyyys!"

I chuckle at the idiot.

"Now, for the rules: You can choose truth or dare in the first two rounds. If you choose dare, only one of you must carry it out, until the final round, which is a dare only, and you will both have to complete it. If you all succeed, the audience will vote on who carried out the final dare the best. Easy?"

We all agree, so Paul approaches the two guys who were last to the stage. "What are your names?"

The taller one leans into the microphone. "Darius," followed by the other, "Levi."

"Are you friends? Partners? Family?"

"Brothers," they say simultaneously.

"Where are you from?"

They bump fists again and holler, "Brooklyn!"

"Well, brothers from Brooklyn, good luck to you." Paul shakes their hands and then moves on to the older pair. "And who do we have here?" He points the microphone at the woman, and I'm not even sure she answers. "Sorry. I didn't quite get that," he says, placing his hand to his ear. "Please speak up so we can all hear."

"Iris," she repeats, her face as red as my truck.

He moves the microphone to who I assume is her husband. "And you, sir?"

"Jim."

"Married? Friends? Family?"

"Married," they both say.

"And where are you from?"

"Atlanta."

"Very good!" Paul shakes their hands as well and then turns to face the audience, pulling an "eek" face. "Good luck. I hope you remain married after this."

The crowd laughs as he moves toward us.

"And who do we have here?"

"Riley and Riley," Riles blurts.

Paul stops walking, cocks his head, and gives the audience a that's-strange-as-fuck expression.

They laugh, and I grit my teeth.

Kill me now.

"Married? Brother and sister...?"

"We're just friends," Riles says.

He presses his lips together, his head nodding comically, and I have the sudden urge to punch him. "Okay, Riley and Riley 'we're just friends,' you're up first. What'll it be, truth or dare?"

"Truth," Riles answers.

Shit!

"Truth it is." Paul grins greedily and scans a piece of paper in his hands. "If you were both the opposite sex for one day, what would be the first thing you do?"

My balls bounce into my throat. *For fuck's sake.* I know exactly what I'd do... stare at myself, naked.

Riles taps her lip, then says, "Pee, standing up. Probably outside by a tree."

A few women cheer and clap for her response, and I have to give her credit where credit is due.

Paul nods. "Fair answer. And what about you, man-Riley?"

I smirk. "Pee, sitting down."

Riles glares at me. "Very funny."

I shrug. "What? I would."

"Yeah, right after you stare at yourself naked for an hour," she chides.

Laughter bubbles in my throat.

How does she know that?

I pull the microphone back to my mouth. "Actually, yes, I would do that first. Then I would pee."

Her eyeballs sarcastically circulate her sockets.

"What do we think?" Paul says to the audience. "Did they tell the truth?"

"Yes!" echoes throughout the theatre, and I sigh my relief.

"Stop mucking around," Riles whisper-hisses as Paul moves on to the married couple. "If you lose this for us, I'll lock you out of the cabin."

"You can try."

"Oh, I will!"

"Ease up, Riles. We're winning."

She lets out a muffled growl, and I chuckle. I like when she growls like a cub. It suits her.

Paul asks the married couple what the most embarrassing moment of their life was, and the woman freezes like a deer in headlights, unable to answer.

Her husband says, "This... now!" and she agrees, mumbling the same thing.

"What do we think?" Paul asks. "Are they telling the truth?"

Almost everyone calls out, "No!"

"The people have spoken, and I'm sorry to say, Iris and Jim, but you are out of the game."

Riles whispers, "Yes!" and claps.

"You're such a bad sport," I whisper back.

"I am not. Their answer was stupid."

"I don't know. I think they were telling the truth."

"Oh well. They're out. One down, one to go."

Carlos politely sends the married couple back to their seats with novelty drink bottles, and I'd rather have one of those than my back, crack, and sac potentially waxed at the spa.

"Okay, brothers from Brooklyn, you're up next. What part of your body do you like the most?"

Darius doesn't hesitate, flexing his biceps before kissing each of them, Levi turning his back to the audience, lifting his T-shirt, and clenching his butt cheeks.

The raw whale fermenting in my stomach threatens to rise to my throat.

"Damn!" Riles drawls, nudging my arm. "They're good."

"Come again?"

"The audience likes them." She presses her knuckle to her lip. "Shit! We're going to have to choose dare next to win the audience back."

Hoping we'd avoid that part of the game until the end, I rub the back of my neck, my muscles rigid. "Great!"

"Stop being a pussy," she hisses.

"I'm not," I hiss back.

Paul steps up to us again, crosses his arms over his chest, and says, "Are you sure you're 'just friends'?"

We both grit out, "Yes."

"*Good* friends?" He waggles his eyebrows. "Or friend-friends?"

"We're just friends," Riles assures him, her searing eyes all but boring holes into the poor guy's head.

He raises his hands, and I can relate to the gesture.

"Okay, *just friends*, what'll it be? Truth or dare?"

"Dare!" Riles shouts, tilting her head from one shoulder to the other to loosen her neck.

The audience sounds out an "Oooh!" as Paul leans against Riles's shoulder and winks at her. "All or nothing, huh?"

"Yep."

"I like you."

"I like that spa voucher," she says before glaring and pointing at the brothers. "And you two aren't getting it."

Cackling like an evil witch, Paul rubs his hands together. "Fighting words. I love it! Watch out, boys. This one means business." He cackles again, scans his list of truths and dares, then stares Riles down. "Are you ready?"

She nods. "Yes. Lay it on us."

"Do the robot dance."

A shiver runs the length of my spine, so I drag my hand through my hair, gripping it hard as I step back. I don't dance, let alone on a stage in front of people.

"Where do you think you're going?" Riles says, snagging my T-shirt.

"You asked for dare, so—" I sweep my hand to her. "—take it away!"

Her skin pales. "What's the robot dance?"

"You don't know what the robot dance is?"

"Should I?"

"You're a millennial, aren't you?"

"So?"

"So... you should know the robot dance." I flatten my hands and subtly chop them.

"Oh! The robot dance. I do know that!" Locking her elbows and flattening her own hands, she proceeds to stomp about the stage, turning her head from side to side as she swivels back and forth, one arm swinging like a pendulum when she stops and hunches over.

Laughing, because she's a lunatic—albeit an adorable one—I slow-clap for her, impressed but also thrilled I didn't have to take one for the team.

She straightens her back and steeples her hands in prayer, eyes pleading with Paul. "Did I do it right?"

"I don't know," he says. "Audience, what do we think?"

They all cheer, and Riles throws her arms in the air.

"Great job, C-3PO." I hold up my hand for a high-five, but she slaps it away.

"At least I did it after you chickened out. We're supposed to be a team."

I gawk at her.

"Man up, builder boy."

Jesus!

She stings worse than a bee, perhaps she *is* Muhammad Riley.

"Brooklyn bros, how's it hangin' over there?" Paul scurries toward them and offers the microphone for their response.

"It's hangin' well," Levi says, glancing down at his junk.

Riles gags. "Gross!"

"Good to know," Paul says. "So, what will it be? Truth or dare?"

Darius puffs his chest. "Dare!"

"I had a feeling you'd say that."

"Bring it on," Levi goads, gesturing toward us. "We eat guys like them for breakfast."

What a dumbass thing to say.

"Eat this, you marshmallow." Riles pokes out her tongue, then murmurs to me, "I bet they eat steroids on toast."

"Who are you?" I double over, my ribs aching with laughter. "And what have you done with my sweet roommate?"

"She doesn't exist when prizes are involved."

"No shit!"

Continuing to laugh, because I'm actually enjoying myself, I forget about the lights, stage, and the people who are watching. I forget about the shit I've been through, the shit I'm climbing out of, and the shit I've left behind. I forget it all and relax, even though I'm going to have to swallow my balls and complete a dare sooner rather than later.

Paul scans his list, then waggles his eyebrows at the audience. "I dare you to do a handstand and walk across the stage."

"I got this, bro." Levi smacks his brother on the chest and moves him aside while Darius claps above his head, coaxing the audience to join in.

"Pa-leease," Riles groans, crossing her arms over her chest, her hip jutting. "This dare is rigged. He probably walks like that to the bathroom."

She makes a valid point; it does seem rigged, especially when Paul starts singing lyrics to "Be Faithful" by Fatman Scoop and the Crooklyn Clan while Levi slowly hand-walks.

Riles puffs out a harsh breath, her arms falling limp by her sides. "We're done. The audience love them."

"Hey! We're not. There's still one round left." I massage her shoulders. "We've got this."

Sighing, she looks up at me, desperation swimming in her pretty, misty eyes. "We can't lose to them, Riley. They're turnips."

Not exactly how I'd describe them, but yeah... fair call. "I know!"

"I want that voucher."

"I know."

"We need to nail this last dare, so you better pray Paul doesn't ask us to climb into a box."

My blood runs cold. "He could do that?"

"I hope not, or we can kiss that voucher goodbye."

Damn straight we can. There's no way in hell I'm climbing into anything.

"Friends, friends, friends," Paul drawls as he ambles toward us, "the stakes have now risen." He taps his chin and turns to the audience. "What shall we make them do, I wonder?"

"Take your pants off!" Brittany shouts.

"Yeah, love," Ben adds, "get 'em off!"

Shrugging, because I'd rather strip than face the prospect of being locked inside a box, I start to loosen my sweatpants.

"Whoa! Not so fast, Magic Mike." Paul places his hand on my shoulder, then narrows his eyes at the audience. "Who's in charge here?"

"You!" they chant.

"That's right. And I have a much better dare for you, *friends*."

My jaw locks tight, his sinister tone and the glare from his pearly whites unsettling my nerves.

No damn box. No damn box.

"I dare you to kiss—" He pauses, grin stretching. "—for twenty seconds."

Snapping my head to Riles, she inches back a step, the color draining from her face, her eyes wide, her mouth open. And for the first time since setting foot on stage, she looks ready to give up, leap off it, and run.

I reach for her hand. "Oh no you don't, sweetheart!"

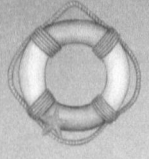

chapter fifteen

RILES

My face heats to the boiling point, my knees almost giving way.

Did he just say kiss... for twenty seconds? As in kiss, kiss?

The audience roars to life, their cheers deafening. I stare at them, then at Paul, then at Riley, my jaw dropping, my hand shooting up to cover it, and then I shake my head so fast I think I pull a muscle.

Riley steps closer, reducing the distance between us, his eyes on mine, mine unblinking.

Shit! Shit, shit, shit!

How much do I want that damn spa voucher and trophy? Enough to kiss him in front of an auditorium full of people? I try to weigh it up, but I don't get the chance when he reaches for my face, his hands gentle but strong as they cup my cheeks and guide my lips to his.

The cheering stops. At least, I think it does; I can't hear it over the thunder of my beating heart. I hold still, hands splayed by my sides, body rigid, eyes locked on his.

Heat surges from my head to the tips of my toes, and they curl of their own accord within my shoes. I gasp ever so slightly, closing my eyes and parting my lips. He releases one hand against

176

my cheek, presses it to my back, and holds me to him as his tongue gently sweeps mine. My body awakens, sparks, sizzles like a bomb, effervescent as if a thousand tiny bubbles have burst beneath my skin.

Never in my life have I kissed or been kissed like am right now. These kisses don't exist except for within the pages of the books I often read. A fantasy. A fairy tale. A fictitious magic trick.

Elevating like a ballerina en pointe, I drape my arms over his shoulders, my fingers climbing his nape until they're tangled in his hair. My chest tingles against his, my mouth hungry for everything he's giving me. Every touch, sweet exhale, and gentle sweep of his tongue. I want it all. I want him. I want to twist, turn, climb, and fall.

A deep growl passes his lips, and the hand pressing my back slips to my side, his fingers kneading the soft flesh above my hip as he lifts me from the ground, my feet dangling, my mind counting down like a rocket, ready for take-off.

"Three. Two. One!"

The audience hoots and cheers, and I blink, the countdown not of my body, instead from our spectators.

Panting, I pull away and drop my hands to his chest, staring at his heavy eyes and glistening lips.

Holy peanut freaking butter!

He stares back but releases his grip and gently plants me on my feet again.

"Phoa!" Paul fans his face, and I'm tempted to ask him to fan mine as well. "Does anyone else think it's hot in here?"

What just happened?

Embarrassment arrests my limbs, and I step away from Riley, side-eyeing him while tracing my lips with my fingertips.

He kissed your damn socks off; that's what happened.

"Just friends?" Paul quips. "Just. Friends?" He laughs. "Not anymore."

"Did we win?" I bite out.

"Did we win, she asks." He gives the brothers a pitiful look. "I guess we're about to find out."

Confused, angry... and slightly turned on, I don't know what to do or say. Do I slap Riley for invading my mouth without permission? Because if anyone else had just done what he did, I wouldn't hesitate in getting slappy. Do I grab him and kiss him again? Because that was, without a doubt, the kiss of a lifetime. Or do I brush off what just happened? Because we didn't really have a choice, and it was a game, and I wanted to win, and... and....

Yes, pretend it was nothing. No big deal, right?

It's what's best for him; he has a lot going on with his divorce, and I certainly don't want to add to that. I just hope I can remain indifferent and not melt into a puddle at his feet, because... wow! He's a phenomenal kisser.

"Great job, Fabio," I choke out, winking as I elbow his side. "Those marshmallow jerks don't stand a chance now."

His eyes narrow, the skin between his brows bunching as he rubs his beard. "Y-Yeah. They're going down."

Relief floods my body. Thank God he's as impassive as I'm pretending to be. "That was so embarrassing," I add, faking a laugh. "Longest twenty seconds of my life."

He doesn't say anything, his eyes still narrowed as he studies my face. I look away. I have to, because if I don't, I'll reveal how I really feel, my fingers, lips, and toes still tingling.

Darius and Levi jump on the spot, shaking their limbs like those creepy person-shaped kites at a car dealership.

"Your twenty seconds starts now!" Paul says.

The brothers hold still, Levi asking, "You want us to kiss too?"

"Yes." Paul gives Carlos an animated look. "It's only fair."

"I'm not kissing my brother."

"Come on, Lev. Just a peck. We can do this." Darius closes his eyes and leans forward, lips pursed.

I smirk as Levi hesitantly inches closer, pulls back, and then inches forward again.

"Nope!" he says, raising his hands. "I can't. They win."

Victory.

Squealing, I bounce up and down, grab Riley's hand, and hold it up. "We did it! We won!" I say, bumping his hip with mine. "Suckers!"

"Congratulations, *friends*. You're our winners of Truth or Dare." Paul takes an envelope from Carlos and hands it to me.

I flap it about, waiting eagerly for the trophy.

"Great job, you two." He pats my shoulder. "You may take your seats again."

"Wait!" I frown. "Where's the gold ship trophy?"

Paul covers the microphone with his hand. "You don't get one. They're for trivia, karaoke, and dance competitions."

"But I did dance. I did the robot."

He stares at me as if I've grown a second head. "Sorry, but that doesn't count."

Doesn't count? My shoulders slump. *What does a girl have to do to get a damn gold trophy?*

"One more round of applause for our, *friends*," Paul says, ushering us off the stage.

Disappointed, I follow Riley down the stairs, my legs Jell-O-like with every step to the floor. "I can't believe we just did that," I say, scurrying along the aisle to match his swift strides.

"You wanted to win," he mutters.

"I did! Didn't you?"

He stops at our row and gestures for me to take a seat. "I didn't care either way."

Edging past him, my stomach knots.

Is he mad about the kiss? Did he hate it? Oh my God... was I terrible?

The kiss certainly didn't feel terrible to me; it was amazing. Sweet. Passionate. Mesmerizing. If anything, it was *too* amazing.

Utterly mortified that perhaps I kiss like a wet fish, I sink into the plush velvet chair next to Brittany, my mortification made worse by her fuming stare drilling into the side of my head.

"I think I'm hard," Ben says, adjusting his crutch. "You two need to bang one out."

"Shut up!" Riley and I both snap.

"Whoa!" He chuckles. "Just go and fuck and get it over with."

Riley turns in his seat, his torrid eyes targeting on Ben, his nostrils flared. He looks ready to launch over me and hit the imbecile, and even though Ben probably deserves a fist to the nose, I don't want Riley to be the one to do it. Not over this. Not over me. It's my fault we played the stupid game and were forced to kiss, and clearly, he's far from impressed about it.

"Thank you, everyone," Paul announces. "You've been brilliant as always. I'll see you back here tonight for the magic show with our resident magician Darren Banes. In the meantime, let me leave you with this joke. What vegetable do we not allow on cruise ships?"

I think about it for a moment, my mind wandering to cabbage, because... well, it stinks.

"Leeks!" Paul yells. "We can't have leeks on the ship."

Half the auditorium groans, and the other half laugh, including me—it was clever.

Riley shoots to his feet and storms out of the theatre, and again, I scurry after him. "Hey! Wait up."

He refuses to slow down, so I reach out and touch his arm. "What's your problem?"

"I don't have one."

"Uh... yeah, you do."

"I don't."

Feeling as if I've been punched in the gut, but also guilt-ridden for pushing him to win at all costs and kiss me when he may not have been ready to kiss another woman, I apologize for the mess we seem to now be in. "I'm sorry, okay? I never thought we'd be asked to kiss. But... you didn't have to do—"

"It's fine, Riles. We won. You got your spa voucher."

"You mean *our* spa voucher."

"I don't care about the damn spa."

I clasp his T-shirt, dig my heels into the ground, and force him to stop walking. "Riley—"

"What?"

Taken aback by his harsh tone, I let go.

He sighs, his eyes finally settling on mine as he places his hands on my shoulders. "It's fine. I'm happy we won."

Searching his face for answers, for why his jaw is tense and why his delightful crinkles are no longer there, my heart pinches; I miss his crinkles. Every fiber of my being wants to cup his cheek and bring his lips to mine again, to feel what I felt on stage, but... I don't. I wouldn't dare. The game is over.

"It was just a kiss," he says, swallowing heavily, his hands falling to his sides. "Nothing more, nothing less."

"Yeah." I clear the lump in my throat. "You're right."

"Good. Now, can we just forget it and move on?"

"S-Sure. Of course."

"Great."

"Great."

We continue walking until I can no longer bear the dreadful silence. "Uh, I'm just going to go back to the room for a little bit and do some work, so I'll... I'll see you later."

"No sweat."

Nodding, I peel away from him, tears threatening to fill my eyes. I should go to the stupid spa and use my stupid voucher on a stupid facial, or maybe on something to help my tear ducts dry the hell up. Acupuncture, perhaps. God knows I need something, anything. Ever since Mom passed away, I've been drowning, my emotional control a delicate thread. Gossamer in the wind. The ability I once had to keep myself grounded and focused has vanished, and that's an awful feeling, especially for someone who's always had her sensibility in check. It is despair in full throttle. You know the crash is imminent, yet you have no way to apply the brakes to prevent the collision. So, you crash. You crash and surrender to the helplessness and pain.

I consider going to the spa for some form of remedy, but all I really want to do is speak to Mom, to tell her what happened, how it made me feel, and to ask for her advice. She was always good at that.

Rushing to the cabin, I enter and beeline for the safe, carefully cradling the urn as I take it out and hug it to my chest.

"Hey, Momma. How are you?"

I feel absurd every time I talk to her, knowing she can't answer, but I do it all the same. Albeit nonsensical, absurdity far outweighs not talking to her at all. It's all I have left. The only piece of her I can cling to.

"I kissed Riley," I explain. "Or he kissed me. Or—" I slump onto my bed and scrub my face with my hand. "I don't know who kissed who, but we kissed, and it was incredible." Sighing, I roll onto my side and prop my head up with my hand. "But I think he hated it. He's getting a divorce, and us kissing probably messed with his head. Either that or I kiss like an overexuberant donkey." Mortification once again swirls through my veins, and I slap my hand to my head. "Ugh! Mom, I feel like such an idiot. What am I going to do?"

"Who are you talking to?" Riley asks from behind, startling the heck out of me.

Rolling like a tumbleweed, I hide the urn behind my back and scramble to my feet. "What are you doing here? I-I... didn't hear you come in?"

He takes a step closer. "Who are you talking to?"

"No one." Blood rushes to my face, and I panic. "Haven't you heard of knocking? Get out!"

He narrows his eyes and tries to look past me, to what I desperately don't want him to see. "What's behind your back?"

"Nothing!"

His voice softens. "Riles...?"

"It's..." I edge away from him, the overwhelming pain in my chest tearing open as I choke back a sob. "It's nothing."

"You said Mom."

The room tilts, and I'm not sure if it's from a swell or my

buckling legs. I stumble, heat surging to my head, as everything around me spins.

Riley reaches out, his strong hands steadying me before I fall, his eyes kind but concerned. "You can talk to me, Riles."

"I—" A sob rips past my throat, tears blurring my vision as I present the urn from behind my back. "I was talking to my mom. She died six weeks ago."

He stares at the pot, then at me, and just when I think he's going to call me crazy and flee the room, he pulls me into his arms, rubbing my back soothingly as he presses a kiss to the top of my head. "I'm so sorry. I had no idea."

Shocked, I pull back and wipe my face with my sleeve. "Why would you? I've been hiding her in the safe."

His eyes close momentarily. "That's why you didn't want me to have the code?"

"Yes. I can't trust you with her. You lost my bathing suit. You might lose her too."

Pain etches his face as he gently presses the pads of his thumbs under my eyes. "I won't use the safe. I promise. I won't go near her."

Nodding, I sniffle and take a seat on the edge of my bed.

"Are you okay?" he asks, sitting beside me.

"No. Not really."

He hugs me to his side, and I don't fight his comforting embrace. Comfort isn't something I've felt since Mom's death.

"What happened?" he asks, but then adds, "You don't have to tell me, of course. But speaking from experience, believe it or not, talking helps."

I stare at the urn on my lap. "Pancreatic cancer. She was gone within months."

"Jesus," he says on an exhale.

"It all happened so fast. One minute, she was happy and healthy, and the next, she was tremendously sick and then... gone." I burst into tears again. "Sorry. I'm hanging on by a thread."

"Don't apologize for your grief, Riles. You'll always be coming to terms with it. Then, now, next month... ten years from now. Grief doesn't have a time limit; it lasts forever."

I blink up at him and nod.

"Losing someone you love is the hardest thing you'll ever endure. That type of pain is brutal."

I wipe my face. "Tell me about it. She wasn't just my mother; she was also my best friend."

"Dad was my best friend too, so I know how you feel."

I angle toward him. "I don't think you do. I mean, I know you know how losing a parent feels, and I'm in no way measuring your grief against mine, but... you have your mother, Veronica, and Poppy. I have no one. Just an empty apartment and a job I now resent."

He gently squeezes my arm. "I get it."

"Do you?"

"Yeah, Riles."

"I'm just so... lonely. And mad." Fury bubbles to the surface of my skin, blistering before bursting. "I've spent years dedicated to *me* and *my* future, working my ass off to please Georgia and get ahead. Years I should've spent appreciating Mom. And what's worse, Mom knew what I was doing, and she supported me... for the most part. She never complained when I didn't make it home for dinner, never got angry when I canceled things we planned to do together. She just smiled and said, 'I'm so proud of you,' even though she wanted me to experience and enjoy life beyond my path to success." I grip the urn, my fingers trembling. "She bought me this cruise ticket... on her damn deathbed. She begged me to leave New York and see the world, knowing I'd never do it of my own accord. And she was right. I wouldn't have, because I'm a fucking workaholic."

"Don't," he says, voice harsh.

"Don't what?"

"Don't punish yourself."

"Why not? I deserve it."

"Would your mom agree?"

I stare at him, knowing she wouldn't, my throat hoarse when I say, "No."

"Then don't do it. For her. This is your chance to give her what you think you didn't when she was alive."

"I don't think, Riley; I know. She wanted so much more for me, and I dismissed it because I thought I knew better. So, yeah... I *know* I didn't give her what she wanted when she was alive. I know it to my core."

"Well, you can give it to her *now*. You're seeing the world like she wanted you to, and you should do it without punishing yourself. She wouldn't want that—you said so yourself. So stop being selfish."

I recoil. "Selfish?"

"Yeah."

"How is regret selfish?"

"Because your mother didn't want you to feel regret. That's why. So stop. Forgive yourself for what you think you didn't give her, and respect her wishes. Be kinder to yourself, Riles."

"Respect her wishes?" I laugh sardonically. "Want to know what one of her wishes was? To sprinkle her ashes in the Atlantic." I glance out the window at the murky ocean beneath the murky sky. "I don't want to. I want to keep her, with me. Always." I scoff. "You're right. I am selfish."

"I didn't mean it like that."

"It's true though. I am."

"You're not."

"How would you know?"

"Because I do. You're just grieving and afraid to let go."

Drawing in a deep breath, my chest quakes as I exhale. "I miss her, and this urn is all I have left."

"So sprinkle her ashes and keep the urn, then you both get what you want." He rubs his beard. "Are you even allowed to scatter ashes from a cruise ship?"

"Yeah, you are. But... I'm running out of time... and ocean.

And I can't actually scatter her ashes. I have to toss the entire urn."

He pulls a "that's weird" face.

I nod sarcastically. "Uh-huh. I have to pitch her like a baseball. Actually," I add, laughing softly, "she wanted me to shoot her like a free throw."

Riley chuckles. "Your Mom sounds fun."

"She was. A little loco here and there, but lots of fun. She did the research of disposing of her remains and presented it to me like a sales pitch."

He chuckles again. "Really?"

"Yep." I sniffle. "Pictures, detailed instructions, diagrams, and all."

"Jesus!"

"When I'm ready, I have to go to Guest Services, book a date and time for her 'free throw,' and weather permitting, a member of the crew will assist me." Staring out at the icy ocean again, my blood runs just as cold. "I'm not ready. I'm not ready to say goodbye for the final time."

"But that's the thing, Riles," he says, his finger gently grazing my chin as he turns my head toward his. "You'll never be ready to say goodbye. No one ever is."

I swallow hard. "So how do I do it?"

"You just..." He holds my stare, strength from his supportive eyes pouring into mine. "You just do."

chapter sixteen

RILEY

R iles clutching her mother's urn shattered my heart. I've
been where she is, holding onto my father's coffin for dear
life, hellbent on not letting go before he was lowered into the
ground. I know her pain, her guilt, her regret.

I know her fear and despair.

What I don't know is her loneliness, because she was right... I
did have Mom and Roni when Dad passed. I still do. And
although I've never felt as lonely as I do now, her solitude and
mine are different.

Stepping forward, next in line, I wait my turn at the Guest
Services desk. Riles shouldn't be alone in grief, and it kills me
knowing she has no one to turn to or to help her through the
toughest moments of her life. We've only just met, but I can't
stand aside while she crumbles and breaks. That's not who I am,
as a fellow human being, nor as a man who just had his world
rocked by her lips.

That kiss. Jesus! It sparked a fire within me that I thought had
long burned out, nothing left but ash and angry embers. A fire
Krystal used to ignite but instead extinguished with her ice-queen
heart. I suspected kissing Riles would spark something, because

I'm wildly attracted to her, but never did I imagine it would light the fuse it did. In fact, I think it's still crackling.

When she so effortlessly dismissed the kiss and the effect it had, I'd been royally pissed. Hurt even. And in my usual false I-could-not-care-less attitude, I pulled out my asshole card and sent her running to get away from me. I don't want to do that anymore. All it ever achieves is me in a bar, licking my wounds and drowning my guilt and sorrow. It pushes me ten steps back, when I'm supposed to be moving forward.

When I followed her back to the room to demand that she too admit she felt something, *anything*, I never expected to walk in on the situation I did. But if I hadn't, I would never have overheard her telling her mom she thought our kiss was incredible.

And it was.

It damn well stopped time.

And I plan to stop it again.

Just not now. Not... yet.

"Next please!" the crewmember behind the desk calls, the same guy from embarkation day, his demeanor pleasant until his eyes land on mine.

I stroll forward, and his shoulders straighten as if he believes I'm here to complain again. "Mr. Wilson, how can I assist you today?"

Resting my elbow on the counter, I lower my voice. "I have some questions about burial at sea."

His brows shoot toward the ceiling, his eyeballs bulging. "What would you like to know?"

"What's the process?"

"Do you have remains you'd like to inter?" He clicks his computer mouse and studies his screen, I assume to check my passenger profile to that effect.

"Yes." I shake my head. "I mean no. I'm just curious what's involved."

"Oh! Very well." He stops clicking. "Because to disperse remains at sea, you must advise the cruise line prior to sailing that you wish to do so, together with presenting a death certificate and a letter from the crematorium stating the urn is biodegradable. Without these documents, I couldn't authorize nor organize the ceremony."

"Ceremony?"

"Yes. If the captain is available at the time, she will oversee the ceremony and say a few words if you wish her to do so. If she's not available, one of her first, second, or third officers will officiate in her place. She'll also take note of the ship's precise location and then compose a lovely letter with coordinates."

"I see," I say, nodding. "And how about flowers?"

"Fresh flowers can be arranged on board, but artificial flowers or wreaths with ribbon or non-biodegradable matter are not permitted."

I rub my beard.

"Was there anything else I can help you with?"

"Yes." I stop rubbing and lean closer. "Do you remember my roommate?"

"The other Riley Wilson?"

"That's the one. She's carrying her mother's remains with her, and I'd like to arrange some flowers for the ceremony, as well as flowers delivered to the cabin for her."

He resumes his mouse-clicking again. "Yes. I can see Ms. Wilson has notified us of her mother's remains and her intention to inter them at sea. However, the ceremony hasn't been scheduled."

"That's because she hasn't scheduled it yet."

"Right." He pouts, the same puppy dog pout he did the first time I saw him. "What I can do is make a note in the system to organize the flowers for when she does make final arrangements. Would you like me to do that now?"

I nod. "If you don't mind."

"Of course." He starts typing, his fingers artfully tapping his keyboard. "Did you have a particular bouquet in mind?"

"Uh...." I scratch my head.

Shit! I wouldn't have a clue. I don't know her mother's name, much less what her or Riles's favorite flowers are.

When I don't answer, his expression turns sympathetic, or patronizing—I can't quite tell. "We don't have a huge selection on board, but our Eternal Remembrance bouquet is the most popular. It has a neutral pallet and—"

"That will be fine. Two of those, please."

"Certainly. And would you like to leave a personalized message on both bouquets?"

I think of Riles and what she said about her mom. "How about 'A loving mother and best friend'?"

"Lovely. And the bouquet for Ms. Wilson?"

"Uh... 'Sorry for your loss'?" I shake my head. "No. That's too generic." Riles didn't *lose* her mom like a set of car keys, just like I didn't *lose* my dad either. "How about 'You're not alone.'"

"Splendid." He touches his chest, pouts again, then continues typing. "All done. Was there anything else I can help with?"

"No, not today." I push off from the counter and give him an appreciative nod. "Thank you. You've been very helpful."

He straightens his shoulders again and smiles. "My pleasure."

Once I leave the desk, I head back to the cabin but pause before opening the door, remembering to knock first.

"Come in," Riles calls out, stepping in from the balcony as I enter the room. "Oh! It's you!" She cocks her head, her puffy eyes amused. "You remembered to knock."

"I did." I smile.

Chewing the inside of her cheek, she wrings her fingers together. "Thank you."

"No sweat." I slump onto the sofa and stretch my legs out. "How are you feeling? Because if you need more time, I can disappear for longer."

"No. Please don't leave on my account." She takes a seat beside me, angles her body in my direction, and presses her knees together, her hands resting on her lap. "I feel... okay. A little embarrassed, but okay, I guess."

"Why are you embarrassed?"

"Because you caught me talking to my deceased mother."

"And?"

She looks down at her hands. "And that's embarrassing."

"No it's not. I still talk to my dad."

"You do?"

"Yeah, when I'm in the workshop. And I swear the stubborn bastard talks back to me, especially when I screw up the job I'm working on."

She lets out a mild laugh, and my heart dances a little.

"I swear Mom talks back to me as well."

Not sure whether now's a good time to playfully bait her, I decide to do it anyway. It'll probably backfire on me, but if it takes her mind off her sorrow, it'll be worth it. "What did she say when you told her about the kiss? By the way, you weren't an... how did you put it? An overexuberant donkey?"

Riles's cheeks bloom as pink as Poppy's bedroom walls, her mouth forming an O. "You heard that?"

I try not to gloat but fail. "I did."

"What else did you hear?"

I scratch my head. "Can't remember."

"Oh my God!" She shoots to her feet, pacing while she buries her head in her hands.

I chuckle; I can't help it.

"It's not funny, Riley. You should've knocked like you just did. It's the rule, damn it!"

"Yeah, one you broke as well, remember?" I grin like a greedy fucker, remembering the way her eyes practically licked the droplet of water from my chest.

She stops pacing. "Let's not talk about that."

"Why not?"

"Because there's nothing to talk about."

I call bullshit. She likes me; I can tell. But I need to tread carefully, for her sake more than mine.

Raising my arm, I rest it on the back of the sofa and prop my head up with my hand. "So you enjoyed the kiss, huh?"

"What?"

"It was—" I pretend to think about it. "—incredible?"

"Riley!" she shrieks again. "You just said you couldn't remember what you heard!"

"I remember that part."

She growls her adorable cub growl and turns her back on me. "I can't believe you."

"Ease up, Riles. I'm just playin—"

"No!"

"It was a great kiss."

"So what if it was?"

I smile and wait for her to continue, because I know she will, especially if I don't say anything.

"Regardless of if it was or wasn't," she says, fiddling with the daily newsletter, "it won't happen again."

My smile plummets. "Why not?"

"Because it can't. We're sharing a room, and... and..." She turns to face me again. "You're getting a divorce."

"What's my divorce got to do with it?"

"They're messy and complicated. Plus, I'm not a rebound, Riley. I never have been, and I never will be." She crosses her arms over her chest in a show of defiance. "And I don't do one-night stands. They're not for me."

I smirk. "They're not for me either."

Her eyebrow rises, insinuating I'm lying, and it pisses me off. I don't do one-night stands, much to Roni's and Ben's encouragement. But one night can lead to two, and two can lead to three, and so on and so on, so you gotta start somewhere if you want to go anywhere.

Dying to put forward my very logical and valid point, I choose to let it go instead. Now's not the time to take this further. I've succeeded in distracting her from her thoughts of her late mother, but there are other ways I can continue to do that, ways that don't potentially lead to her severing my head from my neck.

"Let's get one thing straight," I say calmly, eyes locked on hers. "When I say I don't do one-night stands, I mean it. They don't interest me." I snag the TV remote and press the On button.

"What are you doing?" she asks, giving me a quizzical look.

I give her one back. "Watching TV."

"You're not going to the magic show?"

"Nope. That doesn't interest me either."

Riles chews her lip, and I once again internally praise my distraction skills.

"Well," she adds, a little flustered. "What are your plans for dinner then?"

"Room service."

"Oh." She combs her fingers through her hair and twists it. "I was going to have that too."

I cross my legs at the ankles. "Good."

Turning in a circle, she then snatches up the in-room menu and retakes her seat beside me. "Good."

Not "good," sweetheart. Great!

WE ORDER A MEXICAN FEAST AND WATCH A MOVIE, AND Riles eventually falls asleep at the opposite end of the sofa. I consider carrying her to her bed, but I don't want to overstep and freak her out if she were to wake up in my arms. She's already accused me of drugging my niece beyond just giving her milk, so I don't want to risk her thinking I've somehow roofied her. I'd like to believe she wouldn't go there, but... who knows with Riles.

Pacing before her, deliberating my best course of action, I stop and grip my hair. I could just wake her up—she has no problems waking me most mornings—or I could just leave her to sleep where she is. It looks comfortable enough, and when she awakens and finds I haven't touched her, perhaps she'll trust I'm not a one-night-stand type of creep.

I collect her bedding, then gently ease her head from the arm of the sofa, her body a dead but featherlight weight. Her eyelids flutter, so I pause and hold my breath, her soft cheek resting against my palm. Riles's lashes aren't spidey like Brittany's, so I assume they're not fake and won't fall off into my hand, which is a relief. Body parts shouldn't easily detach, and if any of Riles's happen to snap free, I'd probably squeal like a piglet.

Barely exhaling, I carefully slide the pillow beneath her head before covering her with a blanket and stepping back, pleased with my stealth-like efforts. Thanks to Poppy, I'm experienced in this do-not-disturb artform. I've performed it many nights with astounding success.

I quietly rub my hands together, then head toward my bed when I remember Riles needs the AirPods.

Fuck! How the hell am I going to manage this?

I grip my hair again and scan her bedside table for the white case, finding it next to her cell.

Double fuck! She needs the app too.

Putting Poppy to bed is a shit-ton easier than this, and I suddenly regret ever whining about the process. I'll take a six-year-old firecracker over an emotionally fragile and scarred woman any day. Cranky Poppy, I can handle. Cranky Riles, not so much.

Tiptoeing to her bed, I collect the AirPods and cell, and then I use her fingertip to activate the screen and gain access to the app. Heaven help me if she were to wake up at this precise moment— me hovering above her, trying to break into her phone. She'd no doubt forcefully eject me from the room to deck three... or call security to detain my ass.

Jesus Christ! I should just sleep in the bathtub.

I draw in a breath, tap on the white nose sound she listened to last, and then take an AirPod out and slowly guide it toward her ear, my hand trembling worse than a SWAT team member about to diffuse a bomb. Memories of playing Operation with Roni when we were younger flick to the forefront of my mind, and that only fries my nerves more. I sucked at that game. Touched the sides every time.

Gently puffing out my breath, I steady my wrist, carefully inch closer, and close one eye when I slot the AirPod into her ear.

Riles shrieks, her hand whipping up and cracking me in the nose.

"Fuck!" I groan, stumbling back.

"What the hell, Riley?" She scrambles to sit up, her wide eyes bouncing from me to various parts of the room as she secures her blanket to her chest. "What are you doing?"

"I was trying to put your AirPod in," I mumble into my cupped hands.

"What?" She touches her ear. "Why?"

"Because you fell asleep. And because I didn't want to move you. Jesus! I should've just whacked you with a pillow instead."

She giggles. Fucking giggles.

"Are you okay?" she asks, raising her knees and hugging them to her chest, her bottom lip clamped between her teeth.

Blinking a few times, I wiggle my nose. "I was a minute ago."

"Sorry," she says, continuing to giggle.

"Yeah, so am I."

"Do you need to see the nurse?" she quips.

"No."

Slowly rising to her feet, she reduces the space between us. "I'm sorry, but that," she says, pointing to my face, "was your fault."

"Mine? I was trying to do the right thing."

She tenderly touches the bridge of my nose, trailing her fingers to the tip before honking it. "You'll live."

"Ow! For fuck's sa—"

"Stop whining." She pats my cheek for good measure, and I have the mind to haul her cheeky ass over my shoulder and throw her onto her bed. I almost do, right before she places her hands on my shoulders and says, "Thank you for trying not to wake me. But next time, maybe just give me a gentle shake."

"A gentle shake?" I ask, bemused.

"Yes. I live alone now, remember? I'm not used to someone poking something in my ear while I sleep."

Good point.

"Noted," I grumble.

She bites her lip, face scrunched. "Do you need me to get you some ice?"

"No. Like you said, I'll live."

"Good. Because I couldn't handle another person I care about dying." She turns back to the sofa, collects her bedding, and climbs into bed, pulling the covers over her shoulder.

My mouth falls open.

"Turn off the light," she adds.

Ignoring her, I instead stand there and grin. "You care about me?"

She groans. "Yes, Riley."

"What do you mean by *care* exactly?"

"Light!" she grumbles.

I do as I'm told, switching it off before lowering onto the edge of my bed, waiting for her answer, nothing but darkness and the distant sound of waves lapping the ship. The cabin softly shudders as the stabilizers work to reduce the opposing motion of the swell, my mind shuddering along with it. When Riles still doesn't answer, I climb under the covers and try to settle myself, uncomfortably twisting and turning.

"What?" she grumbles again.

"Nothing. I didn't say anything."

Her bed creaks as she rolls over or sits up. I'm not quite sure; I can't see shit.

I sit up too, blinking as I lean forward.

"Riley?"

"Yes?" I blurt.

"Thank you for today. It meant a lot."

"No sweat."

She inhales, long and deep, before exhaling again. "And yes, I care about you. Perhaps more than I should."

A fuzzy excitement warms and tremors my chest in unison with the quaking cabin, my heart's own stabilizers kicking in. "I care about you too," I say, thrilled as fuck to also reveal how I feel. "Perhaps more than I should."

Desperate to go to her and press my lips against hers, to show her exactly how much I care, the deafening silence instead chains me to my bed.

"Riley?"

"Yeah?" I blurt again.

"Goodnight."

Smiling, I lay back and thread my hands beneath my head. "Night."

chapter seventeen

RILES

When I wake up the following morning, I'm a bowl of emotional cereal: some flakes of humiliation, a sprinkle here and there of rapture and delight, and a rather large splash of disconsolate milk. One minute, I'm coping, then the next I'm somewhat thriving, and after that I'm completely overcome with sadness. Not to mention Riley is burrowing underneath my skin, and I'm not sure if that's a good or bad thing. I don't normally allow burrowers, especially those who burrow for a short-term residency. Nor do I allow myself to be a rebound, one-night stand.

He says he isn't about that either, but I'm not convinced. It hasn't been long since his marriage of fifteen years crumbled to pieces, and he's probably as emotionally confused as I am but for different reasons. How could he not be?

But my God, his burrowing is hard to obstruct. Not only is he sweetly and annoyingly persistent, but having someone show concern, humility, and interest while I'm at my lowest point is irrefutably comforting. A comfort I can't help but selfishly cling to.

A comfort that could do more harm than good.

"It's soggy," he says, snapping me from my thoughts.

I look up at him. "What?"

He gestures to my bowl. "Your cereal. It's soggy. Please tell me you're not a weirdo who prefers their cereal swampy."

I push my bowl aside. "No, not particularly."

"Well, you might want to get some more and eat it without stirring a hundred times over."

"I'm not hungry anyway."

"Riles," he says, his piece of bacon midway to his mouth. "You need to eat something."

I lift my mug of caffeinated bliss. "I am."

"Something solid. Something substantial. We'll be up and down corridors and stairs today during the ship tour. Coffee ain't gonna cut it."

Rolling my eyes, I brush him off. "I'll be fine."

"Here," he says, offering me what's left of his bagel. "Have this."

"No. It's yours."

"If you're worried about boy germs, then sorry, sweetheart, you've already got mine."

I narrow my gaze on him, snatch the bagel, and shove it into my mouth, mumbling, "Happy?"

"For now." He licks his knife, his stupid, crinkly eyes sparkling with amusement, and if I didn't like them as much as I do, I'd look away, ignoring their existence. But I do like them, a lot. They're like a shining light on a foggy night.

"You want to kiss me again, don't you?"

Blinking, I divert my gaze from his stupid eyes and arrogant smirk, then launch my napkin at him before standing and pushing my chair back. "In your dreams."

"That's funny," he says, following after me. "Because last night, in my dream, your lips were—"

"Riley! Stop joking around."

"Okay, okay." He falls into step beside me. "No more kiss jokes."

"Good. Because you're already at three, and it's not even midday."

"Only three?" He huffs. "I thought I racked up more."

Sighing my frustration, I dodge other passengers juggling bowls and plates of food from the buffet, one child in particular not watching where he's walking, instead licking the maple syrup off his waffle.

"Whoa, little man," Riley says as he swoops in front of me and reaches out to balance the boy's plate before it topples onto my dress. "You nearly dropped your waffles." He blows out an exaggerated breath and wipes his brow. "They're safe. Crisis averted."

The little guy looks at him and then at his plate before he ducks his head and continues licking the syrup.

I laugh; I'd probably do the same if I were his age.

Chuckling, Riley helps him to his table, scruffs the little boy's hair, then pushes his chair in for him. My heart melts into a pool of hormonal lava, my ovaries crying out like the Wicked Witch of the West when Dorothy doused her with water. *"I'm melting. I'm meltiiing!"*

I tell my ovaries to shut up.

So what if he'd make a great father and is no doubt an incredible uncle? Why's that any of my reproductive organs' concern?

Ugh! He's like a groundhog. Stop burrowing, damn it.

Striding toward me, his navy T-shirt snug against his chest, his caramel-colored jacket the perfect accompaniment, I give him points for his sense of style. Burly but smart. Understated but eye-catching.

"I'm melting. I'm meltiiing!"

Allowing myself to dissolve just a little, I chew the inside of my cheek, smooth down my dress, and try to remain unfazed, undazed... and uncrazed.

He stops before me and smirks again. "You want to kiss me, don't you?"

My melting solidifies. "Oh my God! Will you quit it?"

"I'm only at four. My goal is to reach ten by day's end."

Groaning, I turn away and head toward Guest Services, our meeting point for the ship tour.

"Ease up, Riles."

"You ease up."

"I would if it wasn't working."

"Trust me, it's not."

He coughs out, "Bullshit," and I'm tempted to take the elevator to piss him off.

But I'm a kinder person than I perhaps should be right now, so I take the stairs instead. "You can cough bullshit all you like. It's not working, so you're wasting your time."

He scoots down a few steps and stops in front of me, his head level with mine. I gasp at his close proximity to my face, my eyes locked with his before they dip to my lips.

"Are you sure?" he says, voice low and sexy as hell.

No, not really.

He smells delicious, like minty flowers: fresh, clean, and...

Recognizing the scent, I lean forward as if to give him the kiss he wants, instead brushing the tip of my nose against his cheek and sniffing his hair. "Have you been using my shampoo?"

He rears back, eyes wide as he swallows. "No."

I cough out, "Bullshit."

Stepping back, he turns and continues down the stairs, so I chase after him.

"You have, haven't you?"

He speeds away. "I don't know what you're talking about."

Irritated, but also delightfully triumphant, because I can play *and* beat him at his own game, I slow down, pleased I just won that round. Do I want to kiss him again? Yes. But it's not a good idea. We still have to share a room, and if things turn bad, it'll ruin our cruise. I simply can't risk that.

Taking the last step to Deck Four, I round the corner to where Riley is chatting with Manny and Hugo.

"There she is," Hugo says, waving animatedly.

I wave back and smile—the shampoo conversation *will* be revisited later.

"Hi, guys," I say. "Are you doing the ship tour as well?"

"We are. Manny's been looking forward to it ever since we boarded. He likes engines and grease, and all that dirty stuff. Me, on the other hand? I just want to see how the galley works... and I don't mind a man or two in uniform." He winks.

I nudge his shoulder. "Me too."

Riley cocks a brow, then says to Manny, "Engines, huh? So what is it you do for a living?"

"I'm a dentist." He flashes his pearly whites and taps one of them.

"A dentist? That's not what I thought you were going to say."

Hugging his husband to his side, Manny elaborates, "My love of engines comes from my grandfather. He was a mechanic, so I spent many days in his garage, watching him work."

Riley nods with interest, slides his hands into his pockets, and rocks back on his heels, which I've noticed he does here and there. Not that I'm complaining; I like when he does it. It's suave and—

"Earth to Riley."

Blinking, I turn to Hugo. "Sorry, did you say something?"

"I said your dress is lovely."

"Oh." I twist my hips, letting the floral material swish. "Thank you. It's one of my favorites."

"A versatile number indeed."

"Yes, very much so." I kick my legs out. "Boots and tights for now, sandals for when we get to London. I only packed one suitcase, so I had to be smart."

"One suitcase?" Hugo touches his chest dramatically. "Are you crazy?"

I giggle. "Yes, sometimes."

Raising his hand to the side of his mouth like a shield, Manny whispers, "Hugo packed two... for himself."

"You're lucky I didn't use yours as well."

"You did."

Hugo dismisses his husband. "Only a small section."

Snickering, my heart warms as Hugo links his arm with mine and leads me toward our guide, who is issuing colored wristbands.

"Why must they be a godawful neon tangerine?" He wrinkles his nose. "They could've at least gone with vermillion or coral. Tangerine looks dreadful with magenta." He glances down at his shirt, then at my dress. "At least you won't clash. That cobalt-blue is divine."

Impressed with his colorful knowledge, I ask, "Do you work in fashion?"

"No, dear. Interior design."

"Really? You and Riley would get along well. He's a carpenter. He has his own business, designing and building signature furniture."

"He does, does he?" Hugo pokes his arm out for his wristband, so I do the same, waiting while our guide secures them.

"I haven't seen any of his pieces," I add, "but he's very passionate about it, so I can only imagine they're brilliant."

"What are you two gossiping about?" Riley asks, separating us with his body.

Hugo points at him. "You."

"Me?"

"Yes. Riley tells me you build and design furniture."

"I do," he says, his expression appreciative. "Been doing it since I was a kid."

"What's your business called?"

"Wilson and Son."

Hugo grabs Riley's arm. "In Buxtonville?"

"Yeah. That's me."

"I've bought a few of your pieces for my clients. They're delightful."

Eagerly ditching me for Riley, Hugo commandeers him as our guide instructs us to follow her to the service elevator.

"I'm afraid you've lost him for the duration of the tour,"

Manny says, chuckling. "My husband can talk all day and night about furniture and decor."

I happily shrug off the abandonment. "I bet Riley could too. He must feel so proud right now, knowing an interior decorator sources his art."

Manny presses his lips together in agreement, then clasps his hands behind his back. "So how's it going, sharing your cabin? The two of you seem to be getting along rather well."

"We are. We had a few hiccups at first, but nothing we're not working through."

"I bet you did. What a shock to find out you both weren't cruising alone as planned."

"Shock is an understatement. But to be honest, I'm enjoying the company."

He holds the elevator doors open for me, so I step in, craning my neck to find Riley crammed in at the back, the poor thing paler than he was a minute ago. I wince, hoping Hugo's continuous rambling provides the distraction Riley needs.

"Welcome to the Behind-the-Scenes tour, folks. My name is Gabriella, one of your Guest Services staff, and I'll be your guide today. Our first stop on the tour will be Deck Two, where we'll find the i95, also known as the crew passage, which is a large laneway from one end of the ship to the other. It allows the crew to move about quickly and freely. It's also where the crew quarters, medical facility, laundry, and food stores are. From there, we'll head to the engine room and desalination plant before visiting the galleys and then the bridge. Video recording and photography are strictly prohibited, but please feel free to ask as many questions as you like."

"This is exciting," I whisper to Manny as the doors open again and we funnel out.

Stepping aside, we wait for Hugo and Riley, Riley's shoulders relaxing as they both join us.

"You okay?" I murmur to him.

He playfully coos. "Naww, you really do care about me, don't you?"

Drawing in perhaps my one-hundredth frustrated breath for the morning, I huff it back out again. "I'm reconsidering."

"You are not."

"Yes, I am."

"Gather around," Gabriella instructs, ushering us closer. "Don't be shy; we're all friends here."

We bunch together like a bouquet.

"As you can see, to my right is the medical facility, which staffs two nurses and one physician. It's equipped to treat minor non-emergency conditions as well as stabilize patients with life-threatening illnesses. It has an ICU, testing lab, pharmacy, and yes... a morgue. For obvious reasons, we cannot go through the center, but you'd be wise to avoid this amazing place anyway. A visit here could set you back hundreds to thousands of dollars."

A few people whistle their astonishment, and guilt once again washes over me for having a hand in Brittany paying a visit... and a price.

"Don't," Riley hisses.

I side-eye him. "Don't what?"

"You know what."

Annoyed he can so easily read me, I frown and move forward, following Gabriella along the i95, which is roughly ten-feet wide with many safety protocol posters on the walls and doors lining the sempiternal passage. One has a list of emergency codes, some phonetic and others with colors, so I pause for a moment to study it.

"Let's pray we don't hear Code Kilo announced," I say to Riley. "If we do, according to this, it means we're going to be evacuated." I scroll down the list. "Or Code Bravo. Oh my God! Could you imagine if there was a fire on board?"

My body shudders.

"I'm more worried about that one," he says, pointing to Code PVI.

I read the description and laugh. "You're more concerned over someone vomiting in a public area than the ship going up in flames?"

"Yep. I don't do puke."

I shake my head at him.

"As we head toward the stern to the laundry," Gabriella calls out, "please stay to your right, and watch your step. The laundry is one of the ship's busiest hives of activity, and you'll soon see why."

We huddle along, past the crew quarters, until we stop in front of a room with many metal-caged carts that are stacked with freshly cleaned linen lined up along the passageway, crewmembers greeting us in their various dialects as they edge past.

"Before we enter, please note it may be hard to breathe from the steam. If any of you are uncomfortable, let me know, and I'll escort you out." Gabriella opens a door, and we file in behind her. "Let me just see if I can find our Chief Housekeeper. I swear she never leaves this room."

A musty, sharp ammonia scent hits my nose, the room humid and noisy, several industrial machines working relentlessly. White linen as far as the eye can see is bunched on benches, piled in large plastic tubs on wheels, and is neatly folded and stacked in at least a dozen caged carts. Crew members hustle about, sorting and folding, and I watch in awe at the sheer volume of fabric being laundered and at how diligently they go about it.

Guilt once again washes over me, this time for using my towels once before placing them on the floor for our cabin steward to collect. These incredible worker bees have enough labor to do without me unnecessarily adding to it.

"Thank you for waiting," Gabriella says, returning with a vivacious older woman. "This is Sophia, our Chief Housekeeper. The cleanest lady on the ship."

Sophia chuckles at her colleague, then holds her arm out. "Welcome to the laundry. We are very busy, eh?"

One of the women on our tour points to a machine folding sheets. "Oh, I need one of those."

"Ah, yes. My favorite," Sophia says, lovingly patting the stainless-steel contraption. "Folds into perfect squares. So clever, eh?"

The women nod, the men less enthused.

"The laundry is most important. Without it and my crew, the ship would not function. The restaurants would not have clean napkins, and you... no clean towels and sheets." Sofia gives us a "blergh" face.

"How many towels do you clean per day?" the same woman from before asks.

"Ah, sometimes we launder ten thousand towels a day."

"Wow!" I whisper.

"And twenty thousand napkins."

Twenty thousand? Holy shit!

"But as you see, we don't do it all by hand, thank goodness. We have many machines to wash, steam, and fold the linen for us, as well as a hard-working staff to collect, sort, and deliver them." She straightens her shoulders, proud. "Impressive, eh?"

Most of us nod, and after a few minutes of watching the laundering process, we're escorted back out into the passageway, the fresher, cooler air most welcome.

I lift my hair from the back of my neck. "That was eye-opening."

Riley murmurs, "Hmm."

"I think we should use our towels more than once from now on."

"Say what?"

"I'm serious. Look at all that laundry. It's the least we can do."

"It's what we pay *good coin* for," he says, mimicking Ohio Oscar's voice yet again.

I release my hair and facetiously elbow him in the ribs.

"Now, just up ahead are the food stores," Gabriella says, glancing back over her shoulder as she strides forward. "One of the most popular Behind-the-Scenes tour places to visit." She stops in front of another door and asks us to wait while she enters in search of the Food and Beverage Director.

My stomach rumbles.

Riley smirks. "Hungry, are we?"

"Do you blame me? All this talk of food stores will do that to a person."

"Not me." He rubs his belly. "I had a substantial breakfast."

"Shut up," I grouch just as Gabriella returns and ushers us inside, boxes of bottled oils, canned goods, and various pantry items stacked to the ceiling.

"I'd like to introduce you to Leon, our Food and Beverage Director, who has one of the most difficult and vital roles on board."

Leon steps forward, his hands clasped behind his back. "Thank you, Gabriella. Welcome, everyone, to the ship's treasure trove. In here, you'll find many food stores, each dedicated to different food groups. As you can see, this is one of our pantries. To your right, through that steel door, is one of our meat freezers, and beyond that is another freezer—my personal favorite, dedicated solely to ice cream." He waggles his eyebrows.

"It's my favorite too," Gabriella adds.

"Why do you have a freezer just for ice cream?" Hugo asks.

"Mostly to prevent cross-contamination. We must follow strict Vessel Sanitation Program criteria, as well as health and safety guidelines, for your protection and for ours. We don't want an outbreak of food poisoning on board just as much as you don't." Leon lifts his chin. "Any other questions?"

Most of us shake our heads.

"Very well. If you'll follow me, I'll show you one of our fridges."

We shadow him along a hallway into another large room, again stacked almost to the brim with boxes of pantry items, several steel doors circling it.

"In those two fridges, there are fruits and vegetables. In the fridge over there is where we thaw our proteins. And in here," he says, opening the door, "is where we keep our dairy and eggs." Leon gestures for us to enter, a few at a time, and I almost stop in my tracks at the mountain of egg cartons.

"Wow! How many eggs do you order for a single cruise?" I ask.

"We can go through ten to fifteen thousand eggs a day."

"Jesus," Riley murmurs.

Leon chuckles. "Eggsactly!"

I giggle. "Do you ever run out?"

"Never. I'm too good at my job." He winks. "And if I ever did run out of eggs, Executive Chef Bruno would have my head on one of his fancy silver platters."

He draws his finger across his neck and then escorts us to the alcohol storeroom.

"Oh, praise the Lord," Hugo says, eyes wide. "That's a lot of wine." He turns in a circle, admiring the hundreds of cases. "Manny, darling, you can just leave me here. I'll be fine for a few hours."

"Here is the last place I would leave you," Manny says, taking hold of his husband's hand. "I'd never see you again."

Hugo sighs. "This is true."

Smiling wistfully at how in love the two of them are, I allow my eyes to lock with Riley's when he steps into my line of vision, leans in close, and whispers, "You want to kiss me again, don't you?"

My wistful smile dissolves faster than an ice cube on a frying pan. "No!"

"Don't even think about stealing my wine," Leon jokes, pointing at Riley. "I have a black belt in Jui Jitsu." He presses his feet together, slaps his hands by his sides, and bows.

Riley raises his hands. "Wouldn't dream of it."

After the food stores, we thank Leon and say farewell to him, then make our way down a flight of precariously narrow steel stairs to the engine room and desalination plant. And although hot, pungent, and uncomfortably noisy, I find it interesting learning how the ship uses four enormous generators to produce enough electricity to power and drive the ship, as well as the process involved in desalinating sea water and treating human waste—all thirty-thousand gallons of it.

We head back above sea level to one of the galleys, where an army of chefs prep food for this evening's dining sessions, some of them artfully sculpting flowers from carrots.

"Last stop on the tour," Gabriella announces, "is the bridge, where you're all lucky enough to meet Captain Katarina, who I'm told is currently there. Please keep noise to a minimum. And I know it goes without saying, but no touching the instruments."

We enter the bridge through glass sliding doors, a panoramic view of the ocean glistening in the sunlight as far as the eye can see. Navigation and communications systems are stationed throughout the spacious room, together with several officers in uniform, all of them acknowledging our arrival with friendly greetings and nods.

Hugo fans his face. "On second thought, dear husband, leave me here."

"Over my dead body," Manny quips.

I giggle.

"Welcome to the bridge," Gabriella says in a hushed voice. "This is, of course, where the captain and her officers drive the ship and monitor weather conditions to ensure a safe journey from port to port." She glances over at the captain, who holds up one finger, Gabriella nodding before continuing, "At night, the bridge is pitch-black except for the illuminated controls. This allows the captain and her officers to easily see other vessels by using binoculars. Each officer can only be on shift at night for a maximum of four hours to avoid fatigue, so while you all sleep, rest assured you're in very capable hands. And speaking of very capable hands, please say hello to Captain Katarina, my boss. The best captain on the seas."

We all murmur, "Hello," and for some reason, I feel a little starstruck. Perhaps it's the tailored white uniform, naval hat, and the stripes on her shoulders. Or perhaps it's because she's a woman in a "man's" world. Regardless, I feel the need to stand to attention and salute. Which I do, sans the salute.

"Hello. Welcome to the bridge," she says. "Have you enjoyed the tour?"

We all nod, some of us saying, "Yes," me included.

"Excellent. She's a beauty, isn't she?" Katarina lovingly rests her hand on a station. "Now, who would like to steer the ship?"

My hand shoots up of its own accord, and I mentally try to wrestle it back down again. I can't even steer a shopping cart.

She points to me. "You, yes?"

Peanut freaking butter.

Tentatively stepping forward, I'm encouraged by Captain Katarina to join her behind the smallest wheel I've ever seen.

Shocked, I ask, "This steers the whole ship?"

"Yes."

I place my hands on the wheel, excited but nervous.

"Just don't crash, okay?"

"Crash?" I look directly ahead at the vast ocean. "What is there to crash into?"

She gestures toward the horizon. "Icebergs."

"What?" I immediately let go of the steering wheel. "Where?"

"Don't let go!" she shouts.

Shrieking, I grasp the wheel again, almost releasing a little scaredy pee into my panties.

Captain Katarina clutches her abdomen and then pats my shoulder. "I'm joking. You're not steering the ship."

"I'm not?"

"No. Do you think I'm crazy?" She points to one of her officers at a different station. "Second Officer Franco is navigating. This little wheel here is just for show... and to play tricks on my passengers during the tour."

Haha... ha... ha.

"You got me," I say as everyone laughs at my expense, Riley included.

Winking, she pats my shoulder again, then instigates a sympathetic round of applause as I trudge back to my spot, mortification burning my cheeks.

"I like her," Riley murmurs. "She's... funny."

Grumbling, I cross my arms over my chest.

"Ease up, Ri—"

"Don't," I grouch.

He chuckles. "You want to kiss me again, don't you?"

"If you say that one more time—" I grit my teeth. "—you'll be kissing my knuckles."

Riley turns to face me, lifts my hand, and inspects it. "They look like nice knuckles."

I go to snatch my hand back, but I'm not given the chance when he leans forward and places a soft kiss against my skin, his eyes not leaving mine. "Is this what you had in mind?"

"I...." I try to speak, but no words form, my knuckles tingling, my hand as immobile as my tongue.

Damn you and your magical lips.

chapter eighteen

RILEY

If all goes to plan, she'll say yes to kissing me again. And the odds are, the more I ask, the better chance I have.

I'm desperate to taste her lips, feel her warmth, and confirm our kiss on stage and what it did to me wasn't just a figment of my imagination. Because, if our next kiss is as mind-blowing as the first, I can't possibly ignore what it could mean. Alternatively, if kissing her again sparks nothing—which I highly doubt will be the case—I'll back down and stop pushing her, as I'm not about a one-night stand, irrespective of what she thinks.

I'll be her roommate, her friend, and nothing more.

I'll be the perfect gentleman.

When I kissed her knuckles on the bridge, I thought I was finally in luck, that she'd give in, say yes, and then press her lips to mine. She looked interested, and it *was* a romantic location after all, perhaps a once-in-a-lifetime opportunity. But she hasn't said more than a few words to me since, and now I'm worried I pushed a little too hard, too soon.

"Idiot!" I murmur to myself as I tie the laces of my shoe.

I'm in over my head; I just don't want to accept it. I've never "chased" a woman, only a girl. And back then, I wasn't much older than sixteen.

You don't have a clue, dickhead. You should stop embarrassing yourself. Save some face before it's too late.

Standing up from sitting on the edge of my bed, the door to the bathroom opens, and Riles steps out in the evening dress she unpacked the day we met, the purple satin material skimming to just above the floor, splitting like a curtain and falling on either side of her leg.

My composure lodges in my throat, and I try to swallow, my throat thick as my eyes climb her body to her bare shoulders, her hair tied up, showcasing her stunning face.

All thoughts of stopping my pursuit whisk past me and out the door.

Embarrass yourself, dickhead. Do whatever it takes.

"Uh... would you mind helping zip me up?" she asks, voice timid as she clutches the dress to her chest.

"S-Sure." I clear my throat. "Of course."

She turns her back to me, her smooth skin a magnet to rival the earth's, gravity pulling my fingers toward her. I reach out to clasp the zipper but ball my fists instead, clenching them before relaxing. "You look... incredible."

"Thank you." She glances over her shoulder. "You look very handsome too."

Scrubbing my hands together, I warm them up then take hold of the zipper and slowly pull it higher, itching to kiss her shoulders and neck but not daring to, instead gliding the tab along the track until it's secure. "There you go."

She spins to face me, her steel-gray eyes sparkling with amusement. "Thank you."

I run my hand through my hair and step back, needing distance to prevent me from taking her into my arms and proving our lips, together, do fucking shift the earth on its axis.

"You want to kiss me again, don't you?" she asks seductively.

My dick stirs within my pants, and I'm about to say "hell yes" and pull her to me when she shoves my chest and laughs.

"Just kidding." She twirls back around like a stormy tornado and collects her lanyard from her bed. "We're gonna be late, and I hate being late."

Fuck me! Did she just play me at my own game?

Blinking as she struts past in her hot-as-fuck heels, her temptress perfume intoxicating me through my nostrils, it almost strips me of what sense I have left.

"Riley! Are you coming?"

I look up to where she impatiently waits by the door, which is propped open by her arm and hip.

Am I coming?

If I stand here a second longer with her, I will be. I'll be coming for her, in her, and all over her.

An animalistic growl rumbles up my throat, so I force it back down and choke out, "Yes."

WE JOIN HUGO, MANNY, THE FAMILY FROM OHIO, AND Ben in the dining room for the formal evening, the men dressed in black suits—with the exception of Hugo in red velvet—and the women in evening gowns. I've been to my fair share of charity gala events with Krystal, organized by her law firm, so I'm no stranger to the glitz, glamour, and over-the-top bullshit.

"Evening, everyone," I say while pushing Riles's chair in for her before taking my seat.

"Long time no see," Hugo says, raising his glass of wine.

I acknowledge him with a friendly nod then turn to Ben, ready to ask him what he's been up to.

His jaw slackens, his eyes greedily devouring Riles. "You lucky—"

"Don't," I warn.

"But—"

"Don't."

He drops his hand to his lap, cups his junk, and rearranges it.

"Will you control yourself?" I hiss under my breath. "You're not fifteen."

He quivers and neighs like a horse before waving a waiter down. "Give me the strongest drink you've got. I'm gonna need it. And anything else for these fine people here."

Impressed he didn't say something along the lines of "And get these bastards a drink too," I inform the waiter I'd like a beer, then rest my hand on Ben's shoulder, thanking him for his generosity with a squeeze. "So what'd you get up to today?"

"Buried myself balls-deep."

I remove my hand. "Charming."

"That's me. Prince effing Charming."

"You're not Prince Charming!" the Ohio daughter exclaims. "You're too fat."

"Avery!" her mother scolds. "Don't be rude."

Ben points at the girl. "So are y—"

I punch his thigh, eyes wide and piercing.

"Motherf—!" He frowns at me, then shoots Avery a challenging smile. "So are *youuu*... going to draw me a picture of what Prince Charming *does* look like?"

"Yes." She flips over a page of her sketchbook and begins scribbling like a little maniac. "And he won't look like you."

Ben pokes his tongue out at her, and she returns the gesture.

"Sooo," Riles says, glaring at Ben before turning toward Avery's mother. "Have you enjoyed the cruise so far, Kathy?"

"I didn't like Greenland. It smelled fishy, and there were too many bugs and dogs. Dirty place, really."

"Oh, that's a shame. I loved Greenland. I got to fly over a glacier, which I'm still pinching myself over." Riles unfolds her napkin and lays it across her lap. "I agree with you about the bugs though, and I'm sure Riley does too. He ingested some."

"Not voluntarily," I add.

"You weren't the only one," Hugo says. "Manny ate a few too."

"A few? More like a few hundred." He takes a long sip of his wine. "I can still taste them."

Yeah, you and me both, buddy.

"So what's everyone's plans in Reykjavik tomorrow?" Riles asks.

"We're taking a tour to the Strokkur geyser," Kathy says, her eyes scanning the dining room for a waiter. "By bus. I hope it has heating."

Her son mumbles, "Boring."

I'd like to tell him there are many not-so-fortunate children around the globe who wouldn't find the things he does "boring," but I don't. The ungrateful little shit will learn that lesson at some point.

"We're spending the day in the city," Hugo offers. "What about you?"

"Riley and I are going to the Blue Lagoon," Riles says. "I can't wait. It's supposed to be stunning."

"Oh, it is. We visited there the last time we were in Iceland. Smells awful, but you get used to it after a while."

Manny wrinkles his nose. "Awful is putting it mildly."

Great! Sounds like will be visiting Satan's ass.

Riles winces. "Thanks for the warning."

Our drinks arrive in no time, so I lift my glass at Ben. "What about you? What are your plans for tomorrow?"

"I have tickets to the Iceland and Team USA FIBA friendly."

"No shit? In Reykjavik?" I prompt.

"Yeah."

My sports-loving heart deflates. I'd much rather see that than a smelly lagoon.

"Is DeRozan on the USA roster this year?" Riles asks.

"He is, love."

"I like him. Great player."

"You would say that. He's almost a bigger ball hog than MJ."

"Ben," she chastises through a sigh, "are we really going to do this again?"

He lifts his drink and winks at her. "Yes, love, we are."

"Are you sure?"

"I am."

She sighs again. "Fine. Answer me this. Who was the best team during MJ's reign?"

He scoffs. "The Bulls, of course. But that doesn't make MJ the GOAT."

"I'm not finished." She raises her finger, silencing him. "Who was the best team during Kobe's reign?"

"Lakers."

"Correct." She leans forward, her pretty eyes intense. "And who is the best team during LeBron's reign?"

Ben opens his mouth but then closes it again, eyes narrowed.

"That's right—the Warriors." She leans back in her seat again, sips her Cosmo, then elegantly places it on the table. "Does Lebron play for the Warriors, pray tell? No, he doesn't."

I smirk; she's got him.

"LeBron is the GOAT," the Ohio teenage son mumbles.

"See?" Ben snaps his fingers at him. "Even the kid knows his shit."

"Hey, Zach," Riles says. "Do you know who Kareem Abdul-Jabar is?"

He looks up from his screen and shrugs.

She picks up her glass, sips her Cosmo once more, and mumbles, "I rest my case."

"You rest nothing, love. No one born this century knows who Kareem is."

"But someone 'who knows their shit' would, and clearly, Riles knows her shit."

Ben snaps his head to me. "Whose side are you on?"

"Hers." I drape my arm over the back of Riles's chair, purposely cementing my choice.

He scoffs. "Yeah. I can see why."

"Okay," Hugo announces, clapping his hands together. "Let's change the subject."

"Yes. Let's do that." Kathy massages her temple. "All this talk of basketball gives me a headache."

"I'm hungry," Zach whines.

His father glares at the waitstaff. "That's because they're taking their sweet time."

"I agree," Kathy says, elevating her ass off the seat as is she's preparing to tackle a waiter.

Just when I think this dinner couldn't possibly get any funnier, Avery lifts her drawing of a stick figure with an enormous crown and shoves it toward Ben. "That's Prince Charming. Not you."

He grins at her. "Kid, I have a big crown too."

I facepalm. *Jesus!*

"You do not," Avery argues.

"Do so."

"Princes are handsome and rich. You're not."

"I fucking am."

"Ben!" we all cry.

"What?" he murmurs, sulking. "I am!"

AFTER OUR DINING SESSION ENDS, RILES AND I MAKE our way through the atrium and past groups of photographers posing passengers in front of ritzy, painted backdrops as if they're members of the royal family.

"Those poor kids," she says, pointing at one of the setups. "They look as stiff as boards."

"I'm more worried about the father. I don't think he's breathing."

She giggles and grabs my arm. "Let's get our formal photo taken. We can act snobby and pretentious."

Reluctantly allowing her to drag me to the spot next in line, I cringe at the fake chandelier and grand staircase props. "This is stupid, Riles."

"I know!"

"So why are we doing it?"

"Ease up, *Riley*. It'll be fun."

"Fun?" I point to the nearly-passed-out father. "He doesn't look like he's having fun."

She ignores me, her voice posh. "If only I had my tiara and a glass of Chardonnay."

"You have a tiara?" I ask, confused.

"No!" She blinks her pretty lashes at me. "Do I look like I own a tiara?"

I eye her up and down. "Yeah, you kinda do."

Playfully scowling, she once again drags me forward when we're called for our portrait.

"Good evening," the photographer says. "Please, have a seat, ma'am." He ushers Riles to a stool and positions her, slightly angled, her knees pressed together, her hands neatly resting on her lap. "And you, sir, stand behind her and place your hand on her shoulder."

I do as I'm told, feeling outright ridiculous.

"Excellent! Very nice." He snaps a few shots and then checks his screen. "Now, ma'am, raise your right hand and place it over his. Yes, like that. And now look up over your shoulder and into his eyes. And you, sir, lean forward and look into her eyes too."

For fuck's sake. Does anyone actually buy these stupid portraits?

Awkwardly bending down, I lock eyes with Riles.

"Perfect!" the photographer says.

Riles blinks rapidly, her face tense and strained as if she can smell something unpleasant. I sniff, but all I can smell is her perfume.

Her nose wrinkles.

My eye twitches.

A snorty crackling sound bursts from her throat, much like a pinched balloon releasing air.

"What the hell was that?" I ask, jerking back.

She clutches her waist and bursts out with the laughter she'd been desperately trying to contain. "You look constipated."

"I feel constipated," I say through gritted teeth, "leaning over like this. This pose is unnatural."

Fanning her face, she wipes tears from her eyes and puffs out a breath. "Okay. I'm sorry. Let's try that again."

"Do we have to?"

"Yes!"

"Then stop laughing so we can get it done already."

"I'm sorry! I just... I can't keep a straight face. We must look ridiculous."

"You think?"

Glancing down at her once more, I attempt to remain poker-faced while her mouth spasms, her brow bunching as she fights her pending hysterics.

"Don't laugh," I whisper, trying not to move my lips.

Her balloon-like screech slowly bubbles in her throat again.

"Don't."

It grows louder and higher, and I can't hold my composure any longer, both of us bursting into laughter, Riles nearly falling off her seat.

"I can't," she says, gasping for air.

Bracing her in my arms, I hold onto her as she cackles like a hyena. "Clearly."

"I'm sorry."

The photographer waves his camera at us. "Try dipping her."

In what... ketchup?

I frown at him. "She's not a french fry."

"Dip," he insists. "Like a dance." Nodding, pleased with his recommendation, he tries to demonstrate by throwing his head back a few times, twitching like a zombie.

I stare at him in disbelief and murmur, "What dance does he want us to do... 'Thriller'?"

"No." Riles giggles. "One of those romantic dips you see on movie posters."

"Why?"

"Why not, I guess." She guides my arm behind her back and clasps my other hand. "Are you ready?"

I grunt. "As ready as I'll ever be."

She goes to lean back but pauses. "Don't you dare drop me."

A devilish grin stretches my face. "Never."

"I mean it!"

"I won't. Just.... Let's just get this over and done with already."

Dipping her a fraction, my eyes chasing hers, I deliberately let her fall a tiny bit before securing her again.

"Riley!" she squeals, nearly crushing my hand with hers.

"Jesus." I chuckle. "I won't. I promise. I've got you."

She shoots me a menacing look, then relaxes, so I lower her again, this time slowly and steadily, her head falling back, my spread fingers supporting her nape. The skin of her collarbone glitters in the light—perfect, smooth, no doubt delicious. I stare at it, wondering how it would taste, and if I did press my lips to her skin, would I be able to remove them again?

All humor and antics dissolve, my heart pounding at an unnatural speed.

"Uh... Riley?"

"Yeah?" I reply, still staring at her delectable skin.

She lifts her head, neck strained. "I think we're done."

Shit!

I'm tempted to seize the opportunity while she's helplessly trapped in my arms by kissing her as I did in the theatre, but despite what my mind and body want, I don't do it. She might kick, scream, and cause a scene. And the last thing I want is to erase the progress we've made.

Lifting her enough for my mouth to graze her earlobe, I nudge her neck with the tip of my nose and whisper, "We're done... for now."

She gasps ever so slightly, her fingertips biting into my forearms as I spin her onto both feet again, her chest rising and falling as she smooths the satin of her dress down her thighs.

"Excellent!" The photographer claps. "Good dip, yes?"

Riles touches her ear, her cheeks rosy, her eyes ghosting mine. "Yes. A very good dip."

He hands her a ticket. "You take this to the gallery."

"Thank you. I will."

"You're not seriously going to buy one of those portraits, are you?" I ask her, stepping aside for the next lot of dummies to pose.

She cocks her shoulder and hugs the ticket to her chest. "I might."

Chuckling, because she probably will, I ask, "Where to next?" hoping it's back to the cabin, or somewhere private at least.

Riles fixes the lapels of my jacket, slots the ticket into my breast pocket, and links her arm with mine. "I made a reservation today at a bar on the top deck. Thought it would be nice to have a quiet drink before seeing the Northern Lights. Care to join me?"

What feels like a mild current of electricity jolts through my body. It's been so long since I've walked with a woman on my arm. That sense of pride, purpose, and possession.

I grin. "Lead the way."

"It involves an elevator ride," she taunts.

"I'm sure I can handle it."

She grips my arm tighter. "I'm sure you can too."

We make our way to the top floor, and I barely notice the walls caving in, my mind at ease with Riles by my side.

"What did you mean by 'we're done, for now' exactly?" she asks as the doors slide open and we exit.

I side-eye her, thrilled my promise is lodged in her head. "I meant that, when you're ready to kiss me again, it'll happen."

She stops at the entrance of the bar, her stare trained dead ahead. "What makes you think I'll be ready to kiss you again?"

As I did downstairs, I lean in, graze my lips against her earlobe, and nudge her neck with the tip of my nose.

She gasps.

"That," I whisper.

"You think my shock indicates I want to kiss you?"

"I do."

"That's rather presumptuous."

"Is it?"

Chewing the inside of her cheek, she lets go of my arm and explains to the front-of-house crewmember that she has a reservation. We're then shown to a lounge, my hand happily resting on the small of her back until she takes a seat in a high-backed velvet wing chair.

"This is lovely," she says, wiggling her ass on the cushion.

I remove my jacket, drape it over the arm of my seat, and roll up my shirtsleeves as she scoops up the menu and studies the list, her tongue darting out and wetting her lips.

"Oooh! I know what I'm having."

I suppress a groan and sit, resting my ankle over my knee. "What's that?"

"The peanut butter cocktail. Yum!" She leans across the small table between us and hands me the menu. "How about you?"

Scanning what's on offer, I opt for something strong. I'm gonna need it if I'm to respectfully keep my hands to myself. "An Old Fashioned."

"Are you?" she asks, lips pursed as she crosses her legs.

"Am I what?"

"Old-fashioned?"

I admire the curves—hers and the chair's. "With some things, yes. With other things, no."

Her brow hitches.

I smirk. "You seem shocked."

"Oh, believe me, I'm not. You definitely give off both vibes."

"How so?"

"I don't know." She moves her hand to her hair and twirls a loose tendril with her finger. "You just *seem* old-fashioned, but you also don't."

"In what way?"

Our waiter arrives, so she lets go of her hair, appearing relieved for the interruption. "Can we order an Old Fashioned and a Peanut Butter Mudslide, please?" she asks.

"Certainly. Whiskey or bourbon?"

Riles snatches up the menu and reads over it again, confused.

"Whiskey," I insert.

He scans our lanyards and leaves.

"I was worried for a moment," she says, setting down the menu. "I thought he meant *my* cocktail was the one with either bourbon or whiskey. Yuck. Thank God it was yours." She winces.

I nod.

She smiles nervously.

I smirk.

"Sooo..." Her pretty eyes divert from mine to scan the room. "This bar is lovely."

I rub my beard, enjoying that I've made her nervous... in a good way. "You said that already."

"Did I?" She uncrosses her legs and then recrosses them.

I nod again.

"Well, it is." She points up. "Look at that sunset."

Arcing my head back, orange hues illuminate the sky beyond the glass-domed ceiling above, ornate pendant lights hanging from mirrored beams separating the many windows curving around us.

I have to agree with her; the bar is impressive—nineteenth-century décor with a modern twist. But I'm more concerned with the response she never gave me.

My eyes meet hers again. "You're avoiding my question."

"What question?"

"About how you think I'm *not* old-fashioned."

Her mouth quirks. "Oh yes, that."

"Well?"

She twirls her hair again. "Well... you just seem not old-fashioned too."

I chuckle. "Come on, Riles. You're a publisher. You can do better with words than that."

Huffing, she relents. "Fine. If you must know, you seem old-fashioned because you respect the simple things in life. And you're kind, caring, mostly well-mannered—"

"Mostly?" I interrupt, pretending to be offended.

"Yes, mostly. You're... chivalrous, I guess, but you're also unabashed, impudent, and... liberal."

Regretting telling her to use her "publisher" vocabulary, I have no idea what she means, so I just go with it. "And that's a bad thing?"

"No, I never said that. There's nothing *bad* about you."

I grin like the Cheshire cat. "Nothing? Is that because you *care* about me more than you should?"

She squirms in her seat.

"What did you mean by that, exactly?" I ask, throwing her question back at her.

She straightens her shoulders. "What did *you* mean by it? You said it too."

"I did."

"And?"

"I asked you first."

"Really, Riley? How old are you?"

"I told you already. Thirty-six."

She rolls her eyes and cub growls.

"I like when you do that."

"Do what?"

"Growl like an adorable baby lion."

Our waiter delivers our drinks, but I don't let him distract her, my stare intently fixed on her exasperated eyes. "Just tell me what you meant, Riles."

"I meant exactly what I said," she murmurs before taking a sip of her milkshake-looking drink. "I care about you more than I should."

"Then let me kiss you again."

Sighing, she places her drink on the table. "It's not a good idea."

"Why not?"

"I told you already. You're getting a divorce."

I lean forward and pick up my whiskey. "I am, but what's that got to do with it?"

"Divorce is emotionally taxing. I don't want to add to that."

Her concern over my mental wellbeing is sweet—I can't deny that—but it shouldn't deter her from "caring" more than she should.

"You're right," I say, reclining into my chair. "It is emotionally taxing. The past two years have been some of the hardest of my life." I swirl my drink, watching the ice cubes circulate within the glass. "But for the first time since everything went to shit, I know I can move on from Krystal. To be honest, I already have. I wasn't ready to accept that before, but I am now."

"Why?"

"Because of you."

"Me?" She cocks her head. "But how can you honestly think that? We don't know each other."

"I wouldn't say that."

"Riley, it has barely been a week."

"A lot can happen in a week."

"I know, but—"

"Fine. You think you don't know me? Ask me anything. What do you want to know?"

"I-I...." She blinks as if it's a stupid solution.

It's not.

"Ask me whatever," I prompt. "That's how it works."

"I know how it works," she deadpans.

"Then fire away. I'm an open book." I wink. "And you like books."

Smiling somewhat sarcastically at me, she crosses her arms over her chest. "Okay. Why are you getting a divorce?"

My gut twists, but if I'm to have a chance with Riles, I need to share the details of my life that I don't want to share. The pain, the anger, the shame. I need to be weak to be strong. "Because my wife cheated on me with her work colleague."

Her jaw drops before she quickly collects her drink again. "That's horrible. I'm so sorry."

"Don't be," I say, burying my resentment. "It's water off a duck's back."

"I hardly think so."

I take a swig of my drink, enjoying the burn as the whiskey slides down my throat. "What I mean is it's for the best. Krystal and I were over before she hooked up with Finn. I just didn't see that at the time."

"Still, that's far from water off a duck's back."

I shrug. "You're right. But I have to forgive and forget to move forward. And I can't do that if I'm constantly bitter about it all."

Nodding, Riles delicately sucks her straw into her mouth, her cheeks sinking into her face as her eyes look from left to right, right to left.

Her awkwardness is amusing, and while I like it, I also want her to feel comfortable.

"What else do you want to know?" I ask.

She swallows, licks her lips, then subtly wipes her mouth. "Do you still love her?"

"No."

"No? But you were together for so long."

"I loved my childhood sweetheart, but she no longer exists. That woman died when our daughter died."

Riles chokes, and for a second, I fear she's consumed her straw. "You okay?"

"Your daughter—" She coughs and thumps her chest with her fist. "—passed away?"

"Yes. Imogen."

Her eyes flick to my arm, to where my sweet girl will forever be inked on my skin.

I glance down at my tattoo as well. "She died before she was born."

Reaching over the table, Riles takes my hand in hers, squeezes it gently, and whispers, "When?"

"Four years ago." I stare at her hand, my mind wandering to the dark recesses that store my pain for my daughter, a void I slip into at any time, any place.

"Jesus, Riley, I'm... I'm so sorry. For you and for Krystal." She sets her glass down, stands, then carefully lowers her ass onto my lap, her arms encasing me in a sweet hug. "Do you want to talk about her?"

Surprised by her bold move, but also appreciating her comfort, I hug her to me and murmur, "Not now. But I will, eventually."

"Okay." She kisses my head much like I did hers when she told me about her mother. "Whenever you're ready, I'm here for you. To listen. To shout at. Whatever you need." She pulls back, rubs my shoulder, and then retakes her seat.

The sentiment squeezes my heart, and a damn tear escapes my eye. I swipe it away, mumbling, "Thanks."

Although painful, I want to break the ice around my heart and tell her more. I want to tell her I did everything I could for my ex-wife and that my everything wasn't enough. That I can fix a broken table but not my marriage. But those details can wait. Saying Imogen's name out loud was hard enough.

"What's your favorite color?" she asks.

I shake my head, caught off guard. "My favorite color?"

"Yeah." Her cheeks lift into a timid smile. "You said I could ask you anything."

Knowing she's deliberately steering the conversation for my benefit, I smile too, my eyes catching on her dress, shimmering in the dim light. "Purple." I tilt my glass at her. "*That* purple."

Her lip quirks. "Liar."

"I'm not. It's the prettiest color I've ever seen."

"Uh-huh."

I clear my throat. "How about you? What's your favorite color? No. Wait. Let me guess. Green?"

"What makes you say that?"

"Your bag, suitcase, and most of your underwear are green."

Her back straightens. "You went through my underwear?"

"No." I raise my hands, chuckling. "I opened drawers to find an empty one."

She narrows her eyes suspiciously. "Fine. Yes, my favorite color is green."

"I especially liked the pale lacy ones."

"Riley!"

We spend the next couple of hours talking about anything and everything—movies, music, food, and growing up. We have similar tastes in most things and are polar opposites with others, but what stands out most is our shared grief. We can communicate it, communicate around it, and not once is that communication coerced, forced, or awkward. Talking with Riles is effortless, therapeutic, and enjoyable.

After what feels like a lifetime but also no time at all, Captain Katarina makes an announcement that the Aurora Borealis may soon be visible, so we leave the bar and head out on deck to a quiet spot at the stern of the ship, the wind sharp and bitterly cold, like tiny shards of ice piercing my skin.

Shivering, Riles rubs her bare arms as she leans over the railing a fraction to see the ship's wake. "So this is what Rose saw on the *Titanic* before she climbed over."

I remove my jacket and drape it over her shoulders. "Want me to hang you over the edge for a more realistic experience?"

"Thank you." She slips her arms into the sleeves. "And no thank you. I'll stay right where I am. Rose was a crazy bitch."

"I could draw you naked if you'd prefer?"

She turns to face me and wraps my jacket across her chest. "Are you any good?"

"Let's go back to the room, and we can find out."

I'm no fucking Picasso, but I'd pretend to be if it resulted in her naked and lying on our sofa.

"Riley, it isn't a good id—"

Stepping closer, I tilt her chin upward with my finger. "Look up."

She complies, then gasps at the green veils of light rippling through the starlit sky. "Wow! It's…. I've never seen anything like it. It's beautiful."

Her eyes dip to mine again and then lower to my lips, my body tingling at the unspoken invitation. It's now or never. A moment you seize or stupidly let pass by. I'm not a stupid man, so I slide my hand to the back of her neck and press my mouth to hers, her breath warm and sweet as she exhales and relaxes into me, her hands gliding up my back before gripping my shirt.

Warmth rockets from my toes to my head, and I groan, kissing her like I did the first time, softly to begin with, my tongue gently lapping at hers, my arms holding her to me.

Riles moans and pulls back, and just when I think she's going to object, she sucks in a ragged breath and tugs my head back to hers, our kiss now frenzied, our mouths nipping and hungry.

"Fuuuck," I growl, trailing my lips down her neck and back up again, the taste of vanilla, peanut butter, and Riles making me wild.

My greedy hands creep underneath my jacket, sliding across the satin on her back before dipping to her ass, her cheeks firm but supple. I clench my fingers, and she inhales sharply, gripping me tighter as she lifts her leg and presses it against my hip, my hand moving to her thigh and holding it in place.

"Mommy, Mommy! Look at the pretty lights," a little girl says in the distance.

Panting, Riles breaks away from me faster than a speeding bullet and palms my chest, her breasts rising and falling, her eyes scanning the deck for where the interruption came from.

Pissed but also fucking thrilled, I hug her to me and kiss the top of her head.

I knew it!

Her lips against mine once again shifted the earth on its axis.

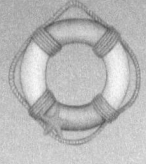

chapter nineteen

RILES

Sweet mother of passionate lip-locking!

Slowing my racing heart, I snuggle into Riley's chest, delighting in his scent and body heat. Delighting in simply being in a man's arms again. I can't remember the last time I felt the way I feel now, able to count on one hand the men I've been intimate with. Men I've shared more than a bed with. Men I've cried over while throwing their toothbrush in the trash. And yet none of them felt like this... like a home I never knew I had.

Turning in his arms, I face the stern again as he hugs me under the mystical skies above. Thank God a family joined us for the spectacular view, because without their interruption, I don't think I would've had the strength to stop when we did.

And we needed to stop.

He nudges my neck with his nose, his breath hot against my ear. "Was that kiss *incredible* too?"

I smirk. "Yes."

"Good. We're on the same page then."

Grasping the railing, I clench it tight, needing it for balance, my legs trembling. His hands glide across my waist, tugging me to him, his erection pressing into the apex of my ass.

I bite my lip. "And what page is that?"

"The page where we see where this leads."

Mesmerized by the twinkling stars and verdant glow, a palpable magic fills the air, a magic I can't ignore, because moments like these happen for a reason. "Are you sure that's what you want?" I whisper. "You've been through a lot. And you're still working through—"

"Never been surer."

I draw in a deep breath then let it out again, wanting to believe him. But what he shared with his ex-wife—their many years together, the loss of a child—none of that goes away in the blink of an eye, no matter how hard you try to bury it out of anger.

"Stop, Riles," he says, resting his head on my shoulder.

"Stop what?"

"Stop filling your head with negatives."

"Negatives are important."

"So are positives."

A memory of Mom, standing in our living room with a box full of my stepfather's things, bursts into my mind.

"Why aren't you mad?" I asked, sad and angry enough for us both. "He can't just up and leave like this."

"He's not just upping and leaving, Riley. We've grown apart. It happens."

I pressed my head against the window and looked out at the street below. "I don't understand."

Mom set down the box and took a seat on the ledge beside me. "I'm not mad because I choose not to be. Life goes on, darling. It twists and turns, and we must twist and turn with it. If we don't, we end up staying still, miserable and bitter." She rubbed my leg. "Gary and I don't want that for each other. We want to move on and be happy, and we can't if we're holding on to the negatives."

I pulled my leg closer and hugged it to my chest. "It's not fair."

"It's not a question of whether it's fair. It's about saying goodbye to what was and being brave enough to welcome what else may be."

"Okay," I say, my voice barely audible.

"Okay?"

I turn my head and search his face. "Let's see where this leads. But we take this slow. Because I—"

He kisses my temple, his delicious lips stealing my words. "As slow as you need."

I roll onto my back, desperate to keep my eyes shut, memories of Riley and me cuddling on a lounge chair under the Northern Lights a dream I don't want to wake up from. A dream that was reality.

Against my better judgement, I'd given in, helpless not to, and we kissed again, a kiss I could still feel to my core. We snuggled together in silence under the ethereal sky, and after neither of us could endure the bitter chill of the arctic air any longer, we returned to the cabin, kissed each other goodnight, and then fell asleep in our respective beds.

He never argued that request. Never pushed for more. And that only enforced his growing stronghold on my heart.

Sighing, I feel his lips on mine, a splendid recollection, until his tongue delicately grazes my teeth.

My eyes shoot open, my hands landing on his chest, shoving him back. "What—"

"Morning, sweetheart."

"What are you doing?" I shriek, blinking all the blinks.

"Continuing where we left off last night." He leans forward again.

"No!" I hold him at bay and cover my mouth with my hand, mumbling, "I haven't brushed my teeth yet."

"I know." He chuckles. "I could taste your morning breath."

"Riley!"

Scooting back onto my elbows, I glare at him, my annoyance dissipating when he presents a steaming mug of coffee.

"I ordered room service for breakfast," he says.

"Oh." I sit up, pleasantly surprised as I take the mug from him and cradle it in my palms. "Thank you."

"Did you sleep well?"

Eyeing him over the rim, I gently blow the steam before taking a welcoming sip. "I did."

He comfortably lounges across my bed and props his head in his hand. "I mustn't have snored."

"How do you know that?"

He grins, all teeth, perfectly straight and pearlescent. "Because you didn't use your AirPods."

Reaching up to my ear, I feel their absence. "You're right. I completely forgot to put them in."

"That Aurora Borealis is some magical shit."

Laughing, I can't disagree. Last night was transcendental.

"Hurry up," he says, bounding up from the bed before placing down a breakfast tray with eggs, bacon, and pancakes. "I need to buy us new swimsuits before we leave for the Blue Lagoon."

"What time is it?" I flick my wrist and read my watch.

"You have an hour."

"An hour?" I kick off my comforter. "That's not long enough to get ready and do my makeup."

"Eat your breakfast, Riles," he says, reaching over the bed and snagging my arm, pulling me back down to sit. "You don't need to paint that pretty face of yours. It's perfect the way it is."

I touch my blushing cheeks. "Thank you, but I don't *paint* my face for the likes of you... or anyone else for that matter." Which is a lie, because Georgia insists on a full face of makeup in the office, which has become an expensive habit. "I *paint* it for me. Because I like to, and because it makes me feel good."

He raises his hands. "You can do what you want. All I'm saying is you're stunning with or without it."

Unable to suppress my smile, I lift the fork from the plate and stab a piece of bacon. "I know!"

He belly-laughs.

"What?" I ask, frowning.

"Nothing. I like your confidence. It's sexy."

A little vexed, I grumble. "Confidence shouldn't be about sex appeal, Riley. It should be about self-worth and appreciation. If more women uplifted themselves instead of trying to live up to what others subjugate, their world would be a much better place." I slide the bacon off my fork with my teeth and mumble, "I'm not 'stunning' because you think I'm sexy. I'm 'stunning' because I know my self-worth."

"Whatever you say," he says, booping my nose with the tip of his finger. "Nevertheless, you're still sexy."

Swiping his hand away, I scarf my breakfast and almost choke when he walks to the closet and wrenches his boxer shorts down, his delicious bare ass gloriously spotlit by the morning sun streaming in though the balcony window.

A cough bursts from my throat, so I pound my chest with my fist, praying I dislodge the piece of bacon now stuck there.

"You okay?" he asks, leaning back and smirking as he peers out from behind the closet door.

"Yes!" I slam my eyes shut and raise my hand at him. "I'm fine. Stay there."

"Why? I can perform the Heimlich maneuver if you need me to."

"No! What I need is for you to get some pants on."

"What's wrong? I thought you were an advocate of confidence," he taunts.

"I am. But there's confidence, and then there's—" I swirl my finger, hoping I'm pointing in his direction. "—that."

Continuing to shade my eyeballs in darkness to protect my we-take-this-slow approach, my spiraling finger suddenly jabs his rock-hard... chest. I splay my hand. *Yes, that's his chest.*

"What are you doing?" I shriek, retracting my hand.

He grabs my wrist and splays my fingers on his abdomen, warmth surging from his skin to my palm, igniting my core. "I'm being confident."

"Stop it!"

"Open your eyes," he murmurs, his voice as rough as gravel.

Desperately trying not to peek, I clench my eyelids more firmly together. "No!"

"You won't regret it."

I sure as shit will... or won't. Damn it! A teeny, tiny peek won't hurt, surely?

Swallowing heavily, I slowly pry one eye open to where he stands before me, shirtless and in a pair of shorts, a grin so roguish the devil would blush.

Frustration sizzles along my cheeks, and I want to stab him with my fork, stab and then take a delectable bite.

"You're not yet ready for all of me, sweetheart, especially *that* part."

You delicious, arrogant son of a bitch!

I'm about to tell him he's a jerk, when he raises my hand to his lips and kisses my knuckles. "Slow and steady, remember? I won't push you to where you're not willing to go."

How sweet.

He cups his crotch and winks. "That part can wait."

How... obnoxious!

Rising to my feet, I slide my hands up his chest and into his hair, tugging lightly to expose his neck, my tongue trailing along his skin. "Can it?"

He shudders.

"I guess it can," I say, letting him go before sashaying to the bathroom.

Two can play at this game. And what a fun game it is!

After buying new bathing suits, we exited the ship and boarded a tour bus before journeying to the Blue Lagoon—a manmade geothermal oasis set amongst a lava field, and arguably Iceland's most popular tourist attraction.

"It looks like blue milk," Riley says as we stand by the edge of the vast, picturesque pool, steam billowing from the surface.

Holding my cell horizontally, I snap a few photos. "It does, but I can assure you it's not milk. It's surplus water from a nearby power station."

"So we're about to bathe in radioactive juice?"

"No!" I laugh and turn toward him. "Didn't you listen to the tour guide when he explained the water is made up of silica, algae, and other minerals?"

"Oh great! So I'm soaking in bacteria today?" Riley wrinkles his nose, then covers it with his arm, mumbling, "Hugo and Manny were right. This place stinks."

"It's the sulfur. And no, you're not soaking in bacteria. This water is good for you."

He scoffs. "Yeah, sounds like it."

"Come on," I say, sliding my hand into his, enjoying the feeling of our entwined fingers. "We have to shower before we can go in."

His eyebrows hitch. "Shower... together?"

"Not exactly."

His eyebrows plummet. "What's that supposed to mean?"

"*You* have to shower, naked, with other men."

Riley digs his heels into the rocky ground. "*That* is not going to happen."

I let go of his hand and clasp his stubbly cheeks. "I thought you were confident with your body."

"I am."

"Then you've got nothing to worry about." I give him a quick peck on the lips, then skip past him. "I'll see you back here in a minute. And hurry up! We've only got a couple of hours before we have to leave again."

Scuttling into the changing room, I snicker to myself for telling Riley he had to shower naked in front of other men. He doesn't, although nudity is embraced by Nordic culture, so I'm not surprised when I find women of various ages, shapes, and sizes hygienically washing in their birthday suits.

Craning my neck, I seek out a cubicle, only to find them all occupied with people waiting their turn.

Peanut butter!

Knowing that if I wait too, I'll be longer than the minute I gave Riley, and he'd no doubt use it against me in his infuriating adorable way. So, throwing caution to the wind, I step into the communal shower. *Screw it!* I'm in Iceland, and Mom wanted me to try new things. Perhaps this wasn't what she had in mind, but... oh well. *You only live once!*

Embracing my newfound bravery, I prop my bag against the wall, strip off my sweats and underwear, and turn the shower on, my nipples beading in the fresh air. Embarrassed, I quickly cover them with my arms, then just as quickly follow the hilarious washing guide on the wall that instructs you on how to thoroughly clean your head, armpits, feet, and hoo-hah. It also suggests you cover your hair with conditioner and keep it out of the water to prevent damage, so I do as suggested and pile it atop my head.

Resembling Pebbles from *The Flintstones*, I thread my new bathing suit on, mildly irritated at the string bikini Riley insisted on choosing because he was paying for it.

In all honesty, I probably would've picked it anyway, because it's green, and the only other choices were a multicolored one-piece or a white bikini with a push-up top. Riley liked that one too, but I lied and told him it was too big.

He unequivocally assured me I was wrong.

I'd growled at him.

Collecting my towel and clothing, I place them in my rental locker and scan the electronic wristband I was given when we arrived, and then I scurry out to the lagoon, slowing my stride when I spot Riley dipping his toe into the water, his long legs lean and muscular, his new black swim trunks shorter than the previous pair, accentuating his well-defined thighs. He rubs his chin as if he's still unsure about the mineral components of the pool and then turns toward me, lips lifting when his eyes find mine.

I perform a catwalk spin for him and laugh. "How was it?"

"If I tell you, you might knee me in the balls."

"Why?" I laugh. "What happened?"

"Well, when you're a man and see something you like, your junk transforms—"

"What?" I shriek, covering my mouth with my hand. "You got an erection in the changing room?"

He rears back. "What the fuck, Riles? No! What are you talking about?"

"What are you talking about?"

"Your sexy spin thing you just did."

Staring at him dumbfounded, I erupt with laughter and facepalm. "I meant how was the changing room?"

"Not *that* good. Jesus!" His eyes rake my body, and I suddenly feel more naked than I was moments ago. "I picked good." He tugs a string at my hip, so I slap his hand away.

"Did you shower naked in front of everyone?" I ask, my smile cheeky.

"No, I didn't."

"I did!"

He holds me at arm's length, his expression perplexed.

"You seem shocked," I say, much like he does to me.

"I am."

"I guess I'm feeling brave today."

He grazes his knuckle down my arm, soft and sweet. "You are brave. Braver than you know."

Shivering at his touch, I collect his hand in mine. "I'm slowly figuring that out."

He lips feather mine, and I melt into him as I stretch up to my tiptoes and drape my arms over his shoulders, deepening the kiss, the friction of his skin heating my body much like the volcanic activity surrounding us.

Knowing I'll erupt if we don't stop, I pull back and ask, "Are you ready to be healed and rejuvenated?"

He rubs his chin. "I'm still not convinced that's water."

"Be brave."

"If I grow a third leg, I'm blaming you."

I flick my eyes to his shorts, then back up again. "I thought you already had one."

Riley neighs like a horse, and I double over with laughter.

"Oh my God! Please don't do that. I'm equinophobic, remember?" I tease.

"Don't you mean Benophobic?"

"Yeah... that."

Galloping forward, he tugs me to follow, and we're soon walking hand in hand across the boardwalk and over a wooden footbridge to a quieter spot in the lagoon.

"Wow!" I gasp, carefully descending the manmade steps into the pool before lowering myself into the fetid yet luxuriously balmy water. "It's so warm and... silky." I submerge to my shoulders, twirling with elation. "I can't believe I'm here. This place is surreal."

Riley pauses on the last step before letting go of the railing and tentatively walking toward me. "Why's the ground squishy?"

"It's silica mud."

"Are you sure I'm not going to turn into a Teenage Mutant Ninja Turtle?"

I giggle. "I'm sure. Although..."

He pauses again. "Although what?"

"Try not to get your hair wet."

"Why?"

"Because it might snap off."

"What?"

"I'm kidding... kinda."

Raking my fingers through the velvety water, I wade to a spot underneath the bridge and crouch down. "I've always wanted to visit here. One of the cover designers at work is from Iceland, and she told me about this place. She said locals don't tend to come here, but tourists love it."

He ducks down too. "Smells like ass, but I can see the appeal."

Taking a deep breath, I attempt to regulate the sulfur scent.

"Did you just willingly breathe in the ass-air?"

"No. I mean, yes. I mean, I'm trying to get used to it."

"And how's that working out for you?"

I exhale harshly through my nose. "It's not."

Chuckling, he inches toward me, his laughter dying off, his pupils dilating. My body instantly reacts, tingling as I swirl around him, his lascivious stare peppering my skin with goose bumps. The luxurious water, the steam, the exotic atmosphere... it's incredibly sensual and like nothing I've ever experienced, especially with a man I'm wildly attracted to. The setting is both alluring and somewhat nerve-wracking.

Kneeling before me, he reaches out and threads his fingers through mine, gently tugging me closer until I'm flush with his chest. "Hey," he murmurs, voice low.

"Hey." I bite my lip and rest my hands on his shoulders, studying the hard and soft edges of his face, his youthful yet weathered skin, the gleam in his eyes, and the kindness of his inquisitive smile.

"You want to kiss me again, don't you?"

Dipping my head, I say, "Yes," then slide my fingers into his hair and press my lips to his, the temperature of my body once again matching our geothermal environment.

His hands creep up my back, holding me firm, his tongue sweeping mine. I grip his hair, then suddenly rear back, realizing what I've just done, my arms shooting into the air. "Oh no! I just contaminated your hair."

"I don't care." He palms my shoulder and urges me close again.

"But it's.... Apparently, it's really damag—"

"Touch whatever you want to touch." He playfully waggles his brows then slides his hands down my back, cups my ass, and guides my legs around his waist.

I wince, fearing he'll regret his decision, but I don't argue, because holy moly his body pressed to mine feels exquisite. "Don't blame me if you end up looking like Edward Scissorhands then," I say, threading my fingers back into his hair.

"I won't."

"Knowing you, you will."

He nips at my chin. "Ahh, see? You do know me."

"I'm beginning to."

"And?"

I shrug. "So far so good."

He clenches me tighter, his fingertips kneading my ass, pleasure surging to my core and undulating my hips. My eyelids flutter, and a delicate moan escapes my mouth. "Slow down," I rasp out, desperately needing to settle my amorous body and all the sexually explicit things it quite obviously wants to do.

Riley instantly relaxes his hands, rests his forehead against mine, and takes a deep breath. "Good idea."

I suck in a lungful of air too. "Yeah."

He nuzzles my shoulder. "Slow."

I breathe out. "Yeah."

He closes his eyes. "Steady."

I bite my lip. "Yeah."

Gently panting, we search each other's eyes before I unwrap my legs and step back to allow our bodies to settle to a rhythm more suitable for a public setting. A rhythm that, hopefully, won't escalate too soon and lead to confusion and regret.

From the corner of my eye, I spot a hut where a woman with a bucket is scooping out white mud for people to lather on their faces, so I turn away from him and head in her direction.

"Where are you going?" he calls out. "I won't bite. I promise."

Needing a little breathing space, I call back, "Mud mask. It's part of the experience."

He follows me as I make my way through the plumes of steam toward the hut, where I hold out my hands for the woman with the bucket.

"*Halló*," she says as she slops a scoopful into my palm.

I twiddle my fingers. "Hello."

"Leave on for ten minutes then wash off in water. Do not get in eyes. And do not eat." She pulls the universal "yuck" face.

I nod. "Okay. No eating and no eyes."

"*Já*." She goes to scoop some out for Riley, but he shakes his head.

"No thanks. I'm good."

"Oh, come on," I goad. "It's just silica and minerals. It's good for your skin."

"But I have hair on my face, and you said it's not good for hair."

"We can avoid your beard."

He lets out a grumble and cups his hand for her, and if my fingers weren't covered in oozing mud, I'd clap with excitement.

"You do me, and I'll do you," I say, stepping up to him.

His sexy eyes crinkle.

"You know what I mean, Riley," I huff out. "Follow my lead, okay?"

Using my pointer finger, I paint the white silica mixture onto his cheeks, nose, and forehead, carefully avoiding his eyes and making a wide birth around his neatly trimmed upper lip, jaw, and chin. When I'm done, I stand back, admiring my artwork, before bursting into laughter. "Now you definitely look like Edward Scissorhands."

He stretches his face. "And this is meant to be good for your skin? It feels like plaster."

"Yes." I lift my chin and press my lips together. "My turn."

Riley dabs my face as if he's pushing buttons.

"You have to swipe not poke," I explain, blinking with every dab. "And don't get it up my nose."

He pauses. "I won't if you stop talking."

"Sorry."

"Stop."

"Sorry."

"Goddamn it, Riles. Shut up!"

Pressing my lips together again, I desperately try not to laugh, my throat squealing under the restraint.

He pauses again. "Go on, let it out."

Shaking my head, I gather my composure instead.

"You sound like a monkey."

How rude!

"I do not!" I exclaim, jerking my chin down, the tip of his finger probing my nostril. I flinch and cover my face with my hands. "Ow! You just picked my nose."

He throws his head back, his shoulders shaking with laughter. "Sorry. But you gotta shut up and stop moving!"

"And you need to stop treating my face like a touch screen."

Continuing to chuckle, he finishes his assault and leans back. "There. All done, panda girl."

"What?"

"You look like a panda. You have black shit all over your eyes."

"I do? Oh, crap! My mascara!"

"I told you not to worry about makeup. You don't need it."

"And I told you it's not a matter of needing it or not," I grouch, wiping my eyes and regretting it the moment I do. "Peanut butter! It burns."

"Peanut—? How would that help?" Chuckling, Riley clasps my flapping wrists. "Hold still."

I do as I'm told, my eyelids fused together as he swishes his hands in the water, then gently wipes the pads of his thumbs across the tops of my cheekbones.

"Damn it!" I whine. "I'm going to go blind in Iceland."

"No, you're not."

"Yes, I am. It's Karma for what I did to Brittany."

"Not that again. Jesus, Riles, why are you so hard on yourself?"

Slowly blinking, I pry my eyelids open. "I'm not."

He crouches down, scans my eyes, and then wipes them one last time. "You are."

"I... I don't mean to be," I stutter, a little taken aback.

"You're a good person, so ease up and give yourself a break."

Nodding, I hang my head. Perhaps I am too hard on myself. My expectations have always been high, but that's what happens when you constantly strive for success. If they're not high, you never rise.

He lifts my chin and gives me a quick peck on the lips. "You don't have to always impress and please everyone around you. Surely, that's exhausting."

"It is."

"Then stop, and be kinder to yourself."

I pout. "I am kind to myself."

"Be kinder."

Nodding again, I bite the inside of my cheek. "Okay."

He boops my nose. "Can I remove this shit from my face yet?"

"No."

Riley grumbles, and I have to give him credit for being a good sport. "Do you want me to do your chest?" I ask, sliding my slimy hands into his.

He throws his arms out wide, flexing his pecs, both of them dancing up and down.

I giggle. "I'll take that as a yes."

"Is this white shit good for genitals?"

I playfully slam my palms onto his pecs, delighting in the feel of him as I glide my fingers over every dip, bump, and groove. "Your chest hair is going to hate this."

"My chest hair loves it, trust me."

When I'm done, I pry my hungry hands from him and mimic his stance, arms out wide. "My turn."

Grinning like an imp, he gathers most of the mud I've just applied to him, rubs his hands together, and then caresses my shoulders, neck, and collarbones, his fingertips and palms gloriously hypnotic, a low growl reverberating from his throat as his hands dip to the top of my cleavage.

"Behave," I warn. "There are children here."

"Believe me, I am behaving." His hands curve around my bikini until they're slipping beneath it.

"That's enough," I whisper, reaching down to hold his wrists.

He leans forward, his mouth ghosting my earlobe. "For now."

I swallow, my throat dry. "I need a drink."

"You and me both."

"Yes. Good." I hold our hands away from our bodies. "Getting a drink is platonic. Safe. PG-rated."

He smirks. "Is it?"

Growling, because he's one-hundred percent correct. Now that we've agreed to "see where this leads," nothing seems platonic anymore. And I'd be lying to myself if that didn't worry me.

"You're doing it again," he says.

"Doing what?"

"Negatives."

Argh!

Intermittently wading, floating, and splashing, we make our way to the pool bar, order some drinks, and then cozy up together in a rocky alcove, me comfortably perched on Riley's lap and sipping my lavender blueberry smoothie, when Brittany and Whitney paddle by, Brittany performing a double-take.

"Riley, is that you?"

We both give her a docile wave, but I suspect I'm not the Riley she's talking to.

She waves back, her eyes dipping to his hand resting on my thigh. "Oh, I—"

"Hey, Brit," Whitney says, lifting her phone while she poses with a peace sign. "Take a selfie with me."

Brittany's shoulders slump, and she trudges away.

"I think we just broke Tittney's heart," I murmur as I sip my smoothie.

He gently squeezes my leg. "You gotta stop calling her that. She's just a kid."

"She's older than a *kid*, Riley."

"Not by much. She's only Twenty-three."

I jerk back. "Really?"

He nods.

"Did she tell you that?"

"Yeah, when I filled out her paperwork in the med center."

"Oh...." *Shit!* I feel awful now. I mean, I knew she was young, but not that young.

"So whether her heart is broken or not... yeah... she's a kid, and far too young for me." He creeps his fingers up my thigh. "You, on the other hand...."

I smack them away. "Are you saying I'm old?"

"I don't know how old you are. Mom always taught me never to ask a woman's age, weight, or bra size."

I laugh. "Well, if you must know, I'm thirty-two. And no, I'm not telling you what I weigh or how big my boobs are."

He glances down at my chest, then says into his beer, "You don't need to tell me."

I poke him in the ribs. "Riley!"

"What? You don't!"

Snuggling into him, an unusual calmness settles over me as I gaze out over the misty lagoon toward Mount Þorbjörn, the volcanic landscape eerily beautiful. "Do we have to leave? Can we not just stay here like this?"

"And let your Mom sail away without us?"

My stomach tightens.

Mom!

Bile rises to my throat, and I swallow heavily. I know I need to lay her to rest; it's what she wanted. But I don't know how I'm going to get through it, to finally sever that tie and let go of the only part of her I have left.

But... I must.

It's time.

Resting my head on his shoulder, I close my eyes. "I'm booking her interment for tomorrow."

His arms tighten around me, and it's the only response I need.

chapter twenty

RILEY

"What the fuck have you done to my hair?" I call out from the bathroom. "I could be Bart Simpson's long-lost brother."

"Bart never had a brother." Riles peeks her head around the door and stifles a laugh with her hand. "Oooh... I warned you."

"Yeah, but I didn't believe you."

"That's your fault, not mine." She slips in front of me, runs her delicate fingers over my face, and giggles. "But your skin is incredibly smooth and divine."

I growl, clench her ass, and lift her onto the sink. "Want to know what else is incredibly smooth and divine?"

What the fuck, Wilson? Why would you say that?

I don't know what's gotten into me. I'm like a horny teenager, saying stupid sexual shit every time Riles speaks. It's embarrassing, and I need to stop.

She flicks the waistband of my sweats.

Hello! Maybe not.

"You need to shower and take care of that."

I cup my junk and adjust myself. "I do."

Fuck me, I can't help myself.

"Not that!" She slaps my chest and slides off the vanity to her feet. "Your hair."

What I really need to do is take care of both.

"I'm just going to head out for a minute." She scruffs the matted, wiry mess on my head then kisses my cheek. "I'll be back by the time you're done."

Smiling like a kid in a candy store, I lean back and watch her leave, uncharacteristically agreeing with Ben. I am a lucky son of a bitch, and I can't remember the last time I was this happy. After my life went to shit, I was convinced I might never be this happy again and that second chances at love didn't exist. Not that I love Riles, but I mean, I could... one day. And just knowing that's possible is fucking awesome.

I grip my hair, and it crunches between my fingertips, so I carefully let it go then sniff my arm, the stench of sulfur wrinkling my nose. Visiting the Blue Lagoon with Riles was one of the best experiences of my life, and had it not been for her, I would never have even tried it. She makes me want to try new things, to explore possibilities, and to let go of what's held me back and made me bitter and angry. It's refreshing and liberating, and for the first time in a long time, I feel whole again. Optimistic and absolved.

Sniffing again, I'm done smelling like ass, so I shower, get dressed, and check the cruise app for tonight's events when she enters the room, a tear teetering in her eye.

"What's wrong?" I ask, striding toward her.

"I did it. I booked Mom's ceremony."

I hug her to my chest and press my lips to her head. "I'm proud of you."

"Thanks." Her shoulders slump.

"And your mom is too. I hope you know that."

"I do," she mumbles before leaning back and blinking up at me. "You used my shampoo again, didn't you?"

My balls withdraw into my stomach.

"Just admit it. I know you did. I can smell it."

"I didn't bring any of my own. And the complimentary stuff smells like dish soap."

"It's fine. Use what you like. I don't mind." She unlocks her hands from behind my back and collapses onto her bed, and my heart breaks a little, no stranger to the battle she's fighting within.

I take a seat beside her and squeeze her knee, wanting to distract her from her anguished thoughts. "What do you want to do tonight?"

"I don't know," she drones. "Get drunk?"

"I thought you weren't a drinker."

"I'm not. But if there's ever a time to give it a shot, I'm guessing now's that time."

"Are you sure that's what you want to do?"

"No, not really, but...."

"There's a good chance you might regret it tomorrow. Just sayin'."

"Regret will be high on my list tomorrow anyway, so screw it. I'm getting wasted."

My churning gut tells me this is a bad idea, but I'm no hypocrite. I've turned to the bottle a few times as well, especially after Dad died.

Riles sits up like a vampire rising out of its coffin, a blood-thirsty grin on her face. "Let's go to the casino!"

I wince.

"Don't give me that look!"

"I'm not."

"You are!" She scoots off the bed, spins toward me, and holds her hands out. "Please, Riley. I never do anything I'm not *supposed* to. Never gamble, never drink until I can drink no more. I'm never late, and I never steal. Hell, I don't even jaywalk or jump the line at Starbucks. I'm Miss Goody Two-Shoes, and I... I don't want to be her tonight. Just this once, I want to be someone else. Someone who isn't about to lay her mother to rest. I want to forget. Pretend. I want it all just to go away for a night."

Understanding exactly what she's saying, even though I know

what she wants to do won't magically erase who she is or what she must face when the alcohol wears off, I take her hands in mine. "Then let's go. Let's gamble and get shitfaced."

Riles nods, more to herself than to me. "Give me one second though. I'm just going to tell Mom my plan... and apologize in advance."

I bite back my amusement—she couldn't be a rebel if she tried —and pick up my cell, pretending to busy myself as she collects her mother's urn from the safe, heads outside onto the balcony, and begins her confession. And regardless of what I just said, I have absolutely no intention of getting shitfaced. She's going to need me to look after her, and I can't do that with a belly full of liquor and a head clouded in the fumes.

"THIS ONE," RILES SAYS, PLACING HER COCKTAIL DOWN and clapping while taking a seat at the Roulette table. "I'm excited!"

Amused, I sit beside her.

"So, how do we play?"

"Place your chips on what you want," I say, gesturing toward the betting layout.

"Is that it?"

"Not exactly. But let's start simple, yeah?"

She nods, eyes wide. "Okay."

"This is a one-dollar table, so you have to bet at least one dollar each time."

"And my chips are worth a dollar each?"

"They are."

"Oh, good. That's easy."

She sucks her drink through her straw, so I take her chips from her hand and stack them on the table.

"What are you doing?" she exclaims, protectively shielding her stacks. "Someone might steal them."

"Riles, there's no one else here."

Her eyes narrow suspiciously at the dealer.

"He's not going to steal them," I tell her.

"How do you know that?"

"I just do. Trust me."

Relaxing, she sits back. "Why are your chips green and mine pink?"

"We have different colors so the dealer can tell whose chips are whose."

She frowns. "Oh. Still... it's sexist that I ended up with pink."

"I don't think it was intentional."

She scoffs. "That's what a man would say."

"Do you want to swap colors?" I ask, knowing her favorite color is green, all while trying not to laugh.

"I do!"

After trading her chips for mine, I drape my arm around her shoulders and explain the different bets. "You can choose a single number, a range of numbers, or one of these three groups of dozens." I point to various spots. "You can also choose these outside bets, either red or black, or odd or even." I set a chip on Odd and place a few more on individual numbers.

"There's so much to choose from." She taps her finger to her lips, then places one measly chip on Black. "Always bet on black, right?"

I chuckle. "Yeah, something like that."

The dealer spins the wheel, and Riles claps again, her head circulating as she follows the ball.

Leaning forward, I toss another chip down before the dealer calls, "No more bets."

She frowns at the guy and whispers, "Did you just get in trouble?"

I chuckle again. "No. I can bet until he says that."

"Oh." She happily stirs her drink with her straw. "This is fun!"

The ball bounces a couple of times, then slots into number seventeen.

"It's black." She throws her hand into the air, turns toward me, and bounces in her seat. "I win!"

I smile at her cuteness. "You did!"

"How much?"

Not wanting to burst her happy little bubble, I don't have a choice, because she'll no doubt accuse the dealer of cheating. "One dollar."

"Is that all?"

"Yeah. The outside bets pay even."

"That's ridiculous. I should win more." Riles sucks another large mouthful of her drink through her straw and then scratches her head. "So which numbers pay more than even?"

"If you choose a column or one of the groups of dozen, it'll pay two to one." Pushing one of my chips onto the table, I stop it at number twenty-five—Imogen's birthday. "The individual numbers pay thirty-five to one."

"Oooh, that's good." She slams a chip on eleven. "That's my lucky number."

I place a chip on fifteen: my birthday; one on three: Roni's birthday; and one on twenty-six: Poppy's birthday. "What day were you born?" I ask.

"The seventh."

I place one on seven too.

"Hey! I was going to choose that."

"Ease up, Riles. You still can."

"Good." She slides a chip next to mine. "What day were you born?"

I point to fifteen.

She slides a chip on that number too.

Once again smiling at her cuteness, I ask, "Are you finished betting?"

"Yep."

The dealer spins the wheel, and she quickly slams a chip onto twenty-one while mischievously eyeing him over the rim of her drink.

He sweeps his hands across the table. "No more bets."

"Mom's birthday," she explains.

I kiss her temple and hug her to me as the ball once again rolls around the wheel, bouncing a couple of times before landing on seven.

"We won!" she shouts, shooting out of her seat and almost choking on her cocktail.

I laugh. "We did!"

"How much?"

"Thirty-five dollars each, plus the dollar we bet." I scan the table and do the math in my head. "But I lost four dollars on the other bets, and you lost three."

She sits back down. "That doesn't matter. We still won."

Technically, it does matter; a loss is a loss. But I don't argue.

"What's up, kids?" Ben says as he plonks himself on the seat beside me, his eyes instantly magnetized to my arm draped over Riles's shoulder. "You two finally fucking?"

I glare at him.

"Jesus, Ben. Not everything is about fucking," Riles snaps, before saying, "Sorry," to the dealer.

A shit-eating grin spreads across Ben's face as he nods at me. "Time biding. I get ya."

"What's he talking about?" Riles grouches.

I grit my teeth. "Never mind."

Ben studies the table, then scrunches his face like a puckered asshole. "High rollers, I see."

"Riles is just learning."

"Fuck that! Come with me and play like the big knobs do. My treat."

She raises her hand at him. "No, Ben. Thank you, but no. I want to gamble my own money."

"That's not money, love. That's change."

"I don't care. It's my change."

"Suit yourself, kids." He slaps my back and stands. "Happy *biding*, fucker."

Clenching my fist, I want to deck the dickhead. But again, I think better of it. I'm happy. Riles is happy. And knocking some sense into the mouthy idiot would only destroy that.

"What did he mean by 'biding'?" Riles asks as he walks away.

I lie. "Who knows what Ben is talking about half the time?"

"True." She cocks her head and continues sipping her drink, the straw echoing the empty contents of her glass. "Peanut butter. I'm out."

Peanut butter? What is she talking about?

Frowning, she flags a waiter down and orders us both another drink, and when she no longer has the ability to notice—which, at the rate she's going will be sooner rather than later—I plan to slow my consumption down.

"Let's try the slots," she says after playing another round of Roulette.

I don't argue—this is her night, after all—so we cash in our chips, and I follow her to machine after machine, hilariously entertained by how she selects them for their colors and themes until she eventually gets bored.

"I don't like gambling. I keep losing."

"Yeah, that happens a lot."

Spinning like a record to face me, she almost blankets me with her drink. "I know what we can do."

I step back to a safer distance. "What's that?"

"Karaoke!"

My ears shrivel.

She grabs my arm in a death grip. "Yes! It'll be fun."

"You can't sing, Riles."

"Hey!" She pokes her finger into my chest. "Says who?"

"You, remember?"

Staring past me, or perhaps through me—who knows—she shakes her head. "That doesn't matter."

It does. Because I also vaguely recall her saying she doesn't want to make a fool of herself. But then, she also said she doesn't want to be *her* tonight, so I guess she'll forgive me tomorrow for allowing this to happen.

"Where's Ben?" she blurts. "He'll come with me."

Riles marches off, finding Ben when he hollers from the other side of the room, a small crowd gathered around him, applauding.

I grip my hair and follow after her.

"Did you win?" she asks, her hand resting on his shoulder.

Eyeballing her twiddling fingers, I have the overwhelming urge to remove them and thread them with mine, keeping her close.

"Yeah, love. Look at my stack." He waggles his eyebrows.

"We're going to the karaoke bar. Want to come?"

"No can do. I'm on a roll." He holds his fist over his shoulder. "Kiss my bones."

Kiss his what?

I step forward, ready to crush his hand, when he twists his wrist and opens his fingers, presenting a pair of dice. Riles stares at them, confused, and then shrugs and gives them a peck.

Tossing them onto the table, Ben hollers, "Seven, seven, fucking is heaven," his posse cheering him on.

The dice bounce off the sides, tumbling until they slow to a stop. I crane my neck, then rub my beard.

Ouch!

Ben slams his palms onto the edge of the table. "Motherfucker!"

Riles nudges him. "Peanut butter!"

He frowns at her.

She frowns back. "What just happened?"

"Your kiss sucked, love. That's what happened."

"My kiss does not suck!"

"It did."

She gives him a shove. "You suck."

He spins his chair around, face stretched with animation. "Are you drunk?"

"No!" She swipes her hand at him. "I've only had a couple of cocktails."

I count the empty glass in her hand and hold up five fingers at Ben.

"Karaoke bar, huh?" The corners of his mouth lift higher. "Count me in. This could be fun." He turns back to the dealer and snaps his fingers. "Cash me out."

"HOLD THIS FOR ME," RILES SAYS AS WE ENTER THE dimly lit bar. "I need to pee."

She passes me her empty glass and kisses my cheek, then shuffles off to the bathroom, past a group of passengers studying song lists. Backstepping, she snatches one up, then takes it with her.

I chuckle and hand her glass to a waiter as he strolls by, and then I take a seat on a stool at one of the last available high-top tables.

"Easy fuck tonight," Ben says, nudging my shoulder and holding up his fist for me to bump.

I smack it away. "What is wrong with you?"

"Nothing. Just stating the obvious."

"I've told you before, I'm not about an 'easy' fuck, and you shouldn't be either."

His eyes bulge. "Do you have a vagina?"

Ignoring him, I scope the room, spotting Carlos taking song requests near the stage area. "Riles is going through a lot. The last thing she needs is a dickhead trying to take advantage of her."

"But you're not a dickhead."

I should say "thanks," but I don't. "I would be if I were after an easy fuck, Ben."

"Are you saying I'm a dickhead?"

"Yes."

He frowns. "That's a bit harsh."

"Then stop trying to get into every woman's pants."

"But I *want* to get into them."

"And I want a cock the size of Texas, but that doesn't mean I should go and get one."

"You should," he says, adjusting his crotch. "They're great!"

I cross my arms over my chest and tip my beer to my lips. "You try too hard."

"It's better than not trying at all."

"Is it?" I take a swig.

"Damn straight." He gestures toward the bathroom. "So what's her story?"

I debate telling him, deciding to give him the condensed version. "Her mother recently passed away."

"That's shit."

"Yeah."

"So she's drownin' her sorrows?"

"Sure is."

"And you don't want to fuck her?"

"I never said that."

He nudges my shoulder again.

I smirk. "I like her... a lot."

"Feelings and shit?"

"Yes, Ben, feelings and shit. So stop being inappropriate toward her."

He raises his hands. "I'm bowing out, brother. She's all yours."

I give his shoulder a patronizing squeeze. "You were never in."

"Sure I was."

I shake my head sympathetically.

"I wasn't?"

"No."

He slams his glass down. "Ahh, fuck!"

"So, where's Brittany and Whitney tonight?" I ask, my eyes trained on Riles as she slowly makes her way toward us, her head buried in the song list.

"Don't know. I think they've ditched me. Haven't seen them since I got back from the basketball game."

"That reminds me, how was it?"

"We killed 'em."

"I'm not surprised."

Riles bumps into a dude and apologizes, his hands lingering on her arm longer than they should.

"Back off, fuckstick!" Ben shouts. "The lady's with us."

I choke on my beer.

"I got your back, man. No one touches her but you."

Jesus!

"So whatcha gonna sing, love?" he asks as she stops at the table.

Sighing, she plonks herself onto a stool. "I don't know. I'm not drunk enough yet."

"Then let's fix that." Ben snaps his fingers at a waiter.

"Don't do that," Riles scolds. "It's not very nice. And you *are* nice; I know it in my tummy."

He grins. "Are you sure you're not drunk enough?"

She looks at me for an answer. "Am I?"

"What's the capital of Norway?"

"I don't know." She giggles. "I didn't know the first time."

Suspecting that was the case, I wrap my arm around her back so she doesn't topple off the stool.

"What'll it be?" Ben asks when the waiter arrives.

"Peanut butter," Riles says.

I go to ask her why she keeps saying peanut butter, when Ben butts in.

"Who drinks peanut butter?" He scrunches his face. "Give us two rounds of Jager Bombs."

"Not for me," I say.

"I never said they were for you." He glances at Riles. "She needs this."

My gut churns yet again, even though I agree.

"I need what?" she asks, not looking up from the sheet of paper in her hands.

"Liquid courage, love."

"Yes, yes, I do."

Several minutes later, four Jager Bombs are lined up in front of Ben and Riles, Ben instructing her on how to drink them.

"Fill your glass up halfway with the Red Bull and drop your shot in, like so. Then, all you do is chug." He raises his Jager Bomb. "Ready?"

"Yep."

They clink glasses, Ben's empty within seconds, Riles politely sipping as her eyes squint.

He lets out an "aaah" and wipes his mouth with the back of his hand. "Stop playin' with it, love. Chug faster."

She tips hers higher, swallowing like crazy until her empty glass is slammed back onto the table, remnants dribbling down her chin.

I offer her a napkin, and she takes it.

"That tastes like medicine."

Ben grins. "It does."

Riles licks her lips. "I like it."

"Thatta girl." He pours another two, and I want to tell him to slow down. I know she needs this or, more accurately, wants this, but I'm concerned she'll be in no state to do what she must tomorrow.

"Bottoms up!" he hollers, clinking her glass yet again.

They both chug, Riles almost beating him, her hands shooting into the air not long after his. To say I'm impressed is an understatement, so I kiss the side of her head as a burp bursts from her throat.

"Beg my pardon," she says, covering her mouth, eyes wide.

Ben clutches his gut and belches as well before offering her a fist bump. She giggles, balls her fist, and taps his.

God, help me!

"So, what's it gonna be, love? Elton and Kiki?"

Her eyes light up. "You're going to sing with me?"

"Damn straight I am."

Clapping, she slips off the stool and latches onto Ben as they walk toward Carlos, both of them soon on stage, illuminated in a blue glow, their voices murdering "Don't Go Breaking My Heart" along with my eardrums.

Laughter dances in my chest as they joke around, pretending to gift each other their hearts, Riles twirling and forgetting all her sorrows, Ben the perfect accomplice. And as the night wears on, I realize I'm going to have to drag her out of the bar.

"I think she's done," Ben says as Riles drones to the lyrics of "Just Smile" by Nat King Cole. He clears out his ear with his fingertip, rolls a ball of earwax, and then flicks it onto the ground.

Yep, I think we're all done!

I slide my stool back, sigh, then make my way to the stage, when Riles snags my arm and tugs me next to her, her head resting on my shoulder as she slurs about smiling instead of crying.

"Sing, you pussy!" Ben hollers.

I grit my teeth at him, nearly losing an eye when Riles's floppy arm shoves the microphone at my face, her wrist limp, her voice box broken... or asleep. And after reluctantly murmuring the closing line for her, I scoop her into my arms and hand Carlos the microphone, mouthing, *"Thank you."*

He nods as if a mourning woman pouring her alcoholic heart out isn't new to him—and it probably isn't.

"You need a hand getting her back to the room?" Ben asks.

I shake my head. "Nah. I'm good."

"You sure?"

I nod. "Thanks, man. I appreciate your help tonight."

"Any time, brother."

We part ways, and as I make my way to the elevator, Riles tries to lift her dangling head while slurring, "Sssmile."

"Yes, sweetheart. Smile."

"I sssang for Mmmomma."

"I know you did."

We pass passengers, most of them giving me a wide berth, as Riles waves at them, still slurring, "Sssmile."

Some of them chuckle while others are etched with concern, and I can't say I blame them. I'd probably be suspicious of a man carrying an inebriated woman to God knows where as well.

Feeling highly uncomfortable, I elbow the Up button, take the elevator, and hurry as fast as I can to our cabin.

"Riiileyyy?"

"Yeah, Riles?" I prompt, fumbling with my sailing card.

"I don't feeeel good."

Say what?

Swiping it like a madman, I shove the door open with my ass when it unlocks, then swing us into the bathroom and place Riles on her feet, holding her hair back just in time for a fountain of puke to plummet into the toilet bowl.

I dry-heave but hold her steady until she's done, and then I clean her face and carry her to her bed, gently laying her down before removing her shoes and slipping her dress over her head.

"I'm sorry," she murmurs, voice cracking.

"Shhh. It's fine."

She lets out a sob. "But y-youuu don't do puke. And I—" She bursts into tears. "—puuuked."

Slotting myself beside her, I smooth her hair back from her face. "I don't do puke, but I'll do it for you."

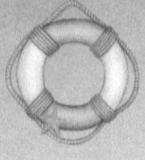

chapter twenty-one

RILES

Forcing my eyelids apart, I immediately shut them again when the morning sunlight beams into my eyeballs, my head vibrating like a taiko drum. A stale, earthy, foul funk coats my tongue, so I gag then lick my lips, my throat dry and revolting. *What the hell happened last night?*

Groaning, I try to roll over but hit a log. A hot, solid, snoring, man-log.

My eyes spring open, and I slowly turn my head before going dead-still while Riley snorts in a breath and then exhales, his arm coming to rest across my chest.

Delicately pinching his wrist, I lift his arm and lay it beside him, then raise my comforter and peek beneath it.

"Thank you, baby Jesus!" I whisper, because my underwear is still on.

"Don't thank him, sweetheart. Thank me."

I shriek and grasp at my chest.

"What time is it?" he asks, scrubbing his hands over his face.

"Uh... time you tell me what the hell happened last night, why you're on my bed, why I'm in my underwear, and why my mouth tastes like ass?"

He rolls onto his side, his lazy eyes finding mine. "You got wasted like you wanted to."

"Yes, I remember the 'getting wasted' part. What I don't remember is what happened after."

He collects my hair with his fingers and tenderly tucks it behind my ear, the pad of his thumb caressing my temple. "How's your head?"

I all but sigh, his sweetness infectious. "It has more pounds than a pound cake."

"That bad, huh?"

"Affirmative."

Swinging his legs over the bed, he sits up and stretches.

"You're still in the clothes you wore last night," I say, confused.

"I am."

"So we didn't...?"

He whirls back around, his brow pinched. "No! We didn't. Who do you take me for?"

"Right. Yes. Sorry. I didn't mean...."

Chuckling, he stands and stretches again, then grabs a bottle of water and fishes some Tylenol out of his bedside table before handing them to me. "Here. You're gonna need these."

"Thank you." I take the pills and swallow them, the fresh cool water like liquid heaven. "I forgot about the aftermath of drinking. How on earth did I forget about the aftermath?"

His mouth quirks as he shrugs.

"It's not funny," I grouch.

"I never said it was."

"You don't have to. Your face says it for you."

"That's because you hit it hard last night. And it was... amusing."

"Amusing?" I frown, trying to recall said amusement. "I can't remember anything after singing... with Ben. Wait! I sang with Ben?"

"You sure did. Twice."

"Twice?"

"And four solos."

"What?" Flopping back on my bed, I groan, "Kill me now."

"My personal favorite was 'My Humps' by Black Eyed Peas."

"Nooo." I wrench my head back up, regretting it the moment I do, the room spinning. "Why'd you let me sing?"

"Because you wanted to."

"No, Riley. No, I didn't." I close my eyes momentarily, remorse twisting my already twisting stomach. How I thought drowning my grief with liquor was a splendid idea is beyond me. Grief doesn't drown; it floats. Never swimming. Never sinking.

Riley disappears behind the room partition to where the TV and desk are, returning with his hands behind his back before presenting me with a gold ship trophy. "Your 'singing' earned you this."

"No way!" I scramble out of bed and snatch it from him. "I won karaoke?"

"You did."

"Huh." Proudly holding it up, I marvel at my prize until I become acutely aware I'm standing before him in nothing but my underwear, his eyes leisurely roaming my body.

"Turn around!" I shriek, covering my lady bits.

"I've seen you in a bikini, Riles."

"I know, but underwear is different."

"I've seen you in your underwear too."

"You have?"

"Yes."

"When?"

"Last night, when I put you to bed."

My eyes bulge. "*You* undressed me?"

"I had to."

"Why?"

"Because you were in no state to do it yourself."

"Right. I suppose I wasn't." I scratch my head. "But you were drunk too."

"Nope."

"Yes, you were. I remember you drinking with me."

"I had four beers, then stopped."

"Why?"

He lifts one solitary eyebrow, and I know what it means. He stopped so he could look after me, to make sure I didn't do anything stupid... other than embarrass myself with a microphone, apparently.

I groan again. "Ugh! Thank you."

"You're welcome."

Bending down, I snatch up my dress from the floor and cover my body with it. "So, are you going to tell me what hap—" The stench of vomit hits my nose, and I blink profusely, hoping my fluttering eyelashes fan it away. "What's that smell?"

He nods at my dress.

I tentatively lift it higher and take a whiff. "Is that... puke?"

"It is."

"Oh, Jesus!" Tossing it aside, my eyes widen before finding his again. "Ohhh! Shit! I puked?"

"You did."

"Were you with me when—"

"I was."

"Did I puke on y—"

His eye twitches.

Feeling outright horrendous, I cover my mouth with my hands. "I'm *so* sorry, Riley."

He lays his palms on my shoulders, presses his lips to my forehead, turns me toward the bathroom, and gives me a gentle shove. "Go take a shower. You stink."

Absolutely mortified, I trudge my walk of shame.

This day is going to be... hell.

CRADLING MOM TO MY CHEST, THE WARM OCEAN breeze whispers across my face, the water calm, tranquil, and somewhat calling, as if it knows it will welcome an angel today. We journey through the Irish Sea tonight and dock in Dublin tomorrow morning, so it's now or never to grant Mom her final wish, a wish I must grant because she deserves nothing less.

"They're ready when you are, Riles," Riley says as he sits beside me on a park-style bench out on deck.

I wipe a tear from my eye and nod. "I just need a couple more minutes."

"Take as much time as you want." He tenderly squeezes my knee and goes to stand.

I clasp his hand. "Please, stay."

Lowering to sit again, he slides his arm behind my shoulders and hugs me to him, his warmth and presence a comfort I in no way fathomed I would desperately need. Never in my wildest dreams had I expected to do what I'm about to do with a man I've known for less than two weeks. I do everything on my own; I pretty much always have. But Riley doesn't feel like a sympathetic stranger, obliged or coerced to console a damsel in distress for her own selfish needs. And if he did, I certainly wouldn't have asked him to join me today. I'm still trying to figure out how and why, but he feels like a part of me that's been hiding deep within, waiting to surface and show me I'm not alone in the world.

"Thank you," I murmur, my fingers gripping the urn.

"How's your head?"

"Less pound cake."

"Good." He nods toward the horizon. "So your mom loved the ocean?"

"She did, but I didn't realize how much until she explained her wishes. It was a shock. It still is. I mean, we took vacations to Florida, and many day trips to Long Island when I was younger, but she never truly expressed her fondness for the sea." I pick at the seam of my dress. "And now I fear I didn't know her as well as I thought I did. Never paid the attention I should have."

"I don't think that's the case, Riles," he says, rubbing my shoulder, eyes trained dead ahead. "We all hold a truth for ourselves and only ourselves, but that doesn't mean your mom didn't love or trust you enough to share that truth with you, or that you were too preoccupied to see it. Perhaps her love of the ocean was simply *her* truth. That one precious thing she kept for herself."

Shifting in my seat, I turn to him and simply stare, his explanation surprisingly sobering. "I... I suppose it was."

"Seems that way," he says, dragging his focus from the ocean to me.

Tears pool in my eyes as I recall one summer at Corey Beach.

"Look, Mom!" I squealed.

"What did you find, Smiley Riley?"

"A hermit crab." I scrambled up the sandbank, almost falling onto my nine-year-old face.

"Show me!" Mom put down her book and gave me her full attention.

Carefully pinching the shell, I proudly presented it to her. "Can I keep it?"

She pouted. "No, darling. It doesn't belong with us. It belongs here."

"But I want a pet crab."

"Do you think the crab wants to leave the beach and live in the city?"

I shook my head.

"Of course it doesn't. It wants to be in the sand and water with the other crabs. That's its home. That's where it's happiest."

"But I love it."

"Then you have to put it back. To love is to give, and to give is to love. Do you understand, my precious girl?"

I nodded sullenly.

"Go on then... show the crab how much you love it."

Trudging back to the water's edge, I set the crab down, waving as it buried itself under the sand. "Goodbye. I love you."

A SOB RIPS FROM MY CHEST, TEARING IT OPEN AS ONLY deep love can. "I'm ready."

Riley kisses my head and stands, offering me his hand. I take it and rise, legs trembling as we walk to where the captain waits patiently, a large bouquet of flowers on a table covered in a white cloth, a single note reading **A loving mother and best friend.**

Confused, I read the note again before snapping my head to Riley. "Did you do that?"

He nods once, then links his hands behind his back.

Pressing Mom to my chest, I step up to him, hug him tight, and whisper, "Thank you. That's so unbelievably thoughtful of you."

"It's my honor, Riles."

Tears flood my eyes and stream down my face, so I wipe my cheeks and step back, not wanting to stain his shirt with my running mascara.

"Ms. Wilson," Captain Katarina says, "if you're ready, I'll say a few words and then give you some privacy to commence with interment."

I nod.

"Very well." She fixes a pair of reading glasses on her nose and raises a sheet of paper. "Today, we interment Grace Diana Wilson to sea. Beloved mother of Riley Alessandra Wilson, and a courageous woman who was taken far too soon. May you rest peacefully, Grace, and move with the ebb and flow of the ocean, your memory remaining, forever in the hearts you touched so deeply." She sets down the paper. "In your own time, Ms. Wilson, you may proceed to the railing."

I slide my hand into Riley's and urge him forward with me, not wanting to do this alone. "Would you mind carrying the flowers for me?"

"Of course."

"Thank you."

Strolling to the railing, Mom pressed to my chest, I breathe in the sea air, committing to memory how it smells and feels: tepid but fresh, salty but clean. The distant laughter of children and adults hums on the breeze several decks above, a joyous soft melody. It draws a smile I didn't think I was capable of today, because Mom loved laughter. She would always tell me it's the world's strongest medicine. An everlasting cure. When she was sad, it was never for long, because she'd find ways to laugh. I thought she was crazy, but... she was just pure like that.

"Okay, Momma," I say, wiping my face. "Are you ready for your free throw?"

If she were here, she'd say, *"Don't miss,"* and then she'd cheer me on like a manic spectator.

I won't, Mom. I promise.

Raising her urn to my lips, I give her one last kiss, position her at my breasts, then take a deep breath, closing my eyes and whispering, "Goodbye, Momma. I love you always and forever."

Exhaling, I draw as much strength as I possess, open my eyes, and set her free, my chest seizing as she sails through the air and splashes into the ocean, the ship's wake a bubbly cradle, carrying her to her final resting place. Unbearable pain ruptures my heart, the loss and emptiness so overwhelming that I want to reach out and take her back, to never let her go again. But I know I can't, and that thought alone is the greatest devastation I've ever endured.

"Nooo," I sob, my knees buckling, my hands slipping from the railing.

Riley encases me in his strong arms, preventing me from crumbling to the deck below my feet, his voice soft as he murmurs, "I've got you."

I hold on to him as if he's the only thing I *can* hold on to, as if he's the only thing left in my life worth holding on to. Because without Mom, I have no one left, no one to turn to, to share with. No one I love and who loves me.

"You did it, Riles. You gave her what she wanted. You set her free. I'm so proud of you."

I rest my head on his shoulder. "I want her back."

"I know." He squeezes me tighter. "Do you want me to jump in and go after her? Because I will, for you."

Sadness and laughter simultaneously bubble in my throat. "No. Please don't."

He sighs with relief. "Thank Christ for that."

I wipe my eyes and straighten my shoulders. "She'd swim away from you if you tried."

"Ahh, so that's where you get your stubbornness from?"

I force a proud smile. "Like mother, like daughter."

"Would you like to release the flowers now?" he asks, handing them to me.

"Can we do it together?"

His damp blue eyes glitter, a mirror of the water below, and I know whenever I look upon them from now on, I'll remember this moment forever.

I'll remember he was here with me.

I'll remember I wasn't alone.

THE REST OF THAT DAY AND THE ONE THAT FOLLOWED were kind of a blur. And in the moments when my despair reared its ugly head, Riley was there to help me confront it or bury it deep where it belonged. He gave me space when I needed it, made me laugh when laughter seemed impossible, and he refrained from arguing when I deliberately pushed to fight, my ill-directed anger unfairly boiling profusely.

He'd been a friend, a punching bag... my saving grace. And I was eternally grateful.

We visited the Long Room in the Library of Trinity College

in Dublin, a grand Georgian architectural masterpiece—Riley's words, not mine. Sadly, all I can remember through my fog of grief is the floor-to-ceiling oak bookshelves stacked with a vast, priceless collection of books, one in particular dating back to 800 A.D, each majestic column headed with a marble bust. The library was used as inspiration for Hogwarts, which was fitting, considering I also remember meandering about it, parentless, like Harry.

Staring at the flowers Riley arranged for me after Mom's interment, an exact replica of Mom's bouquet, I push off the end of my bed and slide out a single white rose, resting it on my lip as I inhale the lovely scent. Only two other men have bought me flowers during my thirty-two years—one of them an ambitious jerk with an ulterior motive, the other an incorrigible imbecile.

Smiling, I pick up the card and read it for, quite possibly, the hundredth time. **You're not alone.**

"I mean every word, Riles," he says as he slides his hands around my waist and rests his chin on my shoulder.

I breathe him in, enjoying the scent of my shampoo in his hair. "I know."

"How are you feeling?"

"Better today."

"You'll have good days and bad days. That will never change."

"Today will be a good day. I'll make sure of that. It's what Mom wanted."

He kisses the side of my head, and every nerve ending fizzles to life. I love it when he kisses my head. It says so much without saying anything at all.

"So today will be a good day, huh? Good enough to come with me, now, no questions asked?"

Turning in his arms, the rose still dangling from my hand, I narrow my gaze. "That depends."

"On what?"

"Where are we going?"

"Did you not hear the no-questions-asked part?"

Truth is, I don't need to ask. After the pillar of strength he has been for me, I'd go anywhere with him. And that should terrify me, but it doesn't. When I'm in his arms like this, his crinkly eyes searching mine, his sexy stubble twitching, terror is the last thing I feel.

Pressing my lips to his, I murmur, "Lead the way."

He growls, his tongue lightly grazing mine, his hands creeping underneath my T-shirt. "On second thought, let's stay exactly where we are."

I don't object. I can't. My body is more than happy to remain attached to his.

Riley pulls away, runs his hands through his hair, and eyes me heatedly. "We need to leave right now, or—"

I pout. "Or what?"

"Or so help me God, I will strip you naked."

My jaw drops.

My core clenches.

I wait for him to continue, but he doesn't. He just continues gripping his hair, and I fear for a moment that he might actually rip it out.

Biting my lip, I take his fingers in mine and lead him toward the door. "We better go then."

chapter twenty-two

RILEY

Jesus Christ, my balls are gonna burst.

J   I want her beneath me so badly, writhing and screaming my name. Our name.

Damn, that'll be weird.

It's going to happen at some point though; there's not a doubt in my mind. The way she reacts to my touch... the chemistry between us. Even Roni would be scientifically impressed.

But Riles is too fragile right now for me to do all the things I want to do to her, and I can't rush what could possibly be the best thing to happen to me for as long as I can remember. I also need to sign my divorce papers. Until that chapter is closed, I can't in good faith start another.

Smiling to myself, I know Riles would like my literary metaphor.

"Why are you so happy?" she asks as we exit the elevator.

"Can't a man be relieved he didn't just die in a death box?"

She laughs. "I guess he can. Although you've been nailing your fear while on the ship. You should be proud."

I drape my arm around her shoulders, loving her praise and how she feels tucked beneath my arm. "It's so nice to hear you genuinely laugh again."

"Mom wouldn't want it any other way. She loved laughter. Hated sadness."

"I don't think anyone likes sadness, Riles."

"I know, but Mom despised it. She insisted we have the power to destroy it because, with everything in life, there is balance." She playfully rolls her eyes. "She was a true Libra. Always just. Always harmonious. If we're sad, we can be happy. If we're angry, we can find peace. If it rains, there'll be sunshine. That was how she lived, day in and day out. I, on the other hand, am an Aries. So Mom was my stabilizer."

"Aries, huh?"

She grins up at me, her steel-gray eyes presumptuous. "You seem shocked, Riley."

Chuckling, because she's getting good at tossing my words back at me, I say, "Not one bit."

"What's your sign?"

"You tell me."

"What sign is the most annoying?"

We stop in the atrium, and I rest against a pillar before reaching out and drawing her to my chest. "The goat one."

"Capricorn?" She giggles, her delicate fingers finding the hair at my nape. "Why are they annoying?"

I shrug; I don't really care for the zodiac. "Because goats are pests."

"So, you're a Capricorn?"

"No. I'm not a pest."

Her chin wrinkles, her eyes mischievously disagreeing with me.

I pinch her hip. "Are you calling me a pest?"

"If the sign fits...."

"If you must know, I'm a Cancer."

Riles stiffens in my arms. "A crab?"

"Yes."

"I once loved a crab." Her cheeks flush with color, before she quickly blurts, "A hermit crab... when I was nine."

Grinning, I'm about to probe for more information about her love of crabs, when she leans back and takes in our surroundings. "Anyway, enough about star signs. Why are we here?"

My insides squirm. "Irish dance lessons."

"What?" She bursts into laughter and pushes out of my embrace. "Are you serious?"

"Unfortunately, yes."

"Do you know how to Irish dance?"

I shake my head. "God, no."

"Oh." The sparkle in her eyes dims a little. "So you want to learn?"

"God, no."

She narrows her gaze. "Then why are you here?"

I roll my neck and mumble, "Because I was coaxed into it. And I can't dance for shit. And after seeing your efforts while you sang karaoke, I figured you can't dance either, so it will make me feel better about doing this if you're with me."

Riles's mouth forms an O, as if she's offended, and she probably should be. I did just call her out on her lack of rhythm and then admit I lured her here so that I don't look as bad.

Waiting for her to punch me or storm off, she instead palms her face and peeks through her spread fingers. "Did I really dance that night?"

"You did."

"To what?"

I smirk. "Beyoncé. Then again, I'm not sure what you did could be classed as dancing."

"Oh God!" she groans. "Was it 'Single Ladies'?"

"It was."

"Pleeease don't let me drink that much again."

I pull her back into my arms. "You're allowed to let go every once in a while and dance like a freak."

"Gee, thanks."

Holding up my hand, I twist it from side to side, impersonating Beyoncé's dance move.

She slaps my shoulder.

"Ease up, Riles. You were... adorable. And you enjoyed yourself. That's all that matters."

"Sounds like I did more than enjoy myself."

I nod. "You could say that."

She scrunches her face and fiddles with the button of my shirt, avoiding eye contact. "I'm so sorry about the puke."

"Don't be. Most of it landed in the toilet bowl."

"Most of it?"

I wince.

"Oh, my God!"

Chuckling, I tip her chin up and press my lips to hers, the earth once again tilting.

"Top of the morning to you, cruiselings!" Paul announces, his overenthusiastic squawk breaking us apart.

Skipping and hopping into the atrium, his suit greener than freshly mowed grass, a four-leaf clover pinned to his chest, he stops and throws his arms into the air. "Who's ready to get their Michael Flatley on?"

I snicker at the hippity-hoppity frog man. "Who's Michael Flatley?"

"You've never heard of him?" she gasps.

"No. Should I?"

Riles snaps her head to me. "*Lord of the Dance*?"

"I know *Lord of the Rings*." I shrug.

She crosses her arms over her chest and pinches her chin. "You really have no idea what you signed up for, do you?"

"I told you—I was coerced. And Mom insisted I do at least one dance lesson while onboard. It was her only request, and trust me," I say, a subtle growl exiting my throat, "she'll ask me to demonstrate when I get home."

Giggling, Riles bites her fingernail. "I like your mom already."

A warm sense of relief washes over me, because I know Mom will like Riles as well. In fact, she'll more than likely love her. Roni and Poppy too.

"Okay, Riverdancers." Paul skips up a few steps onto a circular landing at the base of the grand staircase, upbeat Irish-style music playing through the speakers. "Gather around and form multiple lines on the dancefloor."

"Let's go!" Riles snags my hand and drags me to the front, her back straight, her game face firmly set.

I swallow. *Shit! Not that look again.*

"Just friends!" Paul calls out.

My blood runs cold, regret locking my two left feet into place as I raise my eyes to his. If he thinks I'm going up there, he can fuck right off to Leprechaun land.

Not. A. Chance. In. Hell.

He points his microphone at us and winks. "Good to see you again."

Riles waves, and I secure her animated fingers to prevent her from drawing extra attention to us. "I think we should stand at the back."

"Nonsense. You'll see better from here."

"No, really. The back is perfect. I'm tall. I'll see just fine."

"Riley Wilson," she drawls, turning to face me. "Was it not you who just said to me moments ago that it's okay to let go every once in a while and dance like a freak?"

Annoyed with myself for saying stupid shit, I scratch my beard and grumble, "I meant you, not me."

She raises one solitary eyebrow. "Perhaps you should take your own advice."

Knowing I've dug my own grave, I twist around and look at the flock of passengers lined up behind me. "This isn't my idea of fun, Riles. I'm only doing it because I have to."

"Ease up."

Damn it!

"Relax. It's not a competition." She clasps my hand and tugs me to face forward again, which is when a glimmer of gold catches my eye as Paul produces a ship trophy and waves it about.

"Who likes prizes?" he singsongs.

My stomach plummets.

I side-eye Riles.

"Relax," she repeats. "I already have one."

Exhaling, because hopefully she won't turn into Muhammad Riley again, I loosen my shoulders and crack my neck as Paul welcomes a woman to stand beside him.

"Have you all met Michelle?" he asks, holding out his arms as if presenting her on a game show. "She's one of our fabulous entertainment crewmembers and our resident Irish Dancing Queen. She'll be teaching you all a basic jig." Michelle crisscrosses her legs, jumps, and then curtseys. "At the end of your lesson, we'll choose our best participant."

The crowd gives Michelle a round of applause, and she reciprocates. "Hello, everyone. Thank you for joining me today. Are you ready to have some fun?"

The atrium roars with cheers; I groan.

"Now, before we get into the steps, I want you all to familiarize yourself with the beat of the music by bouncing on the spot, like this." She proceeds to jump like a pogo stick, encouraging us all to copy.

What the fuck?

I have half a mind to bounce the hell out of here. I'll tell Mom the dancing classes were fully booked, or that I had temporary paralysis or some shit. She won't believe me, of course, but I'll come up with something and then ply her with duty-free gifts, which may work. At least, at first.

As I try to slip past Riles, she snags my hands as if we're kids at a playground and coaxes me to join in, her chest springing about in her top. "Jump!"

I stare at her breasts.

"Come on." She tugs my arms up and down. "It's easy."

Happy to stay where I am, because jiggling boobs, I begrudgingly give in and bounce with her until Michelle stops and stands like a demented penguin.

"Now, place your feet like mine," she instructs. "One in front of the other, pointing in opposite directions. Right foot forward."

I try to angle my feet like hers and nearly fall on my ass.

"Oh, this is going to be so much fun," Riles says, steadying me by grabbing hold of my shirt, laughter bubbling out of her.

"For you or for me?" I grouch.

"Probably me."

Wobbling, I try once more to stand heel-to-toe, one foot pointing left, the other right. "Is Irish dancing some form of ballet? Because this feels like ballerina shit to me."

Riles giggles. "Not really." She pauses and taps her lip. "Well, maybe a little. It's less graceful, of course, and it involves light tapping, like tap dancing."

"Tap dancing? Are you shitting me?"

"No."

"So I've signed up for ballerina, tap dancing crap?"

She shrugs and lets out a "meh" sound.

"Now that we're all heel-to-toe," Michelle continues, "I'd like you to jump again and land in the same position."

Riles springs up effortlessly, landing exactly as she started. I give it a go too, surprised when I manage it without fault.

"See?" She playfully nudges my ribs. "Don't knock it 'til you try it."

"Very good!" Michelle praises. "Keep going. Bounce to the beat." She claps and counts in rhythm, enthusiastically encouraging us all to look like idiots.

I sneak another glance at Riles's chest and smirk—at least something good is coming out of this.

"Now switch feet, everyone! Left in front, right behind. And repeat! One, two, three, four."

Internally groaning, I do as I'm told. "Do they really dance like this in Ireland?"

Riles twists as she jumps, facing me when she lands. "Uh-huh." She then jumps and twists back as if she's a damn professional.

I hold still and spear her with my damnation. "Have you done this before?"

"Uh-huh."

Heat rises to my cheeks, but I can't help but be impressed. Just like the woman who signed me up for this bullshit, Riles has swindled me too.

Michelle gives us another round of applause, then rests her hands on her hips. "You're all doing so well." She positions her right foot in front of her left again. "This time, I want you to jump once, and on the second jump, hop on your left foot while lifting and bending your right leg. So, jump, hop."

Practicing it slowly, I murmur, "Jump, hop."

"On the third count, you're going to jump, hop, back-front, back-front," Michelle instructs.

Confused, I shake my head and grip my hair.

"Here, I'll show you," Riles says while whacking my arm, demanding I pay attention while she demonstrates the move. I turn to face her, cross my arms over my chest, and admire the view. "Are you watching?"

"I am."

"My feet, Riley. Watch my feet."

"I can't. I'm distracted."

She gives me a gentle shove back into line. "You're incorrigible, you know that?"

I do, but I refuse to admit it. Ever.

"Jump, hop. Back-front, back-front," Michelle repeats, circling her platform.

Positioning myself yet again, I give it a try and don't fuck it up.

"You did it!" Riles beams, her eyes flicking from my feet to dead ahead, her hands straight by her sides.

Confident I can put this Michael Flatley dude to shame—whoever the hell he is—I jump up again, hop, and then do the step-back-and-forth move when I lose my balance, my arm instinctively flinging out and hitting the woman beside me in the head.

"Shit!" I gasp. "I'm so sorry. Are you okay?"

She rubs the spot and glares at me before forcing a fake smile and stepping over a safe distance to allow me extra space.

Smart woman. I'd move away from me too.

Feeling awful, I hunch over and rest my hands on my knees.

"Hey, don't give up," Riles says, stifling her laughter.

"It'll be safer if I do. I nearly knocked that poor woman out."

She glances at my victim, then swipes her hand. "Don't worry about it. She's fine."

I sneak a look too. "Yeah, for now."

"Here, if you're worried, swap places with me." Riles shuffles me to the end of the row. "And try putting your hands in your pockets like Leo did in *Titanic*."

I do as I'm told, because securing my hands is a good idea. "Wait!" I gasp, twisting in her direction. "Is that how you know how to do this... because of *Titanic*?"

She grins, nodding maniacally. "Yes! After watching the movie, I begged Mom for lessons."

My jaw tics. "How many lessons did you have?"

She side-eyes me. "A few."

"And you didn't think to tell me this before we started?"

"No. You insulted me and said I couldn't dance."

I did, damn it! "Do you have any other talents I'm unaware of?"

Riles kicks her feet out and turns in a circle, exactly like Rose and Jack did in the movie. "Maybe."

Amusement lifts my face; she's good. "Care to elaborate?"

"Not yet. But if you keep going, I might show you what I can do with a banana."

The banana in my pants jerks to life.

She winks.

"After you've stepped back onto your front foot for the second time," Michelle says, "you'll start the sequence again by jumping and bringing your back foot to the front, to the same position we started in. So jump, hop, back-front, back-front, then jump, switch, hop, back-front, back-front, and so on."

I'm so fucking confused. Jump. Hop. Leg up, leg down. Switch. Who invented this shit show? And to top it all off, I now have images of Riles in my head, seductively licking a goddamned banana.

I stop hippity-hopping and turn toward her. "What can you do with a bana—"

"Don't worry about that," she says, turning me forward again. "Just keep going."

Groaning, I slide my hands into my pockets and count to the beat. "You better show me this banana trick."

She giggles. "I will! Now focus."

Following Riles's lead, I'm soon jigging like Leo. Sort of. Less Leo-ish and more Riley-ish—heavy-footed and uncoordinated.

"Brilliant, everyone!" Michelle shouts. "You're all naturals."

She's lying; we're not. There are at least three other unfortunate dudes worse than I am, one of them resembling an electrocuted donkey, his dance space much broader than what the woman I assaulted gave me. I feel sorry for him. Or more accurately, I share his pain.

"Now, to finish the dance, after the fourth hop back, we're going to then hop onto our left foot and then rock onto our front, then back, and then front again. Like this." Michelle demonstrates. "And that's it!"

Blinking, I shake my head, once again lost.

"Are we ready?" Michelle claps above her head, eyes wide with anticipation. "Let's give the full routine a try."

Wait! What?

Riles and most of the others eagerly call out, "Yes!" but I know I'm going to fuck it up. It's a foregone conclusion, like day and night, life and death... me and Riles. And if I'm going to look like a complete and utter fool, I might as well do it in style. *My* style. The Riley-can't-dance-for-shit style. At this point, I've got nothing to lose.

Sucking in a deep breath, I puff it out again as Michelle counts us in, and as if a herd of elephants is storming the ship, the atrium rumbles with our stomping feet, the thunderous noise attracting people to stop and watch from the decks above. They point and clap, cheering us along, no doubt grateful it's us and not them.

Jolly music fills the atrium, and Paul bounces about like a frog, Riles deviating from the steps and performing her own fancy variations, my eyes glued to her spirited chest. It throws me off, and I fumble a step, completely mucking up the routine, my legs and arms flicking out like a circus clown.

"What was *that?*" Riles asks, bursting into laughter as she bends over and clutches her waist.

I keep going, wobbling my head like a dickhead and murdering the dance, my limbs flinging here, there, and everywhere, because I have no idea what part we're up to or what I'm doing.

Standing straight again, Riles tries to continue but fails, her body bowing once more, her knees pressed together, tears streaming down her face. "Stop! I can't. I'm gonna pee."

I'm tempted to just give up, for her sake more than mine, but Riley Wilson, Lord of the flies... rings... dance... whatever, is not a quitter. I finish what I start, even this hippity-hoppity bullshit.

"Nearly there," Michelle calls out. "One more time!"

Jumping a safe distance from Riles, just in case she does lose control of her bladder, I prepare for my finale, springing up like a spasming dolphin before spinning and dropping to one knee, arms out wide.

"Oh, my God!" She stumbles back, bends over, straightens, and then bends again, her entire body wracking with hysterics as she gasps for air. "That's the funniest thing I've ever seen."

I hang my head, mortified yet thrilled I can make her laugh as much as she is, her damp eyes sparkling, her face overjoyed. It drowns my heart with happiness—a death I'll gladly give it if this is the outcome. And despite the utter pile of dance dung I just performed, I can't help but feel proud. I let go and danced like a freak... for Mom, Riles, and for me.

Stepping forward, she holds her hands out and tries to pull me up, but I finally burst into laughter and fall on my ass, taking her with me.

"You're insane," she chokes out, tumbling off my chest until we're both flat on our backs, spectators still cheering several decks above. "Hilarious, but insane."

I scrub my hands over my face. "I'm not even going to argue with that."

"That's because you can't."

"Well, tickle me pink," Paul announces. "I think we have our winner."

Raising my head to where he stands before me, the gold trophy outstretched in his hand, I accept it from him and then flop onto my back again, holding it with one hand in the air, the other covering my eyes.

Riles's lips crash down upon mine, and even though I have no doubt embarrassed myself to within an inch of my life, I couldn't care less.

I haven't had this much fun... probably ever.

"Now we both have one," Riles says as she positions the two trophies side by side on the desk in our cabin. "They're twins!"

I step up behind her and dangle a banana over her shoulder.

"What the...?" She snatches it and whirls around to face me. "Where'd you get this?"

"The buffet." I smirk. "On our way past."

"You sneaky son of a—"

I waggle my brows. "So, this banana trick...."

"Riley!"

"A promise is a promise."

"But—"

"No buts."

"Fine," she huffs out. "I'll show you."

Greedily rubbing my hands together, I take a seat on the sofa and lean back as she kicks off her shoes and walks a lazy circle in front of me, her fingers delicately caressing the banana's tip.

Heat waves over my body, my pants tightening at my groin. I shuffle to get comfortable, subtly adjusting myself as I swallow.

She flicks her eyes to my hand, then bites her lip seductively. "I haven't done this in a while," she says innocently, a faint blush warming her cheeks. "I'm not sure I remember how."

"That's—" I choke on my words before clearing my croaky throat. "That's okay. Take your time."

Riles smiles as if she's playing with me, as if her memory is perfectly fine, and it excites me all the more. I love her modesty, especially when she's faking it.

"You chose a big one," she says, rotating the banana in her hand as she assesses its size.

I swallow again. "I did."

"It might be too big."

"I'm sure you can handle it."

What the fuck am I saying?

I have no idea what she can handle or how she plans to handle it, so I should shut the hell up.

Her brow hitches before she twists at the waist from one side to the other, her fingers splitting the top of the banana ever so slightly. "I used to practice this a lot, at home, by myself," she confides, her eyes flicking back to mine before she lowers to the ground, lays it by her foot, then leans back on her hands and opens her legs.

Fuck me, why isn't she wearing a dress, or better yet... nothing at all?

I run my hand through my hair and swallow yet again, my throat thick, my cock hard.

"Do you like bananas?" she asks, licking her lips as she toes the length of it, her shiny, ink-colored toenails setting my body on fire.

A low growl escapes my mouth. "I do."

"Me too. They're so smooth, soft, and sweet."

Continuing to watch her toe-fuck the banana, I have no doubt in my mind she's smooth, soft, and sweet as well, my patience to find out almost nonexistent until she scissors her toes, clasps the banana, and fucking peels it... with her other foot.

"Ta-daa!" Lifting her leg, she offers me the fruit. "Hungry?"

I blink, close my eyes, and... laugh.

"No?" she teases. "It'll be a shame to waste."

Burying my frustration, I snap my eyes open and launch off the sofa toward her. She screams and tries to scurry away, but I clasp her ankles and twist her onto her back, dragging her to me until she's straddling my lap, my arms firmly secured around her.

"That was..."

"Talent?" she offers.

"...not what I was expecting."

Giggling, her eyes mischievously chase mine, lips closing in a fraudulent pout. "But you said you liked bananas."

I nip her shoulder, then trail my tongue up her neck, tasting her delicious skin.

"Ohhh," she drawls, voice breathy, eyelids fluttering. "So you thought my talent was something else, huh?"

I nibble her earlobe and murmur, "You could say that."

She ghosts her lips over mine. "Maybe it is."

My body sizzles like a firecracker, my hips bucking, desperate for her to show me, until her fingers slide beneath my waistband.

"Fuck!" I grit my teeth and hold her hand still. "Wait!"

Her body stiffens. "Wh—"

"Before we go any further, there's something I have to do first."

She retracts her hand, her pretty eyes cautious.

"Trust me, sweetheart. If we're going to do this, we're going to do it right."

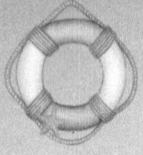

chapter twenty-three

RILES

C onfusion ices my body when Riley lifts me off his lap and turns his back on me. I'm ready to take things further, and I thought he was too, but maybe I was wrong.

Nervously fixing my hair, I wait for him to explain when he walks to his bedside table, opens a drawer, and collects some documents and a small box.

"I brought my divorce papers to sign when the time was right. And that time is now." He takes a seat at the desk, flips a page over, and scribbles his signature.

Shocked, because I did not see this coming, I rub my wrist, awkwardly fiddling with the beaded bracelet he bought me in Greenland. "Do you want some privacy? Because I can—"

"No. This will only take a second." He folds another page over and signs again, as if what he's doing is nothing more than endorsing a check.

I take a seat on the edge of my bed, keep quiet, and wait for him to officially end his marriage, knowing how hard this is for him, whether he cares to admit it or not.

He flips the pages back and slides the document aside before picking up the box and turning in his seat to face me, his fingers caressing the velvet. "And I brought my wedding ring to toss into the sea."

My jaw drops, my spine rigid. Although different from my own farewell, the similarity that he too is on this trip to say goodbye in his own way pinches my heart.

"This once sat proudly on my finger," he says, popping open the lid and staring at the gold band. "A symbol of my love and devotion. A decorative promise. And while I kept my end of that bargain, so to speak, Krystal did not."

I wince at the pain in his voice. "I'm sorry, Riley."

"You and me both." He snaps the box shut. "But as I said the other night, it's for the best."

Not wanting to say what I'm about to say, because it could spell the end of what he and I have started, I say it anyway. "Are you sure about that?"

His eyes meet mine, soft and sincere. "Yes. Absolutely. I did everything I could to save my marriage, but when all was said and done, there was nothing left to save."

Nodding, I drag Mr. Snuffles onto my lap and hug him to me.

"When we lost Imogen, Krystal crumbled. And while I crumbled too, I knew her pain was different. A mother's always is. Her bond with our daughter was on a separate level from mine. I understood that. It was tethered deep in her womb, and I could never compare my own grief with hers. I didn't even try." He looks down at the box again and rotates it in his hand. "So, I shielded her from my pain... to an extent, of course. She didn't need to deal with it on top of her own. I worked as much as I could so that she didn't have to, so she could grieve without any added stress. And I did whatever was within my power to help her heal the parts of her that could be healed. When she shut herself off from the world, I let her but kept her safe. When she blamed me, I took it."

"Why would she blame you?" I ask, my voice timid.

"Deep down, I don't think she did, but she had to blame someone at the time. And if that someone was me, then so be it."

Patting my hand over Mr. Snuffles's ears, my heart breaks for Riley having to endure that while drowning in his own grief. "God, that must've been so hard for you."

"It was. But her wellbeing was my priority, so I made her see our doctor, because she was fading away to nothing. She was a shell of her former self and incredibly bitter. She hated the world and everyone in it, and I mean *everyone*. She would verbally attack not only me but also Mom and Roni. Even Poppy. And Poppy was just a toddler."

I stop patting and frown. "That's awful."

He scoffs. "Yeah, and I could no longer stand for it when she screamed at Poppy and asked why she was here and Imogen wasn't, and when she slapped Roni for being a mother when she couldn't be."

"Jesus." I press Mr. Snuffles to my chest. "Sounds like she was in unbearable pain, and the only way she could deal with it was to lash out."

"She was. And that's exactly what she did." He closes his eyes and takes a moment before opening them and staring at me as if desperate for me to know what happened wasn't his fault. "Our lives became toxic, Riles, for her, me, and our families. The Krystal who was lashing out wasn't the Krystal I loved and married. Before Imogen, she was never aggressive and hurtful. Sure, she was a little self-indulgent and never shied away from a discussion she was passionate about, but she was always sweet and kind about it. She never attacked. Was never vicious." He squeezes the velvet box. "I insisted she see a shrink to properly deal with her grief. And it helped at first, but then... something just snapped. And while her bitterness eased and she stopped blaming everyone around her, she also stopped being *her*." He draws in a deep breath, holds it, then lets it out again. "She became someone else. A new Krystal. Determined. Ambitious. But... withdrawn."

Hanging on every word he's saying, I place Mr. Snuffles beside me and inch closer to the edge of the mattress.

"I knew something was still wrong, but I was so relieved that she was eating again and leaving the house to do the things she loved. She would meet up with friends for coffee and dinners, and she applied for a position in a high-profile law firm in Manhattan. I didn't like the idea, because it meant we'd spend less time together, but it was what she wanted, so I was happy for her. If this new change would bring her back to me, then it was a change I was willing to adapt to, to support and encourage."

"Of course," I say, agreeing with him.

"Things were okay in the beginning. She would talk about her cases, and she was constantly shopping for new clothes and taking care of her appearance, which she'd always done *before*. It was just... different this time around. Her clothes, hair, and makeup were more—" He clenches his jaw. "—provocative, you know?"

I nod but wince.

"Don't get me wrong, Riles. I loved that she was empowering herself by looking and feeling a certain way. She had every right to, and it's not my place as a man to say otherwise." He smiles at me. "Trust me, Mom and Roni have made that very clear for as long as I can remember. They've drilled into me that how a woman looks is none of a man's business."

I smile back, impressed with his answer and the strong female influences in his life.

"So, I wasn't mad or insecure about the *new* confident her. I was just unsettled for reasons I later found out were valid."

Biting my fingernail, because I know where this is headed, I want to go to him and offer comfort with my embrace, to show him I care about his pain. To show him *he's* not alone. But I stay where I am, instead giving him space to say everything he needs to say, because verbalizing your pain is vital in letting it go. I know this from my own experience, having kept my pain internalized. And while it felt the safer option to do so, all it did was allow it to grow, watered by tears and compartmentalized trauma. I don't want that for Riley; he's been through enough.

To successfully say goodbye, we must thread our thoughts into spoken words and then set them free. We must talk, confide, confess. Muted pain is our enemy. To give it a voice is the only way we can truly move on.

"What happened next?" I ask, prompting him to continue.

"She was rarely home, and when she was, she wasn't. She never asked about the business or the family. Never suggested we go anywhere or spend time together. She just switched off from me and the life we once had, as if it had never existed. We stopped being intimate, stopped holding hands and kissing each other goodnight. We stopped being us. I was devastated but also numb, knowing we were done and that there was nothing else I could do to change it. And when I tried one last time, she finally put me out of my misery and was honest about everything she'd been doing with Finn." A sarcastic laugh passes his lips. "Well, her honesty didn't put me out of my misery, of course. It caused more. Much, much more."

"You didn't deserve that. At all. But... grief changes people. And while I certainly don't condone what Krystal did, the grief you shared changed you both in different ways."

He stands, walks to the closed balcony door, and stares out across the sea, the velvet box clutched in his hand. "You're right. Grief does change you, and I was so fucking angry about that. But what I didn't understand until this cruise is how change, whether you want it or not, is inevitable. I thought we controlled the change if we really wanted to, but it's not the change we control. It's how we go about it. Krystal's change—her growth, recovery, transformation... whatever you want to call it—wasn't within her control. What was though, was her decision to hurt me during the process, and while I respect her for surviving the hardest thing she would ever endure, I'll never forgive her for *how* she survived it. And she knows that."

I get up from the bed and stand by his side. "Do you still talk to one another?"

"We do."

"Is it amicable?"

"Mostly."

"That's good, Riley."

"Yeah, I know."

"What about her family? Do you still talk to them?"

He shakes his head. "Not really. Communication was always strained because she married me so young."

"That must've been hard." I slip my hand into his while following his line of sight as he continues to stare out to sea, the sunlight glittering on the surface of the water.

He glances down at our entwined fingers. "It was, but Mom and Roni somewhat filled that void for her. Like you, Krystal is an only child, except her parents were more concerned with their place in society than they were with supporting her decisions. Until she married me, she was their shiny, obedient trophy. But I guess Krystal wanted that lifestyle after all. To be a top-notch attorney, someone her parents could once again be proud of."

I snap my face toward his. "Her parents would be proud that she cheated on you and destroyed your marriage?"

"My guess is they don't know that part, and they probably never will."

My jaw drops. "But that's... that's not fair."

He turns to face me and gently tucks my hair behind my ear. "It doesn't matter, Riles. I don't care what they know and what they don't know. All I care about is that *I* know the truth, *Krystal* knows the truth, and *my family and friends* know the truth. If she wants to live a different life without grief or guilt, whether it's real or not, then I'll let her."

"Wow!" I scoff. "You're a better person than I am."

He chuckles. "I don't know about that."

"You are. I would've set the record straight, no doubt about it."

"I want her to have peace, if that's what she thinks peace is. She's been through enough."

Sliding my hand onto his face, I cup his cheek and peck his lips. "You're incredible, and you should be proud of your strength and selflessness. Not many people could do what you've done."

He jerks back and smiles. "Mom said the same thing."

I wink. "That's because she's smart, like me."

"You're a lot like her, you know. Except for the eating meals part. Mom loves meals. Big meals. Three times a day. She'd be horrified to know you don't."

I pinch his cheek. "Hey! I do like meals, just not all the time."

"We'll see about that." He opens the door and steps out on the balcony, and I can't help smiling because it means he plans to be around in my not-so-distant future, at the very least.

Knowing that fills me with joy and hope, hope that we just might be able to make *us* work.

Staying put while Riley takes a moment outside, I twist my bracelet as he wrenches his arm back, rocks forward, and then pitches the box into the ocean, his hands grasping the railing as he leans over it and watches his ring splash into the water.

"Chapter closed," he says, scrubbing his palms together.

I smile at his words but, at the same time, sympathize with his grief and the pain it caused. "The good thing about closed chapters is they set up the ones to come."

He smirks. "Your fancy publisher talk is sexy."

I laugh. "It's not."

"It is." He strides toward me, pupils dilating. "Now, where were we?"

I step back as he reenters our cabin, my arms outstretched and locked, fingers splayed firmly against his chest.

He dips his head. "What's wrong?"

"I just.... I don't think now is a good time... for that."

His shoulders sag. "I killed the mood, didn't I?"

"Yeah." I nod sadly. "You just officially ended your marriage, so maybe let that emotionally sink in first."

"It already has," he says, lifting my hand to his lips and pressing a kiss to my knuckles. "But... I see your point."

"You do?"

"Yeah, Riles. I do."

"Good." I exhale my relief. "Because I don't want you to think I don't want—"

"You don't need to explain." He smirks. "I know you want what I want."

Releasing my hands from his, I cross my arms over my chest and smirk back. "And how exactly do you know that?"

He kisses the crook of my neck, then trails his tongue to the sensitive spot below my ear.

I gasp.

"That," he whispers. "Remember?"

Groaning, I roll my shoulders. "You're making me tense."

"That's not my plan, sweetheart."

"I need a massage."

His delicious, manly hands climb my arms, his fingers kneading delightfully.

I step back, pick up the envelope on the desk, and wave it in his face. "This! I need this."

He frowns.

"Come on," I say, clasping his hand and dragging him toward the door. "Let's get our couples' massage. It would be a shame to waste."

Soft, sensual music fills the room as we enter the Lotus Spa, floral musky steam billowing from a crystal diffuser. I breathe in the ambience, excited for the relaxation to come, and boy do I need it. As much as I wanted to continue what we started before Riley signed his divorce papers and closed the chapter of his marriage, it just didn't feel right at that moment, despite my body adamantly disagreeing with me.

"Smells like Roni in here," he says, sniffing the air.

I pick up a pamphlet when one of the spa staff approaches, her hair neatly tied back in a bun, black uniform perfectly tailored. "Welcome to Lotus Spa. How can I help you?"

"We won this," I explain, handing her our voucher.

"Congratulations! You're in for a treat. We have a spot available now if you'd like. Or I can book you in for tomorr—"

I clap my hands, excited. "Now would be perfect!"

"I'll just need you to fill out these forms. While you do that, I'll get you both some refreshments." She hands us two clipboards and pens before disappearing along a corridor, returning moments later with two glasses of champagne. "How's it going? Any questions?"

Shaking my head, I take a glass from her and hand her my clipboard. Riley doesn't answer, instead studying his paperwork in the corner of the room as if it's written in a foreign language, so I take his glass from her and step up to him. "Everything all right?"

He points his pen at a specific question. "What did you write here?"

I lean forward and read it. "Are there any areas of your body that you prefer not to be massaged?"

"Yeah. What did you put down for that?"

"I wrote **No**."

"Does that mean it's a free-for-all?" he asks, lowering his voice.

"Free-for-all?"

"Yeah. My entire body."

Laughter bursts from my throat. "I don't know what type of massage you think this is, but I'm confident certain *parts* of you will remain untouched, at least by the staff."

The corners of his eyes crinkle. "At least by the staff?"

"Yes."

"You're not staff."

I pass him his drink and sip my own. "Hand her your clipboard, Riley."

He clinks my glass with his, passes over his paperwork, and picks up a crystal, rotating it in his hand. "Roni likes these fancy rocks."

"Those are not fancy rocks," our hostess says. "They communicate with the energy flow of your body, assisting in realignment and healing."

He stares at it. "This little pink rock talks?"

"Not exactly." She snickers. "It communicates loving energy, replacing negativity and opening you up to self-forgiveness and trust. It's also known to help increase fertility."

He places it down again and murmurs into my ear, "Is she saying I could be pregnant now?"

Subtly elbowing him, I force a smile when she lifts her gaze from my paperwork and hugs the clipboards to her chest. "Perfect! We're all set. Please come with me."

We follow her into a dimly lit room with two massage beds in the center, plush white robes and towels neatly folded on top of them.

"I'll give you both a minute to undress to your underwear, lie down, and cover yourself with the towels provided. Once your massage is complete, feel free to wear your robes and use the spa's other facilities, such as the sauna and infinity pool. We also offer mud baths and—"

"No more mud," Riley blurts, wrinkling his nose as he swallows his champagne. "My hair still hasn't recovered from Iceland."

Laughing, I say, "Thank you. I think we'll just stick with the massage... for now."

"Very well. Your masseuses will be along shortly."

She leaves the room, and I turn in a circle, looking for a bathroom to undress in when Riley discards his empty glass, removes his T-shirt, and starts to unbutton his jeans.

"What are you doing?" I choke out, swallowing my last mouthful.

"Getting ready, what does it look like?"

He wrenches down his pants, then takes a seat on the leather bed, his legs lazily swinging as he leans back on his hands and smirks.

"What are you doing?" I ask again.

"Waiting for you to get ready. What does it look like?"

Unable to drag my eyes off his delectable thighs and abs, the chuckle climbing his throat snaps me out of my daze.

"Turn around," I snap.

"Riles."

"Do it."

"You seem to forget I've seen you in your underwear. Twice."

Growling at him, I set down my glass and remove my top, tossing it at his face before unbuttoning my denim shorts, wiggling them down my legs, and then kicking them aside.

He sits up straighter.

I smirk.

"Come here," he says, voice low.

"No."

"Riles."

Shaking my head, I reach behind my back to unlatch the clasp of my bra, repeating, "Turn around."

chapter twenty-four

RILEY

A feral growl rumbles in my throat as I stare at Riles's delicious body, my hands itching to reach out and take her in my arms. "You're killing me, sweetheart."

She releases one hand from behind her back, brings it forward, and swirls her damn finger at me. "Turn. Around."

"Okay," I say, chuckling at her stubbornness.

"Thank you."

I snatch up my towel and lie on my stomach, obediently turning my head in the opposite direction. "You're not welcome."

The leather of her bed squeaks as she shuffles behind me, which is when I catch her movement in the reflection of the window, her image distorted but clear enough for me to admire.

Waiting for her to remove her bra, my heartbeat thuds in my chest. I should look away. It's the right thing to do. But there's no way in hell I can, even if I tried, even if I wanted to, which I sure as shit don't.

My cock hardens uncomfortably as she takes a step closer, tilts her head, and drags her eyes over my back, her arm reaching out, hand hovering. I anticipate her touch, my skin tingling, but she retracts her hand, presses her fingers to her lips, and then turns her back to me before sliding the straps from her shoulders.

Covering up, she practically barrel-rolls onto her bed, landing facedown. "Okay, you can look now."

I stifle my amusement and turn my head, my breath instantly catching in my throat. "You're so damn beautiful, Riles."

Modesty blushes her cheeks, so I reach out and drag my knuckle along her arm, desperate to feel her soft skin, when a knock at the door halts my hand.

"*Allo*? May we enter?"

"Yes," Riles calls out, voice strained.

Rearranging my position so I'm not spearing the bed with my hard-on, a cool breeze settles over my back as two women enter the room, each of them positioning themselves by our sides.

"Welcome," one of them says. "Are you both comfortable?"

I squirm again. "Not particularly."

The woman closest to me bends down, blocking my view of Riles, her stern but pleasant face mere inches from mine. "First time?"

"Yes."

She smacks her hands together, links her fingers, then stretches her arms away from her body. "Relax. You enjoy. I make you feel good."

My eyes widen.

"Face in hole," she adds.

Face in what?

She points to a towel underneath my head and then parts it, revealing an opening in the table. "Head down."

I stiffen. "Put my head in that?"

"Yes."

"But it's not big enough."

"You fit."

Slowly pressing my face into the gap, what feels like a thousand tiny pins prick the length of my spine, my chest tightening, my hands restless and clammy.

I instantly jerk back, damned if I'll be doing that again.

"What wrong?" She squirts oil onto her hands, rubs them

together, and then places her palms on my shoulders, coaxing me down.

I push against her.

"He's claustrophobic," Riles mutters.

"Just turn to side then," the woman says, clasping my face with her slimy fingers and gently rotating my head.

Riles giggles, and I want to toss a ticking clock at her until she reaches for my hand and rests the side of her head on her towel, facing me. "Don't worry. It's not just you. I don't particularly like the hole either. I end up with a headache and weird indentations on my face."

"And this is supposed to be enjoyable?" I ask, confused.

"It will be. Just relax. Stop fighting it."

Reluctantly doing as she says, her soothing misty eyes chasing mine, I lose myself in their depth while our masseuses massage our shoulders and necks. Riles's heavy eyelids fall shut, her hand slipping from mine as her arm falls limp by her side. I close my eyes as well, peace immobilizing my body and mind, my breathing shallow, the tension from signing my divorce papers and discarding my wedding ring squeezed, kneaded, and worked out of me.

I allow the purge and let go of everything I've been through, the loss, the lies, the fallout, relief a comforting blanket when the crushing weight of it all literally lifts from my body.

"Ohhh, gaaawd," Riles murmurs, a soft, sensual moan escaping her lips.

I snap my eyes open and blink, her body gloriously oiled, her expression erotically sated.

She moans again, and my cock stirs in response.

"Turn over now," my masseuse instructs.

What? Hell no!

Slamming my eyes shut again, I pretend to be asleep.

"*Allo?*" She pats my shoulder. "Wakey wakey."

If I "wakey wakey," you'll see my "snakey snakey," and there's no fucking way I'm allowing that.

"Riley," Riles whispers, her fingers gently squeezing my arm. "Wake up. It's time to roll over."

I play dead, a game I'm a seasoned champion at, thanks to Poppy.

She jiggles my arm.

Damn it!

"Riiileyyy!"

Shut up!

The masseuse karate chops my back, making me bow and spring up to my elbows. "Jesus!"

"*Allo!*" She bends down, her face once again mere inches from mine. "You wake up now."

"We're finished?" I ask, not waiting for a reply. "Brilliant! I feel like a new man. Thank you very much."

"No! Not finished." She lifts my towel. "You lie on back now."

I snatch it from her. "No. I'm done."

"No. You lie on back."

"No. I stay on front."

Riles raises her head and rubs her eyes. "You need to turn over so they can do your quads."

"My quads are fine."

"Uh-ah," the woman says, her fingers painfully digging into my hamstring. "Much tension in legs. I help with that."

I wince and shake her off me. "No, thank you."

Riles rises to her elbows as well, and I catch sight of the side of her breast before she covers up with her towel and flips onto her back.

Jesus Christ, sweetheart. You're not helping my case.

She frowns. "What's wrong?"

"Nothing."

"So turn over."

"No."

"Why not?"

"I can't."

"Of course you can."

I give her my best I-have-an-erection face.

She gives me the same face back.

What the hell?

Blinking at her, I'm ready to just stand the hell up and own it, when her eyes shoot toward my groin, then back to my face.

"Really?" she asks.

"Yes, really."

"Oh!" She presses her lips together, clasps her towel to her chest, sits up, and blurts, "Thank you. That was wonderful, but we're done."

My masseuse shakes her finger. "No. Not done."

"Yes," Riles affirms, "we are. You were both fabulous."

Muttering something in another language, the woman shrugs at her colleague before they wash their hands and leave the room.

"Thank fuck for that," I say, hanging my head.

"Sooo, you *enjoyed* yourself then?" Riles drawls.

I pin her with my stare. "I *enjoyed* listening to you."

"Me?"

"Yes. You were moaning."

"Was I?"

I roll my neck. "Yep."

"Sorry. It was... good."

"I could tell," I deadpan.

Sliding off her bed, she moves closer and trails her fingertip down my back. "Turn over."

I almost choke. "What?"

"You heard me."

"Given my current state, that's not a good idea."

"I think it's a very good idea."

"Riles," I warn.

"What?"

"Don't tease me. My restraint is thin."

"So is mine."

"I thought you wanted to wait."

She drops her towel.

Fuuuck!

Slowly rising, my eyes not leaving her milky skin and pebbled nipples, I plant my feet on the ground, slide my hands onto her hips, and tug her closer, my hard-on pressing against her stomach. She sucks in a breath and reaches down, cupping her hand over me and gently squeezing.

I hiss. "We need to leave."

"Do we?" she prompts, her voice raspy and sexy as hell.

"Riles"—I crawl my fingers up her side and palm her breast— "I can't do all the things I want to do to you here. So yes, we're leaving." I smash my lips to hers while fumbling with the robe at the end of her bed. "Put this on."

"Shouldn't we get dressed?"

"What's the point?"

She contemplates my answer. "True."

After throwing on my robe, I grab our clothes and shoes and secure her hand, dragging her out of the room and along a corridor, passing staff members as they move aside.

"Thank you," Riles calls out, waving at them as she shuffles behind me.

I try to wave too but drop her bra, so I bend over when she crashes into me, both of us tumbling onto the floor.

"Shit! Are you okay?" I ask, rolling her giggling body onto her back before hovering over her.

"Yes. Are you?"

The lapel of her robe falls aside just slightly, so I run my finger along the seam.

A woman clears her throat.

We both look up.

"Is everything okay here?"

Riles scrambles beneath me, her knee plowing my balls into my gut. "Yes," she blurts, kicking me off her. "Sorry, we fell."

"Jesus," I cough out, cupping my nuggets while slumping onto my side.

She gives me an "oops" face.

"It was her fault we fell," I say, voice strained.

"It was not." She gets to her feet and begrudgingly helps me up before collecting her bra. "We were just leaving."

"I see," the woman bites out, then presses her lips together and steps aside, so we hurry past her, me hobbling like an old-timer, Riles's head downcast.

"Did I break your balls?" she whispers.

"Almost."

"Sorry, but they were in my way." She picks up her pace and calls out, "Hold the door!" as the elevator begins to close.

We bundle into the death box, both of us staring straight ahead, Riles nibbling her lip in an attempt to chew back her amusement.

"I'm glad you found that funny," I murmur.

"It was."

I clench my jaw, beyond ready to get back to the cabin to finish what we started, to get her naked and—

"Mummy, why are they in pajamas?" a little girl with the cutest Australian accent standing behind us asks her mother.

"They're not, sweetie."

I glance over my shoulder while Riles stifles a giggle.

"He has hair on his face like Uncle Will."

I rub my beard, and Riles bursts into laughter.

"Shhh, little Minty," the mother says, lifting her daughter and settling her on her hip. "I'm so sorry. She takes after me and blurts out whatever she's thinking."

The doors open, and I exit the elevator faster than the first time I ever stepped foot in one, expecting Riles to do the same when she turns around instead, tickles the little girl's knee, and says, "Byyye."

Crossing my arms over my chest, I wait while Riles waves and backs out of the elevator, the mother waving her daughter's hand in return.

"Naww, how cute," Riles says as she turns around and slams straight into my chest. "What—"

My eyes flare.

She rears back.

Grinning like the devil, I squat down and secure her waist before tossing her over my shoulder.

"Riley! Put me down!"

"No can do, sweetheart."

"Stop it! I'll flash people."

I lift her robe, slide my hand underneath, and rub her ass as I carry her along the corridor.

"Oh my God! Will you stop it!" She growls and tries to wriggle free, but it's no use—she's not going anywhere.

Stopping at the cabin door, I pat my robe with my free hand, realizing I don't have my lanyard. "Shit!"

"Problem?" she asks, a cocky tone to her voice.

"Where's the damn card?"

"I have it."

"Hand it over."

"Put me down."

"Riles," I warn.

"Riley!" she warns back.

Gritting my teeth, I glide my hand up the back of her leg and slap her ass.

"Ouch!"

"Open the door. Now!"

"You just smacked—"

"Riles," I warn again. "If you don't open this door, I'll fuck you right here in the hallway."

She scoffs. "You will not."

I gently sink my teeth into her thigh. "Try me."

"Okay, okay. Here, take the damn card."

Snatching it from her, I fumble with the slot until it unlocks, then push the door open with my foot and stride inside.

Riles straightens her body, slides down my front, and before her feet even hit the floor, she shimmies her robe from her shoulders and slams her lips to mine, her hands wild in my hair, her knee lifting to press against my hip.

I grunt into her mouth, clench her ass, and lift her up, spinning us until her shoulders hit the wall. She gasps and locks her ankles behind my back, her head arcing and baring her neck. Never have I wanted to taste skin so badly, to bury my head into a woman and get lost in her scent.

Bracing my hand against the wall, I lean forward and nip the soft spot below her ear, nibbling and kissing before trailing my tongue to the top of her cleavage.

She moans, and I close my eyes, savoring the sexy sound. *Fuck, I've missed this.*

Palming her breast, I rub the pad of my thumb over her nipple before gently pinching it. She gasps again, so I press my mouth to hers, swallowing her pleasure and soft, shallow pants.

"Riley," she rasps out, her hands cupping my cheeks.

I pull back, my breathing heavy. "Tell me what you want."

Her eyes chase mine, her tongue darting out to lick her lips. "You."

"You already have me," I whisper, smiling as I nudge the crook of her neck with my nose.

Because she does.

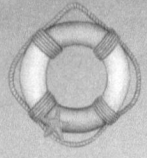

chapter twenty-five

RILES

A wave of ecstasy, belonging, and yearning rushes through my blood as I capture Riley's mouth with mine, desperate for more.

He pushes off the wall and carries me to his bed, gently placing me down as his eyes devour my body, anticipation peppering my skin as I squirm.

Climbing onto the mattress, he hovers over me, his perfect lips kissing and nipping a trail down my neck to my breast, the soft stubble of his beard a delightful tickle. I draw in a ragged breath as he sucks my nipple into his mouth before flicking it with his tongue.

"Oh, God!" I cry out, my voice breathy as I grip his hair, clenching it tight, my hand gentle as it uncontrollably pushes him lower.

He chuckles and inches back toward the foot of the bed, his fingers slipping beneath my panties as he collects them and slides the cotton down my legs. Parting my knees, he clears his throat and rubs his beard, his devilish eyes the shade of midnight.

I swallow.

He looks up at me again, and just as I think he's going to say something, he clenches his jaw instead, slips his hands beneath my ass, and wrenches me toward his mouth, breathing in deeply when his lips touch my skin. I gasp at the feel of him, my back bowing and lifting from the bed, my fingers gripping the sheets as he licks, sucks, nips, and kisses.

My core tightens, and I cry out his name.

My name.

Our name.

Huh. That's weird.

Standing up, his lips glistening, a sinister yet sexy gleam blaring from his eyes, I don't give our name a second thought when he wrenches down his underwear and leisurely fists his length.

Oh, dear Lord! I push up to my elbows and lick my lips as he opens his bedside drawer, pulls out a condom, rips open the foil packaging with his teeth like an animal, and then rolls it on so seductively that I almost incinerate.

Following the hard edges of his collarbone, down his arms, to the rigid lines of his stomach, my body shudders with heat. It's been so long since I've been with a man, a decent man, one so deliciously impeccable. And for quite possibly the first time in my life, nerves over what we're about to do tangle my stomach.

"Don't look so scared, Riles," he says, a grin twisting his lips.

"I'm... I'm not."

He climbs onto the bed and positions himself between my legs. "I'll be gentle."

As he slowly pushes into me, I relax around him while he rocks his hips, the feel of him glorious and strong, his movements heightening as I pant and moan into his mouth.

Lips seek lips, tongues lapping, our hands feverish as they caress, squeeze, and claw at each other's skin.

"You feel so good," I murmur.

"The feeling is mutual, sweetheart."

Heat blooms in my core, so I clench his hips with my thighs, scrape my nails along his back, and hold him tight as he pistons my body, over and over until my orgasm rockets through me, stars, lights, angels—I'm not sure what—bursting behind my eyelids, my muscles tightening around him, underneath him, and with him.

"Yes! Peanut butter. Yes!" I cry out.

Riley spears me deeply, long and sharp, his body stiff as a guttural groan rips from his throat. I capture his mouth, our tongues once again frenzied until they lose the ability to move, our breathing heavy, our limbs limp.

Panting, he drags his lips to my cheek, forehead, nose, and then my mouth again, peppering me with soft kisses, his eyes arduous but alight, the corners crinkling. "Did you just say 'peanut butter' while I made you come?"

I blink all the blinks. "What?"

"You screamed 'peanut butter.'"

"I did?"

"Yeah."

I burst into laughter and cover my face with my hands. "Oh my God! I did, didn't I?"

"Not gonna lie, I've never heard that before."

Peeking through my spread fingers, I push through my embarrassment and explain. "I'm not allowed to say mothereffer."

"Motherfucker?"

"Yeah. Peanut butter."

He stares at me.

I scrunch my face. "Mom hated it."

Dropping his head, his shoulders quake as he laughs. "I think I'm speechless."

"You?" I giggle. "Speechless?"

"Yes. It doesn't happen often, but that... this... you, you've stripped me of words."

I trail my hands up and down his arms. "I'm good at stripping words."

Muttering, "Peanut butter," he rolls off me and onto the bed before tucking me into his side, both of us sated and soothed with the gentle rocking of the ship, my arm over his sweat-dampened chest, his finger drawing lazy circles on my shoulder.

"That's actually quite cute, Riles."

"It's not. It's habit."

"A cute habit."

"Shut up. I thought you were speechless."

"I was. Not anymore."

"Shh."

He chuckles. "I thought maybe you were hungry."

"After that," I say, looking up at him, "I am."

"What do you want for dinner?"

I'm tempted to say, *"You,"* but my tummy has other ideas. "Pasta. A big, fat bowl of pasta."

"Keep talking like that," he says, kissing my head, "and Mom is definitely going to love you."

I smile, but the uncertainty of what will happen after our trip of a lifetime ends tightens my chest. We were supposed to take this slow and steady for that exact reason, but I screwed that up, unable to restrain myself any longer. "About that, Riley. We dock in Le Havre three days from now. Our cruise will be over. What... What happens next?"

"We fly back to the States."

I roll my eyes at him. "You know what I mean."

"We'll fly back to the States and then take each day as it comes. Easy. It's only a two-hour drive from Buxtonville to Manhattan."

I nod and snuggle into his warmth, even though I'm unconvinced it will be as "easy" as he says. Long-distance relationships are hard, or so I've heard. They require commitment, effort, and travel. Lots and lots of travel.

"This isn't it, Riles. I told you I don't do one-night stands, and I don't plan to start now. I want to see you again. And again, and again, and again." He tips my chin up and places a soft kiss on my lips. "We'll make it work. Whatever it takes."

Sighing at the promise in his eyes, I tether myself to his sincerity and roll on top of him. "I like the sound of that."

"I should hope so." He combs his fingers through my hair. "When are you flying home?"

"Midnight. The day we disembark."

"JFK or LaGuardia?"

"LaGuardia."

"My flight to Philly is an hour before yours."

Pouting, I can already feel his absence, my heartbeat an irregular rhythm.

"We could always change our flights, stay in Paris for a few days, and fly back together?"

"I wish I could," I say, smoothing out his chest hair. "But I can't. I have to get back to work."

"Ah, yes. You mustn't upset Georgia the Torturer."

Playfully glaring at him, I pluck one solitary hair.

"Ow! That wasn't very nic—"

"Speaking of work, I have to put in a couple of hours tonight. I'm behind on the manuscript."

He draws in a deep breath, lifts his arms, links his hands behind his head, and exhales while staring at the ceiling.

I sit upright, straddling his lap. "What was that for?"

His eyes flick to my chest. "What was what for?"

"That frustrated puff thing you did."

"Puff thing?"

"Yes."

"I don't *puff*, sweetheart. I'm not the big, bad wolf."

Slapping his chest, I grumble and climb off him. "I'm gonna take a shower."

"You need more shampoo."

"What?"

"There's not much left."

"Riley!"

"It's good shit."

"Yes, I know. That's why I buy it."

He rolls onto his side and props his head on his hand, his greedy eyes raking my body. "Are you sure you don't want to stay in Paris with me? I'll make it worth your while."

"I'm sure you would, but I can't. I've been away too long already, and I have no doubt I'll have to pay for that in one way or another."

His eyes narrow before he falls onto his back again.

Sighing, I step into the bathroom, close the door behind me, and lean against it, my head and heart at war. I'd give anything to stay with him in the city of love, wrapped in sheets with the Eiffel Tower beyond our hotel room window. I've never wanted anything more... besides having Mom back.

But like resurrection and winding back time, what he's asking for is out of my hands. My job is my life, and if I don't return when I said I would, I won't have a job to go back to. I've learned so much as Georgia's slave, and I need to keep saving my pennies so I can eventually free myself of her entrapment and accomplish what I've worked so damn hard for. Until that happens, I'm chained to her every whim, and as much as I want to throw caution to the wind with Riley, those chains are stronger than my heartstrings.

MUCH TO RILEY'S ANNOYANCE, I WORKED MOST OF THE evening while he channel-surfed and seduced me, his seduction eventually winning over. We had sex again, and I was most pleased with his victory, even though I still had more work to do, which was now going to have to wait, because today, we travel to London after docking at Southampton in the early hours of the morning.

"How exciting! We're in Winchester," I say as the train passes underneath a brick, arched bridge. "This place is rich in history." I drag my eyes from the lush green bushland and glance at Riley. "Did you know it was once the ancient capital of England, known

as the Kingdom of Wessex? It's also where Jane Austen is buried."
Scooting forward on my seat, I press my forehead to the window
as we slow to a stop. "Parts of Harry Potter were filmed here too."

"Do you want to get off and take a look?" Riley asks as the
doors slide open, commuters embarking and disembarking in a
flurry to get to their destination.

I do want to see Winchester, but I also don't. I'm not fond of
the idea of rushing our time in London. There's so much to see
and do there. Perhaps, one day in my distant, distant future, I'll
get the chance to return.

I sigh. "I'd love to meander about, but we won't have time."

"There are trains leaving Waterloo Station and returning to
Southampton as late as eleven thirty tonight."

"I know," I say, snuggling into him, "but it's too early to stop
here. Nothing is open. And I don't want to get back too late. I
barely made a dent in that second manuscript last night."

"Riles, you're on vaca—"

"Please don't."

"Don't what?"

"Don't give me a hard time."

He raises his hands. "I just want you to do what *you* want
to do."

"I am. I'm here, aren't I? And anyway, how about you? What
do you want to do and see? When we planned our trip for today,
you let me pick all the places."

He settles his hands again, one on my shoulder, the other on
his lap. "That's because they were the places I wanted to see as
well."

"So we're not omitting anywhere you wanted to visit?"

"No. I want to see Westminster Abbey, Windsor Castle, and
the Tower of London. We're going to all of them, so I'm happy."

Biting the inside of my cheek, I conclude he's telling the truth.
"We can't stop here, even if I wanted to. We booked our admission to Windsor for nine, and we'll arrive there not long before

that time. If we get off now, we'll have to cancel and reschedule. And we might miss out."

"Do you always do everything by the book?"

"Mostly, yes. I like to be organized."

"I can tell."

"You say that like it's a bad thing. It's not. Especially when in a foreign country."

"All I'm saying is it's okay to be spontaneous every now and again."

"Need I remind you that I have been spontaneous, and it resulted in puke... on you."

The train pulls away, so I scoot forward again and get lost in the rolling hills and countryside, the landscape so different from what I'm used to. Serene. Earthy. Beautifully verdant. It provides a sense of peace, and I wonder if I lived here in a previous life. Perhaps I was a blacksmith's daughter, a tavern whore—hopefully not—or a highborn woman?

Imagining my life as a fictional character, I get lost in the fantasy until we're disembarking at Windsor Station.

"I wonder if the king is here," Riley says as we walk the cobbled paths past quaint shops to the castle.

I look toward the cylindrical tower. "He's not."

"How do you know?"

"Because the royal standard flag isn't hoisted."

"What's a royal standard flag?"

"It signifies the presence of the monarch."

"How do you know that?"

"I read... a lot."

Releasing my hand, Riley shows the admission clerk our tickets when we get to the gate, and once we pass through a security checkpoint, we're granted entry beyond the stone and brick fortress walls into the grounds.

I turn in a circle. "Wow! I can't believe I'm here, where kings and queens have lived for centuries." Rushing to a stone wall no higher than my waist, I lean over it. "Isn't it magical? And how pretty are the gardens? They're so well-kept."

"That's because they cut the lawns with scissors."

"What?" I snap my head to him. "No, they don't. They mow them with lawnmowers."

"I'm kidding, Riles."

"Oh. Well, they probably did cut them with scissors at one point or another. I wouldn't be surprised if Henry VIII ordered them to be snipped one blade of grass at a time."

"Was he the dude who beheaded his wives?"

"Yes," I grumble. "Philandering murderer."

Riley rears back a little. "That's a bit harsh."

"Harsh? He was a terrible king and husband. Treated his wives like dirt. Except for Jane Seymour. He liked her, but she died shortly after their son was born." I point to St. George's Chapel. "They're both buried in there."

"And you know all of this from reading a lot?"

"Yes." I lift my chin, proud. "And because Mom was a big fan of Tudor history. After I started my internship, I managed to chase down a first-print copy of Philippa Gregory's *The Other Boleyn Girl* for her. It was her prized possession, besides me, of course."

Linking my hand with his, I practically swing our arms and skip to the door of the chapel, excited I can tell Mom what I'm about to see.

My feet falter to a stop.

"What's wrong?" Riley asks.

"I just realized I can't tell Mom what I see here today."

He tugs my hand. "Sure you can."

"How? I tossed her into the ocean, remember?"

"Riles—" He smooths my hair behind my ears. "—you scattered her remains at sea, as she wanted you to. You still have her memory, so talk to that. That's how I talk to Dad."

"Did you cremate your father as well?"

"No. But I talk to his memory more than I talk to his headstone."

Huh. Nodding, I contemplate giving it a try. I still want to talk to her and tell her everything I experience. And she would love to know about this visit.

Stepping inside the nave of St. George's Chapel, I hold my breath at the white marble architecture and stained-glass windows. St. Mary's Basilica was grand and beautiful, but it pales in comparison to this. "Holy moly," I whisper.

"Peanut butter," he whispers back.

Laughter bursts from my throat, and I have to stifle it by muffling my mouth with my hand. "Don't make me laugh in here."

"I couldn't exactly say mother"—he mouths *"fucker"*—"could I?"

"No." I giggle. "You most certainly could not."

Dragging me toward the quire, he steps onto the checkered floor tiles and rubs his beard, his head circulating like a windmill. "The carvings in here are out of this world. So detailed and intricate."

I let go of his hand, fairly sure he doesn't even notice, and leave him to it before strolling along until I'm standing over the plaque that marks the vault in which Henry VIII and Jane Seymour are interred. A surreal sense of intrusion settles over me as I stand above them, so much so that I can't help but keep moving, until I realize the entire building resides over vaults and comprises surrounding chantries of royal remains: King Edward IV, Queen Elizabeth Woodville—Mom liked her—HRH Prince Philip, and more recently Queen Elizabeth II.

I take a moment to pay my respects and then head outside for some fresh air, the weight of the moment overwhelming.

Waiting beside the door, the morning sunlight bounces off my face as I watch the Changing of the Guard ceremony.

"You okay?" Riley asks, stopping beside me.

"Yeah. I just needed some air. It was viscerally spiritual in there."

He doesn't probe any further, instead nodding toward the men in their red uniforms and black fluffy hats as they march by. "What's going on?"

"The guards are changing."

"Changing what... their clothes?"

"No, silly. Changing shifts, so to speak. You might see it when we go past Buckingham Palace too."

He crosses his arms over his chest and rubs his beard. I want to rub it too, but I take his hand in mine instead and walk up the hill toward the Upper Ward.

"Where are you heading now?" he asks.

"Inside the castle."

"You can go inside, even though the royal family lives here?"

"Of course you can. But they only allow entry to certain parts."

"Sweet!"

His interest is endearing, so I squeeze his hand tighter as we step inside St. George's Hall, overjoyed that I'm not experiencing this on my own.

"Nice," he murmurs, looking up at the gothic-inspired high-pitched ceiling, beautifully constructed and covered with crests, red carpet blanketing the vast floor below.

"Did you know this place was destroyed by fire in the nineties?" I say.

"No." Riley reaches out to touch a statue but is politely berated by a security guard, so he snatches his hand back like a naughty child. "That would've sucked. There are a lot of fancy paintings in here."

"Apparently, most of them were already removed because the castle was under renovation. That's how the fire started, you know? An industrial lamp ignited a curtain, causing the blaze."

"Peanut butter."

I whack his arm. "Stop it."

"No. It's my new favorite saying."

Ignoring him, I continue along the passageway. "Many state-rooms were destroyed as well. Thankfully, the royal library was untouched. Oh my God, that would've been horrific. All those priceless books."

"I'm guessing that would be your worst nightmare."

I wince. "More or less."

We explore the rest of the castle, including the Crimson Drawing Room, grand staircase, and Queen Mary's Dolls' House, before boarding another train to London. And when we pass by Big Ben to visit Westminster Abbey, Riley playfully covers my ears as we walk beneath the clock.

I swat at him.

We then take a double-decker sightseeing bus past Buck-ingham Palace and Hyde Park, where we stop for a late lunch in a flower-covered tavern before reboarding the bus and continuing through Trafalgar Square to the Tower of London.

Standing on the south wall of the ancient fortress, I gaze wist-fully at Tower Bridge as it spans the Thames. "It's so pretty."

"Pretty? That river looks dirty as shit."

"Not the river. Tower Bridge."

"I thought it was called London Bridge?"

"No. London Bridge is boring compared to that beauty. It's upstream from here. We'll go beneath it when we catch the river ferry to the London Eye."

"Let me guess... you know that through lots of reading as well."

"Uh-huh." I look down to where a group of people on a walking tour follow their guide along a path. "Don't worry, I orig-inally thought that was London Bridge too, until I researched my trip. Most non-citizens do."

"Glad to know I'm not dumb then."

I smirk. "You know the capital of Norway. You're not dumb at all."

He pulls me into his arms, my back pressed to his chest, his head resting on my shoulder. "I only know it because of Roni. She's the geography nut. She always wanted to travel to Europe."

"Why doesn't she? Why didn't you travel here together?"

"Because she didn't want to take Poppy out of school, and she couldn't leave her behind."

"That's a shame. I'm guessing you would've loved sharing this cruise with your family."

"I would've, but... I'm glad I'm sharing it with you."

I twist my head back. "Me too. It's been interesting. Interesting but nice."

"Only nice?"

"More than nice."

It's been phenomenal. Something I'll always treasure.

"If it weren't for you, Riles, I wouldn't have seen half the things during this trip that I've seen so far."

"Really?" I ask, delightfully shocked.

"Yeah. I wouldn't have visited the *Titanic* exhibit in Nova Scotia, trashed my hair in a pool of mutant mud, or stood in a library with some of the best woodwork I've ever laid my eyes upon."

"You went to the museum?"

"I did, but not for long. I was looking for you, and when I couldn't find you, I left."

Turning in his arms, I link my hands behind his back. "Why were you looking for me?"

"Because I promised I wouldn't leave you behind."

Warmth flitters through my chest at his dedication and self-lessness, and I wonder for a split moment how on earth Krystal let him go. "There's another *Titanic* exhibit in Southampton. We can go there tomorrow after Stonehenge. I can teach you all about it."

"I'd like that." He dips his head and presses his lips to mine. "You're sexy when you're relaying historical information."

"Oh, am I?"

"Yep. Reminds me of this hot teacher I had in school."

"Riley!" I punch his arm and free myself from his grip. "That's disgusting."

"She wasn't *that* old."

We stroll atop the wall, then stop at Tower Green where two of King Henry's wives were beheaded, among other prisoners, and I find it hard not to imagine the gruesome, cruel place this once was. But it was also a mint, a zoo—so to speak, containing a menagerie of exotic animals gifted to kings—and the heavily guarded home of the crown jewels. So it's not all grim and murder.

"I can't believe those were *the* crown jewels," I say to Riley as we enter the White Tower. "I thought they'd be fakes with the real ones stashed away in some high-security vault, the location known only by the monarch. Seems risky to have them there on display for the public."

He stops by two suits of armor, one enormous, the other tiny. "How do you know they're real? It could be the royal family's greatest and best-kept secret. Just because they say those are the real crown jewels doesn't mean they are."

I frown at him, but he has a point.

We move into King Edward I's bedchamber—a brightly colored room that looks oddly childish for a monarch, and Riley stops in his tracks at a sideboard. "I think I'm in love."

I scrunch my nose at the hideous thing. "Isn't she too old for you? Then again, you did say you liked older teachers."

He rubs his beard, eyes glued to the deteriorated wood. "No. She's perfect."

"Would you two like to be alone?" I offer.

He side-eyes me before tugging me to his chest. "I'd much prefer to be alone with you."

"We are alone."

Riley surveys the room, a devilish grin lighting his face. "Great! Let's try out the bed."

"Wha—" Before I can step out of his embrace, he bear-hugs

me and lifts my feet from the ground, walking us closer to the ropes cordoning off the bed. "Riley! No! We can't."

"We can."

"Put me down!"

Chuckling, he sets me on my feet again. "Ease up, Riles. I'm not that game nor stupid."

I shove him back and smooth my T-shirt down. "I'm glad, because if one could be beheaded in this day and age, something tells me it would be here."

"This place creeps you out, doesn't it?"

"Kind of." I roll my shoulders, my skin prickling. "I mean, I love the history, but terrible things happened here for centuries. And those ravens outside only add to it."

"They're just birds."

"Yeah, creepy birds. And when there's more than one, their collective noun is an 'unkindness.' Enough said."

He gives me an *"interesting"* face.

"Exactly! I think they're also known as a 'treachery.'" I take one last look at the room, then edge toward the door. "Have you seen everything you want to see here?"

"I have."

"Can we go then? The sun will be setting soon, which is the perfect time to ride the Eye. It'll be lovely."

Hand in hand, we leave the medieval, polarizing castle before sailing along the gentle waters of the Thames, past Shakespeare's Globe—which is smaller than I imagined it to be—before docking across the river from the Eye.

"That's one gigantic Ferris wheel," Riley says, his neck arched back, his hand shielding his eyes from the sun.

"Don't tell me you fear heights as well?"

"I don't, but... I'm not sure I can get in one of those glass egg-looking cages."

Shit! I didn't think of that.

"Oh!" My heart deflates. "We don't have to ride it if you don't want to."

He runs his hand through his hair. "You should do it. If I weren't here with you, you would."

I take his hand from his head and clasp it in mine. "But you are here."

Drawing in a deep breath, he holds it before puffing it out, his cheeks akin to deflating balloons.

"It's fine," I say, not wanting him to feel pressured as I pull my cell out. "Let me just take a couple of pictures, and then we can head back to the ship."

He scratches the back of his head, then drops his gaze to mine. "If I die up there, promise me you'll give Poppy the souvenirs I bought her. And tell Mom I won a dance contest."

I laugh. "You're not going to die."

"I am."

"Seriously, we don't have to do—"

"Fuck it." He bounces on the spot and jerks his head from side to side. "Let's do this before I back out."

Riley strides to the ticket booth like a man on a mission, and we purchase our passes, then climb aboard, the doors soon closing, the glass pod slowly lifting.

"See?" I say, clasping his hand firmly in mine as we sit on the oval wooden bench in the center of the pod. "It's only us in here. That's good. We're not cramped."

His eyes suspiciously survey our casing, and I feel awful for his unease.

"And we're hardly moving," I add. "It's as if we're not moving at all."

"It's not the moving part that bothers me, Riles. It's the 'not being able to get out if I want to' part. And I'm going to want to."

"No, you're not. You're going to be fine. Think of it as being on the train. You can still stand and walk about freely. You just can't get off until we get there."

"Not helping, Riles."

"Sorry."

Sweat slicks his palm, dampening mine.

I give it a squeeze and stand. "Walk with me. We'll keep moving while we're moving, as if we're walking along the street." Continuing to talk to him, I try not to give him enough time to think about his confinement. "That garden over there is pretty." I point at it, forcing him to focus beyond the glass. "And look at the river. It's like a murky latte. Oh my God! I'd die for a coffee right now. How about you? Coffee would be perfect, right?"

He nods.

"Oh, look!" I point at Big Ben and usher us to the other side of the pod. "Isn't the clock magnificent from here? And Westminster Abbey? And—"

"Riles."

"Yes? Do you need to sit again?"

"No."

"We can sit if you'd prefer."

"It's okay. You can stop rambling."

"It's not helping distract you?"

"It is, but it's also giving me a headache. You sound like a chipmunk."

"I do not sound like a chipmunk," I squeak out.

He cocks an eyebrow.

Peanut butter.

When he drags me closer, our chests collide before his lips meet mine, his hand cradling the base of my head. I fall languid against him, my arms limp, my legs wavering. If this moment froze in time, everlasting and eternal, I certainly wouldn't complain.

Blinking as my eyes focus on his, I realize that, for the first time in my life, words evade me.

He doesn't speak either, simply searching my face before giving me a quick peck. "Turn around, sweetheart."

"Huh?"

Riley gestures toward something beyond my head.

Curious, I swivel to face the most glorious sunset I've ever seen, swirls of pinks, oranges, purples, and blues lining the sky as far as the eye can see.

"Wow! Just—" I swallow. "Wow."

He crosses his arms over my chest. "Yeah."

Sighing, I rest my head against his pecs. "What a perfect day."

chapter twenty-six

RILEY

Each day with Riles gets better and better, yesterday especially. Being with her, around her, inside her, fills a void I did and didn't know needed filling. After ending it with Krystal, I somewhat enjoyed the single life and was enlightened to discover who I am, not as a husband but as me. I learned my strength and resilience. Embraced independence and solitude.

If I wanted to be on my own, I could. But... I don't. I want to share my life with someone else. Laugh with them, eat with them, sleep with them. I want to watch the sun go down with someone in my arms, someone who appreciates me and what we share. And I want that someone to be Riles.

Our vacation is coming to an end though, and I'm not naïve enough to believe what we have now, here, on this cruise, will be the same once we return home. She's a city girl; I'm a country boy. She's ambitious and lives to work; I work to live.

Our livelihoods are chalk and cheese.

If I were a poetic fucker, I'd say my heart sings when we're together, that she's the missing piece to make it whole again. But I'm not poetic. I am a realist. And what Riles and I have together is as real as I've ever known, chalk and cheese be damned.

When we returned to Southampton the night before, she was

so exhausted that she fell asleep on the train. I'd been tempted to carry her back to the ship, but she no doubt would've ripped me a new one when she realized what I'd done, so waking her was the safest option, this time without poking something in her ear.

I expected we'd grab a bite to eat, then call it a night, but she insisted on working until the early hours of the morning. While I appreciate and respect her ethics and dedication to her career, and how she strives for excellence and success at all costs, I've seen first-hand what that does to a person. I've experienced the fallout, and I don't want to experience that again.

Life is all about balance. Perfectly weighed scales. It's too short to have it tipped one way and one way only.

"So, I was thinking," Riles says, a yawn billowing from her mouth. "When we get back from Stonehenge, and after we've been to that car museum you wanted to go to" —she stretches her face, forcing her eyelids apart—"if you're still interested, we can visit the *Titanic* exhibit at the SeaCity Museum as well."

I bury my frustration at how tired she is after working her ass off on *her* vacation. "Sure. Whatever you want to do."

"Perfect!" She yawns again and snuggles into my side, but then sits upright again, points out of the bus window, and blurts, "We're here. There it is!"

I lean over her for a better look, not particularly impressed. They're just rocks in a field.

"Cool," I say, sitting back.

"Cool?" She gives me one of her *Are you insane?* looks.

I give her one back but smirk.

"This place is more than just cool. It's mystical. Spiritual. Magical."

The bus continues driving for a short distance before it pulls to a stop outside a visitor information center, where we exit into the parking lot.

"I thought they didn't know why it was here or who built it?" I prompt, fixing my Philly's cap on my head.

"They don't. That's why it's mystical and mysterious." Riles

331

lifts her hair from the back of her neck and secures it in a low clump. "They do know it was a burial site though, and its positioning links it to the summer and winter solstices."

I don't know what that means, but I'm sure I'll find out by the time we leave.

"Do you want to walk to the site or catch the shuttle bus?" she asks.

"I don't mind."

Riles pulls her sun hat out of her bag and sets it on her head. "Let's walk. Our tour guide said it takes roughly thirty minutes but that it's an easy walk through those fields."

Smiling, she hikes her bag higher on her shoulder and holds out her hand. I happily take it in mine, and we follow the path to the first field, closing a gate behind us as instructed by a sign.

"Wait!" Riles stops. "There are cows in here."

I spot a few grazing up ahead. "Yep."

"Do you think it's safe?"

I chuckle. "Cows aren't bears, Riles."

"I know that, but they're big and—"

"Have you never been close to a cow before?"

"No. We don't exactly keep them as pets in Manhattan."

"You'll be fine," I say, tugging her along, when her cell phone beeps within her bag.

She stops and pulls it out. "Give me a second. I need to check my email. It might be Georgia."

Inhaling deeply, I let go of her hand and huff out a breath as she scrolls her screen, her face scrunching as she reads.

"Damn it."

"What's up?"

"Nothing." She shoves her cell back into her bag, clasps my hand, and keeps walking, her pace less tentative than before.

"In a hurry, are we?"

"No. It's just... hot, and I don't want the cows to bother us."

"I think it's the other way around. Us being here bothers them."

"We should've just caught the shuttle bus," she mutters.

Narrowing my eyes, I suspect her agitation has something to do with her boss, but I bite my tongue, knowing if I suggest such a thing, she'll more than likely direct that agitation at me. Plus, I'd rather distract her from what she just read and bring her attention back to why we're here.

"Have you always wanted to come to Stonehenge?" I ask.

"No, not really." Her smile is crooked. "I mean, yes. I've always wanted to travel and see the world, but it was never a priority. Only a dream."

I splay my arm out, emphasizing where we are. "It's no longer a dream, Riles. You're here."

"I know," she deadpans.

"So live in the moment. Enjoy it."

"I am enjoying it."

We exit the field and step onto a path, the Stone Age relics peculiar among the desolate landscape, yet also strangely fitting.

"I thought they'd be bigger," she says as she steps up to an information plaque.

I read the description. "Given when they were constructed, I'd say they're big enough."

"You're right." She scratches her head. "How on earth were they moved back then?"

"Isn't that one of the mysteries?"

"Yeah. There are, of course, assumptions based on archaeological findings, but they really don't know for sur—" Her cell beeps again, interrupting her cute history lesson, and she grumbles.

I side-eye her. "Do I even need to ask who that is?"

"No. It's Georgia."

"And...?"

"Before I went to bed last night, I sent her two of the manuscripts she wanted me to work through, and instead of thanking me, she's now asking where the other two are. The thing is, when she originally gave me the time off, she requested that I only do two. Not four."

"So, ignore her."

"I can't."

"Sure you can. You just switch your cell off."

She rolls her eyes. "It's not that simple."

"Why not?"

"Because it's not," she says, moving along to the next plaque.

"So she's expecting you to complete another two manuscripts in... what? Two days?" I ask, following her.

"Yes."

"That's ridiculous."

"I know."

Wanting to shake some sense into her for her own good, I begrudgingly let it go instead. It's not my place to do so, and I'd rather enjoy our time here than make it about her pesky employer.

We complete a full circle of the stones, and at first, things are good, until Riles pauses less frequently to read the plaques, her excitement and interest appearing to have vanished. It pisses me off; she wanted to come here and see this, and now she's preoccupied.

"Are you done here?" she asks, stopping to take a drink from her water bottle before offering it to me.

I am done, but I'm more concerned about whether she's truly done or not.

Taking a swig, I glance at my watch. "Yeah. But the tour bus doesn't leave for another hour."

She rests her hands on her hips and huffs. "I know."

"So we can stay here a bit long—"

"No. Let's catch the shuttle bus back to the visitor center. By the time we've had a quick look around, the bus will be ready to leave." She shoves her bottle back into her bag and marches for the parking lot.

I clench my fist and follow behind her, and after waiting fifteen minutes in line to board the shuttle, Riles constantly scrolling her cell, we arrive back at the visitor center, the air-conditioned building tempering my heated blood.

"Do you want to check out the exhibit?" I ask.

She takes a seat on an egg chair, staring intently at her cell when it rings. "Peanut butter."

Her stupid saying makes me smile until she fumbles with the cell and quickly shoves it to her ear.

"Georgia! Hi, how are y—" She winces, her cheeks blooming red, her brow furrowing. "Yes, I know, but—" Riles holds up one finger to me, indicating she won't be long before she shoots to her feet, covers her free ear with her other hand, and turns her back on me, pacing by the window.

I stay within earshot, listening as she tries to get a word in but is cut off every time until she's just answering with, "Yes. I understand. Yes."

Anger crawls the surface of my skin. We only have thirty minutes before we leave, and at the rate Riles is going, she'll miss out on the rest of the tour.

Fuming, I stride up to her, snatch her phone, reject the call, and hand it back.

"Riley! What—" Her eyes widen as she stares at the screen. "No! No, no, no! You just hung up on her."

"I did."

She grips her hair. "Why?"

"Because she's taken up too much of your time already."

"You can't just do that," she hisses, her fists clenched by her side, knuckles white. "You have no right."

I reach for her hand. "Riles—"

"Don't." She recoils. "I need to call her back. Now!"

"You don't need to call her back. You're on vacation!"

"This is none of your business!"

"I'm here, aren't I? And you're here with me. So yeah, it is my business."

Her fingertips of one hand massage her temple as her other thumb manically taps and moves about the screen of her phone. "Just... Just go outside to the exhibit without me. I'll catch up when I'm done."

"But *you* wanted to see the exhibit, and you won't have enough time if you're stuck talking to her."

"Jesus, Riley!" she snaps. "It's just stupid huts and rocks and crap. You said so yourself. I don't care about them."

"You do!"

"No, I don't. What I care about is getting Georgia back on the phone, so I don't lose my job."

My eye twitches.

"You have no idea what you just did." She storms off, then disappears behind a wall.

Fuck!

Settling my hands on my head, I grip my hair and make my way outside, wandering about the exhibit until Riles eventually steps up beside me. I want to look at her, to see if she's okay, but I pretend to read about the Neolithic way of life instead.

"Did you lose your job?" I ask like a smartass.

"No. But thanks to you, I could have."

I scoff. "I doubt that."

She turns on her heel and heads back inside, so I grit my teeth and hurry after her.

"Riles, wait! I'm sorry." I grab her arm and turn her to face me. "I shouldn't have hung up on your boss. You're right; it was none of my business, and I was out of line."

Letting out a shaky breath, her shoulders slump. "You can't interfere with my job, Riley."

"I know." I pull her in for a hug and kiss the top of her head. "I just don't want to see you...." I hold her at arm's length, my eyes searching hers. "Never mind. This is the last day of our cruise. Let's just enjoy it, yeah?"

She nods but averts her gaze, so I tuck her into my side as we head back to the tour bus.

DURING THE TRIP BACK TO SOUTHAMPTON, RILES FALLS asleep again, her head on my shoulder, her drool on my shirt. Like puke, I'm not a fan of spit, especially someone else's, but I'll deal with it, because Riles isn't just someone else. In the short time we've spent together, she's become a part of me, a part of my life as I now know it and want it to be moving forward.

Her puke is my puke.

Her drool is my drool.

I wince.

Well, not exactly. But it's less stomach-churning if I keep telling myself that.

"Wake up, sleepy head," I say as we pull into the dock not far from the ship.

She lifts her head, wipes her mouth, stares at my damp shirt, and then wipes that too. "We're back already? That was quick."

It wasn't. Fifty-seven minutes in a bus full of noisy people is far from "quick."

We collect our things, amble along the aisle, and descend the stairs, stepping out of the path of other passengers as they disperse.

"We still have five hours before we set sail," I say, clasping her hand, "which should be enough time to visit the car museum *and* the *Titanic* exhibit."

"About that." She holds her ground, our arms outstretched. "I can't. I need to go back to the room and read through—"

My heart deflates, and I let go of her hand.

"I'm sorry, but Georgia insisted."

"Have fun. I'll see you later." Turning away from her, I make my way toward the city center.

"Riley!" she calls out. "Please don't be mad. I'm sorry."

I lift my hand in a wave, refusing to look back, not wanting to argue. Am I mad? Yeah... livid. But I'm more disappointed than anything. We don't have a lot of time left together before we have to say goodbye, and who knows how long that goodbye will last. A few days, a week, a month? I have no idea. Judging by how easily Riles sacrifices everything for Georgia, my gut tells me it could be the latter. I hope it's not. I hope we can make this work. We won't know until we try, of course. I just pray I'm not the only one trying.

Been there, done that, and I won't do it again.

After leaving Riles on the dock, I jump in an Uber and visit the National Motor Museum, where I bump into Manny and Hugo, a decent consolation for Riles's absence. Manny shares his automotive knowledge, and Hugo eagerly chaperones me through a thirteenth-century Gothic manor, which forms part of the grounds. We admire the furnishings and décor, and I appreciate his expertise and ideas, some of them inspiring ideas of my own for when I return to my workshop. I've missed the smell of wood, varnish, and even the sawdust, but I've also appreciated the change of scenery. The escape. The adventure. It was exactly what I needed, and I have Roni—and Riles—to thank for that.

Sliding my sailing card into the door of our cabin, I push it open and enter the room. Riles looks up, rubs her eyes, and immediately shuts her laptop, pushing it aside before standing.

"Hey," she says, voice timid. "Was the *Titanic* exhibit good?"

I take a seat on the edge of my bed and rest my elbows on my knees. "I didn't go there."

"Oh." She frowns. "Why not?"

"I chose not to."

Taking a seat beside me, she fiddles with the bracelet I gave her in Qaqortok and then places her hands in her lap. "You're mad."

"I'm not."

"Lies."

"I'm not mad, Riles," I say, voice calm. "I'm worried."

"Worried?" She gently squeezes my thigh. "Why are you worried?"

"Because you're already in a relationship, and I fear there's no room for me... or us."

"What are you talking about?" She leans back, angling herself away from me. "I'm not in a relationship with anybody."

"You are. With Georgia."

"That's—" She stands up and walks to the desk, tidying the stack of daily newsletters before facing me again. "That's just stupid. She's my boss; I'm her assistant. That's all. We're not together. How could you think that?"

"I don't mean you're seeing each other, Riles." I chuckle, unable to help it. "What I mean is you're obsessed with pleasing her. If she demands, you comply, even when it means sacrificing your own happiness. You said so yourself that she's stolen too much of your time, time you can't get back, and yet you're still willingly giving it to her."

Her mouth opens, then closes, her eyes bouncing about their sockets like pinballs.

"So yeah." I sigh. "I'm worried you'll let her steal *our* time, which she did today."

Chewing the inside of her cheek, she dips her head and stares at the ground.

I stand and tilt her chin up with the tip of my finger. "I've just ended a relationship that was one-sided, and it almost destroyed me. I don't want that again."

"I'm not your ex-wife, Riley." She swipes my hand away. "And I never will be."

I tilt her face back to mine. "I know that. You're nothing like Krystal."

"Then stop comparing us."

"I'm not."

"You are."

I cup her cheeks. "I'm comparing the situations."

"It's the same thing."

"It's not."

"It is."

Goddamn, beautiful, strong-willed, frustratingly stubborn woman!

"Riles—"

"Riley."

My jaw tics, and she cocks an eyebrow.

"All I'm saying is stop letting Georgia dictate your life beyond what is reasonable... and lawful. You're smarter and stronger than that. You deserve better. And if we're going to try to make this work, I deserve better too."

Tears well in her eyes before she blinks them away.

"I don't want to argue, sweetheart." I press my lips to hers. "This is our last night on the cruise."

She swallows. "I don't want to argue either, but I—"

Dropping my hands, I wrap them around her waist and lift her higher, my lips once again fused to hers.

Where they should be.

Where I hope they'll stay for a long time to come.

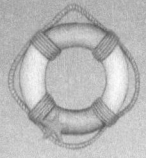

chapter twenty-seven

RILES

He's right, I know he is, but that doesn't change anything. At least not yet. I have a plan, one I've had for years, and I must see it through. If I don't, then what have I accomplished? Failure. I can't do that to myself, nor can I do it to Mom. I know she wanted me to be happy, regardless of where my life takes me, but if I give up what I've worked so hard for, then every sacrifice I've made up to this point will be for nothing.

I'll just have to try harder to accommodate Riley into my life, because he's worth it and because I want him to be a part of it. I can still achieve my dreams, but I no longer have to do it alone. No man before him has made me feel the way he makes me feel, and I desperately don't want to lose that.

I don't want to lose *him*.

"We need to get ready for the farewell dinner," Riley says, placing me on my feet again before heading to the closet.

Lips tingling, my heart in tatters yet somehow still whole and effervescent, I quit foreboding. "I hope everyone is there tonight so we can say goodbye."

"Even Ben?"

"Especially Ben. I can't believe I'm about to say this, but I think I'm going to miss him."

Riley pokes his head around the open door, his sexy eyes crinkling. "You're right. I can't believe you just said that."

"He's a good person."

"Yeah, I know."

Reaching behind his shoulders, he gathers the back of his T-shirt in his hand and pulls it over his head, his perfectly sculpted abdomen making my mouth water. I chew my lip, admiring the view and how he drapes his black shirt over his shoulders, slides his arms inside, and leisurely secures one button at a time.

"Are you just going to stand there gawking at me, or are you going to get ready?"

I weigh my options. "I choose gawk."

"We'll be late," he warns.

Scoffing, I let my ponytail out and comb my fingers through my hair. "I'm never late."

"Keep staring at me like that and you will be."

I keep staring.

Riley tucks his shirt into his jeans, collects his belt, and turns in my direction, the leather sliding along his hand before he pulls it taut with a snap.

My body startles at the intimidating sound. "What are you do—"

He snaps it again, a fiendish grin lifting his sinister lips.

Backing up, I place myself behind the bed and hold my hands up. "Put that down."

"Why? Don't you like the idea of me tying you up?"

No! Well... maybe. Okay, fine. Yes. Yes, I do.

"W-We don't have time."

Before I can form a convincing defense, he leaps across the bed, secures me in his arms, and loops the belt around my wrists. "I did warn you, sweetheart."

I try not to laugh as I fight him off but happily give up. What's the point? I want what he wants, and more. Much, much more.

Gently laying me on the bed, he lifts my arms above my head, my T-shirt following, his stubble tickling a trail down my chest and over my stomach.

I shudder, my body compliant to his every whim.

I guess we're going to be late.

And quite frankly, for the first time in my life, I could not care less.

"NICE OF YOU TO JOIN US," BEN SAYS AS RILEY PUSHES me in at the table.

My cheeks flush with embarrassment as all eyes settle on my face. "Sorry. I was doing my hair."

Ben rests his hand on Riley's shoulder and gives it a squeeze. "I bet you were."

Pressing my lips together, I second-guess whether I will, in fact, miss the impudent buffoon.

"So when is everyone flying home?" I ask, diverting the conversation.

Hugo smirks behind his wine glass as if he too doesn't believe my excuse. "We're staying in France for a week. And then we're heading to Italy."

I sigh. "That sounds amazing. I'd love to visit Rome one day."

"Perhaps you will." He tips his glass to me and then to Riley. "Sooner rather than later."

Blushing again, I pick up my menu and try to focus on this evening's dishes.

"When are you flying home?" Manny asks.

"Tomorrow night."

His eyebrows hitch. "So soon?"

"Yes." I pout. "No rest for the wicked, I'm afraid."

Riley huffs and fidgets in his seat, prompting Manny and Hugo to glance at one another.

"And you, Riley?" Manny asks. "When are you flying home?"

"Same as Riles."

He smiles fondly at us. "You're both still young. Plenty of time to see the rest of the world."

I squeeze Riley's leg beneath the table. "I agree. There's no rush."

"We leave the day after tomorrow," Kathy says, gesturing at her husband. "Oscar is homesick. He misses his armchair."

"And a decent beer," he adds, wrinkling his nose at the ale in front of him.

"I miss my friends," Avery whines. "And my treehouse."

I set my menu down, excited for her. "You have a treehouse? That's so cool! When I was your age, that's all I wanted, but we didn't have any trees where I lived."

"You didn't have trees?"

"No. I lived in an apartment in a city."

Zach slurps his soda. "Treehouses are crap."

Avery throws her crayon at him. "You're crap!"

He throws it back.

I lean out of the way.

"Stop that!" Kathy laughs and pats Avery's hand. "As you can see, it's definitely time to go home."

Feeling sorry for her, I suspect she hasn't had much of a vacation, given how Oscar seems to just sit there like a potato.

"So, you two hookin' up when you get back?" Ben asks.

I move my elbows onto the table, steeple my hands, and rest my chin on my fingers. "That's none of your business."

"Sheesh!" He winks at Riley. "Just tryin' to help a bro out."

"Thank you, Ben," Riley says, letting out a slow breath. "But we've been through this. I don't need your help."

"You stopped biding?"

Riley glares at him.

"You have, haven't you?" Ben gleams. "'Bout fucking time."

A sense of déjà vu settles over me, so I narrow my eyes at them. "What are you talking about?"

Riley tips his beer to his lips. "Nothing."

"He's been dying to get into your panties for weeks, love."

I recoil.

"Benjamin!" Hugo exclaims.

"What? He has."

"Will you just shut up. It doesn't concern you."

"No." I lift my hand at Hugo. "It's okay. I want to hear this."

Riley shifts in his seat and gestures toward the children. "Are you sure that's wise?"

It's not. But funnily enough, I've come to respect Ben's brute honesty. It's refreshing, despite the language he uses to convey it. No falsities. No shame. No tact, of course, but mostly no fear of expression. He doesn't hide who he is or what he wants to say. And judging by how disinterested the Ohio family are—Oscar flagging down a waiter; Zach buried in his phone; Avery cramming a bread roll into her mouth, with Kathy chastising her as she picks and dusts crumbs off her daughter's dress—now's probably the best time for Ben to speak.

I'm about to tell him to go ahead, when he does so anyway.

"Just so you know, love, I wanted in your panties too, but my man here really digs you. Has since day one." He swigs his drink, then wipes his mouth. "Told me to back off, because he was biding his time."

My brow lifts. "He did, did he?"

Ben scoffs. "Yeah."

"This really isn't the time nor plac—"

I press my finger to Riley's lips. "Shush."

Ben continues, "Said you were off limits."

"Off limits?" I drawl.

Smirking, Riley removes my finger and covers my hand with his. "You are... now."

I narrow my eyes and try desperately not to return the smirk.

"So, I backed off, love. Not because I wanted to, but because my man had first dibs."

"First dibs?" I choke out, turning to Riley. "First. Dibs?"

"Uh-oh," Hugo murmurs.

345

I try to tug my hand back, but he holds it firmly in place. "That sounded a whole lot worse than what it was."

I blink. "You think?"

"I told him to just fuck you," Ben continues, "but he's a gentleman and doesn't—"

"Okaaay!" I lay my napkin on my lap. "Thank you, Ben. I've heard enough."

He shrugs, turns his head, and surveys the room.

"The only thing you should take out of all of that," Riley says, turning my head to give me a chaste kiss, "is the word gentleman."

I pat his cheek a little harder than necessary. "We'll see about that."

Our waiter sets our meals in front of us, and something catches Ben's eye, the corners of his mouth lifting as he raises his glass in a salute. Leaning back in my seat, I follow his line of sight to where Whitney is eating dinner with Brittany, her eyes downcast as she mutters something behind her hand. Brittany twists to look at us, then quickly twists back around, neither of them acknowledging Ben, even as their Tiffany bling glitters from around their wrists and necks.

He frowns and sets his glass down, his shoulders slumping.

Anger settles in my chest, my heart pinching for him. Despite the way he goes about seeking a partner, he deserves better than to be used for his money. "Hey, Ben!" I say, dipping my spoon in my soup. "Maybe you and I can catch a game together when the season starts up again."

Riley snaps his head to me, and Hugo almost spits out his salad.

Ignoring them, I challenge Ben with an eyebrow waggle. "It'll be fun. Knicks and Lakers, what do you say?"

He glances around the table, then straightens his back with pride. "It's a date, love."

It's not, but I'm looking forward to it all the same. I haven't been to a game in years.

AFTER SAYING GOODBYE TO EVERYONE, RILEY AND I stroll the deck, hand in hand under the moonlight, before spending our last night together, hearts, minds, bodies, and souls passionately locked between the sheets. He worships every inch of me, and I do the same, committing to memory the lines and grooves of his muscles and how they feel flexed beneath my fingers. We move in unison, breathe in unison, neither of us mentioning the following day or what's to happen next. We simply share the moment, *live* the moment, and eventually fall asleep in each other's arms until the sun casts its rude awakening at dawn.

Clasping the handle of my suitcase, I pull it up and take one last look at our cabin as a sob escapes my lips.

"Don't," Riley says, hugging me to him while kissing my head. "Not yet. We still have a full day together."

"You're right." I blink back my tears, let go of the handle, and blot my cheeks. "I'm just.... I'm going to miss it. All of it. Mom included."

He takes my hands in his. "Me too."

"You're going to miss my mom?" I ask with a cheeky grin.

"Of course." He winks. "She was my roommate too."

Taking another look around, melancholy flutters my heart. "Is it just me, or does it feel like a lifetime ago that we were standing right where we are, arguing over who this cabin belonged to?"

He chuckles. "You were so adorable. Majorly pissed and a little scary, but also adorable."

"Hey! You were angry too."

"Not at you, Riles. I was angry at life in general."

I cup his cheek. "And you're not anymore?"

"No. How can I be? I met you."

My body hums with warmth. "And I met you."

"Best vacation mix-up ever."

I burst into laughter, drop my hand, and clasp the handle of my suitcase again. "We're still getting that damn refund though."

"Already have."

"Really?"

"Yep. Mine landed in my account this morning."

Rummaging through my handbag, I collect my cell and open the app for my bank as he holds the door for me to exit. "Will you look at that? Mine's there too!" I internally clap with glee as I slide my cell back into my bag. "Now I have some spending money for when we hit the Champs-Élysées."

"What's a Shawns Elysay?"

I giggle at his pronunciation, which, to be honest, is nearly as bad as mine. "It's where all the high-end and touristy stores are in Paris."

"Greeeat!" he drawls, less enthusiastic. "So we're going shopping?"

"Of course. Who goes to Paris and doesn't go shopping?"

"I figured you'd want to visit museums."

"Oh, I do. The Louvre is on my list." I shove my case with my foot and roll it along the corridor. "And I want to climb the Eiffel Tower, and walk under the Arc de Triomphe, and climb the steps to Montmartre." Pausing, I turn back to him. "Oh, oh, and let's not forget Notre Dame and that bridge you put a padlock on."

He smiles like my mother often did on Christmas morning and nods beyond my shoulder, gesturing that I keep walking, which I do, continuing to run through my Paris bucket list.

"I want to eat a big baguette with lots of cheese, and we should try escargot." I stop and turn to face him again. "On second thought, I don't think I can eat snails."

Riley comes to an abrupt halt, his suitcase nearly crashing into my shins. "Riles, stop stopping!"

"Sorry! I'm just excited."

"Yeah, I can see that."

"There's just so much I want to see and do."

"Then keep walking, or we won't have enough time to see and do it all."

I swipe my hand at him. "Once we arrive in the city, we'll have around ten hours before we have to check in at Charles de Gaulle. That's plenty of time."

"And what are we supposed to do with our suitcases? Drag them along with us?"

"No, silly. Of course not. I booked us two storage lockers at Saint-Lazare Station."

He stares at me.

I stare back. "What?"

"Nothing," he says, smiling as he shakes his head.

"So, should we eat escargot, or not?"

"Riles—"

"We should, shouldn't we?"

"Riles—"

"Oh, I don't know. The thought of it grosses me out."

"Riles!"

"What?"

"Keep moving!"

"Okay! Okay!"

After disembarking the ship, and roughly two and a half hours later, we're strolling by the Bouquinistes along the Seine River, passing cafés with delightful chairs and tables facing the streets, many Parisians enjoying their coffee while people-watching. Soft florals float from open doorways of perfumeries, gold-gilded statues, bridges, and domed roofs glittering in the sunlight. Pooches strut along cobbled laneways, their owners in tow. I soak up the culture, beauty, and tradition, basking in the romance and extravagance.

We visit the Moulin Rouge, and Montmartre, where my breath catches in my lungs for the first time that day. The second time is when we enter Notre Dame. The third, on the top level of the Eiffel Tower.

And the last, seconds ago, when Riley's flight was announced as "boarding."

Pain constricts my chest, and I breathe him in, memorizing his minty, musky scent and how his arms feel wrapped around me, his hands in my hair, lips pressed, our heartbeats syncopating.

I pull away, eyes locked to his, words spilling from them with the same intensity as if spoken.

"Have a safe flight," I murmur.

He cocks his head. "Is that all you're going to say?"

"I-I don't know what to say, but—" A tear escapes my eye, and I bury my head into his warm chest. "—I know I don't want to say goodbye."

"It's only goodbye *for now*, sweetheart. Not forever."

"It's still goodbye."

He cradles my head, leans away from me, and rubs the pads of his thumbs under my damp eyes. "We'll talk tomorrow."

Nodding, I stretch to my tiptoes and give him one last kiss.

"Final boarding call for American Airlines Flight AA755 to Philadelphia, boarding Gate Eleven."

Finding what little strength I have left, I step back. "Go, or you'll miss your flight."

"I can think of worse things."

"Go!" I say, laughing as I slap his chest. "I'll text you when I land."

As he walks backward, his eyes don't leave mine until he bumps into a man in a business suit. "Shit! Sorry, man."

The guy mutters something in French.

"Watch where you're going!" I call out, shaking my head.

"You want to kiss me again, don't you?"

I giggle. "No!"

He frowns and lets go of his suitcase.

Continuing to giggle, I cover my face with my hand and peek through my spread fingers. "Riley!"

The stubborn jerk doesn't budge.

"Go!" I urge him, pointing to the gate.

He shakes his head.

Peanut butter.

Hiking my bag on my shoulder, I run toward him, his arms encasing me when our bodies collide, lips sealing one final time before he sets me down and then disappears beyond the gate.

I stare at the closed door and draw in a deep breath, my heart plummeting like a meteor slamming into the earth's surface, loneliness once again a dark, hovering cloud. A sob rips through my chest, but I subdue it. We'll see each other soon... I hope.

WHEN MY PLANE LANDS AT LAGUARDIA, I MAKE MY WAY to baggage claim and switch my cell back on, a message alert from Riley chiming almost instantly.

> Just landed. Had to sit next to a snorer. It was hell. If I ever snore again, feel free to suffocate me.

I giggle and type my reply, awkwardly dodging other passengers.

> Never! I just touched down too. So tired. Couldn't sleep on the plane either.

Pressing Send, I pocket my cell, then quickly pull it out and type another message.

> I miss you.

The pending message bubble bounces on my screen, sending a weird sense of excitement through me as I wait for his response.

> I miss you more.

Biting my lip, I stare lovingly at his words and sigh.

Lovingly? Golly gosh, it's too soon for that, surely?

I grip my cell and take the escalator to the carousel, waiting impatiently as suitcases pass by, none of them mine.

> Are you home yet?

> Just got in. About to unpack.

> I'm waiting for my suitcase. Oh, I see it. Better go 🤍

I dash a little closer and wrench it off the conveyor belt, nearly taking out an unfortunate man who didn't use enough sense to move out of my way.

"Sorry," I grouch, ridiculously apologizing for *his* stupidity.

Once I clear customs, I hail a cab and settle into my seat, the Manhattan skyline a comforting yet disappointing sight—no rainbow clouds or rippling ocean. No mountains or trees.

Not once in my life has NYC made me frown... until now.

My cell beeps again, so I quickly retrieve it.

> Did you put your shampoo in my bag?

Laughter bursts from my throat.

> I did.

> What else did you sneak in? Jesus! I told customs I packed my own bags. Lucky I wasn't detained.

> Just the shampoo.

> Thanks, but it's empty.

> And whose fault is that?

> You need to bring some with you when you visit.

I bite my nail, excited at the prospect.

> Maybe.

As I'm about to type another message, he beats me to it.

> Gotta go. Mom, Roni, and Poppy just arrived.

My chest pangs, knowing no one will greet me when I arrive home.

> Say hi to them for me.

> I will, but you can do it in person when you meet them.

Heart delightfully pounding with nerves, I can't type fast enough.

> Okay. Does this weekend work?

> It can't come soon enough 🤍

chapter twenty-eight

RILEY

Sliding my cell into my pocket, I open my front door and lower to one knee, arms wide as Poppy comes barreling toward me.

"Uncle Riley!"

She slams into my chest, so I scoop her into my arms and stand, bear-hugging her as I breathe in her innocent scent of candy and playdough. "I've missed you, popsicle. Did you miss me?"

She clasps my face, her eyes giant blue saucers. "Did you buy me a present?"

"Did you miss me?" I repeat.

"Of course I did, silly."

"Then yes, I bought you a present."

"What is it?" she asks, bouncing in my arms.

"Poppy," Roni playfully scolds, "Uncle Riley just got home. Be patient."

"But I want to see my present. What is it?"

I boop her nose with mine. "Soon, I promise."

Roni holds her arm out to relieve me of my niece, but I swing Poppy away from her and lean forward instead, kissing my sister's cheek. I'm not yet ready to put her down, which will no doubt

354

change in roughly five minutes when she doesn't stop asking me about her gift.

"So, how was it?" Roni asks, stepping past me into the entryway hall.

"Yeah. Good." I gesture to the baking dish in her hand. "What's that?"

She cocks one eyebrow. "What do you think it is?"

Smiling like a son who adores his mother's cooking, I set Poppy down to help Mom up the steps to my front door. "Are those cheesesteaks?"

Mom hands me the baking dish she's carrying, then pulls me close to kiss my forehead. "And a Shoofly pie."

"Mom!" I reciprocate the kiss. "You're the best."

"Can't have my boy come home to no food, can I?"

I link my arm with hers and lead her into the kitchen. "Coffee?"

"Yes, please, dear."

"Sit down," my sister orders. "I'll do it. You must be exhausted."

"Thanks. I am." I take a seat, and Poppy instantly climbs onto my lap.

"So how was your cruise?" Mom asks.

I glance at Roni and smile. "It was exactly what I needed."

She twiddles her fingers on the countertop. "Did you sow your wild oats like I suggested?"

"Veronica!" Mom scolds.

"What? That was the whole point of his cruise."

"It wasn't," I correct her. "But yes, I did meet someone."

Mom's shocked face gleams. "You did?"

"Do tell." Roni sets down the mugs and eagerly leans over the counter.

"She lives in Manhattan. She's thirty-two, and her name is... wait for it..." I grin and tickle Poppy. "Riley. Riley Wilson."

"What?" Roni squawks. "You're joking."

"I'm not. We were booked into the same cabin by mistake."

My mother and my sister's heads snap toward each other before snapping back to me. "How on earth did that happen?" Mom asks.

"I don't know, but I'm glad it did, because we shared our room for the entire cruise."

"Uncle Riley—"

Mom delicately touches my arm. "You shared?"

I nod. "Yes."

"But why?"

"Because neither of us wanted to downgrade."

"You"—Roni points at me—"willingly shared with a stranger?"

I frown. "Why's that so hard to believe?"

She scoffs. "Because you're not exactly the sharing type."

"I am so."

"Uncle Riley—"

"And you're a messy pig."

"I am not."

"And you snore."

I chuckle. "Yeah, apparently like a freight train of hogs, or something like that."

Poppy positions her head into my line of sight. "Uncle Riley."

"Just a minute, popsicle," I say, moving to look past her. "I'll admit the snoring was a problem at first, but I fixed it."

"How? By smothering yourself?" my sister quips. "Because that's what I would've done."

I frown again. "I bought her AirPods."

"You did what?" Roni facepalms.

"Hey! It worked."

Shaking her head at me, she pushes off from the counter and turns on the coffee machine. "So what's the other Riley like?"

"She's—" Riles's brown hair blowing in the breeze and her gray eyes shining as she smiles catapults into my mind's eye. "— beautiful. And sweet." A pillow slamming my face also surfaces from my memory. "And feisty."

Mom's brow furrows. "Feisty?"

"In a good way." I pat her hand. "Let's just say she doesn't shy away from putting me in my place."

"I like her already," Roni says, winking. "So when do we get to meet her? Or was it just a vacation fling?"

I grin. "This weekend."

"Oh." Mom sits straighter. "So soon?"

"I wish it were sooner."

Roni glances at Mom, lips pursed. "Someone's smitten."

I gleam; I am.

"You said she lives in Manhattan, dear."

"Yeah, Mom."

"Won't that be difficult?"

"I'm trying not to think that far ahead. All I know is I'm desperate to see her again. We had such a great time together. She pulled me out of my funk and encouraged me to do and see things I wouldn't have. And she made me want to be—" I stretch Poppy's cheek into a smile. "—happy again."

Roni places our coffees in front of us and takes a seat. "Don't worry about the commute. Manhattan isn't that far. Adrian and I managed a long-distance relationship just fine." She stares into her mug, blinks, then looks up. "It can work if you both want it to."

I reach out and cover her hand with mine, her late husband's passing still as raw as the day we got the dreaded news.

"Uncle Riley?"

"Yes, popsicle."

"Can I have my present now?"

Giving my niece my undivided attention, I grin at her adorable, pleading face. "You can if you use the magic word."

"Pleeease!"

I kiss her forehead, stand with her on my hip before taking her to my bedroom, and plonk her on the bed. She scoots across it, practically dives into my open suitcase, and instantly snags the stuffed moose I got her in Nova Scotia.

"Is this my present?" she asks, holding it up.

"One of them."

She gives it a curious look. "What is it?"

"A moose."

"I love him. What's his name?"

"What do you want to call him?"

"Moose."

Okaaay. Not awfully original, but... it works.

I rifle through my case for the bracelets as she hugs Moose to her chest.

"Is this my present too?"

Looking up and seeing the gold ship trophy tightly gripped in her hand, I shake my head and smirk. "No. Uncle Riley won that in a dancing competition."

Poppy giggles and jiggles, and then she tucks the trophy under her arm next to Moose. "Where's my other present? Where's my other present?"

My fingers snag the beads, so I bunch my fists and sit next to her. "Here. Pick a hand."

She points to my left, so I open my fingers.

"A purple bracelet!" Poppy snatches it up and instantly points to my right. Chuckling, I open that hand too. "And a pink one!"

"Do you like them?"

"I love them. Look, Mommy!" She scurries off the bed. "Look what Uncle Riley got me."

Roni pushes off from the doorframe and enters my room. "Wow! They're pretty."

"And this is Moose. And this is Uncle Riley's dancing trophy."

Roni's face puckers. "A dancing trophy?"

I smirk again.

"I'm going to show Nanna," Poppy says, skipping out of the room with her loot.

"Did I hear that correctly? You won a dancing trophy?" Roni hovers over my suitcase and collects the formal night photo I bought without Riles's knowledge.

"You did hear that correctly," I say. "I'm the new Michael Flatley."

My sister bursts into laughter. "Now *that* I would've liked to see."

"Trust me, you wouldn't have."

Smiling at the photo, she takes a seat next to me. "Is this her?"

I nod. "Yep."

"She's pretty."

"I know."

Roni leans over the bed and places the picture on my bedside table. "So... this thing with Riley—God, that's weird. Riley and Riley." She blinks, then shakes her head. "Anyway, this thing with Riley—"

"Riles," I say, helping her out.

"Riles?"

I nod.

"This thing with *Riles*, is it serious?"

"From my perspective, yes."

She frowns. "What about her perspective?"

I rub my beard. "I don't know... yet."

"Oh. Why not?"

"She's extremely dedicated to her work, so I'm not sure what that will mean for us. I'm willing to find out though. She's worth it."

"Good." She pats my thigh. "You deserve to find love again. But finding it and keeping it are two entirely different things. One involves opening your heart, and the other involves sacrifice and dedication."

"You deserve to find love again too, you know."

She scoffs. "Maybe I should go on a cruise and sow *my* wild oats."

I wrench my head back. "Over my dead body!"

"Don't give me that sexist bullshit, young man. What's good for a gander is good for a goose."

"I know, but—"

"No buts. We're all made of the same flesh and blood."

"Not exactly."

She fires me her don't-argue-with-your-older-sister look and lowers her voice. "Riley."

I challenge it like I always do. "Veronica."

Her eyes narrow into harrowing slits, and she damn well clocks me over the head with her open palm.

I playfully clock her back, and we both call out, "Mom!" like petulant children, then burst into laughter.

"Don't hit girls," she says, getting in a second whack before jumping to her feet.

"Goose and gander, remember?"

"Not the same thing."

She's right; it's not, but I huff all the same.

"Riley!" Mom calls out. "Get your dancing butt out here now."

I groan.

Roni shoots me a cocky grin. "She's gonna want a demonstration."

Groaning again, I hang my head. "Yeah, I know."

AFTER MOM INSISTS I TEACH HER THE IRISH DANCING steps that crowned me champion—which I pretty much make up on the fly—we sit down and eat dinner. I fill them in on *most* of the details of my vacation: the places I visited, the ship, about Riles's mother, and what Riles does for a living. And after scarfing down the best Shoofly pie in the history of Shoofly pies, I can barely keep my eyes open.

"He sounds like a piggy," Poppy says, poking my cheek, prompting my eyes to shoot open.

I blink her into focus, her face mere inches from mine. "I do not."

"Yes, you do." She snorts a few times and giggles.

Tickling her ribs, I move her off my lap, stand, and stretch. "Sorry, but I need some shut-eye."

Roni nudges my shoulder with hers. "Yeah, I guess you would."

I give her a playful shove.

"So, should I expect you at the shop tomorrow?" she asks.

Yawning, I nod and stretch again. "I found a lot of inspiration in Europe, and I can't wait to get started."

"Good." She kisses her fingertips and presses them onto Dad's portrait that's sitting on top of my mantle. "We've missed you."

I've missed them and the workshop too, and I'm itching to pick up my tools and tell Dad all about the furniture I can't wait to design and build.

"But," Roni adds, "you're newfound inspiration may have to wait."

I frown. "Why?"

"Mrs. Parberry."

Drawing in a deep breath, I let it out long and slow. "What's she done now?"

"She brought in her Chippendale stool. Split the Cabriole leg."

"She stood on it, didn't she?"

Roni winces.

"I told her not to stand on it, damn it."

"Language," Mom scolds. "Let's just be thankful she didn't harm herself."

True. Although... she harmed that innocent stool.

"Shh," Poppy says, patting Moose's head. "He's sleeping."

I run my fingers along my lips, pretending to zip them shut, when she lets out an almighty snort, her mouth open, her nose scrunched. Thinking she's choking, I panic and lunge toward her, but then she adds, "He's snoring, Uncle Riley! Like you!"

Roni bursts into laughter, and Mom offers me a sympathetic grin.

Where's the damn milk? It's roofie time.

"I might pop into the store tomorrow after cards with Ellis and Lily," Mom says, taking Poppy's hand in hers.

"Of course." I walk them to the door.

"I want to hear more about this Riley who has you blushing."

"I don't blush, Mom."

"Of course you don't, dear," she says, her patronizing hand patting my cheek. "Don't forget to bring my baking dishes with you."

"You didn't wash them?"

She slaps my arm. "The nerve of you."

I chuckle. "I'm kidding. They'll be so clean you'll be able to do your hair in the reflection."

"I doubt that, but good boy."

Kissing her cheek and then Roni's, followed by Poppy's, I wave goodbye from my front door, when my cell sounds an incoming text.

Yawning again, I pull it out, stupid butterfly shit flittering in my stomach when I notice Riles's name.

> Just wanted to say goodnight.

> Goodnight, sweetheart. Get some sleep.
> Because you won't when I see you next.

> Yes, I will. I'll bring my AirPods.

> That's not what I meant.

> I know.

Laughing, because she gives as good as she gets, my fingers start to type **I love you**, but I stop them.

Jesus fucking Christ, Wilson. What are you doing?

The message bubble bounces on my screen, so I quickly type something else so she doesn't think I've left her hanging.

> Did you eat something?

Did you eat something?
"You're an idiot," I mutter to myself while closing the door behind me.

> Stop thin-shaming me.

I laugh.

> I'm not.

> You are.

> Riles!

> Riley!

> Okay, okay.

> ⬜⬜⬜

> Just look after yourself. And call me whenever you want, no matter the time or day.

> I'll be fine. I'm a big girl.

Rubbing my beard, I lean against the wall, suspecting she's not being honest.

> I just don't want you to feel lonely.

My screen stays frozen for what feels like minutes on end until the message bubble once again bounces.

> I don't. Not anymore.

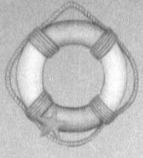

chapter twenty-nine

RILES

Setting my cell down on the wide window ledge I'm sitting on, I bend my knee, hug it to me, and rest my head against the glass as I look at the street below. Truth is, I've never felt more alone in my life.

When I arrived home and opened the apartment door to cold, stale air, what felt like a steel blade pierced my heart. There was no soft light. No brewing coffee. No Mom puttering about, fussing over me, keen to hear every detail of my trip. But then... I wouldn't have taken the trip if she were still here.

Drawing in a deep breath, I turn my head and stare at our life-less apartment, wondering how I'm going to stay here without her and if I can continue to afford the rent on my own. Before she passed, Mom transferred her savings to me to cover funeral costs and to tide me over for a few months. She also mentioned a life insurance policy, and I'm sure she went through the details, but I can't recall any of them. I wasn't interested in listening because, at the time, none of it had been real.

But it is real.

Patting my tear-streaked cheeks dry, I stand, walk to the kitchen, and switch on the oven, preparing to bake Georgia's cookies. All I want to do is unpack and then sleep, but I know my "welcome back" won't be a pleasant occasion, especially because I was unable to complete the final manuscript. She won't be thrilled, but I'm hoping my return to the office will appease her enough, and the cookies *should* help my cause.

I push aside my mail to make room on the countertop for the baking dish when a letter from my mother's solicitor slides off the top of the pile and lands on the floor.

Bending down, I pick it up, knowing I should open it, but I place it back with the others instead. It can wait another day or two; roofie cookies are far more imperative.

The memory of Riley accusing me of drugging my boss quirks my lips. God, I miss him already, which is an unfamiliar but also reassuring feeling, joyous and equally worrisome. It's been less than twenty-four hours, and I'm desperate to see him again, to gaze into his crinkling eyes, run my hands through his hair, and feel his lips pressed to mine. When we're together, nothing else seems to matter, even though I know it does. He just... makes it all worth enduring.

Huh. I pause, turn around, and rest my backside against the cupboards, my hands gripping the edge of the counter behind me. *He does make it all worth enduring: Georgia, my grief, my fears.*

Riley blossoms happiness where there is no sun. To be fair, he also blossoms frustration, but that never lasts for long. We laugh. We bicker. We smooth things over, and then we laugh again. It's all quite... lovely, really.

Sighing, I push off the counter and get to work, soon dead on my feet and covered in flour.

SHUFFLING INTO GEORGIA'S OFFICE, HER GOLDEN LATTE in one hand and a plate with two cookies in the other, I quickly set them on her desk and then straighten her keyboard, files, and pens. She'll arrive at any moment, and when she does, her office must be impeccable and just the way she likes it.

I check the thermostat—a perfect seventy—make sure her trashcan is empty, and I pull out her desk chair, angling it at forty-five degrees.

"What else?" I murmur to myself, straining my brain almost to the point of pain.

Me! Shit!

Scurrying to the mirrored paneling of her storage cabinets, I assess my hair, making sure it's still presentable after my dash from the coffee shop, and then I reapply my lip gloss and step back just in time for her to march into the room.

"Good morning, Georgia," I say, practically standing to attention.

She doesn't respond, instead tossing her coat and Birkin bag on the sofa before sitting at her desk.

Wasting no time in picking them up, I scuttle back to the cabinets and tuck them away, my heart beating erratically when I catch sight of her prized artwork, slightly askew in the reflection of the door as I close it.

"Enjoy your time away?" she murmurs, her tone disinterested as she studies her computer screen.

"Mostly." I inch toward the artwork, correct the imbalance, and then step forward, hands linked at my waist. "Although, saying goodbye to my mother was awfully difficult."

"Hm... I suppose it would be." She looks up from the screen and not so subtly scrutinizes my appearance. "Souvenir?" she asks, gesturing to my wrist as she sips her coffee.

Confused, I glance down, my bracelet incongruous with our surroundings.

Shit!

"Uh... y-yes," I stutter, hastily removing it and hiding it in my bunched fist. "I got it in Greenland."

She cocks an eyebrow. "Interesting choice."

"It's a vibrant place," I explain.

"Yes, and seemingly childish," she mutters, just loud enough for me to hear.

Her passive-aggressive tone prickles my skin, but I push past it as I've groomed myself to do over the years, proceeding to run through her schedule for the day instead. "You have a conference call with Johanna at nine, acquisitions at eleven, and—"

"You seem to have failed to attach the final manuscript to your email."

My blood runs cold, but I knew this was coming, so I straighten my back in preparation to explain. "Yes. It's not yet complete."

"That's—" She glares at the screen, her voice soft but as sharp as a knife's edge. "—unsatisfying."

I grit my teeth. "I was short of time. But I'll get straight to it this morn—"

"Riley." Georgia tips her reading glasses down and studies me over the rim. "You do realize your position here is highly sought after, and the opportunities that come with it are few and far between elsewhere in this industry, correct?"

"I do."

"Then I suggest you take it more seriously." She picks up a cookie, takes a bite, and then dismisses me. "You have work to do."

I fantasize ramming it down her throat but obediently nod before leaving her office.

Bitch! Perhaps I'll add a dash of arsenic next time.

Slumping into my chair, I open my palm and fiddle with my bracelet, comforted by its presence yet also annoyed that I forgot to take it off. It certainly doesn't fit the level of attire expected in the office, but it's not exactly "childish" either. It's unique and has more charm than Georgia has in one single eyelash.

"Welcome back," Tessa from editorial says as she approaches my desk.

"Thank you." I shove the bracelet into my bag and give her my attention. "It's good to be back."

"Is it?" She lowers her voice as she cranes her neck to look past me into Georgia's office. "Because I wouldn't want to be you right now."

I lower my voice too. "Why not?"

She pouts. "Because the wicked witch cursed your absence every day you were gone."

"I'm not surprised," I mutter.

"You'll never get another vacation, you know."

Drawing in a deep breath, I aggressively jiggle my mouse to activate my computer screen. "That's not her call."

Tessa stares at me, mouth amusingly agape.

"It's not," I add defiantly. "She can't keep me here like a caged animal."

"Look around, Riley." She gestures to the office. "There are more caged animals here than at Central Park Zoo."

"You're not wrong." I sigh. "So how did Freya do while I was gone, or do I even need to ask?"

"She lasted two days."

"What?" I blink all the blinks. "Who filled my position then?"

"Me. And Isobel. And Craig."

"Oh. My. God." I bury my face in my hands. "I'm so sorry."

"Don't be. Believe it or not, I like being caged here."

I snap my head up as if she's just confessed a love of cockroaches, which, in hindsight, is probably more acceptable than what she just said. "You do?"

"Yes. A pretty cage full of literature is my kind of cage."

I let out a sarcastic laugh. "I used to feel the same way."

Tessa touches my shoulder. "I'm sorry about your mother, Riley. Had I known before you left, I would've said or done—"

"Thank you," I say, deliberately cutting her off. Talking about Mom at the office is a bone of contention I'm not willing to chew on—they don't belong in the same conversation.

She nods. "I'll let you get back to it."

"Riley!" Georgia squawks. "Where's the list of this week's galleys?"

Closing my eyes for the shortest of seconds, I scrunch my face, almost to the point of pain.

"Let me know if you need anything," Tessa whispers before scuttling off.

Rifling through the paperwork on my desk, I collect the document Georgia is requesting and rush into her office. "It's here."

She snatches it from me and runs her finger down the list, and when she doesn't say anything, I turn to leave.

"I want that manuscript by day's end."

"Yes. It's on its way."

"It won't be if you continue to just stand there, will it?"

"Right. Yes. Sorry."

Rushing back to my desk on the brink of tears, I take a deep breath and compose myself. It's been years since I've had to sneak into the bathroom for fear of crying on the job, and I don't understand why today is any different.

What's wrong with me? Jesus! Get yourself together, Riley. You're used to this. You can handle it. You've been handling it for almost a decade.

"Manuscript," I say to myself.

Manuscript first, cry later.

FOR THE REST OF THE DAY AND INTO THE EVENING, I get lost in the domestic thriller novel, finally typing the closing words of my report. I remove my reading glasses, massage the bridge of my nose, and close my eyes, reopening them to focus on my surroundings. The lights are dim, the only sound a soft hum of a vacuum being pushed around by the janitor. Having been completely focused on my work, I can't recall Georgia leaving, nor anyone else for that matter.

Crap! What time is it?

Picking up my cell—which I put on silent—I blink again,

hoping the time of eight seventeen, a missed call from Riley, and a slew of his messages aren't indeed what's on my screen.

Peanut butter.

My stomach grumbles, so I click Save, email my work to Georgia, and head out of the building, dialing Riley's number as I brave my trek home in darkness.

"Hey, sweetheart," he says as the call connects, his voice gifting me the first feeling of joy I've had all day. "You okay?"

"Yeah. Just had a busy first day back."

"That bad, huh?"

"You could say that."

A cab horn blasts beside me, so I press the phone closer to my ear.

"Where are you?" he asks.

"Walking to the subway."

"At this time of night?"

"Don't worry, country boy. I'm used to it. This city girl can take care of herself."

He doesn't say anything, but I picture him gripping his hair.

"Be careful. You'll snap it."

"What?"

"Your hair."

He chuckles, but there isn't much humor in his tone.

"If it makes you feel better, I'm not the only one who works late in this city. There are plenty of people about. And anyway, I'd much rather hear about your day. Are you back in the workshop?"

"I am."

"I bet you're relieved."

"I am."

"Are you at home?"

"I am."

"Are you just going to keep saying I am?"

"I am."

I sigh. "Riley."

"Riles."

Taking the stairs to the subway, a blast of wind blows my coat apart as I descend underground, so I secure the tie and hug my bag tighter. "I might lose reception soon, so stop with the I-ams. How was your reunion with your family?"

"It was good. Poppy loved her presents."

I smile. "I'm sure she did."

"They're all looking forward to meeting you."

"I'm looking forward to meeting them too. And seeing your shop."

"What about *me*?"

Stopping just shy of the edge of the station platform, I pace a few steps. "That goes without saying."

"No, it doesn't."

"It does!" I playfully roll my eyes. "But if you must hear, then yes, I'm looking forward to seeing you too."

He chuckles. "Not as much as I am you."

My heart skips a beat, then skips another for an entirely different reason when a drunk man hollers something nonsensical and stumbles toward me. Turning my back, I stroll in the opposite direction, closer to less inebriated commuters.

"What was that?" Riley demands.

"Nothing. Just some guy."

"What's he doing?"

"Trying to stand upright but failing."

"Riles, I don't like—"

"My train is here," I say as a beam of light illuminates the tunnel. "Gotta go."

"Keep talking to me."

"I can't. It will cut out."

"Then talk until it does."

"Riley, stop worrying. I'm fine—"

"I repaired a stool from the nineteenth century today," he blurts.

"You did? Wow! That's impressive." The train pulls to a stop, so I step clear of the doors and enter the front car before taking a seat. "Your day was more exciting than mine. All I repaired were sentences."

"Both are equally important, sweetheart. What else did you do?"

"I know what you're doing."

"What's that?"

"Keeping me talking."

"It's working, isn't it?"

I chew the inside of my cheek. "It is, but it's going to cut out any sec—"

The line goes dead as the train pulls away, so I type Riley a quick message, explaining that I'll call him when I get home, then I slip my cell into my pocket. Although unnecessary, his concern for my well-being tugs my heartstrings. He cares, deeply, without chauvinism. A champion for women yet also a protector. It's a desirable balance and one I take pleasure in, because I can still be me *and* fight for me without fear of misogynistic oppression.

Yawning, I recoil somewhat when a man takes the seat beside me despite the plethora of unoccupied rows of seats in the car. I frown at him and huff, irritated, then go to move away when he grabs my arm, his fingers painfully digging into my muscles as he holds me still.

"Give me your bag," he hisses, barely above a whisper.

"Wha—"

"Do it! Now!" He leans closer and presses something hard into my side, just below my ribcage. "Or I'll blow that pretty head of yours off."

Dread freezes me solid, a single breath too distressing to take as I stare dead ahead, my heart manic within my chest.

"No sudden movements, and keep your mouth shut," he hisses again, his breath stale and pungent.

Bile rises to my throat, and I force my trembling hands to release my bag from my shoulder.

"Hurry the fuck up."

"O-Okay," I choke out. "P-Please don't hurt me."

He snatches it and tucks it into his jacket. "Don't fucking move. And don't say another word."

Terrified, I blink back tears and nod, desperate to stay as still and as quiet as possible.

"Look down," he demands as the train slows to pull to a stop. "If you try anything, I'll fucking kill you."

Closing my eyes, I pray to God, to Mom... to anybody listening.

Please! I don't want to die. I don't want to die.

I have so much to live for now: a life with Riley, to make Mom proud, to make *me* proud. And all of it could be ripped away with the single pull of a trigger. A subtle movement. A split-second decision.

Head spinning, I try to calm my breathing for fear of passing out, so I open my eyes and take a deep breath, the pain in my arm subsiding, the seat beside me... empty.

What? Where is he?

I frantically scan the car as the doors close, and the train pulls away, my eyes catching sight of him on the platform, casually ambling by the window as if he's just any other commuter.

"Oh my God!" I say on an exhale, a sob ripping from my throat.

Cowering, my shoulders wrack uncontrollably as I release every ounce of fear I'd suppressed.

You're alive, Riley. Breathe. Just breathe.

"Uh... are you okay?" a woman asks.

Wiping my face, I look up to where she's standing beside me with a man, both of them stumbling as the brakes on the train release. "Y-Yes. I mean no. I was just robbed at gunpoint."

She immediately sits opposite me. "Are you hurt?"

"No. I don't think so."

"Thank goodness," she says, glancing up at the man with her.

I nod, continuing to take deep breaths.

"Is he still here, on the train?" the man asks, eyes sweeping the car.

"N-No. He just left."

They both relax a little, and I wish I could do the same, my entire body quaking.

"What's your name?" the woman asks.

"R-Riley."

"I'm Nya, and this is Perry."

I wipe my cheeks. "H-Hi."

"Jesus! You're trembling." She scoots to the seat beside me and wraps her arm around my shoulders. "It's okay. You're safe now, Riley. We'll get off with you at the next stop and call 911."

Sliding my hand into my pocket, I retrieve my cell and clutch it tight. "I still have this. He didn't know—" I burst into tears again. "I thought he was going to kill me, or... or force me off the train with him."

"Thank the Lord he didn't," she says, gently rubbing my arm.

A chill runs the length of my spine, and my body turns rigid. "He has my keys. And my address. What if...? What if he's there when I—"

"Try not to worry about that. We'll call the police as soon as we can. They'll keep you safe."

"Y-Yes. Thank you."

"And you can change the locks, right?"

Nodding, I draw in another deep breath, exhale, and wipe my face again.

After the train stops at the next station, we get off, and Nya and Perry stay with me while I dial 911 and am met by two officers who take my details and then escort me home. They check that my apartment is secure and wait until the locksmith arrives.

I text Riley, blatantly lying when I tell him I'm fine but too tired to talk. I can't speak to him; I'll burst into tears if I do, and then I'll have to come clean and admit what happened. Knowing him, he'll be furious, and worried, and he'll somehow blame himself despite none of it being his fault, nor mine for that matter.

It is what it is, and it can't be reversed.

Cradling my coffee in my hands, I settle on my sofa, eyes trained to the front door, ears wired to every noise beyond it. Never in my thirty-two years of living in the city have I been this scared and unsettled. So unsafe and unprotected. So lost and misplaced.

A door slams out in the corridor, startling me. I jolt forward and spill my coffee, my heart hammering in my chest.

Damn it, Riley. This is crazy. You're safe. This is your home. He can't get in. He can't hurt you.

Setting my mug on the table, I pluck a few tissues from the box Mom always had readily available and pat my pants leg. Then I turn on the TV, needing a distraction, my restless fingers fidgeting as they settle on my wrist, seeking comfort from Riley's bracelet.

I jerk my hand up when I skim nothing but skin, my bracelet gone.

No! No, no, nooo!

"Fuck you!" I scream at the door. "That was my bracelet, my bag, my...."

Screaming again, I snatch my laptop from the table, open it, and cancel my credit cards. I also order a new ID and finally open my mail, including the letter from Mom's solicitor.

Shaking out the contents from the envelope, another smaller envelope with Mom's handwriting falls into my lap. My breath catches, and I stare at it for a moment before picking it up and tearing it open.

My dearest Smiley Riley,
I'm so sorry, darling. I wanted nothing more than to stay with you in this world and watch you achieve your dreams, but I know in my heart of hearts that

you will, because you've always been a fighter. My little warrior. My determined, resilient daughter.

Tears pool in my eyes, and I scoff. "Resilient? Jesus, Mom. I feel anything but resilient right now."

Plucking another tissue, I blow my nose and keep reading.

Stay strong, Riley, but please open your heart and mind to everything the world has to offer, not just Georgia. You're so talented, and you have so much to give.

It's my hope that after your cruise, and as you sit down and read this, you've discovered there's more to life than constantly giving to her. I don't want that for you anymore. You've fought for too long and given her too much, so... now's the time for me to give to you. For me to take care of your fight.

My life insurance policy is enough for you to set up your own small press. It's what you've always wanted, so take the leap, darling. You're ready. Stop working for that soul-sucking witch, and leave this city. Find a nice place by the beach or in the country, and go out on your own and live your dream. And while you're doing it, fall in love. Get married, have children. Be your own boss, and be happy.

You deserve nothing less.

Love always and forever,

Momma

"Oh, Mom," I sob, tears drenching my cheeks. "You selfless, stubborn, beautiful angel." I blink up at the ceiling and shake my head. "You've always known what's best for me, whether I admitted it or not."

Wiping my face, I open the letter from the solicitor... and nearly fall off the sofa.

Peanut freaking butter! That's a lot of money.

AFTER STARING AT MOM'S INSURANCE POLICY AND reading her letter again, I'd curiously researched available office spaces in Buxtonville before eventually falling asleep, kitchen knife by my side.

Arming myself in my own home isn't something I want to become accustomed to, but until I feel safe again, I don't have a choice. And that's if I'll ever feel safe here, and I'm not sure I will.

"Excuse me," I say, edging past other people to exit the elevator, Georgia's golden turmeric shit—and my coffee—in hand.

"Do you have a death wish now?" Tessa asks as she falls into step beside me, files hugged to her chest.

"No. Why?"

"Because you're late."

"I know." I wince. "It's only fifteen minutes though."

"Only fifteen minutes? In Georgia time, that's fifteen hours, Riley."

She's not wrong.

"Shit." My stomach feels like it could churn butter. "I was mugged last night. He took my OMNY card, credit cards, everything. I had to search around the apartment to scrounge up enough change to get to work."

"Oh my God, Riley!" She touches my arm. "Are you okay?"

"To be honest, I'm still a little shaken up. He had a gun."

Her footsteps falter. "How terrifying!"

"Yeah, it was, but I'm guessing not as terrifying as what I'm about to walk into."

Tessa cocks her head to the side, her expression sympathetic. "No."

I sigh. "Wish me luck."

"You and I both know it's not luck you need." She cups her chest. "It's breasts of steel."

I can't help but laugh, even though laughing is the last thing I should be doing. "Damn it. Here goes nothing."

She straightens her shoulders and pokes out her chest, gesturing I do the same, which I do to humor her until I'm a few feet from Georgia's desk, my steel breasts now as fierce as deflating balloons.

"Good morning," I say to the back of her chair as she takes in the view of Manhattan beyond her twenty-second-floor window. "I apologize for my tardiness. I was mugg—"

"I don't want to hear your excuses, Riley." She swivels her seat to face me, her makeup precise—bar the feathering of lipstick across her pursed lips. "You've worked for me long enough to know they don't matter."

I hand over her cup. "Yes. Of course."

Narrowing her eyes, she scans her desk, and I realize she's looking for the cookies.

Crap!

Her jaw twitches. "You look disastrous."

I touch my hair.

"Your eyes, Riley. Are you high? Because we have a zero tolerance—"

"No!" I shriek, offended. "I'm not *high*. I've never been high. I was mugged at gunpoint last night, if you must know."

She jerks back a little at my tone, then leans into the leather of her seat and smirks, imperiously tapping the end of her pen on the desktop. "I like you, Riley. But be careful. You're replaceable."

Clenching my fist by my side, I nod.

"Redo that report you emailed me yesterday. It lacked conviction."

What? That's a crock of shit!

Turning on my heels, I storm toward the door but stop dead in my tracks when she adds, "And where are my cookies?"

A rush of heat surges the length of my spine, my eyes closing momentarily, Mom's letter blaring like a beacon at the forefront of my mind.

"Stop working for that soul-sucking witch. Go out on your own and live your dream."

God, I desperately want to, but can I really just leave my old life behind and start a new one... with Riley? Am I brave enough? Strong enough? Do I have what it takes to stand on my own two feet in this industry?

"My little warrior. Take a leap, darling."

Slowly turning back around, I stab my finger at her. "They're not *your* cookies, Georgia. They're *mine*."

"I beg your pardon?"

"You heard me. *Mine*. I bake them, every week." Closing the distance to her desk, I set my palms on the edge and lean forward. "And I'm done. I'm done being your slave. Done putting up with your shit. Done kissing your overbearing, authoritarian ass. Find someone else to kiss it for you."

"Riley—"

"No! You don't get to speak right now. I am. I've given you everything, and I'm not giving you any more. You're not worthy of me, and you never have been. I've wasted so much of my life on you, and it's taken the death of my mother, and a man who's known me for a fraction of the time you have, for me to realize that." I push off from the desk and poke out my breasts of steel. "I quit. I quit you, your tyranny, and your goddammed golden turmeric piss in a cup."

She blinks, her jaw dropping, before she leisurely closes it, and... smiles. The first genuine smile I've ever seen on her icy face. "Finally. Goodbye, Riley. And good luck."

What the peanut butter?

She reaches into her Birkin, and I flinch, thinking she too might pull a gun on me. Instead, she retrieves three hundred-dollar bills, and holds them out to me. "For the train," she states, "and until you get your ID and bankcards back."

I recoil, shocked, but then take them from her because the sharp look in her eyes is scary.

Staring at the cash, I nod... and nod again. Speechless. And then I turn on my heel, pick up my speed, and exit her office for the final time, my colleagues avoiding eye contact and bustling about as if they haven't just eavesdropped on our entire exchange.

"She's all yours, Tessa," I announce as I open the drawer, grab the Memorize This if You Want to Live Bible, and toss it to her. "I really do hope you love your cage. But if you don't, and you can find the key, call me. I have a small press to get up and running."

Winking, I press my fingertips to my lips, kiss them, and then hold them above my head, waving as I march to freedom.

chapter thirty

RILEY

"Stupid piece of shit!" I shout, tossing my scraper across my workbench.

"Language!" Roni shouts back from the store.

I grumble, annoyed at my lapses of concentration, which are causing me to repair my repairs. Ever since Riles was too tired to call last night after she got home at ridiculous o'clock, my mind has continued to wander to dark places: someone hassling her on the subway, Georgia treating her like a slave... her not eating because she's been too busy or exhausted to do so. Krystal calling me first thing this morning with the news she's stopping by to collect the divorce papers isn't helping my foul mood either.

I press my palms down on my workbench and hang my head.

"It's not the chair's fault, you know," Roni says, pushing off from the doorframe before taking the few steps down into the workshop. "What's wrong? Why are you being a pain in my backside today?"

"I'm not."

"You are! I've already had to apologize to a customer for an F-bomb *I* didn't say."

I wince. "Sorry."

"Hmm. So, what's eating at you, little bro?"

"Riles. Krystal. The usual."

"Riles? Has something happened?"

"No. It's nothing like that. I'm just worried about her."

She picks up a hatchet and presses the tip of her finger to it, so I raise my eyebrow, suggesting she put it down. Roni and tools aren't a good match.

Rolling her eyes at me, she begrudgingly sets it back on the bench. "Why are you worried about her?"

"Because she works long hours, and Manhattan isn't safe."

"You're not her father," she says condescendingly.

"No shit. That doesn't mean I can't show concern for her safety."

"I never said that." She picks up Dad's hammer and presses it to her chest. "And Krystal? Why's she pissing you off?"

"She's not. But she is coming by today to collect the divorce papers."

"Ah, I see."

Running my hand through my hair, I turn my back to her and stare out into the yard, the shorter days and longer nights turning the leaves on the trees from green to yellow. I've always loved Fall in my hometown, and not before long, I'll need to set aside some time to rake them all up.

"Krystal coming here to collect the papers was going to happen at some point, Riley. And who knows, you might find it cathartic."

"I just want that part of my life finalized. I've moved on. Krystal has moved on. The divorce still lingers."

"Well," she says, stepping up beside me and handing me the hammer, knowing I treasure it as much as she does, "after today, it won't. So stop swearing and massacring that poor chair. As for Riles, take a deep breath and have a little faith. From what you've told me, she's intelligent and certainly capable of looking after herself."

"She is those things, and more."

"Then stop worrying."

"Easier said than done. How can I protect her if I'm here and she's there?"

Roni punches my arm.

"Hey!" I rub the spot. "What was that for?"

"Stop with the macho protection crap."

"Macho? Wanting her safe isn't *macho*."

"It is if you think you're the only one who can keep her safe."

I narrow my eyes at her. "When are you going back to teaching?"

"When you no longer need me here."

I frown. "Veronica."

"What?"

"Don't stay away from teaching for me."

"I'm not." She winks. "And anyway, working with teenagers is just as awful as working with you."

"Working with me is awful?" I gently shove her toward the store. "In that case, get back to it, slackass."

The bell above the front door chimes, so Roni scoots off, leaving me to now worry over whether she's sticking around for my benefit rather than hers. When Adrian was killed in action, she couldn't bring herself to step foot in the classroom. She said her head was no longer in it, and her students deserved better. At the time, it was the right decision, but she's a gifted educator, and if teaching is really what she loves—and if she's ready to return to it —she shouldn't be wasting her talent here, with me.

Grumbling, I focus on the chair, making a mental note to revisit the conversation when Krystal's voice roots my feet to the ground.

"Still playing with wood, I see."

I look up toward the door, to heels as high as a small dog, a black suit intended to intimidate those who oppose her, and blonde hair twisted in a ball thing at the base of her neck.

"I'm not playing," I snap. "I'm working."

She dismissively laughs and carefully descends the steps. "I'm kidding, Riley. Can't you take a joke?"

I collect a sheet of sandpaper and point it at her heels. "You know those aren't appropriate in here. It's dangerous."

She swishes her hand at me. "I'll be fine."

"Just watch your step. There are cutoffs everywhere."

"You're acting as if this is the first time I've stepped foot into your workshop."

"I just don't want you breaking your damn ankle."

"Naww, he still cares." She cocks her head to the side and pouts.

Despite her flaws and mistakes, Krystal knows how to melt ice around a frosty conversation.

"Of course, I do," I say, finally cracking a smile. "I'll always care. You know that."

"As will I."

The old, bitter Riley would've said something hurtful like, *"Bullshit! You care for no one but yourself,"* but I'm not him anymore. I'm a new and improved, happy Riley, a Riles-has-made-me-a-better-man Riley, so I bite my once hostile tongue and point to the bench near the window, to exactly what she's here for. "They're over there. Signed, sorta sealed, and now delivered."

Precariously treading around the workshop, she picks up the envelope containing our divorce papers and shakes them into her hand. "Any problems? Questions?"

"No."

"Good." She slips them back into the envelope. "I guess it's settled then."

"I guess it is."

Krystal goes to speak but stops, instead swirling her finger through a layer of sawdust coating the bench.

"Was there anything else?" I ask, hand-sanding the chair.

"No. I just..." She sighs. "For what it's worth, I never, *ever,* meant to hurt you. And I know did. Horribly so. I just.... I couldn't be the person who lost our daughter anymore. I had to become someone else. I had—"

I set down the sandpaper. "I know."

"And I hope that, one day, you can truly forgive me."

"I have."

"You have?" she asks, incredulous.

"Yes."

She touches the envelope to her lips, her eyelids narrowing suspiciously before they spring apart. "You've met someone, haven't you?"

"That's none of your business."

"I know it's not, but—"

"My love life is no longer your concern."

"Love?" She smirks, but I catch the moment it falters. A split second of regret.

"You know what I mean," I say, ignoring her lapse in façade. Whether she's repentant or not over our marriage ending doesn't matter to me anymore. It's done and dusted. And we can never go back to what it was.

"How was your cruise?"

"*Great.* You should consider going on one."

"Nah." She brushes her hands together, cleaning the dust from her fingers. "Not my thing."

"I didn't think it was going to be my thing either, but it was."

She points the envelope at me, her eyes shimmering almost as much as the glittery stuff on her eyelids. "You did meet someone. On the cruise!"

"Krys," I warn, just as the bell above the door chimes again.

The jingle-jangle equally annoys and pleases me, because I'm glad the store is thriving, but I also don't have time to stand around and talk to my ex-wife about my future.

"Fine. I won't pry." She moves around the bench until she's standing before me, fixing my collar. "I just want you to be happy, Riley. That's all. I wasn't capable of giving that to you in the end. If someone else can, well...."

I remove her hands and hold them between us. "I am happy. I wasn't for a long time, but I am now. Life changes. We both know that. And I've changed with it."

She nods and drops her gaze to the ink on my arm. "I'm so sorry for losing her."

"Hey!" I squeeze her hands tighter. "You didn't lose her. It wasn't your fault."

She slips her fingers from mine and wipes a tear from her eye. "Deep down, I know that. Trust me, Dr. Hastings has drilled that into me more than enough times, but... it's hard not to blame myself. I was her mother. It was my job to protect—"

"It was *our* job. And we did everything we possibly could. It just... wasn't meant to be."

She scoffs and wipes her eye again. "You would've been a great father, Riley. Better than mine. If Immy had lived, she'd be the luckiest girl alive."

My heart constricts at my daughter's nickname and the love and softness in Krystal's voice, so I pull her to me and cradle her head against my shoulder until the door chimes once again and reminds me I have work to do.

"Are *you* happy?" I ask, leaning back to hold her at arm's length.

"As happy as I'm capable of."

I nod. "That's a start, at least."

"Riley!" Roni calls out.

"I'll be there in a minute," I call back.

"I'll let you get back to play—" Krystal gives me a sneaky grin as she smooths down her suit. "To work."

I smirk at her correction. "Thanks."

"I'll be in touch once these are filed."

"No sweat."

"Take care of yourself, Riley," she says, ascending the stairs and edging past Roni, who's now standing in the doorway. "You too, Veronica."

My sister simply lifts her chin, barely acknowledging her. And even though Roni's disdain pains me, for her sake and for Krystal's, I can't exactly blame her for feeling the way she does. She's a fiercely loyal sister, and Krystal was cruel to her and Poppy, so it's not my place to force Roni to forgive her as I have.

"You too, Krys," I say as she exits the shop. Cracking my neck, I release the tension and focus on Roni. "What's up?"

"Are you okay?"

"Yeah, I'm fine."

She smiles. "I have to hand it to you, bro. You've come a long way since... well, since everything happened. It's nice to see you less savage where she's concerned."

"You can thank Riles for that."

"Speaking of Riles, I think she was just here."

I blink at her. "What?"

"Yeah. I can't be sure, but there was a woman who just came in. She looked awfully similar to the woman in your photo."

Excitement sizzles every nerve ending in my body, my gaze shooting past her shoulder toward the store. "Where is she?"

"She left. Practically fled before I could ask her name or if I could help her."

I rub my beard, slide my cell out of my pocket, and dial Riles's number. It rings a few times and then disconnects.

"She's not answering her—" My blood runs cold. If Riles was here and just saw what she saw, she'd think.... "Fuck!"

"What? Riley, what's wrong?"

I leap up the steps, Roni quickly moving out of my way.

"Where are you going?"

"After her."

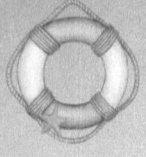

chapter thirty-one

RILES

*H*ow *could I be so stupid?*
Hands trembling, heart painfully pounding, I flee Riley's store and hail a cab, tears stinging my eyes as I open the door and slide onto the back seat. "Manhattan, please."

"Manhattan?" The driver turns to face me, his expression dumbfounded.

"Yes."

"There's a train station just around the cor—"

"I don't want to catch the train. I just want.... Can you take me or not?"

"Of course. But it'll cost—"

"I don't care what it costs!"

"Okay." He turns back to his steering wheel, flicks the turn signal, and pulls away from the sidewalk. "Heading home?"

"Yes."

Home. I stare at the quaint stores as we pass them by, my mind in disarray. Before seeing Riley with who I'm assuming was Krystal, I'd been ready to call Buxtonville home. To call *him* home. A gigantic leap of madness. But the way the two of them embraced, and how he held her to him, it's clear Buxtonville is their home and not mine.

My cell rings beside me, catapulting my pulse to soaring heights, so I slip my hand into my bag, pull it out, and look down through my tear-stained vision at Riley's name and the photo of us at Qaqortok on my screen.

He must've seen me leave. Shit!

I'm utterly mortified, and the way I'm looking at him in the picture—with lovesick Bambi eyes—is a serrated knife slicing my heart.

I hit Decline and wipe my face, exhaling a deep, excruciating breath. I would've liked it here with him. Loved it, even. Peaceful, serene, the opposite of NYC. It was the change my life needed. The change I always dreamed I could achieve one day.

"Are you okay, miss?" the driver asks as we pull to a stop at a set of traffic lights, his concerned eyes catching mine in the rearview mirror.

"Yes." I sniff and wipe my face again. "I'm fine."

Nodding, he slowly taps his finger on the steering wheel, the lyrics of "Risk" by Gracie Abrams humming softly from the speakers. I home in on the tune, almost laughing at the irony, because I was here, risking everything to be with Riley. But jumping in the deep end could lead to drowning, and that's exactly what it felt like as my lungs filled with sorrow.

My stomach tightens as memories of us cuddling at the Blue Lagoon, kissing under the Northern Lights, and strolling the streets of Paris flicker into my mind. How it felt to be in his arms, laughing and holding his hand. The romantic sunsets. His determination. The ocean breeze whispering across our faces. None of those moments felt fake, because they weren't. They were real. *Are* real.

What if what I just saw wasn't what it looked like?

A shiver runs the length of my spine, my damp cheeks trembling.

What if I'm overreacting?

I turn in my seat and look out the rear window along the

street, a sliver of hope threading my heart back together and once again filling my lungs with air.

Should I go back? Should I let him explain?

The threading pauses.

But what if there's no explanation? What if he has decided to give Krystal another chance? What if he and I were only a vacation mix-up?

As if my mother is sitting beside me, her soothing voice caresses my ear. *"You only live once, Smiley Riley. Take a leap. Fall in love."*

"I am in love, Mom," I whisper back, knowing it's true. I can feel it to my core. Every time his eyes crinkle. Every time he rubs his beard. Every time our bodies touch and his soul dances with mine.

"I love him," I blurt.

"Did you say something?"

My eyes once again meet my driver's in his rearview mirror.

What am I doing? Why am I running away?

"I love him," I blurt again.

"Who?"

"Peanut butter!"

The light turns green, and my driver accelerates.

"Stop!" I shout, feeling as if I've been hit by a bolt of lightning.

"What?"

"Please. Stop. Pull over!"

He swerves the cab to a halt, brakes screeching, car horns blaring.

"I've changed my mind," I explain, wrenching open the door and tossing him a fifty. "Sorry."

"Wh-what about your change?"

"Keep it."

Slamming the door, I turn on my heel and… run. I run back along the street, lungs burning a hole in my chest, my bag slipping from my shoulder, my mind unmistakably sound yet filled with utter chaos. But that's what love is, chaos among clarity. A tornado pirouetting around your heart. Love *is* a battlefield... according to Mom and Pat Benatar. It's when you fight until you can't breathe, think, or do.

It's the end, and the beginning.

Clasping my bag, I hoist it back onto my shoulder when a "For Lease" sign in a shop window stops me in my tracks. "This is the one," I rasp out, stepping back and taking in a much-needed breath.

I shade the sun from my eyes, admiring the Victorian-style façade, the same one I'd seen in my Google search. I was going to show Riley after I filled him in on everything that's happened in the hopes he'd want me to move here too.

"It's perfect!" I say, exhaling just as Riley skids around the corner and comes to a stop when he sees me, his chest heaving, sweat dampening his brow.

"Riles, I—"

I stare at him, shocked. "What are you doing?"

He bends at the waist and rests his hands on his knees. "What are *you* doing?"

I smile. "I asked you first."

Holding up one finger, he takes a deep breath, then says, "I'm chasing after you. What does it look like?"

"So you were planning to run all the way to Manhattan?"

"If I had to, yes."

I narrow my eyes at him. "Why?"

He does the same. "You know why."

"Do I?"

Standing straight again, he cocks his head, his expression condescending. "Because I love you, Riles Wilson. And I'll run to the ends of this earth just so we can be together."

My heart skips a beat. "You love me?"

He takes a step forward. "Yes."

"And what about Krystal?"

"I was merely giving her the divorce papers. We hugged. We said goodbye. That's all it was."

Taking a step closer to him, a flush of remorse warms my cheeks. "I know. It just took me a couple of minutes to realize that."

He grips his hair, eyes flaring with exasperation, as if those couple of minutes were the longest of his life.

I burst into laughter.

"You think this is funny?" he prompts.

"Yes. Kind of."

"Jesus Christ, Riles!"

I laugh again.

"Stop it." He chuckles. "I thought I'd lost you."

My laughter dies off, my throat thick as I swallow. "I love you too, Riley Wilson."

Our eyes lock, and he strides toward me until our chests collide, his mouth feverish, my hands wild within his hair. Riley lifts me off the ground, twirling me in a circle, his grip tight, mine tighter.

"Don't do that again," he says between plying kisses to my face. "Don't run without talking first. Promise me."

I rest my forehead against his. "I won't. And anyway, where would I run to?"

"Back to Manhattan, of course."

"Yeaaah... about that. I want to show you something."

His brows draw together, and he sets me on my feet, so I link my hand in his and face the shop.

"What do you think?" I ask.

He stares at the empty building. "I think it's a vacant shop."

"*I* think it's perfect for my small press."

Riley snaps his head to me, his eyes crinkling, his smile all teeth. "Here? In Buxtonville?"

I swing our arms. "Why not?"

"But—" He runs his free hand through his hair. "—what about Georgia?"

"I told her to stick my job up her ass."

He coughs, then chokes out, "You did?"

I smirk. "You seem shocked, Riley."

"I am." He blinks a few times. "I'm... I'm speechless."

"Happy speechless? Or I-don't-want-you-to-move-here-so-soon speechless? Because if you're not ready for that, I underst—"

"Are you shitting me? Of course I want you to move here. I couldn't think of anything more perfect."

"Really? Because if this is all too much, I—"

"Yes! Really!" He lifts me up and twirls us in a circle again. "Is the Pope a religious fuck?"

"Riley!" I laugh and kiss his lips, soft, slow, and with purpose. "We really need to stop speaking about the Pope like that. We'll go to hell."

"Hell is the last thing on my mind right now. You're here... in my arms... where you belong. To hell with hell." He kisses me again, and I lose myself to everything that is him. His smell, his warmth, his undeniable love.

"Mommy, why is Uncle Riley kissing that lady?"

Our heads snap to where an adorable little girl is holding her mother's hand.

"Because that's Riles, sweetie," the woman says, grinning from ear to ear. "Uncle Riley's girlfriend."

I push back and wriggle free of his grip, nervously fixing my hair as Poppy giggles and twists from side to side.

"What are you doing?" Riley asks his sister.

"Chasing after you."

"Who's minding the shop?"

"Mom. Who else?" She gives him a duh-face, steps up to us, and shoves his shoulder. "Stop being rude. Introduce us."

Amused, I offer my hand. "Hi, Veronica. Sorry about before."

Riley frowns. "What happened before?"

I wince apologetically. "I kinda bumped into her when I left the shop."

"I'm Poppy!" his niece says, racing her mother to shake my hand. "Pleased to meet you."

Bending over, I smile and lightly grip her little fingers with mine. "Pleased to meet you too."

She animatedly wrenches my arm down and then up, down and then up again, her bracelets jingling on her wrist.

"Those are pretty," I say, gesturing to them. "I had one just like it.'

"What do you mean *had*?" Riley asks.

I side-eye him. "I was mugged last night at gunpoint, and he stole my—"

"You were what?"

I swish my hand at him. "It doesn't matter."

"It damn well does matter." He reaches down and tips my chin so that I'm looking up at him. "Riles? What the hell happened?"

As I'm about to explain, Poppy pushes her uncle's hand away and replaces it with hers, turning my head back in her direction. She then removes her purple bracelet and threads it onto my wrist.

My jaw drops.

My heart stops.

"For me?" I ask, blinking back tears.

She nods.

I clasp her tiny fingers in mine. "Thank you, Poppy. That's very kind of you."

"Nanna says kindness is rewarded, so what's my reward?"

I burst into laughter, as do Riley and Veronica.

"How about ice cream?" Veronica offers. "Come on, little miss. Let's visit Mrs. Parberry."

Sliding her hands from mine, she retakes her mother's and skips off.

"She's adorable," I say, sighing. "Why on earth would you roofie her?"

"Riles—"

"Georgia deserved roofieing. That little sweetheart doesn't."

"Riles—"

Standing up again, I continue ignoring him. "You better get back to the shop. I'm going to the realtor."

He snags my arm and tugs me to him, fastening my hands behind my back. "You're not going anywhere until you tell me what happened last night. Were you hurt? Are you okay?"

I chew my lip. "I'm fine—at least, I am now. He didn't hurt me. He just stole my bag and fled."

A muscle in his face twitches.

"I promise. He just scared me. That's it."

"And that's why you want to move here?"

"No! Not entirely." I shrug free of my confinement and drape my arms around his neck. "I'll admit I don't feel safe on my own in that apartment anymore, but I want to move here to be closer to you. To spend more time together. To—"

He seals my lips with a kiss, the world melting away as our mouths become one. Love, light, and an insurmountable sensation of belonging surges through my body, and I know I'm where I'm meant to be—here, with him.

"Good," he says, pulling back. "Because I promised you you're not alone, and I meant it. From now on, it's you and me, me and you." He waggles his brows. "Team R 'n' R."

I bury my face in his chest. "That team name is so lame."

"Come on," he says, chuckling as he kisses my head and slides his hand into mine. "I'll introduce you to Buxtonville's realtor."

I squeal. "I'm so excited!"

"She's excited too."

"Who... the realtor?"

Side-eyeing me, he rubs his beard. "Yep."

"But how do you know that?"

"Because she's my mother."

"Oh!"

Peanut butter!

the end

Turn over for a sneak peek at
The Sharehouse Mix-Up,
the second interconnecting standalone
book in The Mix-Up series by K.M. Golland

the sharehouse mix-up

CHAPTER ONE

Kiara

There's nothing quite like the sting of cold hard truth slapping you across the face. Swift. Sharp. Often rude and unsolicited. A blow to your pride. It's even worse when that slap comes from the hand of someone you love, or... used to love.

Okay, so I still love Iliana—my boss and best friend—I just don't like her all that much right now.

"Your work is stale, impatient, and out of touch," she says, eyes locked on mine as she describes my latest opinion columns.

Harsh? Maybe so, but not entirely untrue.

Opening my mouth to object, I'm silenced when she raises her palm.

"Let me finish, Kiara."

"Fine." I sigh, slump back in my seat, and stare out of the window beyond her shoulder.

"What you've been churning out of late in uncharacteristic. You're talented. You know it. I know it. Everyone here knows it."

I ignore her compliment, instead choosing to continue to

avoid eye contact. A childish move? Yes. But I'm simply not in the mood for her psychoanalysis.

"Perhaps you're tired?" she asks, "uninterested and unchallenged? Perhaps it's something else...?" Iliana waits a beat for me to offer up what that something else might be, but I remain tight-lipped. "Okay then," she says with a disappointed tone that cuts through my chest bone. "I've decided you need to go on a sabbatical."

My eyes snap to hers. "What? No!"

"A change of scenery will be good for you."

"But—"

"Kiara..." She steeples her hands over her desk, and Iliana only ever *steeples* when she means business. "If you're not going to tell me what's wrong, I have no choice but to assume it has something to do with that troll who keeps commenting on your columns and harassing you. He's spooked you, hasn't he? Admit—"

"You're wrong," I lie. "He's just a misogynistic, keyboard warrior."

"Nonetheless"—She says gathers some documents in her hands—"I'm sending you on a month-long assignment."

I bolt upright. "To where?"

"I want you to open your eyes and mind to new people, places, and experiences." Iliana slides brochures of Buxtonville, Philadelphia across her desk to me. "You're too comfortable here. Too stubborn and set in *your* ways."

I scoff. "I beg to differ. My penchant for ritualism is safe and familiar."

"Maybe so, but it will spell the end of your career." Iliana covers my hand with hers. "Your work has become one-sided, biased and untrustworthy, and as a journalist, if your words can't be trusted, no one will read them. And if no one reads them, there's no point penning them in the first place."

In all honesty, I agree with her. I am bored and bitter. I've been passtionately stuck in a rut, and I can't deny it's infiltrating my work like a tidal wave of poison. "Fine," I murmur, snatching my hand back. "What's the assignment?"

"I want you to discover how the small-town folk live. Are they happier? Healthier? Is their way of life better than their urban counterparts? And if so, why? Delve deep and break free of your metropolis habitude by broadening your horizons and opinions." She leans back in her leather chair and smirks like a Disney villain, her gleaming teeth icing my veins and cementing my pending torture. "Become a hippy, Kiara."

"A hippy?" I laugh, although it's not the funny kind. "What even is a hippy?"

"Google it." Iliana pushes up to stand. "But, for now, go home and pack. I've booked your accomodation, and a cab will collect you in—" She checks her watch. "—approximately two hours."

"What?" I screech.

She rounds her desk, clasps my shoulders, and pulls me in for a quick hug. "Don't argue. You *need* this. And who knows, it might actually be fun."

"For whom... you or me?"

"We'll soon find out."

"Do I have a choice?"

"No, you do not."

Grumbling, I trudge out of her office—highly freakin' annoyed—and head home. And in less than two hours, I'm being ferried away to my pending doom.

A HIPPY? I REST MY ELBOW ON THE DOOR TRIM OF MY cab, cradle my head in my hand, and sigh. *What even is a hippy?*

Collecting my cell from my purse, I Google the damn word.

According to Merriam-Webster, a hippy is usually a young person who rejects the mores of established society (as by dressing unconventionally or favoring communal living) and advocates a nonviolent ethic.

Offended, I scoff. *Does Iliana think I'm old... and hostile?*

Besides that one time I deliberately swiped a stack of papers off an intern's desk because he emailed my *very* important and highly confidential email to the wrong person, I can quite confidently say I'm mostly pleasant. Non-criminal nor confrontational. And I haven't yet seen my thirty-third birthday, so I'm far from geriatric.

I read the definition again. *Pfft.* Of course I don't reject the mores of established society. Why would you in this day and age? Technology is a gift: a device for sanity and survival. Coffee machines, cell phones, Wi-Fi, and Netflix just to name a few. Surely there's no shame in embracing and enjoying such things?

"Become a damn hippy," I mutter under my breath.

"Did you say something?" my cab driver asks, his eyes catching mine in the rear-view mirror.

I lift my head from my hand and stretch my neck from side to side. "How much farther?"

"We're almost there."

Sighing again, I stare out the window at the lush green scenery, pops of white and pink blossoms creating a beautiful Spring palette—very different to the concrete jungle with highrise buildings I see day in and day out—and I'll admit it's rather lovely. But it's also earthy: dirt, moss, critters, and... nature.

Ugh! Why did I agree to this? I wrack my brain, but it only takes a nanosecond for the answer. *Because I'll lose my job if I don't, that's why.*

Despite being best friends for almost ten years, Iliana won't keep me on the payroll if I don't rediscover my investigative and literary spark. She can't keep me on, even if she wants to because the powers that be would take her job too, and I'm not about to let that happen. I'm too good of a friend to let my demise be hers as well.

So... here I am, traveling to *"Hippyville"* for a mind-awakening experience, which will, hopefully, save my career.

According to Iliana's text, which I conveniently received after being jailed in the cab, I'll be staying in a quaint, riverside cabin, which she'd booked this morning, surprisingly at such short notice. But then... should I be surprised? If the brochures are anything to go by, Buxtonville is a far cry from Hawaii. No tropical beaches, Nordstrom, or Starbucks. Just trees, a river, a corner store, and... trees.

Not exactly a vacation hot spot.

Oh, and apparently, the keys to the cabin are in the mailbox.

Not exactly high-scale security either.

Perhaps hippies are naturally trustworthy and safe, or maybe they're naïve and reckless? I make a mental note to research that particular question, the pending answer intriguing me.

"Here we are," my driver says as he pulls into a gravel driveway before stopping alongside a two-story, mushroom-gray weatherboard cottage.

Peering through the window while he retrieves my luggage, I wrinkle my nose at the dome of maples and oaks secluding the property from the outside world. Ambience: *Blair Witch Project*.

"I better not be murdered while I'm here," I grumble. Although, that would make an interesting news article: *Sabbatical Leads to Death. Stay Home; Stay Safe.* An article I couldn't write, of course, because I'd be dead—Irony at its best.

Reluctantly exiting the cab, my favorite suede boots squelch on the soggy ground underfoot, so I tippy-tap to avoid sinking. "Gross!"

"I hope you bought some rainboots with you," the driver says, chuckling as he points to my feet.

I laugh then lie. "Of course, I did."

I didn't; Kiara Moore doesn't own rainboots.

After collecting my bags, I retrieve the keys from the mailbox —a painted cow made from a rusted tin milk can, which is both weird and artsy—and then I make my way toward the cottage.

A gust of wind spirals leaves from the driveway, each one chasing another along the ground. Birds squawk, the wood paneling of the house creaks, and a concoction of dangling cutlery and empty glass bottles hanging from the porch eaves chime in the breeze. I shiver, the eerie atmosphere sending a chill through my bones.

A bush to my side rustles, so I scuttle up the rickety porch steps to safety in the event that a wild animal dashes out and tries to maim me. I'm not fond of untamed furry things, big or small. Things with teeth, claws... fangs. *Damn you, Iliana. You could have at least chosen a place with little to no threat to my life.*

Setting down my luggage on the warped decking, I sidestep questionably hazardous planks underfoot while dodging pot plants hanging from the awnings, rainbow blooms spilling over the sides like clown wigs. Ambience: Stephen King's *It*. All that's missing is the red balloon.

"Is this her idea of a joke?" I murmur, desperately scanning my surroundings for the punchline.

A wooden love swing lightly sways at the end of decking, facing the Delaware River, sunlight glittering from the water's surface, so I wander toward it, brush the seat clean with my hand, and tentatively lower to sit, lightly rocking back and forth as I draw in a breath and try to admire the ethereal view.

Fresh, unpolluted air fills my lungs, and I can't deny the cathartic feel of it. Clean. Revitalizing. No smog or garbage stench.

I exhale, long and hard. *Maybe this won't be so bad after all.*

It's been years since I've taken some time to myself. Unplugged from the hustle and bustle and switched off from my daily grind. Not that this treechange is a vacation because it's not. I still have work to do. People and places to investigate. Comparative research I must compile and convey analytically. My assignment is to learn how to be a *"hippy"*—definitely not a vacation.

Closing my eyes, I take in another deep breath when the love swing makes a sharp cracking sound. I spring to my feet and stand clear, almost losing the contents of my bladder in the process. *Jesus! Even the furniture is a potential threat to my life.*

I glare at the swing, then quickly scoot away from it to where I left my luggage, my fingers settling on the handle of my suitcase as I read a chalkboard sign beautifully scrawled and etched with drawings, nailed to the wall next to the front door.

Welcome to Treescape Cottage, where strangers become friends.

Eat, play, and be JOLLY.
The MOORE the merrier.

The poem's clever play on words lifts the corners of my mouth into a curious smile because my surname is Moore. It's cute and hospitable, and you wouldn't find such a jovial greeting in the city. At least, I never have. Everyone is always time-restricted, perturbed, and chained to a demanding schedule. Astute and businesslike. You may encounter the atypically pleasant barista or sandwich shop owner here and there, but that's about it.

Maybe there's something in the air here, something warm, fuzzy, and pleasant. I take another skeptical, sweeping glance at my surroundings. *Yeah, probably weed and hallucinate fungi.*

Slotting the key into the door, I go to unlock it when it releases from the catch and pushes open. *Wow! Hippies are definitely not security-wise. Have they never heard of theft, home invasion, or squatters?*

I shake my head, step inside, snib the lock behind me, and abandon my bags in search of the bathroom, scurrying past a lounge with a crackling fire in a stone hearth and some weird cartoon with a blue dog blaring from the TV. My steps falter, eyes narrowing as I look toward the ceiling where the lights are switched on. It's all very odd, but I'm too close to soiling myself to think more of it, instead rushing into a hallway where I find the bathroom.

Wasting no time, I wrench my suit pants down, and squat over the porcelain bowl when the door springs open and a small child bursts in.

I scream, and pee—more out of fright than necessity.

"Hello," the little cretin says as he waves, dimples popping.

My pelvic floor muscles clench.

"I'm Parker. I'm five."

Blinking, just in case I've inhaled said hallucinate fungi fumes, I poke his shoulder to determine if he's real or not.

He giggles and pokes me back. "Who are you?"

"Jesus!" I shriek, tugging my pants to my thighs.

He frowns and shakes his head. "No, you're not."

"Wha—"

"Parker! What's wrong?" The door swings open again, and a man skids to a stop when he sees me. "What the hell?" He yanks the little boy to his side. "Who are you?"

I blink.

He blinks back.

Heat soars through my body like lava and erupts at my cheeks. "Do you mind?" I yell, pointing at the door. "Get out!"

His eyes dip to my lap, then back up again. "Shit! Sorry. We'll just..." He ushers the kid back into the hallway and shuts the bathroom door behind him, and all I can do is stare at it as I clutch my chest, my breathing sharp, my pulse erratic.

"Oh, my God!" I say, panting. "What the hell just happened?"

Springing off the toilet seat, I quickly secure my pants, grab the handle of a toilet brush—the only weapon-esque thing I can find—and take a deep breath as I slowly open the door.

acknowledgments

Before I acknowledge the wonderful people I wish to acknowledge, I want to share with you something that almost destroyed my love and faith in publishing...

Writing a book is a mixture of excitement and chaos, but mostly it's creative vulnerability. Our ideas and how we sew them into a story are deeply personal. They're fragments of our heart, mind, body, and soul. Artistic DNA if you must. And when they're ostensibly stolen and remodeled as someone else's art, the violation is literally gut wrenching.

Sadly, ideas aren't copyrighted. I mean how can they be? *But...* when you pitch them to an a literary agent, you hold dear to the notion they'll remain *yours*. That didn't happen to me. My *"exciting and fresh"* concept—that said literary agent loved—was later published by an author on her list.

Coincidence? Perhaps. But likely not.

Deep, long inhale. Deep, long exhale

As you can imagine, I was shattered. I cried, got really fucking mad, felt numb, cried more, and just... lost faith, as an author and as a human being. But, if I've learned anything during my thirteen years within this industry, it's that publishing is a business and writing is a passion and way of life. One is cutthroat, and the other is a part of *you*.

The point of me telling you this other than sharing my truth is that while imitation is a form of flattery, it's also creative laziness and theft. Don't do it. It leaves a faecal scent trail, and it will rightfully follow you. Also, if you love doing something so deeply—

providing it's ethical, of course—never stop. Keep persevering despite the shitstorm that may or may not accompany it, xoxo.

Now, to my acknowledgments:

Rachael Johns, you were a shining beacon while I wrote this book. Your enthusiasm for the concept together with championing me while I navigated how I wanted to publish was a constant reminder that a precious gem like you is a lifeline for an author in this industry. I appreciate you immensely.

Tiffany from T.E. Black Designs, YOU. NAILED. THIS. COVER! It's just so pretty and perfect, and did I say pretty? I adore working with you and can't wait to share the other covers in this series.

Kayla Robichaux, we've always said we were separated at birth. Each time we discover a new similarity we share, we giggle like teenagers. I wish we didn't live on different continents, because if we weren't on opposite sides of the world, I know we'd be neighbours. We'd blast the same music, wave from our kitchen windows, and no doubt dance in synchrony as we wifed and mothered like badasses. I love you, woman, and I'm so grateful for your editing excellence.

Please know what I wrote above if for you as much as it is for me. Keep going, twinsie.

My beta readers: Kayla, Maureen, Brooke, Staton, Sherry, and Sue. Thank you for volunteering to read an early copy of this book. Your feedback and comments were super helpful, and I appreciated them so much xo Get ready, ladies, because book two will be landing on your kindles soon ;)

Andrew, Blake, Bri, Mum and Dad, you're always there when shitty moments in this business tear me down. You hug me, give me space, and offer words of encouragement. Thank you. I love you xo

Lastly, **to everyone who has read my books**. Thank you from the bottom of my heart. Don't get me wrong, but... I don't write for you; I write for me, lol. I think most authors, at their core, always do. Or at least, they should. If we don't feel, love, respect, and appreciate what we produce, why should we expect you to? So, I write for me in the hope what I've written is for you too.

Your time and money is valuable, so it's an honour you spent it on me and that you continue to do so after all these years.

Thank you xo

also by k.m. golland

about the author

Born and raised in Melbourne, Australia, K.M. Golland is a best-selling author with HarperCollins, and a two-time Romance Book of the Year award nominee.
A lover of doughnuts, bridges, music, and cars, she's also quite happy to support a very healthy high heel obsession.
K.M. lives on a farm in country Victoria with her husband, two children, and golden retriever.

Connect with K.M. Golland
Website
Email

Sign up to my mailing list for the latest news, book releases, and sales.

www.ingramcontent.com/pod-product-compliance
Lightning Source LLC
Chambersburg PA
CBHW030549020726
47494CB00005B/1541